THE SIDEMAN

ALSO BY BRYAN THOMAS SCHMIDT

NOVELS

The Worker Prince (Saga of Davi Rhii 1)
The Returning (Saga of Davi Rhii 2)
The Exodus (Saga of Davi Rhii 3)
Simon Says (John Simon Thrillers)
The Sideman (John Simon Thrillers)
Common Source (John Simon Thrillers-forthcoming-May 2020)

CHILDREN'S BOOKS

Abraham Lincoln Dinosaur Hunter: Land Of Legends
102 More Hilarious Dinosaur Jokes For Kids

NONFICTION

How To Write A Novel: The Fundamentals of Fiction

ANTHOLOGIES (AS EDITOR)

Infinite Stars: Dark Frontiers
Joe Ledger: Unstoppable (with Jonathan Maberry)
Predator: If It Bleeds
Infinite Stars: Definitive Space Opera and Military Science Fiction
The Monster Hunter Files (with Larry Correia)
Maximum Velocity (with David Lee Summers, Carol Hightshoe, Dayton Ward, and Jennifer Brozek)
Little Green Men—Attack! (with Robin Wayne Bailey)
Decision Points
Galactic Games
Mission: Tomorrow
Shattered Shields (with Jennifer Brozek)
Raygun Chronicles: Space Opera For a New Age
Beyond The Sun
Space Battles: Full Throttle Space Tales

THE SIDEMAN

By

Bryan Thomas Schmidt

Ottawa, KS

BORALIS BOOKS
Ottawa, KS 66067

ISBN-13: 978-1-62225-7539 hardcover
ISBN-13: 978-1-62225-7546 paperback
ISBN-13: 978-1-62225-7553 ebook

First Edition: February 2020

Printed in the United States of America

10 9 8 7 6 5 4 3 2 1

Interior Design and Layout by Guy Anthony De Marco
Cover Design: A.R. Crebs
Author Photo: Bryan Thomas Schmidt

Dedicated to

Mike Resnick

John A. Pitts

and Cara Carter,

Gone Too Soon

CHAPTER 1

"TURN LEFT! LEFT!" Training Officer Gilbert Lenz shouted from the passenger seat of the 2025 Ford Explorer Interceptor his trainee, Lucas George, was driving.

A dark-skinned Filipino, short but stocky and mostly muscle, Lenz was an eighteen year veteran of the KCPD with the look of one not to be messed with. His crew cut hair and tattoos testified to his past as a military mercenary and sniper in the Middle East, amongst other places. Lucas, on the other hand, was tall, thin, black, with bright blue eyes, and his uniform, haircut and everything about him was neatly coiffed, pressed, and shiny like the rookie he was. He was also an android, the first android graduate of the Kansas City Police Academy. In fact, the first android student. Gil had been assigned to train him because of his experience, but right now he was wondering how the android had ever made it through training.

"I know that. I can see them right in front of us," Lucas replied, almost matter-of-fact, and spun the wheel, tires squealing as he cut off a box truck and two SUVs, making the sharp turn from 18th onto Main.

Gil winced as the seatbelt bit sharply into his shoulder and grabbed the handle overhead to steady himself. This android might just be crazy. "We're supposed to protect people, not kill them, George!" he said through gritted teeth.

The Explorer bounced as it landed back on all four wheels hard and straightened, but Lucas showed no reaction. He just nodded. "We're police officers! We're not trained to handle this kind of violence!" Lucas quipped, quoting some movie Gil couldn't remember.

The T.O. just glared. Lucas was known for quoting cop movies, not always at the best times. But he'd graduated from the Academy first in his class, and was assigned the fast track to partner up with a veteran Property Detective at Kansas City Central Patrol Division named John Simon. Real cops didn't quote cop movies...much. So Gil had warned him to cut that out, but sometimes the quotes just popped out from habit.

Gil keyed the radio clipped to his shoulder. "146."

"Go ahead, 146," the dispatcher replied.

"146 continuing chase south on Main at 18th," Gil said over the radio.

"146 acknowledged. 144, 133, did you copy 146?" the dispatcher replied.

"144, copy," a voice acknowledged.

"133, copied also," another said.

Gil was happy working patrol. He felt he'd been born to it. He had no desire to move up or jockey for detective like many other officers, but that didn't make him any less irritated at Lucas being the first cop he knew to jump straight from Academy to detective. All that had happened because of a case nine months before that Lucas helped Simon solve, involving the death of Simon's previous partner, the forging of artworks, stolen nanochips carrying top secret data, and both a prominent local businessman and Deputy Chief. The businessman, Benjamin Ashman, had turned out to be innocent and got murdered for it by a trusted associate. The Deputy Chief had gone down in an embarrassing case that the KCPD had been very glad to have overshadowed by both the solving of the case itself and the android's role in it.

"If this guy doesn't want to be caught," Lucas muttered as he made another sharp left and then followed the speeding, beat up 80s Mercury Capri into an alley, "he should have upgraded his ride. He's not even in this century." The perp's car looked like it was barely holding together.

Gil shook his head. "Just focus on your driving, Officer."

"I'm a professional. Don't try this at home," Lucas cracked and slammed the brakes as the Capri tore out of the alley and narrowly missed colliding with an SUV. The SUV skidded to a stop then started off again just as Lucas burst from the alley. The angry driver flipped him off and shouted obscenities after them both.

"Bad language makes for bad feelings," Lucas said, quoting one of his favorites: Robocop.

"Stop it," Gil warned.

Lucas just grinned. "All this over some graffiti," he added.

"The guy's been on our list for two years," Gil said. "First time I ever caught him red handed. He escaped three times just before I arrived. He knows he'll do time and heavy fines. Probably has a record, too."

"Maybe you just scare people."

Gil held back a grin. He liked that idea. "That, too." If only I could scare you, he thought.

He held on again as Lucas followed the suspect's vehicle

through another red light and narrow miss, continuing up the street toward a Metro crossing. Then just as the commuter train approached, the Capri shot across and headed the wrong way down the left side of the road. The train barely missed and Gil saw the frightened engineer's wide eyes and pale face as Lucas narrowed his eyes and sped up on the right side, motioning to the train.

"You keep an eye on him, in case he turns off," Lucas said.

"I'll call it in. One of the others will get him," Gil said. The android did have mad driving skills but that was pushing it. "We need to be safe. You know the regs."

Lucas nodded. "I live my life a quarter mile at a time, bro." *Fast and Furious.* The android continued speeding up as best he could, honking his horn at any driver who got in his way. They cleared the train, just as the suspect turned left onto 22nd Street and raced up hill.

Lucas slammed on the brakes, his body tensing involuntarily even as he struggled to maneuver the steering wheel. The car skidded into an arc, passenger-side first, then Lucas accelerated again and tore up the hill after the Capri. "I got my own skillz, bro," he snapped.

Gil considered for the first time whether he should be wearing Depends diapers during training.

The Capri turned right on Oak and headed south again toward Crown Center.

"146, south on Oak toward Crown Center at Pershing," Gil reported over the radio.

"146, acknowledged. 144, 133, did you copy?"

Even as the units' replies came over the radio, Gil saw the flashing lights of two squad cars up ahead coming toward them. So apparently did Golden Boy, the graffiti king, as the suspect started weaving, then shot up onto the sidewalk and skidded to a stop near the front of Crown Center, pedestrians screaming and rushing clear.

Golden Boy bailed out of his Capri and ran straight for the shopping center, as Lucas and the squad cars pulled up onto the sidewalk nearby, slower and safe. The five cops and Lucas climbed out and headed off in pursuit.

Gil knew he was getting old because his skin was already glistening with sweat after climbing out of the Interceptor and starting the chase. Forty felt older than he wanted to admit. Lucas, of course, quickly outran them, making good headway on Golden Boy, despite the oblivious shopping crowd.

"144," Gil heard over the radio as one of the uniforms running down the stairs behind him called in to dispatch.

"144, go ahead," the dispatcher replied. Two dispatchers usually covered calls for all of Central at one time. Gil couldn't tell by voice which one this was, but she sounded new.

"Pursuit continuing on foot into Crown Center," the uniform said as they ran past Einstein's Bagels and Fritz's with its large train engine out front. "Suspect is Hispanic with bleached blond hair, medium height, tattoos covering the length of both arms and his chest, wearing jeans, a Royals sweatshirt and a black bandanna wrapped around his head. 133 and 146 also in pursuit."

"144, acknowledged. Do you need further assistance?"

"Only if you can make us faster," Gil cracked, each word between breaths as he ran, feeling his age.

"146, sounds like you need youth first," the dispatcher replied.

"146 reminds dispatch of his past record in races at Choir picnics," Gil said. "Ten years running," he added.

"And you sound every minute of it now," one of the uniforms cracked.

Shoppers parted before them, chattering and pointing, a few clearly filming with cell phones, as the officers ran past pursuing the graffiti artist. Gil could see Lucas running, closing on their target now. Golden Boy was just a yard ahead of him. He motioned to the four uniforms, "Let's split up and see if we can get around him."

The uniforms nodded, kept running, and split off in pairs, two heading for the far side of the present aisle while Gil took the left side and the others turning right for the garage stairs, hoping to get in front of the suspect and cut him off. Of course, that would only work if they could move faster on the next floor up. Gil had doubts.

As expected, Golden Boy took the escalator up outside the Coterie Theatre—there was nowhere else for him to go. Lucas was right behind and Gil and the uniforms a few minutes after.

They came up to the wonderful, tantalizing smell of Chip's Chocolate Factory and could see shoppers crowded around, watching a candy-making demonstration even as they hurried past. Lucas followed Golden Boy right and through a narrow passage beside Chip's. Gil and the uniforms went left toward the Kid Oh! outlet and the wider passage and saw the other uniforms running up the hall from the garage in the opposite direction, toward them.

Golden Boy was stuck between, jostling the crowd and pushing people aside in an attempt to get through and escape.

"Police, Golden Boy, it's over!" Gil shouted.

"Hey, that's my daughter, you ass!" a man said as Golden Boy pushed a teenage brunette into the wall she was facing and plowed on. The man whirled and grabbed Golden Boy by the arm, lightning fast, pulling at him, as the girl spun and scowled. But Golden Boy yanked free and wrapped his arm around the girl, pulling her to him and backing toward a stone wall, a knife appearing in his hand and moving toward her neck.

Gil and the uniforms arrived, looking down at them, sidearms locked on Golden Boy as the teenage girl struggled to free herself, yelling, "Get off me! Stop!"

Lucas narrowed his eyes, honing his aim, and Gil knew the android was using his special abilities to target the suspect. "Hold your fire," Gil ordered, then locked eyes with the suspect. "Let the girl go."

Golden Boy shook his head, eyes darting around. "I'm getting out of here, man."

"Only in cuffs," one of the uniforms snapped.

"Drop the knife," Lucas said coldly.

"Fuck you, man," Golden Boy said and spat at Lucas's feet.

Lucas' Glock 19C snapped downward and fired, and Golden Boy screamed as he let go of the girl and fell to his knees, his thigh bleeding. "You shot me, you fuck!"

"No spitting. No cursing in front of ladies," Lucas said as the girl ran and hugged her father. Lucas yanked Golden Boy to his feet, the perp cursing and wincing from pain. The android shoved Golden Boy at the uniforms, who cuffed and Mirandized him.

"Shall we take him in our car?" Lucas asked.

Gil shook his head and looked at the uniforms. "Take him back to holding at Central please."

"Police brutality!" Golden Boy yelled as shoppers around them watched the scene.

"Spitting is assault, be glad you missed," Lucas snapped and turned back to his T.O. as the uniforms dragged a wrestling Golden Boy back onto the escalator.

Gil grabbed Lucas by the arm and dragged him toward the wall nearby. "What the fuck was that?! I ordered you to hold fire."

"A civilian was in danger," Lucas said, offering his trainer a puzzled look.

"As much from you as the suspect!" Gil snapped.

Lucas shook his head, frowning. "My weapon was never aimed directly at her. My aim is quite good. I would never have hit her."

Gil knew the trainee was right. He was not human, not a normal cop. Still, it was an unnecessary risk, and not one he felt comfortable with a trainee taking on his watch. Even experienced cops would have hesitated longer. "What if you had missed?"

Lucas scoffed. "I never miss, sir."

"You never follow orders either," Gil muttered.

Lucas frowned and started to respond but Gil raised a hand. "Just shut up and give me the keys. I'm driving the rest of the shift."

Lucas shrugged and handed Gil the keys then stepped toward the escalator. "Yes, sir."

"Where you going?" Gil asked.

Lucas stopped and whirled back to face him. "The car?"

Gil shook his head and pressed a palm into Lucas' chest. "We're not going anywhere until the Shooting Team's done with us. Just wait here and don't say or do anything." Gil hurried over to where a shopping center janitor pulling a bucket and mop was eyeing the blood stain.

THE CUBICLE FARM that served as the Central Division Property Detectives' squad room was at its busiest in the early morning when detectives were arriving, starting paperwork, and making their flurry of early phone calls, and then again in late afternoon when everyone came in to wrap up before heading for home.

At 4 p.m., when Master Detective John Simon arrived back from the latest scene of what he was sure was a connected string of burglaries, the place was hopping. He glanced down the row of cubicles to where his former partner, Blanca Santorios's old desk was buzzing with activity as Detectives Art Maberry and Jose Correia borrowed it to sort through a stack of files. In between, Detectives Anna Dolby and Martin Oglesby occupied their own cubes, busily typing on keyboards, catching up on the days' paperwork.

As he made his way toward his own cubicle, Simon glanced in the Sergeant's office to see JoAnn Becker sitting at her desk, working the phone. Except for Santorios's desk, it was a routine scene, and as he reached his own cube, Simon stopped to glare over the wall at Maberry and Correia. Slickly dressed, late twenties, and tan, the Brazilian

Casanova Correia paid him no mind, but Correia's partner, Maberry, an overweight nerd with too many Hawaiian shirts and a penchant for letting his facial hair go untrimmed too long, glanced up and shot Simon a puzzled look.

"Hey!" Maberry said, elbowing his partner.

Correia looked up at the annoyed Simon and rolled his eyes. "Boss said as long as we clear it off in time for your new partner's first day, we can use it as long as we want." And he went back to work on the stacked files again as Maberry shrugged at Simon.

Simon scrunched his face, mimicking Correia's whine, "Boss said we could! What is this—third grade? Shut the fuck up and clear out."

Correia looked sheepish. "Well, she did."

"It's been ten months, John. Time to move on," Maberry said, respectful but firm enough to let Simon know they weren't going to bow to his wishes on the matter anymore. "This case is paper-heavy. We needed somewhere to work. Sorry." And then Maberry went back to work, too.

Simon shot them another glare and growled, "I'm sure Santorios would be touched by your sense of loss." Without waiting for a reaction, he slid into his chair and pushed the button to click on his own computer's flat screen LED. They were probably right. It couldn't stay empty forever. And Simon had been a dick about it long enough, out of mourning, respect, and just missing his old partner. But Santorios was dead, and the squad room was close quarters with little space to spare. He let it go and started typing.

"John! What you got?" Becker's voice called from down the row, moments later.

Simon looked up to see the face of his old friend—forties

with the face of a retired model, though she wasn't—a woman who could give any man in there a run for his money in an ass-kicking contest. He grunted and rose from his chair, plodding toward her as the Sergeant turned and retreated back into her office.

Despite the constant piles of paperwork and files covering every available surface, Becker's office smelled pleasant, like the cleanest place in the building. Stacks aside, she kept it dust free and had strategically placed air fresheners plugged into sockets or sitting atop file cabinets or shelves around the room. The scent they gave off wasn't particularly feminine but more of a warm, cozy kitchen essence he couldn't exactly describe.

As Simon took the seat opposite her oak desk, she looked up at him, waiting.

"Another break-in with a hole cut through the wall," Simon confirmed what they'd both suspected when he'd taken the call early that morning. "They took a laptop and a few files, but nothing like the last three. Seems random again, except for the cutting thing. This time they cut a hole in a different spot where the owner couldn't see it from outside."

Becker shook her head. "Imminently adaptable crooks."

Simon sighed. "Yeah, I fucking hate that."

"Certainly seem smarter than the usual burglars," Becker observed.

"Why can't they all just be idiots?" he cracked, but he agreed. These were certainly more sophisticated crimes than many burglaries. Burglars were often clever but rarely smart. They knew their craft well and were skilled at it, but they made mistakes that got them caught. These scenes were the cleanest Simon had ever seen. Even the holes cut in walls and doors to let them in were left concealed and covered over on the exterior—almost professionally done to conceal the crimes until the victims entered the buildings or rooms burgled. It was unique to his years of handling property crimes for sure. None of the other detectives recalled anything like it either.

"What the hell are they after? Seems a lot of effort and thought for random burglaries," Becker said as she leaned back in her chair.

Simon had no answer. He'd been running over and over the list of stolen items for several hours, trying to find a connection. Even the types of locales differed: two businesses, a lumberyard, and now two apartments. The first theft had involved taking some power tools and empty steel drums, the second some wiring and electrical tape and related items. They were fairly certain the same thieves stole a box truck and a bunch of lumber and screws from the lumberyard—the kind of stuff that made them wonder about bombs. But afterwards they'd only hit apartments and taken the kind of stuff burglars always seemed to take—items of convenience: home electronics, files, credit cards, computers, cell phones, bills. It made no sense so far.

"And no evidence any of the items they took were used in the later break ins?" Becker wondered aloud.

Simon snorted. "Power tools? Shit yeah. Likely, but what they took doesn't match the MOs so far as we can tell. Different kinds of tools. So, no. It's weird. Like they started down one path then switched to another."

"They could be stealing extra stuff at the apartments to throw us off," Becker said.

Simon nodded. "Yeah, the electronics would work as triggers for sure. I've got a call in to the bomb squad to consult. See if any bombs have turned up with related components, but they haven't called back yet."

"How many perps do you think we're looking at?" Becker asked.

"Two, maybe three, tops," Simon said. "One could do it, but moving the quantities taken would mean multiple trips—greater chance of being caught, so more than one makes more sense, but more than two or three also would increase the likelihood of drawing attention."

"Agreed," Becker said and shifted in her chair, stretching a bit. "Well, you're on top of it as expected. Just wondered if you had anything new. Let me know when they return your call, okay?"

"Of course," Simon said as he stood and ambled for the door.

"Maybe Lucas can help," Becker said, smiling. "Use his special skills."

For the time in his career, Simon was actually looking forward to a new partner. He'd always dreaded it, even though he'd gotten lucky a few times over his nineteen years with KCPD. Santorios was one example. Although Property Detectives often worked in pairs, they weren't assigned partners per se. But Simon had been the exception, and because of Lucas' special rushed promotion and circumstances, the department had insisted he be partnered with a veteran, so it was natural the guy who'd just lost a partner pair up with him. If they hadn't insisted, Simon would have. Android or not, the guy had saved his life. He was smart, adaptable, and had great skills and instincts. Plus, they'd worked a case months back when Santorios was killed and become friends, despite Simon's dislike of new technology. Even Emma, Simon's fourteen-year-old daughter, adored the guy. And he'd been joining them once a week for meals and movies since.

In fact, despite his earlier resistance, even the android's annoying habit of quoting movies had won Simon over. Now he was remembering quotes and lyrics just to share them with his new partner—making notes so he'd remember them—in anticipation of their sarcastic back and forth. He'd never done that with any partner before for sure.

"John?" Becker's questioning voice shook him out of his thoughts.

Simon realized he'd just frozen there in her office doorway. He cleared his throat. "Uh, yeah, Sarge. Sorry. I'm sure he can. Look forward to it."

So awkward.

He quickly whirled and strode back toward his cube as Becker's laughter followed him down the short aisle.

Simon had been working less than five minutes on his paperwork when Oglesby called his name. "Hey, Simon!"

"Yeah?" he asked, looking up to where Oglesby was glancing across from the cube next to his.

Chubbier and taller than Simon, Oglesby was a sixteen year vet whose slipped disk led him to spend a lot of time standing in his cube rather than sitting. A fellow divorcee with kids who were older, he was Simon's closest pal in the squad. "Just got a call from Sergeant El-Ashkar down at the front desk," Oglesby said. "Guess who just arrested Golden Boy and shot him in the thigh?"

Simon raised a brow and went back to typing. "Got me. But hell, I've been wanting to talk to him about these burglaries." In addition to his various criminal enterprises, Golden Boy was a fount of information on everything nefarious going on in Kansas City at any time. All the cops who'd been around long enough to have a rapport with him always did what they could to pry such information out of him when they got a chance.

"Lucas George," Oglesby said.

Simon stopped mid-keystroke and stared over at Oglesby. "No shit? Lucas shot someone? Is he okay?"

Oglesby chuckled. "Our metal friend is fine. Golden Boy is crying 'police brutality' and whining obnoxiously about his thigh, though."

Simon smiled as he stood, more relieved than he'd ever admit to hear Lucas was fine. He still felt pangs from the time he'd almost lost him after a shootout. Android or not, Lucas was like family. He mattered. "Yeah, Golden Boy whining. That's a fucking surprise."

They both guffawed again as Simon headed for the door.

"Lucas is still with the shooting team and his T.O., she said," Oglesby added, referring to the female Desk Sergeant.

Simon sighed. "Okay, I'll get the details, I'm sure. Thanks for the heads-up." Moments later, he was out the door headed down the hall toward booking. It was just ten yards away, past the tinted glass double doors leading to the lobby and civilian side of the front desk and right down another short hallway past the desk sergeants who checked out vehicles and radios to the station's small holding cell area.

Simon immediately spotted Golden Boy lying on a bench in one cell, moaning and pressing his hand against the bandaged wound on his left thigh.

"Buzz me in, will you, Leo?" he called to the Sergeant manning the cell block desk. The rest of the cells were empty at the moment.

The Sergeant smiled and nodded. "Have at him, Detective." He pressed a button on the desk in front of him, and there was an electronic buzz as a light above the cell Golden Boy occupied switched from red to green.

Simon pulled on the door and went inside, hurrying to Golden Boy before the crook could react and patting him on the thigh right atop the bandage. "Golden Boy! Long time, eh? How's the street treating you?"

Golden Boy cried out in pain. "Shit! You asshole!"

Simon grinned. "Sit up and let's chat."

"Fuck you!" Golden Boy said through gritted teeth as glanced down at his injured thigh.

"Or I can pat it again and inspect your pain threshold some more," Simon added.

Golden Boy spat, whined, and sat up. "I hate you, Simon."

Simon grinned. "You say the sweetest things." He straddled the end of the bench beside Golden Boy, a couple feet between them and sighed. "What do you know about the people burgling these days?"

"Which people?" Golden Boy asked, wincing as he stretched out his wounded leg and looked at Simon.

"I'm so glad you asked," Simon said and told him.

CHAPTER 2

KARL RAMON WAS a sideman, a sax player. Not that he'd made much money at it. That was just how he thought of himself, no matter what he did for income. He'd been in a lot of bands over the years, too, since he'd taken up the instrument in middle school, back in Salina, Kansas where he'd grown up. Roosevelt-Lincoln Junior High, two early twentieth century brick buildings joined in the 1950s which served the northern population of the small city until it closed after the 2002-2003 school year, when Karl finished eighth grade.

"We closed down the joint," he and his classmates had loved to brag, but in truth, many students were sad to see it go—the place had a lot of memories. After closing as a school, the buildings had been rehabilitated into senior apartments as a new middle school, built across town, replaced it and new generations of students had no memory of Roosevelt-Lincoln.

Mister McMillan, Karl's band teacher, had infected all of his students with his love of music, using an easygoing sense of humor and hearty laugh to soften his dedication to hard work and discipline. Despite the challenges of marching band—practices, extra time, mockable uniforms—McMillan made it fun and his students adored him for it. Many had gone on to lifelong relationships with music, some even professional. Karl had tried to be one of them, but then he'd married and had kids, and though his wife's career as a lawyer provided for a time, she came down with ALS-Lou Gehrig's disease—a neurodegenerative condition effecting nourishment of nerves in the brain and spinal cord—which killed her in five years and left Karl as the sole provider. Although some like famous scientist Stephen Hawking might survive for years with it, Julia had literally wasted away in front of her family's eyes.

Little known to most residents, more than ten percent of the industrial space in greater Kansas City was located "down under," covering about twenty-five million square feet—an area bigger than the downtown business district. With mining limestone for roadways continuing, more space opened up all the time. 5 million square feet of leased warehouse, light-industry, and office space, and a network of more than two miles of rail lines and six miles of roads, made UnderCity the world's largest underground business complex—and one of eight or so in the area. It was a budding industry, one growing in several other states as well, but Kansas City was at the vanguard, with more and more business clients trading architectural advantages like windows and above ground signage for cheaper energy bills and consistent year round temperatures in what appeared like a mix between an over-sized parking garage and a mall. With ten thousand limestone support columns laid out forty feet apart in a grid, pillars replaced corner offices as the most desirable real estate—or so tenants joked—and a whole new subculture and way of doing business had developed there.

With that came more jobs, perfect for a guy like Karl looking for flexible hours paired with decent benefits.

And so the family had relocated to Kansas City when Julia got sick, for better healthcare, and a better job market for Karl. And there they'd stayed, living in a blue collar neighborhood north of Truman Road in Independence, Missouri. Karl commuting every day to his job at UnderCity. He was involved in security and it suited his mood. He worked nights, after his scattered gigs, allowing him to be home during the day to care for Julia and see the kids off to school. And it had worked well. So much so that even after she'd died, he'd kept the position and hours. He was used to it by then.

Karl liked his job, liked his employers, and enjoyed the tenants, many of whom were interesting and innovative people—as anyone had to be to choose such unusual surroundings—and work had become a second home, almost a family for him. Seniority allowed him a few benefits as well, like seven hour days that let him do gigs at clubs before starting work at midnight, great health benefits, three paid weeks off, and more. It had been a godsend he'd stumbled into almost by accident—friend of a friend helping in a desperate hour—and now he'd been there fifteen years.

But still, in his mind, Karl was a musician, and tonight he played the role well, joining his friends in a jazz trio they dubbed the "Blues City Notes"—sax, drums, and piano. Tips were good, the crowd was respectful and appreciative despite also being heavy consumers of alcohol from the well-stocked bar, and life was good. They played two Thursdays a month—six to eleven at a club called The Waterfront, inside a downtown hotel. It was twenty-five minutes from work and home, so fairly convenient, and in the city's hopping Crossroads Art District, so they always had a decent crowd, too.

The piano player, Jimmy, usually took the lead but tonight they'd come in early to play warm-up and cover part of the dinner crowd, so by special request they played a lot of Stan Getz classics and that put Karl up front. They opened with "Desafinado," a bossa nova classic from the famed Getz/Gilberto album and then "Bim Bom" from that album's sequel, Cole Porter's "Night and Day," and eventually closed with an instrumental of "The Girl From Ipanema" with various other standards and a few originals mixed in throughout the night. Altogether, they'd planned three sets, and each song would be played twice. And Karl was on fire the first set, one of his best performances in ages. When he left the stage to head for the dressing rooms, he was flying on adrenaline and sheer joy—the ultimate feeling for a musician who's done well. That all came crashing down when he closed the door to find himself facing a dark stranger with a gun.

Seated in a chair behind the door where Karl came in, the man was tall and bulky—but all muscle—like some kind of warrior, Karl supposed. The intensity of the green eyes cut through him like a blade, and the crew cut hinted at military connections. The gun was a semi-automatic pistol of some sort, black and sleek. Karl didn't know much about guns. His job required him to carry mace and a club but he'd used neither in fifteen years and had neither on him now. Muffled music and chatter echoed through the walls from the dining area and club as Karl caught his breath.

The man just stared, saying nothing, so Karl swallowed and asked, "What do you want?"

That brought a grin, but not a friendly one. This one was cold as ice, an implied threat. "Nice set, Karl. I'm impressed."

"Uh, thanks," Karl said. "You know you're not supposed to be back here. I go out front for a bit after."

"I'm not here as a fan," the man replied, monotone.

"I gathered that from the gun," Karl said as he nonchalantly set his sax down on the sofa and turned back, forcing his body to relax despite the fear charging through it and tensing every limb. "Do we know each other?" Karl searched the face but kept coming up with nothing.

The man grunted. "No, but we're going to become great friends I think."

"Why's that?"

"Because you're going to help me change the world, Karl."

"Change the world, huh? Ambitious guy. How will we do that?"

"That, we will discuss in time," the man said. "But first, let's just say you have information we need. And when I'm ready, I'll be in touch. And you'll be ready to provide it."

"I guess that depends what it is."

The man laughed. "And I guess the survival of Julie and Matt depends on your full cooperation." His eyes cut into Karl again, and Karl winced with imagined pain.

"You leave my kids alone," he said, his voice shaking with a mix of anger and fear.

"That all depends on you, Karl," the man said. "You just wait until we contact you."

"When will that be?"

"Soon," the man said, with another cold grin as he stood. "Tell no one or your kids will be getting a visit at Nowlin."

The Middle School in Independence Karl's kids both attended. The man moved toward the door and turned to lock eyes again with Karl. "We'll know if you do. You're being watched."

Karl gulped, telling himself it was all a bluff and yet somehow he found it hard to even breathe. He simply nodded.

The man grunted again. "Good. I'm glad we understand each other. Have a good night, Karl."

And then he whirled and was gone, the door shutting behind him so quietly, Karl had to blink to believe it was real. On instinct, he raced and opened it, peering down the short hallway one direction then the other. The guy was gone. Like evaporated water on a summer sidewalk.

Karl took a deep breath and stepped back into the dressing room. What kind of information could anyone want from him, a widowed amateur musician and security guard? It made no sense. Yet they knew his kid's names and their school, too. Who was the guy? Karl felt a sudden urge to race home, but he had two more sets and work at UnderCity after that. Instead, he'd call them and check. Julie would still be up texting with friends. Working quickly, he laid the sax in its case and sealed it carefully, then grabbed that and his coat and headed for the alley to find a quieter place to make a call.

BY THE TIME Simon finished his paperwork and follow up, it was almost eight—a late night for him—but with his daughter Emma at her mother's he had nowhere to be, so he took a stroll down to the locker room to look for Lucas or Gil Lenz. He was almost past the lunch area to the locker room when he heard taunting up ahead.

"Hey, Robocop, don't shoot me, I'm not running!"

"Hey, George, did Sarge write you a ticket for street racing yet?"

"I hear you made the T.O. crap his pants. They should give you a citation."

Simon entered and looked around at the smiling cops— several in clean, pressed uniforms, preparing to start their shifts, and others in various stages of civvies—all smiling and looking at Lucas George, who was sitting on the end of a bench in silence, looking dejected. The room was warm with humidity from the showers and smelled of sweat, aftershave, deodorant, foot odor, and hairspray.

"You guys are very funny," Lucas said.

"Hell, you should be popular as a partner—for anyone wanting early retirement," another cop pitched in from around the corner then Simon heard more chuckling as several smiling faces peered around the edge of the painted cinder block wall.

Simon stopped beside his friend and future partner, ignoring the others. "You okay?" Forties, former star running back at K-State, divorced, a fifteen year veteran of the department, he was older than the rest of those taunting his friend and more experienced with the bullshit, too.

Lucas looked up at him and offered a weak smile. "Lenz is considering failing me."

Simon frowned. "That bastard. You let me talk to him."

"I was doing my best," Lucas said.

Simon patted his shoulder. "Of course, you were. It's just your best is intimidating—in a scary way, pal."

That brought a smile. Lucas nodded. "I guess I can understand that."

"Just ignore these assholes," Simon said, then raised his voice, "It's all petty jealousy anyway. They wish they had half your skills."

The comment brought scoffs, shaking heads, and laughter from the other cops, but Simon saw in their eyes he wasn't that far off. He stepped back as Lucas got to his feet.

"They took my gun, too," Lucas said.

"Standard procedure in a shooting," Simon said with a nod. "For ballistic tests. You'll get it back."

"Hey, Simon, you got a real winner there!" one uniform said and slapped Simon on the back as he and his giggling partner moved past and out the door.

"Shit, Swanson, out drive and out shoot you any day. At least, my ass is covered!" Simon called after them. "Good luck with Bays there!" Swanson's partner was widely known as the worst shot in the station, having barely passed his last qualification.

Lucas stood beside Simon, the other cops still jittering around them.

Simon patted him on the shoulder again. "Let's go find Lenz or a drink, whichever is easier," Simon said.

"You know alcohol has no effect on me," Lucas reminded him.

"It makes me feel great though," Simon said. "What else could I ask?"

Lucas grinned and followed Simon out the door.

"You gotta learn to give it right back to 'em, like you do with me," Simon said as they walked down the corridor the way he'd come. "Quote movies or something."

"Lenz ordered me not to do that," Lucas said.

Simon groaned. "Bastard's never had a sense of humor. Ignore him."

"I did. It just made him mad."

Simon grinned. "So? I got over it."

"I want these guys to like me."

"Your being a smart ass won me over," Simon said, totally serious.

Lucas shrugged. "You threatened to shoot me twice."

Simon grunted. "Yeah, almost did, too."

"I can outshoot you now, you know?" Lucas joked, a skill he seemed to be picking up on more skillfully by the day.

Simon shot him a look. "Don't push it, pal. Partners can be changed."

"I'm not worried. The Force is strong with us," Lucas said and grinned.

"Shut the fuck up," Simon teased and they headed up the stairs.

At the booking counter, Simon nodded to Sergeant El-Ashkar's replacement, Sergeant Thomas. "Anyone seen Lenz around?"

"He raced out of here once the shooting team finished with his crazy trainee," Thomas said, then noticed Lucas and cleared his throat. "Uh...sorry."

"Shit, Bob, you really want anyone reviewing your

driving record from back in the day?" Simon fired back. Thomas had developed a rep as a rookie for going through the most black and whites in a month.

"Damn, John, that's cold," Thomas said, shaking his head.

Balding Sergeant Wallace chuckled from a chair behind Thomas. "Wrecking Ball Thomas, wasn't it?"

Thomas screwed his face up and blushed as Wallace nodded to Lucas. "You got the bad guy and the car's fine," Wallace said. "You're still ahead of Thomas, George."

Lucas smiled. "Well, I'll do my best to keep it that way."

Wallace and Simon laughed. Thomas, white, short, bulky, was the opposite to Wallace's tall, thin, black presence and about ten years his junior, too. He glared at them both then nodded to Lucas. "Better day tomorrow, Officer George."

"I hope so, sir," Lucas agreed.

Simon patted Lucas on the back and headed for the door. "Time for some alcohol, gentlemen."

Wallace grunted. "Have fun now!"

As they headed for Simon's classic 1985 Dodge Charger, Lucas looked worried. "Don't worry, we'll catch him tomorrow," Simon said, back to the topic of Lenz. "If it was a righteous shoot, nothing to worry about."

"If it was?" Lucas said.

Simon nodded and met his gaze with a reassuring look. "Relax. I believe in you, but not everyone knows what you can do. Give them time."

Lucas nodded. "Where are we going?"

"Out for some fun," Simon said. "You need to get your mind off of this."

"If you want, I can drive," Lucas offered as he stopped beside the Charger while Simon continued around to the driver's side.

Simon shot him a look. "I already said I believe in you. Doesn't mean I want to die."

"Those two statements seem contradictory," Lucas said.

Simon raised an eyebrow. "I'm an enigma, pal. Now get in and relax."

Just to taunt his future partner further, Simon let off a rebel yell as he peeled out of the lot, tires screeching, and turned sharply right onto Linwood, headed downtown.

"Where are we actually going?" Lucas asked as the car straightened and he rocked back hard in the passenger seat.

"Golden Boy gave me a tip I want to check out on the case, but it's a bar, so I figure we can kill two birds," Simon said.

"Killing birds is how you relax?"

"Still haven't learned that one, eh? Remind me to work on your knowledge of colloquialisms, See Threepio."

"I prefer Artoo-Detoo," Lucas said.

"Artoo couldn't talk," Simon said.

"Yeah, but he was cooler. Less annoying."

Simon grunted. "Why do you think I picked Threepio?"

After that, Lucas fell into silence and within ten minutes they'd pulled up in a small lot outside a corner bar that bore the name "Jimmy's" flashing in blue neon, smaller signs advertising "Bud Light" and "Corona" below it on the brick wall beside the plain entrance. Simon parked and led the way as they got out and approached the building.

"Have you been here before?" Lucas asked.

Simon shook his head. "Not a cop bar. Supposedly a rough place sometimes, though it's early. Just watch my back and let me do the talking."

"Is there karaoke?" Lucas asked, naming a favorite pastime he'd discovered on their last case and pursued ever since.

Simon stiffened, raising a palm in objection. "Don't even think about it. This is not the kind of place we want to stand out. Blend. Like I do."

Lucas smiled. "And I was going to ask you to dance."

Simon shot him a warning look. "So very much not that kind of place."

As soon as they walked into the dimly lit, smoky room filled with cracked leather booths and faux marble plastic tables, a long Oak bar taking up the entire north wall, Simon hoped Lucas got the point. The place dripped blue collar machismo. A few regulars and the bartender stared up at them as they came in, but the rest couldn't be bothered. Oldies blared from a jukebox in the corner, loud enough to drown out any eavesdropping on conversations without going right up next to the locations where they were being held. Instead, Simon headed for the bar and Lucas followed.

Sliding onto a red, cracked leather stool, Simon nodded to the bartender. "Corona, bottle, please."

The bartender grunted and leaned down under the counter to open a short cooler and retrieve the requested item. Simon dipped his hand in a bowl of salty peanuts on the bar and shoved half a fistful in his mouth, chewing.

"I don't know you," the bartender said, sliding him the beer.

Simon caught it and nodded. "First time."

"What brings you here?" the bartender's growl was almost pirate-like, his face scrunched up with his displeasure at dealing with strangers. Fifties, thinning hair, medium height, with an ever-expanding beer belly, he looked like he enjoyed his own fare as much as his customers. His upper arms bore tattoos of an anchor, crossed swords, and an Uzi. Although he radiated unfriendliness, Simon found his attempt to appear intimidating almost laughable.

Simon tipped back his head and took a long sip of the Corona. "Looking for someone," he said with a sigh when he lowered the bottle again.

"Ain't we all," the bartender said. "Your friend want something?" He motioned to Lucas who had leaned his elbows and back against the bar and was taking in the room.

"Him? Nah, he doesn't drink," Simon said. "You wouldn't want to see him drunk."

The bartender issued a cocky snort. "I'll bet I've seen worse."

Simon laughed. "You might be surprised."

"Your types never surprise me," the bartender said, his face returning to an unfriendly glare. "What makes you think I'll know the person you're after?"

"Can't hurt to ask," Simon said nonchalantly, as he took another sip from the beer then wiped the foam casually off his mouth with the back of his arm. Golden Boy had given him a name, an odd one, but someone who fenced lots of stolen goods and usually knew everyone active in burglary in the town. A player Simon surprisingly hadn't encountered before which meant he'd either changed his name or was new. Didn't matter. Golden Boy's info was almost always worth checking out, so Simon said the name, "Guy named Weasel."

"Weasel?" the bartender scoffed. "That's an animal, not a person."

Simon shrugged. "Takes all kinds, you know?"

"Don't know him," the bartender replied quickly. Too quickly but he kept his eyes locked on Simon's and offered no clue if the guy might be in the room. The guy was good.

Simon sighed and took another sip, finishing the bottle, then set it back on the counter with a bit of a pop. "Okay then. We'll just ask someone else."

"My customers don't like other people in their business," the bartender said. It was a warning.

"I can understand that. Not too fond of it myself," Simon said, in a way that made it clear the bartender getting in his business wasn't welcome either.

The bartender raised both palms in surrender and turned, walking off toward the opposite end of the bar.

Simon nodded his head to one side at Lucas and turned, finding himself face to face with the roughhouse version of Mr. Clean. The guy was bald, in a white shirt and spiked leather jacket with torn jeans and steel-toed boots beneath.

"You want Weasel?" the man demanded, his voice a deep growl.

"Friend of a friend," Simon said innocently. "Might have a job for him."

"Weasel don't like friend's fucking friends," Mr. Clean said, crossing his arms over his puffed chest and blocking Simon's way.

Simon stepped right and tried to go around him but saw three other tall, bulky types approaching from behind him.

Lucas slipped into ready mode beside him.

"I'm not looking for trouble," Simon said. "Just a referral."

"Weasel don't take fucking referrals," Mr. Clean insisted.

"You have quite the vocabulary, friend," Simon said.

This time the answer was a fist flying at his face, a dagger glinting in the dim light. Simon ducked and rushed, headbutting Mr. Clean in the mid-chest as Lucas reacted beside him.

"KCPD Officers, everyone step back!" Lucas demanded, and Simon wished he'd warned him. It was the exact wrong move.

Chairs scooted back loudly and more toughies closed in.

"We hate cops," Mr. Clean said as he grabbed Simon by the arm and threw him into several more toughies, who were more than ready to join the battle.

"Wrong thing to say, pal," Simon said, looking at Lucas, who was also grabbed by three men and being shoved toward the door. "Look, we didn't come for trouble," Simon continued, turning to make eye contact with the toughies again.

"We did!" one of them said, and grinned—his teeth all steel.

The next few minutes, try as he might, Simon felt like a pin-the-tail donkey at a child's birthday party. Lucas' android strength stood him in better stead, but despite some groans, screams, and cursing, they were outnumbered and soon Simon found himself propelled out the door to land painfully hard on his knees in front of the bar on the sidewalk. Lucas landed beside him moments later and they turned back to see Mr. Clean and four others, arms crossed over their huge chests, blocking the door.

"Don't fucking come back!" Mr. Clean ordered.

Simon groaned, his body aching, but waved Lucas off as his friend tried to help him to his feet. Instead, they stood and faced the men, Simon raising his palms in surrender.

"All right, so no one's seen Weasel. You could have just said that," Simon cracked.

"Fuck you!" steel-teeth replied, glaring.

Simon winced, clenching and unclenching his fists, then rubbing his arms which ached as he stumbled after Lucas and headed for the parking lot.

"You call that relaxing?" Lucas said.

Simon snorted. "I feel fucking great, don't you?" He stumbled and Lucas caught him, leaning him against the Charger.

"Maybe I should drive," Lucas said.

Simon handed him the keys. "Just remember, this isn't city owned. Treat her with respect."

Lucas grinned. "I just follow my instincts."

Simon opened the door and slid into the passenger side, fumbling for the seatbelt.

"Gil Lenz always does that first thing, too," Lucas said as he settled behind the wheel.

"Shut the fuck up and drive," Simon said. "My house."

Without further word, Lucas did just that, driving at a relaxed pace to Simon's relief.

CHAPTER 3

THE BURLINGTON AND Santa Fe Northern Railyard had dominated the central bottoms as long as Simon could remember. Located off I-670 and Kansas Ave, it was a familiar landmark for residents and tourists alike, as three major highways passing through the city converged there, just west of downtown. Originally centered around the Argentine Smelter of the early 1900s, it consisted of miles and miles of converging tracks, switches, sidelines, and more. Rows of old abandoned boxcars were parked on tracks fallen out of use. Others still in use waited there to be picked up or refurbished. Traffic control towers rose into the air, level with the highway overpasses high above the tracks, and on busy days, drivers might see trains loading and unloading, trading cars, switching tracks, or just passing through.

This morning as Simon stopped by on his way to the office, the place was quiet. The early morning trains having passed through already, workers now awaited the next arrival. Apparently no cargo had been dropped or was being unloaded, as Simon saw parked vehicles but no signs of people as he pulled the Charger into a lot and took an open space, then started walking across the tracks.

One of his best confidential informants—or CIs—was a

vagrant who lived in an old abandoned boxcar here. The boxcar was the usual brown though much faded and starting to rust. It rested on a small spur on the south side of the central track cluster that was formerly used for switching cars back and forth between trains. A dirty red rag signaling the occupant was home hung from one of the steps leading up the car's side next to the rust-covered remains of a Santa Fe RR emblem. Simon approached and moved around to the north where other boxcars sat and found the CI's door open and waiting as expected. His real name was Denny but most people just knew him locally as "Mr. Information," because the Meth addict seemed to know everything and everybody, especially about the shipping, smuggling, and criminal activities that intersected with his home area and the downtown he roamed at night.

Stepping toward the car and peering into the shadows inside, the first thing Simon saw were the usual scruffy tennis shoes and ragged jean cuffs. His eyes traced the pant legs up to the ragged t-shirt and thrown over flannel shirt—it was almost like Mr. Information had a uniform. Bedraggled with hair and beard long overdue for trims, Mr. Information was leaned up against the far side of the car, cradling his usual bottle of Absolut Vodka. His eyes stared right at Simon and he jumped up, throwing out a palm as if to warn him off as his eyes darted around warily.

"Oh shit!"

Simon suppressed amusement and shook his head. "Don't worry. He's not with me."

The first time Simon had brought Lucas with him to meet Mr. Information, Lucas had gone overboard imitating Hollywood police techniques and held the vagrant's head out the side of the car, inches from a passing train to make him talk. In the year since, every time Simon came to talk,

Mr. Information would panic, his eyes darting around looking for the crazy android.

"He better not be, man," Mr. Information said, relaxing only a little. "You know how I feel about him coming around me."

Simon climbed up into the car and nodded. "I know. Respect, Denny."

"Damn right. Respect." The vagrant eyed him again, suspiciously. "What you want now? I ain't heard much lately. Been sick the past month on and off."

"Really? Did you see a doctor? I hope it's cleared up," Simon said, genuinely concerned. As much as it seemed Mr. Information and vagrants like him were beyond help, they were often victims of circumstances beyond their control and a series of missteps and bad decisions that led them to live a life trapped in addiction and poverty. Despite CI's often unseemly appearance, cops tended to grow fond of their informants, at least the noncriminal ones, and while he might be guilty of drug use and the occasional opportunistic petty theft, Mr. Information was an ex-Gulf War vet in his fifties, mostly honest, and fairly harmless to anyone but himself.

"Free clinic gave me antibiotics and some nasty tasting liquid thing," Mr. Information said. "Didn't go well with the Vodka, so I threw it out."

Simon fought back a groan and nodded. "I hate that."

"What you need?"

"You ever hear of a guy calls himself 'Weasel'?"

Mr. Information frowned. "Like the animal? What a stupid name."

"I think so, too, but to each his own," Simon said with a

shrug.

Mr. Information thought a minute. "Doesn't ring a bell."

"Can you ask around for me?"

"What you want him for?"

"His name came up from another CI," Simon said. "May be a burglar. Need to check him out."

Mr. Information sighed. "I'll ask a few. Come back in a day or two. But bring me more Absolut, or I ain't saying shit."

It was his usual demand. Simon didn't always comply but it had been a while. "Sure. You got it."

Mr. Information grinned. "You must need him bad, that was too easy."

Simon smiled. "Eh, been a while since I let you win. Besides, Lucas lives near here and can bring some by after work."

Mr. Information's eyes turned cold and he backed away, glaring. "That shit ain't funny, Simon."

Simon laughed. "Just funning you, Denny. Relax."

"Some things you shouldn't joke about."

Simon raised his hands in surrender. "You're right. I'm sorry."

"You bring me Absolut, all is forgiven. Big bottle, though. Don't go cheap on me."

Simon grunted. "Yeah, I know how you roll. You go asking. Be back soon."

Mr. Information was already sliding back down the side of the car and reaching for his bottle as he mumbled in reply.

Simon simply turned and headed back for his car. Mr. Information was discrete enough so no one would know who was asking. He'd play it off like he was connecting people or had a scheme in mind, so if word got back to Weasel, he wouldn't have any clue his name was in play with the cops. That's why Simon liked him so much as a source. That and his information usually panned out as quite useful.

Climbing into the Charger, Simon turned the radio to a rock station and rolled out, headed for Central Patrol. With a start like this, it might actually be a good day. He always liked that.

KCPD'S CENTRAL PATROL DIVISION was based in a triangular, elongated, white brick monstrosity built in the early 90s at 1200 E. Linwood. Remodeling in 2023 had added interrogation rooms, better detention facilities, two conference rooms, and updated lighting and wiring but the walls remained the same blue they'd always been. When Lucas arrived that morning he went straight to the interrogation block and waited in the room marked '3' for the Shooting Team to arrive and question him.

As was mandatory, he'd been given a week off after the shooting and had to meet at least once with a department psychologist plus answer the Shooting Team's interrogatories. The psychologist was pointless in Lucas' case but obligatory according to policy. For most cops, the post-incident process was such a rare occurrence that it was hardly routine. Many had never even been through it, though Lenz and Simon both had offered him a few tips in preparation for the meeting.

Two female officers, an odd pairing known as "the two BBs"—Bahm and Beebe—arrived within ten minutes and sat across the table from Lucas. Both Simon and Lenz had told him of their run-ins with the pair and they'd done so as warnings. But now, looking at them, Lucas found himself intrigued. Neither looked that scary. Marge Bahm, the older of the two, had her gray hair up in a bun, giving her a grandmotherly, school teacher look, while Lena Beebe wore her brunette hair cut shorter and straight. Beebe looked about ten years younger and was six inches or so taller. Whereas she wore new, expensive looking modern suits, Bahm's suit looked like she might have been born in it—well out of fashion from another decade.

The women settled in across the table, setting twin datapads and a digital recorder on the desk, and sitting up straight in their chairs. Only Beebe smiled at him. Bahm just nodded, coldly. So much for the grandmotherly vibe. As they did, a Police Union Rep, Officer Doaa came in. Thirties, long dark hair in braids, uniform crisp and clean, she was a patrol officer from Metro Squad whom Lucas had seen around but never interacted with. She took a seat beside Lucas and nodded confidently.

Lucas nodded back. "Good morning." He then nodded to the BBs and maintained his smile.

"I think we're ready now," Doaa said, looking at the Shooting Team.

Bahm reached over and turned on the recorder, stating the date, the names of those present, and the time and location of the interview.

"Okay, Officer George," Beebe said, taking the lead. "Why

don't you tell us about the events leading up to your apprehension of the subject"—she glanced at her datapad—"Golden Boy?"

Doaa added, "Suspect's real name is Marcus Crebs."

"Okay," Beebe said, eyes locked on Lucas with a friendly look.

Lucas began recalling the events of the afternoon before in vivid detail, giving times to the exact second, describing every street intersection, etc. All three women exchanged looks of surprise and perhaps annoyance? But Lucas figured he must be misreading it. After all, the more detail the better to clear him, right?

When he was done, he leaned back in his chair with a satisfied look.

Bahm shook her head. "That was the best demonstration of overkill I think we've ever heard."

"Excuse me?" Lucas frowned and leaned forward, assuming she was talking about the shooting itself. "I shot him to protect the girl and get the situation under control."

Doaa put a hand on his arm. "Nothing wrong with being detail oriented, right? This is an important process."

Beebe smiled and nodded. "Yes, it was fine."

Bahm looked annoyed. "We'll get to the shooting itself in a minute."

Lucas relaxed again as Doaa's eyes met his with reassurance. "Okay," he replied. "I'm sorry."

"Officer George, you said the suspect grabbed the girl and threatened her with a knife, is that right?" Beebe resumed.

"Yes," Lucas said.

"And you believed neither you nor any of the other officers present could talk to him and convince him to surrender?"

Lucas hesitated a moment, mind racing. "I assessed the situation and believed it best to diffuse it before anyone got hurt. There were numerous civilians around us."

"All the more reason not to rush into firing your weapon," Bahm said, face cold and unemotional.

"I did not rush," Lucas said. "I took my time."

Bahm flipped through data on her datapad with a finger. "But the other officers on the scene, including your Training Officer, reported the entire confrontation took less than two minutes."

Lucas nodded. "There abouts, yes."

"How can you say you took your time when the incident was only two minutes?" Bahm said. This time she looked annoyed.

"Two minutes, thirty-six seconds to be exact," Lucas said after quickly onsulting his memory banks. The two BBs offered no reaction. These people were so intense. Lucas had never felt comfortable around humans who were overly emotional. He'd never met these woman, yet he felt sure Bahm, at least, hated him. Beebe and Doaa were friendly but reserved. His instinct had become to lighten the mood, cheer them up with humor. Disarm their discomfort as his non-humanness or unfamiliarity with a quip or a quote.

"He brought a knife to a gunfight," Lucas said, then smiled, hoping to break the awkward silence with some humor. The three women shot him puzzled looks, so he added, "He was a cowardly son of a bitch."

All three women scowled this time.

Bahm's eyes narrowed, her brow furrowed. "Do you find something funny about this, Officer?"

He'd clearly miscalculated. She seemed only angrier now. Like his T.O., she apparently didn't like the quotes. He could think of no way out but the truth. "No, ma'am," Lucas said. "They are from movies. Sometimes they pop into my head."

"Officer George, shooting incidents are serious matters," Beebe started to say, but Bahm cut her off.

"Do you just say everything that pops into your head whenever it comes to you?" she demanded.

Lucas shrugged. "No. Sometimes."

"Just like sometimes you just do whatever pops into your head and shoot a suspect without even talking with them first?" Bahm said next. It was angry, an accusation.

Lucas shook his head. "That is not what happened."

"Did you offer him movie quotes, too?" Bahm added.

"Officer Bahm, that is not appropriate," Doaa said quickly.

Bahm scoffed. "I'm not at all certain we'd all agree what is appropriate, given the Officer's statements."

Doaa looked at Lucas, "Officer George, please stick to answering the questions asked. This is important."

"I'm sorry," Lucas said. "I meant no disrespect."

"Tell that to Mister Watkins," Bahm snapped.

"Bahm!" Beebe scolded as Doaa glared.

"We can take a break and reconvene later if necessary," Doaa said.

"No, we're fine. Please continue," Lucas said. "I did not

mean to be inappropriate. I apologize again."

The ladies leaned back in their chairs and took deep breaths, sitting a moment, then Beebe nodded and continued, "They taught you at the academy about the department's guidelines for use of deadly force, Officer?"

"Of course."

"And under what circumstances is deadly force authorized?" Beebe asked. Unlike her partner, her emotions had not seemed to change. She exhibited none of the anger or hostility of Bahm. She was just distant. Not exactly cold, but not friendly either. Businesslike, he believed was the term.

"Force may be used only to the extent objectively reasonable to accomplish lawful outcomes," he said, repeating the policy statements he'd captured via his visual sensors—effectively photographic memory. "This Department and its members recognize and respect the value of human life. In permitting members with lawful authority to use force to protect the public welfare, and for the apprehension and control of subjects, a careful balancing of all human interests is required."

"Do you believe, Officer George, that it's in the interest of public welfare to discharge your weapon carelessly in a crowded area surrounded by innocent civilians?" Bahm asked.

"Department members are authorized to use deadly force in order to protect themselves or others from what they reasonably believe is an immediate threat of death or serious bodily harm," Lucas answered, repeating another policy. "The girl was being threatened with a knife. I believed her life and possibly others might be endangered, so I decided to disable the suspect in order to render him harmless."

"Using your service weapon?" Bahm added.

"Yes, but only wounding him, in the knee," Lucas said.

"So your claim is you fired exactly where you hit him and you had no intention of killing him?" Beebe said.

"Yes," Lucas said. "I believe if you check my academy records, you will see that I am a precision shooter. Because of my special abilities…" he hesitated a moment. "…I have a targeting computer in my head, ma'am."

"You're saying you use the computer system that is your mind to direct your fire?" Beebe said.

"Yes, ma'am. I do not miss," Lucas said.

Bahm clearly didn't believe him. "What if you had?"

Lucas thought a moment, shaking off another movie quote. "If I had, I suppose I might have hit someone I did not intend to, but this never happens. I am incapable of it."

Bahm scoffed. "You believe you are perfect, Officer?"

Lucas cocked his head and shrugged. "By human standards, I suppose that is accurate."

Bahm laughed. "You've got to me kidding me."

Doaa cleared her throat. "Officer Bahm, you are both aware of the special nature of the current Officer, are you not?"

"We know what we've been told," Bahm said. "That doesn't mean we believe it."

"You think the department misled you?" Doaa asked.

"I think this man's friends and colleagues have more confidence in him than is reasonable under the circumstances," Bahm said. "Given his lack of experience and other factors."

"Officer Bahm," Lucas said, "my academy shooting range

records—"

"I was not talking to you, Officer," Bahm scolded, glaring at him.

"But if you'll only—"

She cut him off with a dismissive wave. "You fired a weapon in confrontation with a suspect within two minutes of engaging said suspect in a public place, with many civilians potentially in the line of fire. Is that not correct, Officer?"

Lucas met her angry eyes a moment, trying to determine that she meant for him to respond this time.

"We're waiting!" she scolded.

"Yes, I did," Lucas said. "But I knew I would not miss, and the suspect was apprehended without injury to any civil—"

"That'll be enough, Officer," Bahm said, cutting him off again as she leaned back in her chair with a smug look.

"But the circumstances—"

"Do not matter to us, Officer," Bahm said.

"Officer George," this time it was Beebe talking as she leaned forward to meet his eyes. "What my colleague is suggesting is that perhaps you did not exercise all appropriate options before choosing to fire your weapon at the subject. And perhaps the result might have been endangering the public and your fellow officers."

"But I knew they were not in danger because my aim—"

"Your own confidence may be misplaced, Officer," Bahm said.

"But you don't understand—"

"Officer," this time Doaa cut him off with a warning look, despite her gentle eyes. "I highly recommend you do not comment further until you've spoken with an attorney."

"An attorney? But I did nothing wrong." Lucas was confused. Did they actually mean to accuse him of wrongdoing? He'd followed all the guidelines to his best understanding, and what he'd learned from his training and fellow officers.

"We do not agree," Bahm said.

"I'm sorry, Officer," Beebe said. "At this time, we must investigate further and your representative is correct. Legal advice would be wise at this time."

"Do you intend to formally charge him?" Doaa asked.

"Not yet," Beebe said. "But we are not clearing him either."

Lucas' eyes darted back and forth between the women trying to understand how they'd come to the idea he'd done anything wrong.

"At this time, we'd like to prepare a transcript of this session for you verify, and then compare it with the statements of other witnesses," Beebe said. "After that, we may have further questions for you."

"So I should just wait here then?" Lucas said.

Doaa looked at him sadly as Bahm glared.

Beebe almost smiled but instead she pursed her lips and shook her head. "You should go home. You have administrative leave pending the outcome of our investigation. Time off, Officer. And you need to talk to the department psychologist as well."

Lucas nodded. "All right. If you think it will help."

"I do, Officer," Beebe said, seemingly sincere, though Bahm's expression made it clear she still had doubts.

With that, Bahm reached forward and turned off the digital recorder and Doaa stood beside him. Apparently the session was over.

CHAPTER 4

SIMON WORKED AT his desk a while, reviewing reports on the various burglaries and assembling a list of things to investigate that might lead to a breakthrough. He left messages for the forensics team wondering what they'd uncovered since they last talked. Then he headed out to the downstairs vending machines to grab whatever looked good for breakfast.

As he rounded the corner and hit the stairs at the back end of the building, he ran into Officer Gil Lenz, Lucas' Training Officer.

"Gil, been wanting to talk with you," Simon said.

"If this is about your metal friend, nothing to say, John," Lenz replied, attempting to walk on past, but Simon stopped him with a hand on his shoulder.

"I've seen this guy in action, checked his academy records—he's a good cop. It was a clean shoot."

"Clean maybe, but only because he got lucky."

"He took down the suspect, saved the girl—it's a win."

"For who?"

Simon bit back his rising annoyance. "For all of us."

"Look, John, I know he's your friend and anointed future

partner, but just because he has special abilities doesn't make him immune from the same rules as anybody else," Lenz said. "If one of our other trainees had tried that, a blatant disregard for procedure and policy on use of force, would we be having this conversation?"

Simon shrugged. "Maybe, sure, if it was a righteous shoot."

"What if he missed?"

"He doesn't miss, Gil, check his records," Simon said. "Guy's one in a million—a perfect shooter."

"And that makes it okay for him to just fire his weapon in the midst of a crowded public mall?" Lenz replied, shaking his head. "It's not just about whether he missed. There's the department's image."

"The department's image of taking down a scumbug who was threatening an innocent girl in front of fifty witnesses?" Simon snapped, letting his annoyance show now. "Oh yeah, we look real bad there."

Lenz smiled smugly. "Next time he might not be so lucky. It's my career if I sign off. Sorry. I can't do it." He started walking away, but Simon followed.

"Come on, Gil, he may need a driving course, but you know he's a good cop."

"Driving? Oh my God, don't get me started on that!"

"I'm just asking you to be fair to him," Simon said. "Test him if you want to. Make him review the policies, test him at the range, but don't just write him off."

They reached the bottom of the stairs and Lenz headed for the vending machine area so Simon kept following. As they passed the station workout room, men grunting and the smell of sweat drifted out the door. Simon crinkled his nose. From the opposite corner, muffled, happy chatter drifted from the locker rooms as officers teased and bantered with each other.

"Doesn't matter anyway," Lenz said. "He blew his Shooting Team interview. Made real trouble for himself."

"What?"

Lenz stopped by the humming machines and met Simon's eyes, chuckling. "He tried some of his movie lines on the two BBs. Apparently they found it as funny as I do. And then he tried to explain how he's special. With Golden Boy and his lawyer crying 'police brutality,' it went over like a lightning bolt."

"Son of a bitch. They know that's bullshit!"

Lenz looked over the machine's contents, choosing in silence.

Simon continued, "He's not like every other cop. The first of his kind. He's special."

Lenz grunted. "Until the department changes policy, the same rules apply to all of us. That's how I've trained them for fifteen years now, and it's how I evaluate them. You don't like it, take it downtown." He meant to administrators at department headquarters.

"Fuck, Gil, don't be an asshole about it."

"Fuck you, pal," Lenz's eyes narrowed, his lips tight. "You don't get to tell me how to do my job. That's all there is to it."

Simon pounded a machine with his fist. "I'm just trying to look out for a friend."

Lenz put coins in the machine and punched numbered

buttons for his selection. "Noted. Have a nice day, pal."

The machine hummed and a candy bar dropped as he slipped more coins in.

Simon fought the urge to shake him, instead turning and heading for the stairs again, but then stopped. He turned back. "Do you at least know where he is?"

Lenz shrugged as the machine hummed again and he reached noisily inside for a bag of chips. "Sent home. Mandatory time off."

Simon turned and hurried up the stairs. His training officer had been a lot more sympathetic. He wished he'd pushed harder to get Lucas assigned to someone else.

LUCAS WALKED, EYES DOWN, not watching where he was going. He'd left the station with no plan, no idea where he was going. He just needed to walk.

He had blown it. He had destroyed his career before it even began. Helping protect people had become his sense of purpose, come to give his life meaning. And now he felt lost, depressed. As if androids could feel anything. He knew most humans would assume that to be ridiculous, yet here he was. His servos felt sluggish, his mind weighed down, and his every move had to be purposeful, because his internal urging was to just stop, lie down and give up. His Maker had told him he was capable of simulating the equivalent of human feelings, under the right circumstances. If this wasn't depression or sadness, he supposed he'd never know what it was.

Since the beginning, he'd found humor to be his best way to connect with the humans around him. Especially once they determined his unusual nature. After all, humanoid robots were still relatively new. His Connelly Labs class of ten had been the first set created. Although another larger class had since been put into service, they were still unique and many people had never encountered them, only heard rumors. So being funny enabled him to win people over, disarm their fears and uncertainty; to fit in. And now it seemed it had also been his undoing.

He had been designed to obey orders, follow programmed assignments and take commands from certain humans assigned responsibility for him. But then he'd witnessed a shootout, found his owner had tried to make him complicit in his crimes, and that violated his programming. In the end, it wasn't his owner but other employees who'd been responsible, so Lucas had left Benjamin Ashman's service with permission and instead sought a career as not a security guard but with the police. Since then he'd never been happier or felt more driven and focused.

Now what was he to do?

So he walked. And walked. He started down Linwood nearly a mile before turning north along Main past Gates Bar-B-Q, just wandering. What had he heard the Australians called it—a walkabout? He'd been so distracted, so needing to just get away from there, that he'd forgotten his car in the station lot.

Oh well. He could get it later. He didn't get tired like humans did.

He'd obeyed his programming. No matter how many times he'd reviewed his actions during the pursuit and its final confrontation, he was certain of that. The basics were Asimov's Three Laws: One, a robot may not injure a human being or, through inaction, allow a human being to come to harm. Two, a robot must obey orders given it by human beings except where such orders would conflict with the First Law. Three, a robot must protect its own existence as long as such protection does not conflict with the First or Second Law. But those had been adapted when he decided to enter law enforcement. First, Lucas would only obey orders of his Maker, Owner, and those they assigned to authority over him. Thus, criminals or other troublemakers could not sabotage or interfere in his work. Second, he could harm human beings in context of the First Law according to the guidelines and policies of the KCPD, which he'd not only had added to his programming but also memorized, line by line. It wasn't his fault his reaction times and enhanced vision and other skills allowed him more accuracy and faster movement than human cops. But it sure seemed like they were blaming him and punishing him for that.

Even in training, Gil had made rules that held him back from using his full capabilities, justifying it as necessary to ensure he was trained equally with everyone else and not just relying on special abilities to slip through without learning the same skills at the same level as other cadets. Gil had forbidden him from using his internal WiFi and computers to access traffic cameras or crime databases—skills Lucas had put to great use while working with Simon on the Ashman case—because the Training Officer feared they were distractions from his focus on other abilities. Lucas suspected his T.O. feared and resented these abilities, as most cops didn't have them. The android was perfectly capable of multitasking on a level no human could accomplish—running through searches of databases, images, maps and more in his head while driving or shooting or executing other commands, but since humans couldn't multitask at that level, they couldn't understand how Lucas could. So he bore the special restrictions without resentment, hoping that with time his full capabilities would be seen as the great benefit and useful tool they were designed to be rather than dreaded or resented by his fellow officers.

He passed the Buick dealer, then a Wendy's, then on past the Bank of America tower at East 31st. He was intent on his thoughts, paying little attention to the other pedestrians or the drivers of passing cars. So this was what it was like to fail then. He supposed it was a more human sensation. After all, he wasn't supposed to fail. He was programmed with the appropriate skills for whatever the task. He supposed Simon would call it ironic that those very skills had led to this disappointment. Sigh. Lucas didn't like irony at all now that he'd experienced it. No wonder it often annoyed humans having it pointed out.

As he finished the thought, tires squealed and he half-turned to watch a brown sedan swerve past and turn sharply to park at the curb in front of a small independent convenience store. Doors slammed as two men climbed out and raced into the store, one of them wielding a shotgun.

Lucas didn't hesitate, he started running immediately for the store.

As he arrived, he found the clerk and several customers with hands raised as the shotgun-wielder shouted orders, while his pal, waving a pistol in one hand, shoved money from the open register into a bag with the other.

"Nobody move and you might stay alive!" Shotgun shouted as the people inside cowered where they stood along the three aisles, all within view of the register up front.

Lucas stepped into the doorway and badged them. "Officer Lucas George, Kansas City Police Department. Drop your weapons and lay down on the ground." It went against his training but he worried about the customers and hoped to distract the men and lure them outside, maybe make up for his mistakes at Crown Center.

The two men spun their heads with incredulous looks, but when they saw he was unarmed, they started laughing.

"This fuckin' guy!" the register man sad, shaking his head and went back to filling the bag.

"How 'bout you get down on the ground and we don't kill ya?" Shotgun said, waving the shotgun in an arc toward Lucas and then back to cover the customers.

As he stood there, Lucas used his enhanced vision to take in the room. There were security wires on the doors and windows and a fire alarm mounted on a column a few feet away, between two aisles.

"I can't do that," Lucas replied as he lowered his badge and prepared to dodge if the man fired.

"We're the ones with the guns, asshole," Shotgun said, smirking. "Get in here and on your knees, now!" he shouted, whirling so the shotgun fully pointed at Lucas now.

Lucas slid the badge in his pocket and walked slowly forward, hands raised. "It's not too late to walk out of here. No one's been hurt."

"Fuck you, buddy!" the register guy said and snickered.

"What're you gonna do about it?" Shotgun sneered.

As he reached the column, Lucas spun and pulled the fire alarm, klaxons blaring, then ducked and rolled toward the shotgun-wielder as he fired—pellets tearing into the column and shelf behind it but somehow missing Lucas—knocking him off his feet.

"Son of a bitch!" the register guy yelled as the customers backed away quickly, out of gun range.

Lucas shot to his feet seconds later with the shotgun and slammed its stock against the back of its former wielder's head, knocking him unconscious, then spun and aimed it toward the register.

"Jesus Christ!" the other robber said, dropping his pistol and raising his hands.

"Step slowly out from behind the counter," Lucas ordered then locked eyes with the clerk. "Call 911, sir, and ask for the police department."

As the clerk rushed to comply, sliding behind the robber as he moved slowly out from behind the counter, Lucas moved forward then called over his shoulder to the customers. "You all get outside, quickly."

The customers rushed for the door, moving behind Lucas except for two old women who were in such a hurry, they rushed between Lucas and the remaining robber.

That robber took advantage and raced for the door, punching an exiting customer in the gut and causing him to double over in the doorway as the robber slid past him onto the street.

"Freeze!" Lucas called and raced after him, but the bent over man and other customers blocked the way. Sirens approached from both sides as Lucas tried to navigate clear.

Tires squealed as the robbers' car pulled away and sped off, the escaped robber at the wheel, then two black and whites and a fire truck pulled up at the curb. Lucas turned back to check the robber he'd knocked unconscious—still lying where he'd fallen. He lowered the shotgun as Gil Lenz and two other officers converged on the store.

"What happened?" Lenz demanded, pulling a small note pad and pen from the upper pocket of his bulletproof vest.

"He saved our lives!" a woman shouted, looking gratefully at Lucas, who began filling Lenz in as the other two cops rushed inside to handcuff the called robber. Nearby, firemen began examining customers for injuries.

"You went in without a service weapon? Are you crazy?" Lenz scolded.

Lucas saw Simon pull to the curb in his official vehicle, a Ford Explorer Interceptor, having left his personal Charger at the station, then hurry across the street.

"I had to act quickly," Lucas said. "I was worried about the customers."

"You could have gotten them all shot!" Lenz yelled as Simon joined them.

"I heard on the radio. Are you okay?" Simon asked, eyes finding Lucas.

"Yes, I am fine," Lucas said.

"What happened?" Simon asked.

"This fucking nut job badged armed men without his weapon and almost got everyone killed," Lenz said, shaking his head.

"But no one was shot, and I apprehended a suspect," Lucas countered.

"By sheer luck," Lenz said. "And one of them got away."

"Without any cash or harm," Lucas said.

"They both would have likely escaped if he hadn't acted," Simon added.

"He could have called us in and we'd have been here in minutes," Lenz said, offering Simon a look of contempt. "You were told to take it easy," he said, turning to Lucas again, "while the shooting is under review."

"But I saw them arrive and rush in with guns," Lucas said. "I could not just stand by—"

"That is exactly what you should have done!" Lenz scolded. "Stand by and make a phone call."

"But I stopped them," Lucas said, looking confused.

"You got lucky," Lenz said. "It could have ended very differently with several civilians and yourself wounded or dead. And don't think the Captain won't hear about this, too!" Lenz gave Lucas one more disgusted look as he finished jotting notes on his pad and turned toward the milling customers.

"What else should I have done?" Lucas asked Simon.

"You're a hero, Lucas, forget about him," Simon said.

"He is going to make big problems for me with the Captain," Lucas said, shaking his head.

"I'll talk to him," Simon said and hurried after Lenz.

Lucas sighed and started walking back up the hill in the direction of his neighborhood. He had given his statement. He didn't want to wait around and cause any further aggravation to his T.O. He still didn't believe his actions were wrong. He'd acted on instinct and diffused the situation, even if there had been a risk. His internal calculations had told him his own faster reflexes would give him an advantage. Worst case, he was bullet resistant and could have survived a blast with minimal damage if need be.

As he walked, the fire truck drove past, returning to its station unneeded. He was almost to a stop light when he heard another car approaching from behind.

"Lucas, stop."

Lucas didn't even recognize the voice at first, until he turned to see Simon pulling up to the curb, across traffic and parking in a yellow zone.

"Come on, pal, talk to me," Simon called.

Lucas hesitated but just kept walking and soon he heard a car door shut and footsteps as his friend chased after him.

Simon moved around him and turned, walking backward, as he said, "Lucas, it's not a done deal. We can fight this. You can change their minds."

"They seemed preconditioned to my failure," Lucas said sadly. "I doubt it."

"So you're just gonna give up then?"

Lucas stopped, meeting Simon's eyes. "Do I have a choice?"

"Fuck yeah. There's always a choice."

"First my T.O., now the shooting team, and then this," Lucas said, shaking his head. "Perhaps I am not cut out for this."

"Sure you are," Simon said. "You've got some things to learn but you're doing fine. T.O.s are always tough on newbies, and as for internal affairs, they're not impressed by anyone. Don't worry about it."

Lucas pursed his lips, thinking. "They did not appreciate my humor."

Simon chortled. "Hell no! The two BBs have no sense of humor! I tried to warn you."

"Humans are confusing," Lucas said.

Simon laughed. "Yeah, some of them. Especially women."

Lucas had to smile. "I thought that was just for you. I have gotten along well with several."

"You got lucky. Especially with Lara." Simon's bitter ex-wife, much like their precocious daughter, had been totally charmed by Lucas from the start, much to Simon's shock. Simon had reminded Lucas that saving Emma's life hadn't hurt, thought it sure hadn't helped him with his ex.

"The policies are not written for someone like me," Lucas said, sad again as he remembered his interview with the Shooting Team.

"I know," Simon said. "They will have to make adjustments."

"Adjustments? To department policy?" Was this possible?

Simon nodded. "You're the first of your kind to serve. Some changes or modifications will be required. It's not legal for them to discriminate against anyone. Federal law. Not to mention state and local."

"Even androids?"

Simon shrugged. "I would think so. You are breaking new ground here. But we can try."

Lucas locked eyes with his friend, who really seemed to believe it. "I thought I was screwed."

Simon laughed. "That phrase takes on a whole new meaning when you say it."

Lucas laughed this time. "I do have screws."

"Maybe we need to tighten some," Simon teased.

"More likely loosen them, if they want me to do things more like humans," Lucas said, shaking his head.

This made Simon laugh harder. Lucas' smile grew. He couldn't help it when he was around his friend.

"It's going to work out, I promise," Simon said then, his eyes sincere, the laughter replaced by conviction.

"They sent me home," Lucas said. "Administrative leave. How am I to work on anything at home?"

"You're not," Simon said. "Leave that to me. Meantime, if you're not doing anything, I could use some help with this burglary ring. I'm getting nowhere. I think some of your special skills are just what I need."

"But the Captain—"

"Just take a look at some stuff with me, I'll deal with her if we need to. You may be 'off duty' but you're still a cop. Cops consult cops."

Lucas decided it sounded good to him. "Okay. I'd like that."

"Then quit sulking and get in the damn car, alright?" Simon said, turning back toward where he'd left the Explorer.

Lucas nodded and followed. "Okay, but can I drive?"

"Not on your life, pal."

SIMON AND LUCAS SETTLED in at Simon's favorite

downtown spot, the City Diner, on Grand at East 3rd, to review the case. A local institution, it offered all the usual fare, the breakfast being what interested Simon at the moment. A long black and white counter separated the kitchen from the rows of white Formica tables and black faux leather chairs. The building itself was a cement square with neon lighting. Simon ordered the 2x2x2—scrambled eggs, 2 bacon, 2 sausage, and hashbrowns with orange juice and coffee to wash it down. It wasn't fancy but it was cheap and less greasy than the old style fare it emulated.

The waitress took her time delivering it, making eyes at Lucas, who she seemed to have taken a liking to. "You're not having anything, sugar?"

Lucas shook his head. "Not hungry."

"He's not into breakfast," Simon said, hoping to keep her from digging.

She tilted her head. "Awww, but our breakfast is special, hon." She smiled at Lucas, her eyes meeting his as she said it.

Lucas showed no obvious awareness of her flirting. "I had toast and coffee earlier," he said.

"Okay, honey," she said, hand going to her hip as she leaned forward over him a bit. "But you don't know what you're missing." Then she smiled again and whirled, looking back over her shoulder as she walked away—hips shaking like some model on a runway.

"I think she's offering you more than food, pal," Simon said.

Lucas' brow furrowed. "She is?"

Simon rolled his eyes. "Girl has the hots for you." When Lucas remained puzzled, he added, "She was flirting big time."

Lucas frowned. "That was flirting? I was not flirting."

"Yeah, she tried hard to change that though," Simon said.

"Perhaps I should order something then," Lucas said. "I wouldn't want to hurt her feelings."

"No, Jesus," Simon said, louder than he'd intended. He stopped and lowered his voice. "If she comes back, she might never leave. She'll get over it."

They glanced over to see the waitress looking back at them from behind the counter, she smiled and wiggled her fingers in a wave.

"I am fully functional, the doctor said," Lucas commented, referring to his creator, Dr. Livia Connelly.

Simon groaned, wincing at the images coming into his mind. "For fuck's sake, shut up. I'm eating here." As he ate, Simon began sharing details of the burglaries with Lucas.

"So they took some power tools at one place, laptops at another, electronics, wiring, chemicals—sounds like potential components for explosives, but beyond that and the holes cut for entry, what's the connection?" Lucas asked.

Simon shrugged. "I don't know yet, but my instinct tells me there is one." He slid some photos onto his iPad and tossed it on the table in front of Lucas. The newfangled device was not his favorite, and he'd always hated relying on technology. But the department had started requiring every cop to carry one six months before, and though he'd been one of the last to surrender, now Simon too had been equipped.

Lucas flipped through the images, using his finger to change between them. They were shots of the holes, including up close images of the marks left by whatever had cut them, plus photos of the various scenes—the destruction left behind from the searches the burglars conducted, et cetera. In the background, waitresses and cooks called back and forth through an opening to the kitchen behind the metal counter as griddles and grills sizzled, plates rattled, and silverware clanked.

"The holes vary a bit," Lucas noted. "Some are large enough for a man to crawl through. Others look just big enough for a hand."

"Those are the ones cut near enough to reach in and unlock a door," Simon said.

"You'd think someone would hear the noise of the cutting or see the holes," Lucas said.

"Yeah," Simon agreed, finishing a bit of delicious, crunchy bacon. "Except they were cut clean and the drywall replaced and repaired so well, it wasn't obvious to anyone not paying attention. The victims discovered the burglaries after they were inside."

"They repaired them all? Even the large ones?"

"No, but those they cut in places away from entrances, hidden from view, so they weren't easily discovered by anyone approaching the building or driving by," Simon said. "They were obvious only once a person looked from the inside." He jabbed a sausage with his fork and tore off a big bite with his teeth, echoing his internal frustration.

Lucas grunted. "Clever."

"They are definitely not as stupid as the usual suspects," Simon agreed.

"Yet the items are random enough as well as the types of targets so as to leave confusion," Lucas noted.

"Which is why we are trying to link them by identifying how the holes were cut," Simon said.

"Oh," Lucas nodded, flipping back to the photos of the holes on the datapad. "They look very clean."

"Yes," Simon confirmed.

"So anything else in common?"

"There's a smell of burning to the surfaces, but no," Simon said. "And so far, the forensics guys can't match it to the pattern of any power tools."

"Power tools would be really noisy," Lucas said. "Not a problem for the warehouses and businesses, maybe, but in apartments that would attract notice."

Simon grunted in agreement as he finished his scrambled eggs, moaning a bit with delight at the flavor. Whatever they added—some butter and cheese combo—the eggs were just right.

"What about laser cutters?" Lucas asked.

"Lasers?" Simon repeated.

Lucas nodded. "They're quiet, compact, and they do burn but rarely leave marks. Might leave a burning scent though, depending upon the material they cut."

"Mobile laser cutters? They have those?" Simon knew lasers had come into more and more common use over the past decades—from surgery to engineering, manufacturing, and more, but handheld, mobile devices he hadn't encountered.

Lucas chuckled. "They are pretty common now. Even pen-sized that clip to your pocket, though those don't come cheap."

"Wait, a laser disguised as a pen?" Simon said, shaking his head. "What the hell—?"

Lucas shrugged. "Lots of people need to cut things and

they come in handy."

"Shit, well those could be everywhere," Simon said.

Lucas shook his head again. "No. They are still pricey. Google sources say slightly larger hand held models are used in autobody work, by plumbers and electricians, and the like."

"So where will we find them?" Simon asked, then finished his orange juice to wash down the eggs before tearing into his hashbrowns.

Lucas looked up, thinking a moment. "Aren't you the Master Detective? We should start with where they sell them. They'd have a pretty good idea who their usual customers are." Lucas' blue eyes glinted as he watched Simon for a reaction.

It was obvious, of course, but Simon had been so distracted trying to picture the devices and wrap his mind around their existence, he hadn't gotten there yet. Still, he tried to cover it. "Hey, I was just waiting to see if you came to the same conclusion."

Lucas laughed, watching Simon. "You have no idea where they sell them, do you?"

Simon smiled in surrender.

"Let me run a search," Lucas said with a smile back.

Simon chewed a bite of hashbrowns and waited. Lucas remained silent, but it was obvious his mind was busy compiling, so Simon just ate and sipped his coffee, knowing when his partner finished, they'd have places to start.

After about five minutes, Lucas grunted and stood. "Ready?"

Simon still had a third of his hashbrowns left. "Just let me eat this last bit."

"Okay," Lucas nodded. "I'm going out to the car. Be sure and leave her a good tip, okay? I like her." He turned and waved at the watching waitress. She giggled, looking about ready to run over, but instead Lucas headed for the door. She gave Simon a sad look to which he just shrugged and looked away, occupying himself with his food.

CHAPTER 5

LUCAS' RESEARCH SHOWED that the number of local sites selling laser cutters had tripled in five years, but that still wasn't saying much. There were eight locations—four of them hobby shops, two industrial equipment firms, and the last two high-end electronic retailers. Lucas directed Simon to a hobby shop which carried handheld laser cutters in the art district, both because it was the closest and one of the oldest such vendors in the city.

Covering seventeen blocks centered on 16th and Southwest Boulevard, the Crossroads Art District was a thriving revived area of downtown Kansas City, Missouri which had lots of spaces for artists, galleries, restaurants, and even housing and attracted a younger, up-and-coming clientele. The hobby shop occupied a refurbished portion of an old brick warehouse at the corner of 20th and Main. Its owner was behind the counter wearing a dirty apron over jeans and t-shirt with the shop's logo and name splashed across the front beneath the stains. In his late forties or early fifties, he had a scruffy beard and disheveled hair covering a well-lined face offset by a warm, welcoming smile.

"Welcome to Randy's Hobby," he said. "What can we do you for?"

"Are you Randy?" Simon asked, flashing his badge.

"Yes, sir. Police huh?" Randy said. "You know, if someone got hurt with something I sold I have this disclaimer." He laughed at his own joke, a rattling sound.

Simon and Lucas stopped beside the counter. "We just have some questions about laser cutters, actually," Simon said.

"Oh yeah?" Randy perked up, clearly a favorite topic. "You wouldn't be looking for lightsabers to fight off high tech criminal empires, would ya?" Again he laughed, quite amused.

Simon merely shook his head. But Lucas nodded and said sotto voce, "I'm one with the Force. The Force is with me."

Randy looked amused and replied, "Right." But when Lucas continued staring at him with total seriousness, his smile faded and he cleared his throat. "The technology is improving so fast we get new stuff all the time." He looked down at the counter and cleared his throat as Lucas winked at Simon. Simon reminded himself to keep working with the android on comic timing.

"We mostly specialize in handhelds for etching, drawing, and such, but we do custom order a few desktop or table models under special circumstances," Randy continued. "What d'ya need to know?" He shot a cockeyed glance at Lucas then quickly looked at Simon.

"Well, what would you use to cut through wood and dry wall if you wanted a really clean cut?" Simon asked.

Randy nodded. "Depending on the thickness of the wood, those might be two different tools. Drywall, obviously, is much easier to cut and takes less force, but the thing about lasers is all of them cut real clean if you know how to use them. That's a big part of the appeal."

Simon shrugged. "You're the expert." Always helped appealing to the person's ego when seeking information. The guy seemed harmless himself, if a little hyper. But then he was discussing his products and he was a salesman. Nothing unusual about that.

"What are you trying to cut through? Raw materials or something already built?" Randy asked.

"Walls," Simon said.

Randy scrunched his face up, thinking. "For what?" He winked. "You trying to break into a place? You know that's against the law, right?"

Simon groaned silently but chuckled at the guy, encouraging him. "Yeah, you know. Sometimes those battering rods we use just aren't enough."

Randy laughed heartily, his shoulders and round belly shaking as he did. "Hell, those would punch right through most dry wall. But okay, so you want to cut a hole in dry wall, pretty much your standard model like a XyKit or Boss would do ya. But for wood reinforced areas, that might take a bit more heavy duty model."

"Ever have anyone come in asking about this before?" Simon asked.

Randy shook his head. "No. Most of my customers are hobbyists or artists. Small stuff—etching, aluminum or metal artwork—that kind of thing. I think if anyone asked me that, I'd suggest they talk to someone with better knowledge about such things."

"But you have laser cutters strong enough?" Lucas said.

"Potentially, yes. All you have to do is swap out the CO_2 cartridge to one with higher wattage. Just not an application I know much about."

"Right," Simon agreed, then thought a moment. "Do you demonstrate any of these handhelds perchance?"

Randy smiled. "Of course, from time to time. And we do etching in house. That's what started us carrying them. Come on in the back with me." He turned and walked down the counter to the right, grabbing safety goggles from a bin and putting them on then handing a pair each to Simon and Lucas, who'd followed. "Put these on please."

Once they had complied, he pushed aside ragged curtains hanging over a doorway. "Just in here."

Randy opened the door and Simon and Lucas followed him into the back room, which had a concrete floor and walls of gray drywall over brick and pink insulation, which peeked out of cracks and up near the ceiling. Long, old-school fluorescent lighting hung from cables above them and a mix of cleaning fluids, chemicals and dust filled Simon's nose. There were two steel worktables with vises attached and various tools laid out on them. A kid in his late teens or early twenties was smoking like chimney as he bit his lip in concentration at a glass table, working a laser to cut aluminum held on each end by a vise over the glass desktop, and he was clearly cutting a large sheet into smaller shapes. The laser was a long tube, attached to a power pack with a focusing lens at one end where the beam came out.

"Fuck!" he said as the others approached.

"Kyle!" Randy said, looking embarrassed. "We have guests."

Kyle turned, his mop top 'do flopping as he squinted through safety goggles looked the newcomers over. "Yeah? I think I just screwed this up, dammit."

"You can start another sheet," Randy said. "We plan for

that, as you know."

Kyle clicked his teeth and nodded, then stood, headed for a nearby bin. "Yeah."

"But first."

Kyle stopped and turned back. "Yeah, boss?"

"I want you to show these gentlemen how we use handhelds to cut shapes and etch," Randy added.

Kyle grinned. "Sure thing. Easy stuff."

"If they have any questions, answer them or send them back to me, okay?" Randy said.

Kyle nodded. "Sure thing."

Randy turned and headed back to the front to man the counter as Lucas and Simon moved to either side of Kyle where they could see what he was doing.

"Easy stuff you just screwed up?" Lucas asked.

Kyle's eyes narrowed and he shook his head. "Yeah, well, it happens. But still. Easy mostly." He came back to the glass table and motioned them closer. "What are your names?"

"Lucas and John," Lucas said.

"Okay," Kyle said. "The magnifier here helps the eyes see the surface as you cut, and you can set the level here." He motioned to some buttons and dials on a control panel on the arm stretched over the table to hold the magnifying lens. "The laser can be held by hand, which takes a lot more skill, or clipped onto this extra arm here." He pointed to an arm similar to the one holding the magnifier. It had hinges and springs and could bend and twist and turn into various positions. He looked up to see if they understood and saw Lucas with a frozen stare and Simon looking lost.

"Yeah, let me show ya," Kyle continued. He grabbed the laser with one hand as he flipped buttons and dials on the control panel with the other then set to work. The laser itself was fairly quiet, just a slight hum, and the sulphury, carbon smell of burning metal rose above the dusty chemical cleaners smell as the metal tore in front them, heating up, reddening and then just melting away clean. Kyle moved the beam slowly with great coordination and focus, carving out a heart shape from the aluminum. The heart slipped down and fell onto the glass below as the edge pieces remained in the vise.

Kyle reached down to retrieve the heart shape with his fingers.

"Isn't it hot?" Lucas asked.

Kyle grinned. "Nah. Cools almost instantly. But I don't grab it by the edges." Setting the heart in front of him atop the glass, he then took the laser and flipped a switch, adjusting its settings apparently, then started etching. It took less than a minute or two before he leaned back, flipped off the laser and had a satisfied look. "Done!"

He stepped back and motioned to the heart. "You can keep that."

Simon and Lucas stepped forward. It was a heart with an arrow sketched on it, the middle part disappearing beneath the aluminum and only the point and feathered ends showing. Written on the middle over it were the words: 'Lucas + Simon Forever.'

Simon scowled and Kyle grinned.

"That's a fast one. I can add much more detail, using a vector drawing," Kyle offered, "but I like the handcrafted touch, and it's fun." It was clearly not something many people could do and he was proud of it. Simon couldn't blame him.

"We can hang it in the car," Lucas said. "The guys at Central will love it."

"Shut the fuck up," Simon growled.

"Anything else you guys want to see?" Kyle said, looking smug.

Simon briefly considered shooting the kid in the foot just to make a point, but then his radio beeped.

"186, 185 requests your presence at a scene at 1223 West 11th for a burglary call," the dispatcher said. 185 was Oglesby and Dolby.

Simon keyed his radio. "186, on my way."

"Copy 186," dispatch replied.

Simon lowered his hand from the radio and smiled at Kyle. "Damn, I was so hoping you'd show us more of those awesome skills, too." And with that, he headed for the front, Lucas following as Kyle watched them go.

THE BURGLARY SCENE was in the West Bottoms, an older area near the Missouri River that had been undergoing a revival and renovations for two decades, bit by bit. Tons of old warehouses and industrial buildings had been abandoned or run-down, but many had been purchased and refitted for new uses, others restored for continuing use for their original purpose. 1233 W. 11th was a Feed and Fertilizer warehouse, or so a painted billboard-sized sign on the side said: Watters Feed and Fertilizer. Watters supplied material to various big box home improvements stores and garden centers around the metro, but this is where pallets were stored before distribution.

Simon pulled up alongside Oglesby's Ford Explorer Interceptor and two black and whites, parked in a small lot out front. The warehouse was bustling with cops and forensics investigators. Simon and Lucas found Oglesby and his partner, Dolby, just inside the large, twenty-five foot garage door that lay open on the west side, just around the corner from where they'd parked. Anna Dolby, unlike her partner, was tall and thin with chocolate skin and long, black hair. A former college track star and amateur model, at thirty-five, she didn't look a day over her early 20s. But she was gritty as sandpaper when she needed to be. She didn't mess around.

The garage door connected to a drive that led to the street and continued inside into a large cement-floored main room with wooden tiered shelves lining three walls. Most were packed full of sacks of fertilizer, seeds, feed, etc. The place smelled of dust, soil, and shit mixed with oil and machinery.

"Whatta we got?" Simon asked.

Oglesby and Dolby turned from where they'd been talking with a disheveled man in his mid-fifties, chubby, with a day or two of brown stubble on his face. He was wearing sweatpants and a sweatshirt and tennis shoes and looking somewhere between disbelief and anger.

"Lucas?" Dolby said with surprise. "What are you doing here?"

"Hi, Anna," Lucas said and smiled. "Martin," he nodded at Oglesby.

"We had just finished breakfast when we got the call," Simon replied as he slid on rubber gloves he'd pulled from his pocket and passed another pair to Lucas. Oglesby and Dolby were already gloved up.

"Good to see you," Dolby said to Lucas, both of them accepting Simon's explanation without hesitation.

"You know, John here's been really bad about getting out of bed early since you went to the Academy," Oglesby teased. "He's gotten lazy."

"Like he was before we met?" Lucas snapped and grinned.

Dolby and Oglesby laughed. Simon frowned.

"Yeah, exactly like that," Dolby said.

"Are we here to investigate or bust my balls?" Simon said.

"We're professionals. We can do both," Oglesby replied.

Lucas joined them in laughing this time.

Dolby shot Simon an amused look then turned serious. "This is the owner," she indicated the disheveled man, "Mister Pierce Watters. He discovered the break in when he came in to open up."

"What'd they take? Cow shit?" Simon asked.

Watters nodded. "Yeah, actually, four box trucks full of it."

"What?" Simon looked around. There was no sign of any trucks.

"They took the trucks, too," Oglesby added.

"Trucks and fertilizer?" Lucas said, shaking his head.

"They were all loaded up to ship out this morning," Watters explained. "A big order for one of our industrial clients. All gone. Thousands of dollars." He almost looked ready to cry. "Who steals that much fertilizer?"

"Maybe they needed the trucks," Simon said.

Watters was not amused but Oglesby and Dolby both covered smiles.

"How did they get in?" Lucas asked next.

"Cut through a door into the office and then let themselves in," Dolby said.

"They disabled the alarm somehow," Watters said, shaking his head.

"Cut right through the wires at the pole," Dolby added.

"The same as they did at other sites," Simon said.

The other detectives nodded.

"We figure it's all related, thought you'd want a look," Oglesby said.

"You taking inventory?" Simon asked.

Oglesby nodded. "Yeah. So far it's just the trucks and fertilizer."

"Which may bankrupt me!" Watters said, voice shaking, shoulders slumped.

Lucas put a gentle hand on his arm. "We're very sorry, Mister Watters. I can assure you we'll do everything we can to find the perpetrators and get your trucks and fertilizer back."

"Fuck! If I'm around long enough," Watters mumbled.

"Where's the hole?" Simon asked.

"Through there," Dolby said, motioning to a closed normal-sized wooden door on the east wall. "Down the corridor straight and then right. Up near the side entrance where we parked."

Simon motioned to Lucas. "Let's go take a look."

Lucas followed Simon across the cavernous room toward the door and into a long, carpeted corridor with light gray walls that passed three small offices and one larger one and then opened into a lobby with a long receiving counter and several chairs for waiting customers. Behind the counter, a desk held a phone with speaker, a flat screen monitor and keyboard, and some filing bins. Several file cabinets lined the wall behind it. Except for dust, it was a very clean work area, and the lobby and corridor didn't smell like the warehouse. They were a bit musky but pleasant.

At the opposite end of the counter from the corridor where they stood, taking in the room, Simon spotted a door with a hole in it.

"Huh. They cut right through the door this time," he said as he moved around the counter and walked over to take a look, Lucas following. They both stopped and knelt beside the door, examining the hole.

"The edges are very clean," Lucas said. "Similar to that of a laser."

Simon picked up a piece of door wood on the floor beneath and held it up. It exactly fit the hole. "Hmmm, glue this back in and it's not that noticeable from a distance."

"Is that what they've done before?" Lucas asked.

"Yeah, one way or another. Glue, caulking, something," Simon said.

Lucas took the door piece and examined it. "You can see the glue here, along the edges." He ran a finger along the wood to indicate what he was seeing. There was a darker stain to the grooves where it had been cut—like some kind of liquid.

"But it must have been fast drying or we'd be seeing the glue itself," Simon added.

Lucas shrugged. "So, same guys. And the fertilizer and trucks to transport it—makes it more likely they are planning some sort of explosive."

Simon sighed. He'd already come to the same conclusion. "Yeah. Something way bigger than we'd imagined from the amount taken, too."

Lucas gently set the door piece back on the carpet, examining the area around it a moment, then they both stood. "I see not many splinters or even sawdust," he commented.

"Yeah, I noticed," Simon said. "Same with all the burglaries. Which is why we've been puzzled about their M.O. How were they avoiding the mess or cleaning it up without drawing too much attention."

Lucas' eyes met his. "Laser," they both said at the same time.

"Has to be," Simon said. "It's quiet, would be mobile."

"But the holes are very straight," Lucas said. "At least this one is. Even at the hobby shop, doing it by hand, the heart was off center a bit."

Simon shrugged. "An expert?"

"Surely someone with very steady hands at least," Lucas agreed.

"Find anything interesting?" Dolby asked from behind them. They turned to find her watching them from the end of the corridor. Simon hadn't even heard her approach.

"You walk too quietly, Dolby," Simon said. "Anyone ever

tell you it's a bad idea to sneak up on cops?"

"Hadn't heard that," she said, straightfaced. "I'll keep it in mind."

Simon motioned to the door piece on the floor. "Smooth cut, no mess. We think it might be a hand laser."

"A laser?" Dolby said, coming over to kneel down and examine the piece and the floor surrounding it. "That would explain why the pieces fit so well going back in."

Lucas nodded. "Apparently they are more and more common."

"I wonder if the lab guys even checked that," she said.

Simon pulled his cell from his pocket. "I was wondering, too. Let me call them and ask."

"Burglars with lasers," Dolby muttered as she stood again, shaking her head. "That's a new one."

"And gathering materials for a bomb," Lucas added as Simon dialed the phone.

"Yeah, Martin and I wondered as well," she said.

"Paul, John," Simon said as the lab tech answered. Paul Engborg was an old hand at the crime lab, and someone the Property Detectives knew well since he was an expert on construction tools and materials and often got involved examining any building damage from crime scenes. "Did you guys ever figure out what made those holes?"

"Not yet," Engborg replied. "Not anything we've found in our files or computers so far. Why?"

"Try hand lasers," Simon said.

"Lasers?!" Engborg said it like he was having an epiphany. "Of course. We hadn't even thought of it. So much more common these days. Less mess. Okay, we may have one around here. Give me an hour or two."

"Call me back," Simon said and hung up, then to Lucas and Dolby, added, "He's checking."

"So now we just have to check out everyone who's bought hand lasers in the area for the past year—" Dolby mumbled, chuckling. It would take forever and likely get them nowhere, they all knew.

"What about the trucks? Did we get plate numbers?" Lucas asked.

"Already called them in," Dolby said with a nod.

"Any logos or distinguishing marks?" Simon asked.

Dolby shook her head. "No. Just standard white. He never went to the trouble."

"So there could be hundreds all over the city on any day," Simon said. "Shit."

Dolby shrugged. "Still checking cameras. Maybe we got lucky and can see where they went and when they left."

"At least part of the way," Lucas agreed.

"All right," Simon said. "You guys got this? I want Lucas to take a look at some crime scenes stuff at the office. See if he notices anything we haven't thought of."

"Sure, we should be headed back in half an hour," she said.

Simon nodded to Lucas and they headed out the door for the car.

"See ya, Anna," Lucas said to Dolby as they went, smiling back at her.

"Good to see you," she replied with a wave.

"If you take me back to the office, when I am supposed to be on leave—" Lucas said as they stepped out into the daylight again, Simon squinting as his eyes adjusted.

"I'll tell Becker you came up with something we hadn't thought of and I just asked you to take a look. Don't worry," he said.

Lucas offered no further argument as they climbed into the Explorer. "Thanks."

"For what?" Lucas asked as he pulled the keys from his pocket and slipped them into the ignition.

"For letting me help you," Lucas said. "I was very depressed after the interview. It's a good feeling being useful."

Simon chuckled. "You were always useful. Fuck the two BBs, pal. You'll get through this. It's a good shoot."

Lucas sighed as he slid on his seatbelt and Simon started the car. "I hope you're right."

CHAPTER 6

T HE MAN WATCHED the feed and fertilizer warehouse from another rundown warehouse down the street, smiling all the while. As usual, the cops had little to go on. White box trucks were a dime a dozen in any big city, and though they might have plate numbers, the traffic camera coverage in the West Bottoms was sparse. None on this block. His team had planned well. He ran his hands through his crew cut hair and took a deep breath. The plan was going perfectly so far.

For months they'd been stealing the items they needed to put the plan in motion, working randomly so as to not create any obvious pattern the police might use to track them. Other than the laser, the types of locations burglarized and the locations and items taken were different every time. That would keep them guessing. They just needed two weeks anyway. Two weeks to Memorial Day weekend and it would all be over.

He chuckled and thought about Karl Ramon—the fear in the man's eyes, the surprise at first seeing him in the club dressing room. Since then, Karl hadn't heard from them but that would soon change, for the information he possessed and his role as security guard at UnderCity was key to their plans. While several team members burgled, others had been tracking his children's movements for weeks, just in case they needed leverage. Taking photos, recording routines, etc. They'd tracked Karl, too, of course, but his routine was less complicated. The kids were very active in various activities and with many friends, so following them actually took more work than their dad who was usually either home, at the club, or at work.

Simple people. Some people had no appreciation for life and their freedoms. No appreciation for what they had. But the plan was about to change everything. A whole bunch of simple people were about to lose all they cared about. If Karl played his cards right, he wouldn't be one of them, but that depended on him. He was a tool they'd discard and write off when his usefulness ended, and beyond that, he wasn't their concern. Be smart and live. Otherwise, pay the price. The cause was so much bigger than a few simple people's lives.

The man had already scouted UnderCity for the right locations. There were several already prepared and up for rental, and others where work was sporadic. He'd found a cavern big enough to store their supplies, box trucks and all, and it was in the perfect location to unleash their plan to maximum effectiveness, too. Memorial Day would see Worlds of Fun and Oceans of Fun packed. The perfect targets. And the massacre and resulting devastation would be something Kansas Citians would not soon forget. The Kansas City equivalent of 9/11. That most of the victims would be children and families made it all the sweeter. They'd go down in history.

They just had to wait a few days until investigative activity died down at the Feed and Fertilizer place, then they'd move everything across the city. He'd go there tomorrow night to make arrangements with Karl. In the meantime, it was fun to watch the police impotently flail about. They were used to dumb criminals. People of limited skills and focus. They'd never encountered a team like his, he was certain, and they'd rue the day for decades to come.

"They're clueless," a voice said over the ear piece he had in his ear, and he glanced over to see one of his men looking out a nearby window, gleeful and relaxed.

"We planned well," he replied.

"Almost time for Phase 2," the other man answered.

"You just get to work on those vans. Get them painted and new plates. I'll worry about Phase 2."

The man's smile faded as he turned, raising his hands in surrender. "Okay, okay, boss. Sorry. Just wanted to enjoy it a minute."

"I think you've had your minute. We can celebrate when we've accomplished our mission. Not before. Much can still go wrong."

The man laughed. "Ah, relax, chief. We got this. They'll never forget us." He grunted and chuckled as he moved off into the warehouse, presumably to follow orders. He'd better.

He himself would take inventory, run the checklist one more. Make sure they weren't missing anything. Make sure everything had been acquired. No more burglaries once they entered Phase 2. That trail needed to run cold, distract the cops, while they did what they needed to do. The two needed to seem disconnected, whether the cops suspect their purpose or not. Surely the signs were there of the possibility of explosives. The materials were mostly common. Too many prior incidents. But once the trail went cold, the city was too big. There'd be no way to find them in time, and time was all they needed.

His mind flashed back to Afghanistan and the Taliban

caves he'd blown up on three different occasions. Locals had cleaned up body parts and debris for months after each incident. He and his team had wiped those terrorist bastards off the map. It was the perfect training ground. But since then, the country had gone to shit. First that eight years under the idiot Obama, then the clown presidency, and after that, weak leadership without purpose. All the while, American culture and values got weakened, destroyed, perverted and watered down until they were almost unrecognizable to anyone who took pride in them. This wasn't the country he'd fought for in his youth. He could no longer look at the public and see people whose freedoms he was willing to give his life to protect. So many friends lost in the name of that cause. So many better people than the bozo citizenship he saw around him now.

Fuck them.

It was time to restore greatness, and that started with reminding people what made America great. The clown president had promised it and failed, mostly because he was too stupid and divisive and worst of all, self-centered. He was too clueless. American greatness came from its citizens' unity against common enemies, the remembrance that they lived in the greatest country in the world and no matter what differences divided them, protecting that and keeping it strong was more important than anything else. America had remembered that for a year or two after 9/11. But 28 years later, it was mostly forgotten again, and the clown president and his predecessor had done a lot to divide people further, not unite them. So men like his would have to do it the hard way. And that was fine. U.S. tax dollars had funded their training in just the skills they needed, and provided the access and networks they were using to carry it out. Striking at the heartland was just the beginning. What the country needed was a reminder that enemies were out there—people much worse than their petty differences—to remind them of what really mattered; who they really were.

So he'd give them a reminder. He'd start the ball rolling at least. And it all began in the nation's heart—the Midwest, Kansas City. He licked his lips and chuckled, almost like a kid on Christmas—he hadn't felt that way in years. It was nice. He'd missed it. His fellow Americans needed to experience that feeling again about their country and themselves. He and his men were here to show them the way.

SIMON TOOK LUCAS straight back to Central Patrol and the bustling Property Crimes Bureau. As Lucas greeted the other detectives and staff, Simon went straight to his desk and dialed the Computer Services Unit downtown, asking for Trevor Welch, the admin in charge of traffic monitoring like traffic cams.

Welch came on the line with his usual business-like tenor, "Sergeant Welch."

"Welch, John Simon." Simon leaned back in his chair, fingers playing his desktop like a piano.

"What's up, Detective?"

"I'm calling about the box vans from the burglary at West 11th," Simon said.

"We're searching for those plates, but it'll take a while," Welch replied. "You got something else?"

"Nah, I need a favor."

Welch paused a moment. Cops always asked for special treatment from the tech guys, because everyone thought their case was rush and top priority. "We're kinda busy up here."

"When are you not busy?"

"What is it?" Welch said with a sigh.

"Remember my associate, Lucas George, who consulted on the Keller-Ashman thing?"

Welch thought a moment, pausing to chatter with someone in the background. "I'll be there in a second, Susie. Gotta go, Detective," he said to Simon as he returned to the line. "The android?"

"Yeah. He's consulting on the burglaries. I want him to take a look at some of the footage."

"Chief sign off on it?"

"Becker's working on it, but come on, Trevor, this can't wait. We think these guys are planning major explosions, and so far Lucas has helped me make more progress today than we've made in a month."

Welch sighed. "I better see that paperwork ASAP, because you know I'll call."

"I'll go remind her right now," Simon promised.

"I'm only doing this because it's actually easier than most requests," Welch said. "Where you want it?"

"The guy's head's a computer," Simon said. "He can just log in wherever he is."

Lucas shook his head and cleared his throat.

"Hang on," Simon said and put his hand over the receiver, looking at Lucas.

"T.O. Lenz forbid me from doing that until I am out of training...," Lucas explained.

"What?" Simon scoffed. "That's bullshit."

"Yes, but I don't need more trouble," Lucas reminded him.

Simon sighed and took his hand off the receiver. "My terminal at Central," Simon said to Welch.

"Give me ten and the link and login will be in your email," Welch said.

"You're the best, brother," Simon said, but Welch was already gone. He grinned and turned to find Lucas waiting behind him. "You can at least see if you can find the vans with your faster-than-light computer brain searching."

"Easier if I know where to focus," Lucas said.

"Yeah, well, start with the Bottoms, see if you can spot them leaving the area."

Lucas nodded. "Okay, makes sense."

"Maberry!" Simon called and stood, looking over the cubicle divider. "Clear Santorios' desk for Lucas. He's helping me out." His old partner had been gone a year but her desk had been empty since and he hadn't stopped thinking of it as hers.

"Ah, come on, John, we're still sorting those files. Nowhere to put them!" Maberry whined.

"Tough shit. It's not your desk," Simon replied.

"We'll remember this next time you need a favor," Correia said, glaring at Simon.

"I'm shaking in my boots, Latin boy."

"You should be. I'm letting him drive these days,"

Maberry said then laughed. Simon joined him. Almost a year and Correia still wasn't living down an incident where he'd almost backed over a man in the station parking lot.

"Fuck you guys," Correia whined then stood and went to work on the files with his partner.

"You clear this with Becker?" Correia said, clearly stalling as he grabbed a stack of files and carried them to his desk. Maberry took another stack to his own.

"Becker will be signing off soon as she gets back," Simon said.

"He's on administrative leave, man," Correia said. "He shot someone. If she says no and you wasted our time..."

"It'll still be just one more fucking thing you can whine at me about," Simon said. He motioned with the back of his hand. "Work faster. I thought you Latinos put our lazy white work ethic to shame."

"That's immigrants, asshole, I was born here," Correia said.

Maberry grunted. "Doesn't stop him from faking a sympathy accent, though."

Correia scowled at his partner, then his voice took on a Cuban lilt. "Hey, mahyn, you're supposed to have my back here."

"Heh, I do when it counts, lazy Mexican," Maberry teased. Typical cop giving his partner shit.

"Hey, I'm a South American American, man," Correia said.

"South American American? Damn, that's some stutter," Simon said. "You should see a doctor about that."

"Shut the fuck up," Correia said.

"Stop stealing my line," Simon snapped, then turned back to his desk as his email inbox dinged with a new email. He double clicked the mouse on the email icon and flipped through. It was Welch with the link and info. Simon clicked the link and motioned to Lucas. "Sit down."

He stood and cleared the way as Lucas took his place.

"Login info's here," he said, leaning down to click the email tab and show him. "You can do the rest."

"Yeah, okay, I'm on it," Lucas said and went to work. His fingers worked the keys lightning fast, his eyes locked on the screen with an intensity no human could match. Simon shook his head watching him. The info flashing across the screen almost made him dizzy so he turned away.

His phone buzzed in his pocket and he picked it up. "Simon."

It was Paul Engborg at the lab. "You son of a bitch, you nailed it. Hand lasers for sure."

"Yeah?"

"Closest match to anything we've got," Engborg added.

"But can you narrow it down to make and model or anything?"

"Nah, not that good. Lasers are cleaner than most hand tools, which makes it worse. No nicks or damage to create a unique signature. They all basically look the same."

"Shit," Simon said. "Well call me back if you find anything else."

"We're working on determining the width of the beam. That should narrow it down some," Engborg added to Simon's relief.

"Great, thanks."

"Do what we can," Engborg said and hung up.

Simon slipped his phone back into his pocket as he heard his name.

"Simon!"

He turned to see Becker glaring at him from her office door. She'd been gone when they came in but apparently had returned. She waved him over sharply.

"Yes, boss?" he said innocently as he followed her into her office.

"What is Lucas George doing working your terminal when he's supposed to be on Administrative Leave for a shooting?" Becker took a seat behind her desk, sipping from a Starbuck's cup as she did, then set it on the desk and adjusted herself in the chair as her eyes locked on Simon's.

"I just asked him to take a look at a couple things," Simon said. "He had a bad interview with Shooting Team and was all depressed."

"Yeah, he made an ass of himself his rep told me."

"You know Lucas, JoAnn," Simon said. "He didn't mean to."

She sipped her coffee again and sighed. "Hardly matters. The two BBs are out for blood it seems. He can't be here."

"We were just having breakfast and I was running some stuff by him, then I got called to that scene in the Bottoms with Oglesby and Dolby."

"Anything promising there?" she asked.

"Crime Lab just confirmed hand lasers were used to cut the holes," Simon said.

She perked up, leaning forward in her chair and cradled her Starbucks with two hands. "Really? All of them?"

"Yeah, it's a match."

"Hot damn!" she said with a grin. "How'd you discover that?"

Simon nodded toward the squad room. "Lucas."

"Hmmm, not something I'd have thought of," she said.

"Me either, but they've really taken off. Lots of applications it seems," Simon said.

"He still can't stay," Becker said.

"He's spinning through footage trying to track the box trucks the burglars stole with fertilizer and all in them," Simon said.

"Fertilizer?"

Simon nodded. "Enough to fuel some pretty big devices."

"Son of a bitch! We gotta find these guys," Becker said, shaking her head and taking another sip from her coffee.

"We've made the most progress with his help we've made in a month, Joann."

Becker sighed. "John, he's in real trouble here. If he'd just kept his mouth shut, but he had to kick the wrong horses."

"Fuck, I know," Simon said, shoulders sagging. "I feel bad for him. He was going for the joke like he always does. To win them over."

Becker snorted. "No one wins over the BBs."

"And I warned him."

She groaned. "It may be time to ask the Feebies in on this."

"FBI? Fuck, no, come on!"

"If we have serious homegrown terrorists or something, they have the resources we don't, John," she said. "We've gotta find these guys."

"They'll run right over us," Simon said.

"We worked pretty well together on the Ashman case," she reminded him.

"Only because we forced their hand," he reminded her.

She shrugged. "So, this is their bailiwick, not ours."

"Give me a few days."

"What if we don't have them? Do you know what those explosives might do to this city?"

Simon grunted. "I know, I know."

"I'll ask the Chiefs about it and about Lucas, but don't hold your breath," she said.

"Go to Melson, okay? He's cool and smarter than most."

Becker laughed. "They're all bureaucrats who've lost touch with the street, but yeah, he's the one I always approach first."

Simon felt relieved and headed for the door. "Good."

"Don't go rogue on me on this, John. It's too important."

Simon turned back and locked eyes with her again. "I know. That's why I wanted Lucas' special skills. We have to find these people. And he's given us more to go on in half a day than we had since we started."

Becker sighed, her eyes confirming she believed him. "If it weren't for his situation…"

"Just ask Melson," Simon insisted. "Have him check his

Academy records and shooting files, testing, etc."

"Okay," she said as she picked up the phone. "But soon as that search is done, keep him outta here so no one sees him and raises hell. At least 'til I clear it."

Simon grinned. "You got it, chief. You know I love to hide."

"Sleeping in your car doesn't count the same, Simon," she scolded then dialed the phone as he headed out the door and back down the walkway to his desk.

Lucas was still tapping away at the keyboard, his eyes scanning the flat screen on Simon's desk as he flipped through images at an incredible rate. As Simon reached for Oglesby's chair in the cube next to him—he saw Oglesby and Dolby coming into the room, looking pleased.

"You got something?" he called.

"Security camera across the street caught the box trucks pulling out," Dolby said.

"Yeah?"

Oglesby nodded. "They turned right and headed down 11th, so maybe we can trace them from there."

Simon nodded to Lucas. "Lucas is already searching the traffic cams. Welch's people are on it, too."

Dolby grunted as she stopped at her cube across the divider, still standing. "We think we've got a face."

"A face?" Simon asked.

"In one of the trucks," Dolby added.

"Don't know for sure until we look at the footage, but the security guy across the street said he thinks he saw one of the drivers when he gave it to us," Oglesby added.

"Well, shit, what are we waiting for?" Simon said.

Oglesby dropped a shoulder bag on his desk and dug out a flash drive, holding it up for Simon and smiling.

"Well, let's see it, big shot," Simon said as Dolby hurried around from the other side.

Oglesby flipped on his monitor and stuck the flash drive into a USB slot. He clicked the mouse and keyboard, opening the files and started the footage playing across his screen. It was a nice shot of the street and drive leading to the Feed and Fertilizer place, but not much was happening. Oglesby fast forwarded. Then the garage door was opening.

"Forensics guys also found some prints, maybe we'll get lucky," Dolby said.

"These guys have been good at cleaning up," Simon noted, remembering the previous lack of fingerprint evidence linking to anyone not living or working at the various burglared sites.

"Worth checking though," Dolby said.

Then, on the screen, the box trucks were pulling out, and turning right. The last one stopped and a hooded, ski masked man got out the passenger door and ran back to shut the garage door. As he did, the driver leaned out of the truck and he had the mask pulled up over his forehead. He squinted and coughed, then looked straight at the camera.

"Freeze it!" Simon said as Oglesby fiddled with the controls trying to do just that.

"Blow that up!" Dolby added.

Oglesby fiddle again. And then they were staring at a face—white, late thirties to early forties, stubble.

"Think we can run facial rec on that?" Dolby asked.

"Fuck yeah!" Simon said, excited.

"You got something?" Becker asked, coming up behind them.

"Yeah, boss, a face from a security camera across the street," Oglesby said.

Becker's brows raised. "Really?"

"You talk to Melson?" Simon asked as Becker joined them and stared at the screen.

"Run facial rec on this guy, or get Computer Services on it ASAP," she ordered.

Simon just waited until she turned to him and their eyes met.

"He's looking into the Academy stuff, but he's of the mind if Lucas is useful, we should use him, but low profile for now," Becker said.

Simon clenched a fist and waved it in victory. "Yes! Can you get Lucas clearance to access traffic cams and crime computers directly? Lenz ordered him not to."

"I'll certainly ask," Becker said and smiled, yet it was anything but triumphant. "He also said to call the Feebies and tell them what we've got."

"Fuck!" Simon said.

"Son of a bitch," Dolby added.

"There goes our case," Oglesby said.

"He'll do his best to keep us on it," Becker said. "They'll need local resources. But best guess is until were sure who we're dealing with, they'll leave it to us. Either way, we have to find them fast, so we'll need everyone we can get." She looked at the face frozen on the screen again. "Not Middle

Eastern, so militia nutjobs or something."

"Homegrown likely," Simon agreed.

"Well, you guys stop standing around and find these fuckers before they start killing citizens, okay?" she ordered. "Correia, Maberry, you guys leave those files and get on this too for now."

"Yesssssss!" Correia shouted.

"Thank you, boss," Maberry said. They'd clearly been bored stiff. Now they looked somewhere between relieved and enthused.

"I'm still lead," Simon reminded them.

"For now," Becker agreed. "Get that footage to Welch's guys and find those damn trucks!" She turned and hurried back toward her office.

"Okay, let's get cracking before the Feds come in and enslave all of us," Simon commanded. And everyone hurried to their desks as Oglesby clicked on the screen to copy the footage onto the shared harddrive.

CHAPTER 7

SIMON TRIED RUNNING the prints through PRINTZ, the KCPD's digital finger print system, but that came up negative. Designed more as a field tool for identifying live suspects with the press of a finger, PRINTZ was connected to not only KCPD's database but other local law agencies as well as IAFIS, the FBI's system. Because these prints were on cards and partials, not live, the system couldn't get a good read, so they had to send them to the KCPD for more efficient analysis than Central's on hand equipment could provide. Despite Becker's request for priority, the fingerprints and facial recognition scans were going to take at least until the next morning, so Lucas spent the rest of the afternoon with Simon, catching up on the case: examining evidence, reading witness and victim interviews, discussing lists of items taken, etc.

He drew up a digital map of the locations, searching his memory banks for a pattern and came up with nothing. He also searched whatever surveillance and traffic camera footage that he could find. He came up with some vehicles and tags, but no further images of the burglars. A search of the tags revealed the vehicles had all been stolen and abandoned later, soon after their use. In most cases, he could track them from the burglary sites and timing and deduction led both him and Simon to conclude they were most likely suspects. In a few cases, he could find no direct connection but they looked like possibilities and he searched anyway. All of the victims had been taken by surprise. No one had been unlucky enough to witness or be present when the burglars came. They would not likely have been witnesses if they had, of course.

When Dolby arrived with blowups of the van suspect's face, the two teams split up and went off to show it to victims to see if anyone recognized him. The first two stops were apartments where no one was home. But the third suspect ran a hardware store and was working the counter. Late forties and thinning hair with two days of stubble, he wore overalls over a t-shirt and cowboy boots. His name was Robert Tully.

After he finished helping a customer at the register, Lucas and Simon stepped forward and Lucas showed him the picture. "Have you ever seen this man, Mister Tully?" Lucas asked. Gentle easy listening music played softly from speakers overhead, the sound mixing with the hum of air conditioning and lights buzzing overhead.

Tully eyed it a moment, thinking. "I have a lotta folks in and outta here all day, you know. Hard for me to remember. He ain't no regular fer sure, but I mighta seen him."

"You don't remember for sure?" Simon asked.

Tully took the picture and looked at it more closely. "Who is he?"

"We aren't sure," Lucas said.

"This one o' the burglars?" Tully asked.

"A possible suspect," Simon said. "We aren't sure about that either."

Tully grunted, then handed Lucas back the photo. "Did you see him on the security footage you confiscated?"

"We're having it checked," Simon said.

Tully smiled. "Well, cameras don't lie, right? It can tell ya fer sure. I just don't remember. Sorry."

Lucas smiled back. "That's all right. We are asking all the victims just in case."

"You guys make any progress?" Tully asked, leaning his elbows on the counter as he swallowed, then sighed.

"No, but we have a couple leads and it's a priority, I can promise you," Simon said.

Tully chortled. "Well, shit. I know what that means. You may stumble onto something but don't hold my breath."

"We're trying," Lucas said. "We take this very seriously, I can assure you."

Tully shrugged as the door opened and a bell jingled, signaling it. Customers had arrived. "Insurance payment came in yesterday. Cost o' doin' business. Sorry I couldn't be more help."

Lucas turned to see a couple of bearded men in torn jeans and t-shirts heading up an aisle, eyes searching the shelves. Neither matched the suspect. "Thank you," he said.

Simon nodded to Tully and they both headed for the door.

"That was useless as usual," Simon said as they crossed the parking lot for the KCPD issue Ford Explorer they were driving.

"Happens a lot though, right?" Lucas said.

Simon nodded. "Oh yeah, we can have hours of fun."

After another two hours, Lucas was understanding human boredom on a new level.

Simon pulled the Explorer into the back lot at Central and turned off the engine, leaning back in his seat. "Well, maybe the prints and facial rec will yield something better by morning. But for tonight, that's all, folks."

Lucas laughed. "You are quoting cartoons. Am I a bad influence?"

"Fuck yeah. You messed me all up," Simon said and grinned. "Sure you still want to be a detective? Such an exciting life?"

Lucas nodded. "It is in my blood."

Simon laughed this time. "Blood, huh? Whatever passed for it in you?"

Lucas thought a moment. "I believe it is a combination of hydraulic fluid, lubricant, and conductive liquids of various types."

Simon made a face, trying to picture it. "What the hell color would that be?"

"A bluish green, I am told," Lucas said. He recalled the greenish pool he'd left behind at the warehouse the one time he'd been shot—the night he first met Simon.

"Ah yeah, I remember," Simon said. "Almost mucousy, too. Gross shit."

Lucas raised a brow. "I believe shit is gross. I never make it."

Simon groaned and opened his door. "TMI. You are far too literal, pal."

Lucas grinned as they both climbed out.

"You need a ride? Have some plans?" Simon asked as they crossed the parking lot for the station. Lucas realized his partner was referring to Lucas' depressed mood earlier as much as making chit chat.

Lucas nodded. "I have to see the doctor—a shrink, I believe you would say?"

Simon grimaced. "Oh yeah, department shrink. Standard post-shooting. That'll be fun. A fucking blast." They stopped at the door. "Just call me if you need me, okay? It's all going to work out."

Lucas smiled. "Thank you. I will."

Simon pulled open the door. "I gotta sign out, do a little paperwork. I'll see you in the morning, okay? Pick you up around eight."

Lucas gave a quick wave. "Okay."

Then as Simon disappeared inside, he headed for his car.

DOCTOR ALBERT GIRTZ, PH.D. had his counseling offices in a strip mall off Southwest Boulevard in Westport, a thriving shopping, dining, and nightlife center of the city near downtown. The shopping center was red brick with white-painted window frames and doors, well kept, and a small parking lot off the street in front. Lucas parked his Outlander in one of the spaces and entered the foyer-entryway, looking for the right office suite number. He found it at the end of the short first floor hall, near the back. Number 5.

Letting himself in, he found a small, empty waiting room with magazines spread on end tables between chairs lining three walls. A receptionist's counter was behind glass in one corner, beside a brown door that led into the back but no one was there now, though the light behind it was on. Lucas considered what to do for a moment, then decided to sit down and wait. At 7 p.m., he was five minutes early for his appointment anyhow, and didn't want to call out in case someone else might be in session.

He sat back in a black, cushioned chair with soft arms and stared at the wall, reviewing the day's events and evidence in his head as he waited. It was two minutes before a medium tall man with white hair, a beard, and a warm smile came out the brown door, his green eyes squinting slightly as he did. "Officer George?"

Lucas stood and nodded. "Yes. Lucas, please."

"I'm Doctor Girtz. Al," the man said, extending his hand.

Lucas shook it.

"Come on back with me," he continued, stepping to one side of the door frame and motioning Lucas inside.

The corridor was wider than Lucas expected with clean, shiny four-drawer file cabinets lining one side and the other decorated with paintings of peaceful soothing scenes to match the calming, gentle tan paint on the wall itself. Girtz led the way about fifteen feet, past another closed door, to a large office with a dark oak antique desk, and several leather chairs, as well as a couch. Packed bookshelves lined two walls, while the other was mostly a large bay window covered lightly by translucent, white curtains that let in light and a shaded view of the beautiful landscaping on the lawn outside.

Girtz took a seat in one of the chairs on this side of the

desk, motioning for Lucas to take another.

"You don't want me to lie on the couch?" Lucas said, looking around the room. The books ranged from psychological and medical tomes to a complete classic set of Encyclopedia Brittanica from the 1990s, and even leather bound classic novels as well as some modern ones. It was quite eclectic. And decorating the shelves in front of the books at various spots were little trinkets—toys, touristy items, etc., presumably from the Doctor's travels or reminders of his life.

Girtz chuckled. "No, that's a cliché."

"Oh," Lucas said, meeting the doctor's eyes again. "So if I get bored, I'm not allowed to sleep?"

Girtz laughed heartily. "Someone has been warning you how fun this is, eh?"

Lucas sat in the chair the doctor had indicated. "My partner-to-be, Detective John Simon."

"Ah yes," Girtz said, nodding with understanding. "Well, I try not to be too boring, but he's not wrong about some doctors in my profession."

Lucas pursed his lips, surprised.

"Hadn't expected me to admit that, had you?" Girtz said.

Lucas shook his head.

"Look. This is a real space where we deal with very real things," Girtz said. "I try to make it as pleasant and comfortable as I can, to make it easier, but I don't shy away from honesty. Honesty is very helpful to what I do."

Lucas liked Girtz immediately. He seemed very reasonable and kind, and he had a sense of humor. Something Lucas always hated to find lacking in human beings and had all too often. "I imagine it would be."

"Yes," Girtz agreed, relaxing in his chair. "So, why don't we start by you telling me why you're here."

"You don't know?" Lucas' brow creased. This was a surprise.

"No," Girtz chuckled. "I know what the file says, but look, they send you here for your health, not mine, not theirs. This is about you. So I find it best to start with what you want to talk about, what you're feeling."

Lucas shrugged. "I feel fine."

"So you are here because they made you?"

Lucas nodded. "Is this not typical?"

Girtz laughed. "I like you. I was told you have a good sense of humor."

"I try," Lucas agreed.

Girtz nodded, waiting a moment hoping for more, but when Lucas stayed silent, he said, "Is that because it warms people up to your unique circumstances?"

"Unique circumstances?" Lucas pondered the words a moment. "My not being human?"

"Well, yes, to put it bluntly," Girtz said.

Lucas nodded. "Yes, it does disarm them. And I like to make people smile and relax. This job can be very intense and emotional for people."

"Oh absolutely," Girtz agreed. "That's very kind of you."

Lucas shrugged. "It is how my creator programmed me really."

Girtz frowned. "That seems a very impersonal way to

think of yourself."

"As a programmed being? But I am," Lucas insisted.

"Yes, but aren't you so much more?"

"What do you mean?"

"You are capable of learning, growing, and becoming more than what you started out to be, right?"

Lucas brightened. It was true, and it made him feel good to be reminded. "Yes."

"Do you think other officers think of you that way as well?"

"As a robot?" Lucas asked. When Girtz nodded, he continued, "Some do. Some tease me about it. Not all, but the ones who do not know me well...yes. I am an anomaly. The first of my kind."

"So you feel isolated?"

Lucas shook his head. "Only sometimes. Mostly I am different, and I accept that."

"Yet we are all different in one way or another, aren't we?"

Lucas leaned back in the chair. "I suppose so, yes. But they have a sense I am especially different...once they know."

"Once they know you are not human?"

"Yes."

"Who tells them?"

"Word gets around."

"So you don't announce yourself? Introduce yourself as an android?"

"No, that would be odd," Lucas said.

Girtz smiled. "I agree. And it sets you aside right off the bat. Which would encourage special treatment."

Lucas hadn't thought about that but nodded. "Yes, I suppose so."

"Do you feel then that they do treat you differently?"

"Sometimes."

"Do you think they've treated you differently in handling this shooting?"

"Some, yes."

"How so?"

Lucas had to admit the doctor was smooth at steering him back toward the topic they were supposed to talk about. It almost felt natural. He had to give him credit. But at the mention of it, he felt tense and awkward for the first time since they'd come back to the office. He pondered his answer, then said, "I have unique abilities. I am not like everyone else. So maybe I should be treated differently."

"How so?"

"I am extremely accurate with my weapon," Lucas said.

"And you feel they have been unfair?"

"They seem more concerned about policy and human standards for response to it than about how that relates to my abilities."

"And that hurts you?"

Lucas squinted, leaning forward to lock eyes with the doctor. "I assume I am your first patient...like me."

"My first android, you mean? Yes. Why?"

"I supposed we have what you might call feelings, but it is not the same."

"Okay, but close enough for our purposes, yes?"

Lucas sighed. "Perhaps."

"You do seem a bit quieter and more reserved than I expected. Is that because you are upset about the shooting?"

"I shot a bad man who had taken an innocent girl hostage and was threatening other innocent people," Lucas said. "That is my job, isn't it? To protect the public."

"In a way, yes," Girtz agreed.

"I did my job, and if I faced the same circumstances, I would do it again," Lucas said simply, with no emotion.

Girtz grunted. "I see."

"Is that wrong?" Lucas looked at the doctor, whose face had taken on a sense of concern.

"Not necessarily," Girtz said. "But you must understand, Lucas, that it won't necessarily be what they normally expect from an officer after a shooting. And that may make them question your reaction."

"Why? They have my academy and range records and know my abilities," Lucas said, truly frustrated. "And they know I am not like everyone else."

"So on the one hand, you admit they don't treat you like everyone else and you resort to humor to help them accept you, and on the other, you want special treatment because you are different."

Lucas shook his head. "Not really."

"That's what it sounded like, the way you described it."

Lucas leaned back in the chair, thinking. "Humans can be

very frustrating and complex."

Girtz chuckled. "Yes, we can. But from what your colleagues say, so can androids."

This time Lucas laughed. "I suppose so."

"Which actually makes you more like them than they think."

"You think so?" Lucas said, pleased.

"Yes. But they have to get used to it and that takes time."

Lucas nodded. "I guess that makes sense."

"Tell me more about the shooting, Lucas," Girtz said. "How did it happen? How did the other officers and civilians react? Break it down for me, please. Maybe I can help you better understand their reaction and figure out a path forward. Does that sound good?"

Lucas had to agree that it did.

"Good. I'd really like to." Girtz smiled warmly again, and soon Lucas began to tell him about the events at Crown Center, replaying the recordings in his heads to ensure accuracy as he did.

THE ENTRANCE TO UNDERCITY looked like a standard man-made tunnel across from railroad tracks off Northeast Underground Road near State Road 210 in Northeast Kansas City. A 'Warning: 16' 3" Clearance' sign hung overhead, and long rows of lights on the ceiling disappeared inside over a two lane road. A row of flags from different nations flapped in the breeze on the cliff side lining the road above, respectfully lit by spotlights to ensure they could be seen even at night.

Karl Ramon had been on duty just under an hour when the man approached the security booth, walking casually through the shadows as if he had all the time in the world. Karl recognizing him, considered hitting the alarm button under the counter that would call the police. But then he remembered the man's cold grin as he'd said the most threatening phrase Karl had ever heard in his life: *"Tell no one or your kids will be getting a visit at Nowlin."*

Karl hit the speaker button and leaned forward in his chair with a sigh. "What do you want?"

"I told you when we met: information." The man's intense eyes and muscular frame almost made it seem as if he might tear right through the bulletproof glass into the booth with his bare hands.

"What kind of information?" Karl asked. "You know we're on security cameras right now."

The man stopped and glanced overhead and then over his right shoulder at the two cameras in line of sight. "No one will suspect anything as long as you treat me like just another late night visitor. Some guy inquiring about the place at odd hours."

"We don't get a lot of those," Karl said.

"But it's happened?"

Karl had to concede the point. "Occasionally."

"Then just stay relaxed and listen," the man instructed.

Karl leaned back slowly in his chair, trying to look normal, but he figured if the man could smell through the glass he'd take a step back. Karl was sweating enough he'd started to stink.

"You're going to find me a big space, some place in here toward the back, where we can do what we need undisturbed for the next two weeks," the man continued.

Karl stared at the white, cut stone walls surrounding the booth and thought, What the hell could the man want with space down here? There were no clients he knew of doing top secret work. The items worth stealing would have to be hauled out past security cameras throughout the tunnel system, and the most direct route was through the north dock entrance, but that was the securest point of the entire complex and never open at night.

"What are you planning on doing with the space?" he asked.

"None of your business, Karl," the man snapped with a piercing glare.

"If I give you space, somebody will want answers," Karl replied, feeling a sudden chill.

"Not if they don't know about it."

Karl scoffed. "You expect me to sneak you in here and hide you for two weeks?" He shook his head. "Security's too good for that."

"You're going to let us in to unload what we need to, and then we're going to pull out, and no one has to know."

"But then how will you get in and out to access the space—you can't just live here?" Karl said and then saw from the look on the man's face that it was exactly what he and whomever he worked with were planning to do.

Karl shook his head more vehemently this time. "That's crazy. Food, bathrooms—you can't just hide in here. It's well monitored."

"Not in the unused spaces awaiting construction," the man said. "The parts the limestone has been cleared from but isn't developed yet."

"Undeveloped space?" Karl said. "Why would you want undeveloped space?"

"I told you it's none of your business," the man said, leaning forward to lock eyes with Karl. "Can you do it or not?"

"This is my job here. I have to know what's going on," Karl insisted.

The man pulled out his cell phone and pushed up, holding it up to the glass. Covering the lit screen was a picture of Karl's children's smiling faces. "One phone call," the man said. "Who's home with them tonight?"

Karl gulped. "You just need it for two weeks and then you'll be gone?"

"Like we were never here," the man said and smiled this time. It was the eeriest smile Karl had ever seen.

"How big of a space do you need?" Karl asked.

"The biggest you've got," the man said, still smiling.

"I can't show it to you right now, but maybe during the day I can arrange something," Karl said.

The man looked at him cockeyed. "You better not be setting me up—preparing to betray me to your bosses or something."

Karl shook his head. "No, I swear."

"You don't work days."

"But I have to come in tomorrow to get my paycheck, and

I get a storage locker. One of the job benefits. Maybe I need to visit it and take a friend to help me."

"They won't be suspicious?"

"Less so than if I left my post and walked in with you now," Karl said. "We'll take my car."

After a moment, the man nodded and smiled again, though it was more of a pained smirk. "You the man, Karl. Now you're using your head. What time tomorrow?"

"I usually come around noon. Can you meet me out front?"

The man grunted. "We'll meet at the gas station up by 210 and drive in together."

Karl nodded this time. "Okay. That's better for sure."

"I'll see you tomorrow, Karl," the man said, then grunted again, turned, and strolled casually back the way he'd come.

Karl felt as if his heart might burst out of his chest, resisting the urge to stare after the man, and instead forcing himself back to his usual duties: checking monitors, noting the man's visit in the computer log, looking alert and vigilant. But inside his mind was on anything but his job. What the hell was he being dragged into? And what would it cost him?

One way or another, he knew he'd regret this. But if it kept his kids alive, he'd live with it.

CHAPTER 8

SIMON PULLED THE Charger onto I-35 from Mission Road, headed for the River Market area in northern downtown to pick up Lucas, when his phone rang with Emma's ringtone. His fourteen-year-old daughter rarely called him before school unless she needed something, so he readied himself as he clicked to answer, hoping it would be unproblematic.

"Headed to the office. What do you need?"

"No 'hi, honey?' Nothing. Some manners, dad," Emma scolded.

"You know I hate it when you sound like your mother," he replied.

"Can't I just call to say 'I love you?'" Emma said with a forced whine. Yep. She wanted something.

"You didn't say it yet," he replied.

"Duh. I just did."

"Not really. You implied you might. Not the same."

Emma scoffed and he could picture her giving one of her usual eyerolls as she said, "I love you, Dad."

"I love you, too, honey. Now, what do you need?" Simon replied.

"Oh my gawd, such a jerk," Emma said, but he could tell she was smiling and he smiled back. "Mom's schedule changed. She's going out of town early. Can you pick me up after school?"

"Like I said, you need something," Simon said, squeezing the phone to his ear with his shoulder as he reached down for his coffee mug and took a sip. Caffeine is good. His ex-wife Lara did this a lot, and he'd recently stopped minding. Since he and Emma had patched up their relationship back when he and Lucas had first met and solved the Ashman case, Simon treasured his limited time with her and any bonus was more than welcome. But that didn't stop him from offering a cursory protest. "You know I hate when she does this."

"Her boss gave her no choice," Emma said, defensively. "Are you complaining about seeing me?"

"No, just being a proper estranged ex," Simon said.

Emma laughed. "You're cute. Here. I'll see ya later. Talk to her. Kisses."

Simon switched lanes, weaving through traffic as he heard his ex's always tired alto on the phone.

"John? I'm sorry for the late notice. Roger only told me last night," Lara said. Once upon a time just hearing Lara's voice had been like a dagger through his flesh. But since they'd started getting along better the past year, the pain had lessened. It still hurt being divorced, feeling that sense of failure and disappointment, but he was also starting to feel okay about it, and Lara being nicer too helped.

"Why does he always do that? Doesn't he know his employees have lives and families?" Simon asked.

Lara sighed. "Why don't you call him and ask? I just work there."

Simon smiled. "At least I can't argue that point. Happens on my job, too."

"Now there's the truth," Lara snapped. She'd grown from excitement at the danger and importance of his job to hating it toward the end of their marriage, and hating him as a result.

Simon sipped his coffee again. "I don't want to fight."

"Me either," Lara said. "No shoot outs, okay?" She'd been saying that almost every time they arranged for Emma to visit since the Ashman case, where Emma had accidentally been in the car and then later his house when some gunman attacked.

"You know that only happened that one time," he said.

"Two times," she reminded him. "And never again, John." Her voice was so stern it reminded him of his mother. He flashed back to childhood scoldings and shuddered at the thought.

"Never again," Simon agreed. "You know I'd never want that."

"Just reminding you," Lara said, softening. "You lead a different lifestyle than we do."

Simon pulled onto the 2Y off-ramp and headed left on 3rd Street toward the River Market. The area was mostly restored industrial buildings turned apartments, nice ones, up and coming revival. "Yeah, I know."

"Okay, I'll be back in ten days," she said.

"Ten days? So they lengthened the trip, too?"

Lara sighed. "I thought you'd be grateful for more time with her."

Simon chuckled. "I am, Lara. Really. Just surprised. I'll see her tonight. You travel safe."

"Okay," she said and hung up without further ado as always. Even with the growing peace between them, Lara never prolonged any conversation with him she didn't have to. He hated that.

"Okay, nice talking to you to," he said, and clicked off the phone. Turning right on Wyandotte, Simon went a short block and turned right on 4th Street, pulling up in front of Lucas' small apartment building. An old brick former factory refurbished into apartments, it resembled a lot of other buildings in the chic River Market area, an area dating back to the 1850s that contained the original settlement on which Kansas City was founded, bordering the Missouri River and just across the highway from the Bottoms. Prostitutes, mobsters, car bombs and more had given this area a rich past, but now it had a thriving farmer's market, restaurants, shops, and a steamboat museum as well as providing homes for the up and coming adults who loved chic areas and access to the street cars and public transportation that made them feel both environmentally and financially conscious as they went out into the world.

Lucas' apartment had been a gift from his maker, Dr. Livia Connelly, and though small, it was well appointed with modern furniture and a few art pieces he'd collected at the nearby market. Simon had only been there a couple times when Lucas had tried modestly to cook his friend a meal and not succeeded. The second time, whatever it was, had at least tasted okay, so Simon had eaten it anyway, but being as Lucas didn't eat, he had a long way to go to cook anything approximating good human cuisine. Simon didn't fault him for it, though.

Today, Lucas met him out front on the stoop and soon they'd turned back onto 35 and headed for Highway 71, which would take them down to Lindell and Central Patrol.

"So, you sleep well?" Lucas asked, making his usual attempt at small talk.

"Yeah? You?" Simon asked automatically, knowing it was a relative term for whatever approximation of rest an android needed.

"I am very recharged and ready," Lucas replied.

Simon chuckled. "Have some coffee. You're way too cheerful in the morning."

"Coffee is to wake up and energize, is it not? How will it make me less cheerful?" Lucas asked, puzzled.

"Well, it's pretty hot," Simon said. "Maybe it'll burn your enthusiasm circuits. Worth a try." He grinned.

"You're in your usual bitter mood. Talked to Lara, eh?" Lucas said.

Simon laughed. "That obvious? Emma's coming tonight. Her mother's trip got moved up last minute."

Lucas brightened. "So more time with Emma. Yay! You love that."

"Yeah, but as usual Lara gave me no notice," Simon said. "Usual shit kinda puts a damper."

"You would drop everything for that kid," Lucas observed.

"Shut the fuck up! You're supposed to be on my side," Simon replied, sipping his coffee as he transitioned off 35 onto 71. "Sometimes a man likes bitching to his partner, okay?"

Lucas shrugged. "I'm like Switzerland. Neutral."

"I'll remember that next time someone's shooting at us,"

Simon snapped.

They both laughed, and Lucas flipped on the radio to Simon's favorite station.

AS SIMON AND LUCAS ENTERED the Central's Property squad room, the place was bustling: phones ringing, detectives chatting, keyboards clicking, drawers sliding. The smell of doughnuts, pastries, and warm coffee filled the air, soft music playing softly from radios at a couple desks.

Dolby spotted them and hurried from her desk. "John! Trevor Welch called about the facial rec and prints," she said.

"We got something?" Simon asked, ignoring Lucas who was being warmly greeted by the other Detectives.

She nodded. "From facial rec. Driver's name is Gregory Ronan. Six known aliases. Long rap sheet."

"We have an address?" Simon and Lucas followed her to her desk and she pulled up information on her terminal.

"Yep. Correia and Maberry are running down known associates now. Figured you'd want to check out last known work and home," she said, pointing to the screen.

"Can you send that to my cell?" Simon asked.

"Morning, Anna," Lucas said.

Dolby smiled at him. "Hi, Lucas." Then to Simon. "Already done."

"What about the prints?" Simon asked.

"So far the owner and a few employees but they're still running a few," Dolby said.

"We'll check this Ronan guy out," Simon said, patting Lucas on the arm. "Come on."

"He always this cheerful?" Dolby teased.

Simon rolled his eyes. "Fucking annoying, ain't it?"

Dolby and Oglesby laughed as Lucas grinned.

"You want coffee or a pastry?" Lucas asked as he stopped beside a small table holding a coffeemaker, cup, and box of pastries and doughnuts.

"Shut the fuck up," Simon teased.

"You want backup?" Oglesby offered from his desk across the divider.

"One guy, right?" Simon said. "I think we can handle it."

"I thought Lucas was acting as consultant," Oglesby said, implying Lucas was unarmed.

"He is."

They all turned to see Becker standing in her office door, watching them. "He better be," she added—a gentle warning. "Oglesby and Dolby, you two keep finding those known associates." She looked at Correia and Maberry. "Art and Jose, you're up."

"All right!" Maberry said.

"Fuck yeah," Correia echoed as they stood from their desks and hurried toward Simon and Lucas.

Simon looked at Oglesby and Dolby with sympathy an apology. But they were the best in the squad at computer research.

"Call if you need us," Oglesby said with a nod of understanding and Lucas and Simon headed for the door with Maberry and Correia close behind.

"Take all precautions on this, people," Becker said. "We're dealing with potential terrorists, not everyday burglars. Consider them guaranteed to be armed and dangerous." They all knew it but she was telling them not to take the usual chances they lived by every day. No matter what it cost the investigation in time.

"We should be okay as long as Maberry drives," Simon teased as he moved past her.

"From what I hear, we should let Lucas drive," Correia cracked.

And the four men hurried out the door, sharing a laugh.

SINCE IT WAS MID-MORNING, the detectives headed for Ronan's last known place of employment—a garden center bearing his name off West 12th and Beardsley near Mulkey Square Park. On the way over, Maberry and Correia followed, as Lucas read the information Dolby had given them about the suspect.

"What's Emma been up to lately?" Lucas asked, changing the subject as Simon pulled off West 12th into a small parking lot in front of Ronan's Greenery and Garden. Lucas and Simon's daughter had bonded quickly upon meeting and he knew Emma often called Lucas to chat and ask for help with various homework or research. Simon supposed, in a way, it was cheating but he didn't mind. Lucas treated her like a kid sister and being an only child, Simon felt having a safe friendship with an older guy was probably good for her. For once, her mother even agreed.

"Homework, boys—the usual teenage drama. I don't know," Simon said. "I expect she'll fill me pretty good over the next ten days, though."

"Awesome," Lucas said. "She hasn't called me in a while."

Simon shot his partner a look as they opened the doors and climbed out of the Explorer. "I thought you talked to her more than I do?"

Lucas shrugged. "I'm safer. I'm not her dad."

"Yeah, well, you just remember who is, okay?" Simon growled, a glint in his eye.

"I'm not going to date your daughter," Lucas said, reading Simon's warning as serious rather than teasing. "Or your ex-wife," he added just to get a reaction.

"You better not," Simon snapped, shooting him a warning look. Lucas started to reply, but Simon cut him off. "You give me that 'fully functional' shit again, and I will shoot you."

They both grinned as Maberry and Correia joined them.

"Ronan," Correia said, noting the large sign over the entrance. "Think the suspect owns it?"

"Guess we'll find out," Maberry said.

"You two cover the back," Simon said. "We'll go ask for him."

The other two detectives grunted in agreement and turned, heading around the side of the building as Simon led Lucas inside. Aisles of plants, bags of manure, seed, and other fertilizer or plant feed, and rows of racks of tools, planters and more filled the large, open space around them. The smell of flowers and soil filled Simon's nose as they passed several employees in red aprons helping customers and moved toward a large counter to the right.

"Emma's more pleasant to talk to than you. She's not so dramatic," Lucas said.

Simon rolled his eyes. "You're not around her enough. Besides, she's nice to you."

Lucas laughed.

"Can I help you?" A bearded man in Dockers and a red button down cotton shirt, a red apron reading Ronan's over the right pocket, stepped from the back room and approached the counter as they arrived. Simon noticed his brown hair matched his brown eyes as he looked them over.

Simon flashed his badge. "KCPD. We're looking for Gregory Ronan."

The bearded man's eyes went down as his shoulders sank in a sigh. "What did he do now?"

"Is he the owner?" Lucas asked.

"No!" the man snapped, anger flaring before he quickly regained control. "I'm the owner, Mark Ronan. He's my younger brother."

"I take it he's had trouble before," Simon said.

"Constantly," Mark said, shaking his head. "If I hadn't promised the old man, he'd never come near this place."

"So he's working today?" Simon said, offering a sympathetic and understanding look.

Mark hooked his finger over his right shoulder. "Out back."

"Thanks," Simon said as he and Lucas headed for swinging double doors leading outside.

"Do me a favor," Mark called after them and they stopped and turned back. The man lowered his voice. "I got customers. Try and keep it quiet and take him elsewhere if you need to. Bad for business."

Lucas nodded. "Of course."

"We'll do our best," Simon added and then pushed through the sliding doors, Lucas on his heels.

The back was dominated by lines of tables containing various plants and beyond them rows of taller, potted plants and seedling trees. To the side, under an overhang, were shelves containing seed, feed, and fertilizer as well as piles of sod. Customers were moving around, inspecting plants or pots, grabbing bags, and chatting with more red aproned employees. Simon immediately spotted Maberry and Correia moving casually through the rows of plants, looking people over.

"Any idea what this guy looks like?" Lucas asked.

"Yeah, I know what you know," Simon said as they walked down a center aisle and joined Maberry and Correia. "You guys find him yet?" he asked them.

"No idea," Maberry said with a shrug.

"What the hell have you two been doing while we were busy in there?" Simon teased.

"Shit. Doesn't look like you had any better luck," Correia said.

"He wasn't in there, he's out here," Simon said. "So what's keeping ya?"

"What's he look like?" Maberry snapped back.

Lucas shrugged. "You know what we know." Simon shot

him a grin as the other detectives scowled with frustration.

As they talked, they wandered down an aisle between tables and came into view of two aproned employees loading sod into the bed of an old pickup.

"You guys aren't done yet?! I could have had this loaded in ten minutes if I'd done it alone!" Someone scolded, and the detectives and employees all turned to see Mark Ronan looking annoyed as he strolled toward them from an exit Simon hadn't noticed under the awnings. Mark looked at the customer. "I'm sorry, Mister Reed. We can do better." He turned motioned to another employee nearby. "Roger, come give Bill a hand."

Another employee grunted from nearby as Mark turned toward the pickup again and pointed at a clean shaven, tall, skinny man who shared his brunette hair and brown eyes. "Gregory, whatever you did this time, cops are here to talk to you."

He motioned toward Simon and Lucas and his brother had an immediate reaction: his eyes went wide, darting around as he stiffened and eyed the detectives. Then he flinched and started running away from them.

"Goddamn it!" Mark cursed, looking after him. "What did you do now?"

"Gregory Ronan, KCPD!" Lucas called as he took off after him, startling employees and customers alike.

"So much for keeping it low profile, huh?" Simon muttered to Mark as he, Correia, and Maberry followed.

"Fuck! I hate when they run," Maberry said.

"My brother's an asshole!" Mark yelled after them.

Gregory Ronan headed straight for the parking lot out

front and Simon heard squealing tires as a blue Ford SUV screeched to a stop, waiting for him.

"Don't do it!" Correia called in warning.

Gregory ran straight for the vehicle and hopped inside as the driver's side window rolled down.

"No respect for cops," Simon said. "What's this city coming to?"

A muzzle flashed as a Mac-10 appeared in the driver's hands and automatic gunfire broke out, tearing up the asphalt, cars, and landscaping out front as the detectives dove for cover and drew their sidearms.

Then the tires squealed again and the Ford rolled away. The detectives fired a few shots after it but then ran for their cars.

"Son of a bitch!" Maberry cursed, looking at the two bullet flattened tires on his Explorer.

Simon was eyeing the shot out windows on his own as he fumbled for the keys.

"I think we found the right guy," Lucas said.

"What was your first clue?" Simon asked as he leaned against the Explorer and caught his breath, hoping the BOLO dispatch was issuing would allow other officers to intercept the suspects. After a second or two, he turned and opened the door to climb in. Lucas doing the same on the opposite side.

"Forget it. They're gone," Correia said.

Simon looked back toward where the Ford had gone and saw it racing up West 12th over the bridge and swerving onto an onramp to I-35 as Correia called it in to dispatch over the radio.

CHAPTER 9

THE MAN WAITED at a Conoco station at the corner of 210 and Randolph Road until Karl picked him up in his beat-up blue Jeep Cherokee, then drove the half mile to the south entrance of UnderCity. Using his credentials to clear security, Karl nodded to his fellow guard.

"Friend is helping me move some stuff from my storage today," Karl said, explaining his companion.

The other guard, a chubby woman in her thirties with dirty blonde hair and poorly done makeup, nodded. To the man, she looked like a sausage squeezed into a uniform that was clearly a size too small, but her smile was warm and she treated Karl like it was perfectly normal, so the man relaxed and slowly lowered his hand away from the concealed Glock it had instinctively inched toward when they stopped at security.

"Have fun, Karl. Enjoy your day off," she said cheerfully.

Karl smiled back. "Thanks, Ali. We'll probably go out the Parvin exit because we're headed that way," Karl said.

Ali nodded again. "Employee privilege is nice sometimes, eh?"

"It sure is," Karl agreed then slipped the Jeep back into

gear as she waved and drove on inside and around the corner to the office. This time the man waited two minutes while Karl retrieved his check before driving them on into the complex.

"Gotta keep up appearances," Karl said, as he turned the truck back onto the main straightaway and headed north. "Payday."

The man grunted but said nothing as the details of an underground world unfolded around them. The road winding through the caverns was two lanes with dotted yellow lines down the middle. The walls were cut limestone, smoothed only by time and age, but bearing all the marks of the explosives and heavy machinery used to extract the rock once attached adjacent to them. At times the road seemed to stretch off into the distance for yards, while at others, it curved into short straightaways before curving again. Rows of long lights centered overhead lit the passage and the man saw occasional security cameras and red, wall mounted emergency phones. They passed numerous alcoves in even the short stretches which led to either offices or storage areas, Karl explained, the storage becoming more common the deeper they went toward the middle as office space with easier access to the outside was more convenient and desirable.

At various places, large limestone pillars supporting the roof partially obscured the alcoves and Karl explained that they were spread evenly throughout UnderCity—the necessary support to keep the place from caving in on itself. They cut through storage units, offices, etc. wherever they needed to be and the tenants had begun treating them like coveted landscape. Offices with a pillar were like corner offices with a view in the world above: privileges of status and rank and a sign of one's importance. The man found it hard to imagine how a pillar in a cave could excite anyone as much as a great bay window with a stunning view, but then his thoughts quickly turned to plans and the importance knowledge of such pillars and support systems would be to his team.

In some places, side roads left the main and headed into other parts of the complex through larger breaks between alcoves. As he glanced at them, the man found they all looked identical to the main road in size and design. It would be quite easy to get confused and lost down here.

"It's like a giant maze until you get used to it," Karl said, noting where his companion was looking. "Most regular tenants need a map for at least a while, and the ones renting storage, who come infrequently, can't do without. The guards and staff have maps on our handhelds that act like GPS systems to get us where we need to go, but in this case, I know the way."

Karl prattled on about the place like a tour guide, almost proudly, despite his obvious nervousness, and after about fifteen minutes, they stopped at a storage area. "I brought a few items to swap out, then we can move on to the space I found for you. Appearances."

The man shrugged.

"Make it look better if you help me," Karl added.

Reluctantly, the man climbed from the truck and went around to the back as Karl unlocked his storage unit's large lock with a key and combination both, then opened the bed of the truck. There were a few old chairs and a table and they moved them into the storage, Karl swapping out a few boxes into the back before he locked it back up. The locker itself smelled dusty and damp, not unlike the road and walls outside it. The place was temperature and climate regulated, the man knew, and he figured most of that was residual or even psychological to match expectations of a cave. It didn't matter for his purposes, of course. As Karl closed the tailgate and headed back for the driver's side, the man turned and headed for his own.

Then their journey continued.

After another ten minutes of winding and another long straightway, Karl turned left onto a side tunnel and entered a zone with many "Danger! Under Construction" signs posted, and orange cones and yellow or black and white warning sawhorses either set up or stacked to the side of various alcoves and entry ways. They went fifty yards or so down a side passage and stopped in a curve, Karl parking the Jeep in an empty alcove which looked finished except for residue of sawdust, and scattered material scraps.

"This oughta be a good place for you," Karl said.

"What about the cameras?" the man asked.

"None installed in this section just yet," Karl said. "Not until construction is finished here and they start renting."

"How soon would that be?"

"Probably a couple months."

The man nodded, inwardly pleased though keeping his expression stern. "Okay. Show me."

Without further ado, they left the Jeep and Karl led them through an unlocked door into a large area that looked like it was room for a cubicle farm or warehouse workroom. There were a few drywall walls set up, painted plain white, with electrical outlets and wiring for computer networks, etc. But no furniture or electronics. A couple corridors stretched off out of the wall across the room from where they'd entered. Overhead, basic lighting had been installed that looked sufficient to light the center of various spaces. Lamps and other things would be brought in to eliminate shadows as desired, he guessed.

"Smaller offices, closets, bathrooms, and a kitchen," Karl said. "All finished and ready to go. Once we rent it they are repainted or decorated per tenant wishes."

The man grinned. "This looks perfect."

"Also, it is just off center, but toward the north end slightly into the unused area," Karl added then nodded toward one of the corridors. "Back there is an open cavern we will either seal off or develop as needed for whomever rents this space. It has two temporary walls over openings large enough for trucks if you need them."

"Oh?"

"Yeah, anyway, the areas near the two entrances rent and develop faster, for obvious reasons, but there is constant demand. Eventually, they tell me, we will probably add another entrance to accommodate some of these tenants for east access and such."

The man nodded. It was perfect, but he didn't want to reveal too much to Karl. "And we can work here in peace?"

"No one will bother you unless you bother them," Karl said. "Construction mostly takes place week days. The crews start at seven. A lot of coming and going amongst them won't raise alarms, but if they see you and ask questions..."

The man locked eyes with Karl. "We won't come and go a lot, and we are good at hiding ourselves."

"So this is what you wanted?" Karl asked, still nervously shifting from leg to leg or scratching at his arms and nose.

"It will do," the man said. "But tell no one."

Karl read the warning menace in his eyes and simply nodded back.

"We'll start moving in Monday," the man said.

"Okay," Karl agreed.

"Now, as for our vehicles…"

LEAVING CORREIA AND MABERRY at the Garden Center to deal with Becker and the other responders, and instructing them not to mention Lucas' presence to anyone but Becker, Simon and Lucas took off for Ronan's last known address.

"He has to go somewhere," Simon had told them, and hoped "last known" didn't mean long abandoned.

Lucas read it off to him as Simon raced up the W. 12th slope toward downtown. "315 Forest Avenue."

Luckily, it was just across downtown. Simon flipped on the lights and sirens and drove Code 1, taking a left on Broadway, then right on Admiral across to Charlotte, where he turned left again and passed under Interstate 29, then right again on Independence Ave to Troost. Turning left, he raced up Troost to 4th and turned right past the Guinotte Manor and then right again into old residential areas not far from the River Market.

Guinotte Manor, being one of The Housing Authority of Kansas City's affordable housing properties, was nothing spectacular or hoity toity as the name might imply. All apartments, government funded and built in the late 80s through 2000s—they all had the same vertical siding, painted shades of yellow, tan, or off white, and the same shingled triangular roofs. Some had double glass doors leading out to fenced in patios or small front stoops, others had faux brick fronts overlooking the tiny grass lawns with little landscaping to keep it as simple for the THA's maintenance contractors to maintain. Most of the complex lining Forest Avenue consisted of duplexes with street parking, but a few had small lots.

Simon pulled to the curb in front of 315, drew his weapon, and raced to the door, with Lucas on his heels. They left the car still running, lights flashing to hopefully scare off overly curious neighbors or passersby. The door was locked, but calling out or knocking would likely just get them shot if this was the right address, so Simon motioned Lucas to one side and kicked the door in, swinging inside with his gun extended in front of him—into a mostly empty room. The faded carpet was somewhere between tan and orange, the walls off-white but showing signs of use—dirty hand prints, scraped paint from furniture or other items brushing against it, etc. There was a rundown flowered couch that looked like even Goodwill would reject it, and three bedrolls laid out in three corners. As they moved in past stairs leading up to the second level, they came to a kitchen, under the stairs off the main room. It had no furniture. Lucas moved in to check the cabinets and fridge. Just a few cans and bottles of assorted types. The place was hardly lived in. Whoever had stayed here, it was temporary. That, or they were on the poorest end of those qualifying for such housing. The place smelled of cigarette smoke, dust, and musty carpet. Probably the same as almost any unit around them, Simon figured.

He put a finger to his lips and then used it to point upstairs, Glock 37 still ready at his side. Lucas nodded.

Simon raised the gun again and led the way back through the room to the stairs, then they climbed together, alertly but quickly to find three empty rooms and a bathroom. Only the full bath showed any sign of use—two ratty towels hanging from bars and another in a heap beside the tub. But the counters and fixtures were all dry. No one was home.

Simon relaxed and holstered his Glock. "Damn it."

"He could still come back," Lucas said.

"Right," Simon agreed. He hadn't really expected a suspect on the run to come straight home—especially when they knew his identity—but still, there looked to be not much evidence to find here either.

"Should we search?" Lucas asked.

Simon grunted. "Search what?" Then he motioned for Lucas to go ahead. Lucas began carefully searching the rooms, starting with the bathroom cabinets and drawers, behind the shower curtain, in the toilet bowl and back, etc. While Simon stood nearby, keeping an eye down the stairs on the front door. In less than a minute, it was clear there was nothing to find, unless they wanted to try pulling DNA and fingerprints off two old toothbrushes.

"Bag 'em?" Lucas asked.

Simon gave a nod. "Yeah, just in case, but we don't even know if he was here, and we IDed him already." He supposed it was possible they'd ID another accomplice.

Simon led the way downstairs where Lucas repeated the process in the kitchen, then searched the bedrolls and couch cushions. Again, nothing significant. Just a few personal items like combs, a CD or two, a lighter, and an empty cigarette carton, plus a candy bar wrapper and two toothpicks. Exciting stuff.

"Ah the glories of police work," Lucas said, smiling.

"It never gets old," Simon cracked.

"Want to call in forensics?"

Simon shook his head. "I'll have someone come sit on it. Unless he comes back and we know he's one of the ones living here, no point, and not even Becker would want to justify those man hours."

Lucas shrugged. "What time do you need to get Emma?"

Simon glanced at his watch. "Shit. Five minutes ago." He headed for the door. "I'll call a unit from the car."

Taking I-70, they got to Nowlin Middle School, off 31st and Harvey, in twenty minutes and pulled up in the curved drive to find Emma waiting.

"Ah, no boyfriend today," Lucas teased, referring to the time they'd pulled up and found Simon's daughter making out, much to her father's disgust and dismay.

"Shut the fuck up and don't encourage her," Simon said as Emma opened the back door and climbed into the Explorer. Looking at the blown out windows and glass on her seat, she shot her father a look.

"What is this—makeshift convertible? How am I supposed to sit?"

Lucas opened his door. "I'll sit back there. You come up here."

"Who did you shoot at this time?" Emma asked, smiling at Lucas as they traded places and she buckled in next to her father, then closed the door.

"Bad guys, like always," Simon snapped, then slipped the Interceptor back into gear and pulled away, around several other tardy parents picking up their own kids.

Emma grinned. "I should text pics to Mom of this. She'll love it."

"Don't you dare," Simon said. The last thing he needed was Lara being reminded of the dangers Emma had been put in before by his job.

"How's the Academy, Lucas?" Emma said, turning part way around to look at the android as Simon turned the car back on 31st and headed back west.

"Fine," Lucas said with a smile Simon knew was forced. "How was your day?"

Emma sighed. "Tiring. I didn't sleep well."

"Oh no," Lucas said with utmost sympathy. "Why not?"

Emma looked at Simon and sighed. "I think Mom's off her pills again."

"What?!" Simon snapped his head around so fast his neck hurt, almost swerving the car and having to turn back quickly and compensate before looking at her again. "What makes you say that?"

"She's been so erratic, high energy, up odd hours, obsessed with cleaning..." Emma said, reciting common symptoms to her mother's illness.

Lara had been twenty-eight and Emma six in 2017 when she'd first been diagnosed. The symptoms had never been as bad as the episode she'd had then. Simon arrived home late from work one night, almost midnight, to find his wife gone, his young daughter crying, cheeks red from tears. He'd tried her cell twice and got voicemail both times, then checked with the neighbors, who'd really enjoyed being woken at that hour—nothing. Then he'd called a fellow cop over to watch Emma and went out searching.

He'd come back two hours later still with no idea where his wife was. He'd tried her cell again to no avail and finally fallen asleep on a Barcalounger in the living room, only to awaken at four a.m. to knocks on the door as two uniforms delivered a bedraggled, dirty, shoeless Lara to the house. She was talking nonsense, something about not having an earthly home, then complaining Simon was abusive. After he'd showed his badge and convinced the Kansas City, Kansas uniforms he was just a fellow man in blue and she must have been drinking, they finally left, wishing him the best. The eccentric behavior didn't stop for three days until he finally had the county attorney issue an emergency detention order and had her taken in. Thus began a two year nightmare with Lara in and out of facilities until doctors got her body chemistry adjusted enough with the right combination of medicines that she settled back into a sense of normalcy again.

The diagnosis was bipolar 2, with a tendency toward mania rather than depression. And though she'd had a couple episodes since, most had manifested in hyper energy and increased anger but none had reached the same level as the first incident, which was why Simon had agreed to let her have primary custody of their daughter in the divorce. Additionally, Lara's hours had been much more conducive than his to raising a child and she was mostly stable. For Emma to bring this up like this was truly startling and worrisome.

"She went on her trip?" Simon asked.

Emma shrugged. "Supposedly. But you know—"

"She hasn't been that bad since the first time," Simon reminded her, shaking his head. "Why would she ever go off those meds?"

"She's been working so many extra hours, even at home,"

Emma said. "With the promotion and all—"

"She got a promotion?" Simon didn't remember.

"Yeah, Dad, before Christmas, remember? To Vice President."

Simon had a vague recollection now and nodded. "This is not good. Have you called her?"

Emma rolled her eyes. "School all day."

"Call her now," Simon insisted.

"What's wrong?" Lucas asked.

"Hang on," Simon said, driving up an on-ramp onto I-70 even as he kept one eye on Emma as she dialed the phone and put it to her ear. It rang several times, then he heard Lara's voice.

"Voicemail," Emma said, then: "Mom. Me. Call me please. Hope you got there safe. Bye," and she hung up.

"Fuck," Simon said, worried. Emma just shrugged. "We'll keep trying her."

"'Kay."

After that, while Simon drove nervously, Emma and Lucas chatted like old friends catching up, which they kind of were. It wasn't until Simon pulled them off 670 at Kansas Avenue that either of them turned to him again.

Emma asked, "Where are we going?"

"Have to make a stop," Simon said. "You two can wait in the car. I won't be a minute."

Simon pulled the car to a stop in the railyard two minutes later, beside an old switchman's shed, and turned off the ignition. "I'll be back shortly. Have to check with a guy. You two should wait here."

"But I've always wanted to look around this place," Emma objected, frowning.

"Keep trying your mother, I'll be right back." Simon closed his door and was gone, hurrying off across the tracks toward Mister Information's residence to find out what the CI had discovered.

THE VAGRANT LOOKED UP from the shadows as Simon climbed into the open doorway of the boxcar. "Who's there?"

"It's me, Denny."

The bum's eyes lit up with recognition and he grinned. "Absolut!"

Simon realized right then he'd totally forgotten. "Not today."

"Not today?" Mr. Information said, shaking his head vehemently. "You asked, I told you two days, but bring Absolut. You're here, two days later, no Absolut." He frowned almost like a child preparing to throw a tantrum. "Go away!"

"Denny, these people are shooting up the city with machine guns," Simon said. "They almost shot me and several others earlier today. And it's just a matter of time. We need to find them." He locked eyes with Mr. Information with urgency.

"You know how it works," Mr. Information said, shaking his head. "We had a deal."

"I'll bring it back tomorrow, I promise, maybe even tonight if I come back by," Simon said.

Mister Information stared at him a moment, thinking, reading. Finally, with a sigh, "These people you want, they are strangers. Not from the city. Just rumors. Not much."

"Anything would help," Simon said, nodding for him to continue.

"Don't got much," he repeated. "One or two of them live over near that HA manor on Troost, I heard."

"We were there today, but they weren't," Simon said. "Less than an hour ago."

"They'll come back."

Simon nodded. "I've got people watching. Anything else?"

Mister Information felt around in the shadows and came up with a bag containing a bottle, just the spout not hidden, and took a long swig. After smacking his lips, he frowned again. "I'd rather have Absolut."

"I know. I let you down." Simon was genuinely apologetic.

"There's rumors of some big plan," Mr. Information said then. "Explosion or something. Some big tourist site. But no one said which."

"Try and find out, will ya?" Simon urged.

"Get me Absolut," Mr. Information demanded.

"Yes. I will."

"Like I said, not much. They work in shadows but I can keep asking," Mr. Information said, then there was the sound of footsteps.

From somewhere behind Simon, Lucas said, "Emma!

We're supposed to wait."

Before Simon could react, Emma hopped up onto the boxcar beside her father and stared at the vagrant. "Whoa! Real life hobo. Cool!" She grinned.

"I told you to wait for me," Simon scolded.

"Ah come on, dad, I've been cooped up all day," Emma whined.

"Who is this?" Mr. Information demanded.

"My daughter," Simon said.

Then Lucas appeared in the doorway and the hobo started screaming. "Not him! I told you! Never him! Fucking no!"

Simon growled. More calmly, he nodded to the bum, "I know. I told him not to come." He whirled to Lucas, pushing Emma toward the door. "Take her back and wait, damnit!"

"She got away from me," Lucas said, shooting him a sheepish look.

Emma struggled to free herself. "Come on, I can just watch or something?"

"You're freaking him out," Simon scolded again.

"Not me, Lucas," Emma said, then with a scream, Mister Information pushed past and leapt from the boxcar, racing away down the tracks, his curses trailing behind as he ran.

"I can get him," Lucas said, turning to run.

"No!" Simon yelled, then calmed himself as Lucas and Emma stared, shocked. "Just leave him be. Damn it. I barely got anything useful. Just go back to the car. I'm coming."

Lucas and Emma said at the same time, "Sorry." And Emma climbed down.

"Fuck," Simon said under his breath and joined them.

HE WAS ON THE phone with the European when Gregory Ronan and Edson Núñez came into the abandoned warehouse looking scared and hurried into the small office to find him. In the background, he heard others working on the trucks, preparing, loading.

"We need to talk with you, Colonel," Edson said.

The man raised a finger to stop him as he listened into the phone. "Everything is going right on plan," he said. He listened again, then, "Yes, and we will move them early next week."

"Boss, the cops—" Ronan said, his voice shaking but the man cut him off with a glare.

"We may have a problem," he said into the phone. "I'll call you back in a few minutes….Okay." He hung up and turned to stare at them. "What happened?" It was an accusation more than a question.

"Cops came to the Garden Center looking for me," Ronan said, unable to meet his eyes.

"What did they want?"

"We didn't stick around to find out," Ronan said. "I ran to the car and we left."

The Colonel's eyes widened as he noticed the muted TV screen behind them. It was a TV news special report and it showed the garden center surrounded by police with a "Shots Fired" banner across the bottom of the screen.

"You shot at them?" he demanded.

"They had us surrounded, coming at us," Ronan said.

"You idiots!" he growled, shaking his head. "You fucking fools!"

"Colonel, we just shot at them to distract them enough to get away," Edson said. "We couldn't have them arresting him."

"How did they even know about him?"

Ronan and Edson exchanged a look, then shrugged.

"No idea," Edson said.

"Gregory?"

Ronan shook his head. "I don't know either."

He glared, then locked eyes with Edson. "Make some calls and find out what you can."

"Okay," Edson agreed.

"Who should we call?" Ronan asked.

"Shut up!" the man said, eyes locking on his in warning. "You just go help finish preparing the trucks and we'll handle this." It was a growl, loud, but he was pissed. "You really screwed up."

Ronan shook again. "I-I know...but—"

"Go!" he yelled, already turning away to dial the phone again.

Ronan and Edson both hurried off. The man known as "the Colonel" made sure to calm himself before European answered.

"What happened?" the European asked in his heavily accented voice. The Colonel thought he was Slavic, but it didn't matter, and wasn't the kind of thing you asked in his circles.

"We're looking into it, but the police came to question Ronan," the man replied.

"How did they know about him?"

"I don't know," he said with a sigh.

"Someone screwed up," the European said firmly, angry. "We're too close. This must not get in the way."

"I'll take care of it."

"No liabilities," the European said, and the man knew exactly what was expected. "Cops, too. Whatever it takes. The project must be completed as planned."

He nodded. "It will. I'll handle it." And the line went dead without any further words. Ronan was done. And when he found the cops, he'd be sending them a message, too. He just had to figure out how to do it in a way that sent them looking away and not toward them.

He stood a moment, pondering the puzzle, then heard voices from the other room as men worked on the trucks. He would say nothing until he was ready. He knew what to do.

CHAPTER 10

SIMON'S MAIN RESIDENCE was a small, H-shaped, brick two bedroom with attached garage that had been built in the '50s and was currently the smallest and oldest house on its block at 5516 Canterbury Road in Fairway, KS. Technically, he was required by department policy to reside in the Kansas City, Missouri limits and so he kept an apartment down near Grandview which he was currently subletting to a graduate student, but the house he'd inherited from his grandmother was where he lived.

As he pulled his Charger into the drive and parked, he climbed out to hear a familiar buzzing. The bright spotlight of a square, black, media drone hit his eyes as the machine hovered nearby and a female voice emanated from it. A gentle breeze tickled the leaves of nearby Oaks and Cherry trees in well-tended yards, as birds' and insects' calls spun a symphony sound drone of their own. The air was fresh and clean and smelled clear and peaceful, a slight hint of pollen adding a sweetness, unlike the tainted city air he was used to working in most of his day.

"Detective Simon, we understand you were involved in a shootout earlier today in the West Bottoms off 12th," it said.

Emma and Lucas had climbed out the other side of the car and hurried out of camera range, now watching him with puzzled looks.

"Are you crazy, coming to my house?" Simon said, moving to block the house from the camera while also keeping an eye on his car and license plates. "Get the fuck off my property!" He scowled and pointed at the street, eyes locked on the drone.

"We just want to confirm a few details off the record," the voice said—some hotshot producer or reporter sitting safe back in a newsroom, letting their station's nasty toys do the dirty work.

"Okay, confirm this," he said, flipping them the bird. "No fucking comment." Ever since drones had become commonplace, legal, and affordable, they'd been intruding on people's lives more and more. The KCPD, like many law enforcement and government agencies, used more sophisticated models, but the press were the ones who'd really taken to them on an obnoxious level. Every crime scene, every station—there they were, getting up in officers' faces, disregarding crime scene tape or boundaries, trying to get the scoop before anyone else.

"But Detective—"

"Call the department's media office like you're supposed to," he said. "I know I will be as soon as I get in the house." KCPD had clear guidelines for dealing with the press, and the stations damn well knew it.

He slammed the car door and started to step away but the drone followed, swinging around with a buzz and hum to keep his face in view. "You show my goddamn house and car on camera and I'll sue you into bankruptcy, bitch," he scolded, flipping the drone off again.

"Wow. Nice language in front of your daughter," the voice said as the drone swung out, lens widening to add

Emma to the shot.

"No! Not me!" Emma yelled, dodging to try and get out of view.

Simon drew his Glock and shot the drone three times, until it crashed to the ground at his feet. The birds and insects went quiet now, though the leaves still whistled around him.

"Hey! You shot at us!" the voice said, muffled and partially buried in static now as the remains of the drone lay on the ground.

"I wish you were here to shoot in person," Simon said. He bent down, grabbed the remains of the drone, and Frisbee-tossed it out into the street. "Send someone to retrieve your piece of shit property. If I see it when I come out again, I'll be driving over the remains."

"I can still see you," the now staticy voice said from the street.

Simon didn't see how when he'd cracked the lens. It couldn't be a very good shot. But just because it pissed him off to have his privacy intruded on and his daughter put at risk, he flipped a switch on his keys, the garage door humming as it began climbing open. As soon as it had risen four feet, he reached under and grabbed a black trashbag from a box on a built-in shelf to one side, then turned and stormed back toward the drone.

Bending down, he snatched it up, wrapped the trash bag around it, and tossed it back on the street.

"Don't ever do that shit again," he warned as the voice objected.

"Hey! The public has a right—"

"You have a right to remain silent," he replied as he marched away and followed Emma and Lucas into the house. He clicked the button to close the garage before slamming the door behind him, then called the media office. Emma answered her own ringing cell in the background as he explained to a very unhappy KCPD PR hack what he'd done.

"You can't shoot the press drones, Detective," she scolded.

"They came to my house, risking revealing my address, my car, license plate, and they put my daughter on screen!" Simon said angrily back. He could almost hear the woman shrinking away from the phone and he suspected she'd pulled it away from her ear. "They do that, all bets are off! No more shooters at my house after last year." The year before his house had been shot up twice by assassins sent by a criminal network he and Lucas had uncovered via Benjamin Ashman's art warehouse and gallery. It had cost him an additional fifty thousand dollars after insurance for the repairs and upgrades and his neighbors were pissed and worried.

"I'll talk to them" was all the PR woman said before she hung up. And Simon knew Becker would be getting a report and complaint. He only hoped the shooting team would go easy on him, since no other humans were involved and he was off the clock.

"You shot a drone," Lucas said as Simon looked at him, taking a deep breath but still tense and furious. The drone in the driveway move had really pissed him off.

"Yeah, so?" Simon replied.

"Anger management, Dad," Emma said.

"Shut up," Simon whined. "Your mother is putting bad

ideas in your head."

Emma grinned. "My friend Julie called. We need to finish our project. Can she come over tomorrow night?"

"Project? What project?" Simon was distracted and had barely registered her words.

"School, dad. That thing you and mom make me attend, even when I don't want to."

"Riiigggghhht," Simon nodded. "It's good for you. Like bran."

Emma rolled her eyes. "Yes or no?"

"Sure. Do I need to pick her up?"

"Well, her dad will come get her, but can she just ride over after school with us?"

Simon sighed, doing his best to let go of the anger. "Sure."

Emma smiled, pleased.

"What's the project?" Lucas asked with sincere curiosity, and with that Simon tuned them out as they launched into chattering like two hens, back and forth, all excitedly. He had a headache. Instead he went into the kitchen for a beer and plopped down in his favorite chair, reviewing the day and the case. He should call Becker and head off the complaint. Also give him a chance to find out what happened with the shooting team at the greenhouse and ask if the BOLO issued for Ronan had turned up anything.

He leaned back, putting his feet on the coffee table and sipped his Pabst Blue Ribbon. "Anger management, huh?" he chuckled, recalling his daughter's words then glanced through the thin curtain over the front window to where he'd left the drone in the street. Neighborhood kids were poking around at it now. He laughed. That oughta be fun for the station lady. At least until one of their P.A.s got here to pick up the pieces.

"Wish it had been you, lady," he mumbled. He'd call when he finished the beer. He needed to relax.

"What?" Lucas asked, moving into the room and taking a seat on the couch nearby.

"Nothing," Simon said and grinned. Then they started dissecting the case again.

THE NEXT MORNING, when they arrived at Central Patrol, Simon and Lucas were called into a meeting in one of the Conference rooms with Sergeant Becker, the other property detectives, along with Sergeants El-Ashkar and Thomas, Captain Snapp, and Major Wilcox of Central as well. They all had taken their seats around the long, plain wooden table, the Captain and Major's presences marking it as a high priority meeting, when Deputy Chiefs Greg Melson and Tony Cardno stepped into the room.

Melson was an old friend of Simon's, they'd come up together, and he'd worked with the Squad on prior cases, including the Ashman-Paulsen case a year before. Medium height, large build with graying blonde hair that betrayed his family's Scandinavian heritage, Melson was calm, professional, and respected the men and women who served under him, treating them like teammates, not just those he could command. Cardno was newly promoted after the corrupt Deputy Chief Kenyon Keller's fall and conviction for his role in that case. Cardno was the first gay man to ever rise to leadership in KCPD's history. Tall, thin, with short brown hair and a plain face that was dominated by piercing green eyes, he was all business, tough. Simon suspected he'd had to be to rise so high given his lifestyle. Modern conventions aside, it would always be hard to be gay in a profession with such a macho-dominated history and prevailing attitude. Maybe even tougher than it was to be a woman. Unlike Melson, he didn't smile. Simply took a seat at the table and waited, as Becker called the meeting to order.

"Okay, we're here because the Ronan case has taken on new priority, and it's time to read in the brass to all the details," Becker said as she looked around the room. While the Major or one of the Chiefs might be expected to lead the meeting based upon rank, Becker's words made it clear she would do so because it was her squad's case. But her slow locking of eyes with each of her people one by one put them on notice that they'd better make her look good. "John, you and Martin bring us up to speed."

So Simon and Oglesby ran down the burglaries and the various evidence they'd uncovered, taking them through by timeline up through the recent shootout with and escape of Gregory Ronan. Along the way, Becker and the officers would occasionally interject with questions or comments, seeking clarification, but mostly they listened, until the two detectives were done.

"So this Ronan is out there and we've issued a BOLO but so far, no one's turned up either him or the vehicle," Simon finished, looking at Sergeants El-Ashkar and Thomas, who could confirm if anything new had come in overnight from the uniforms.

El-Ashkar nodded, leaning forward, too alert for a conference room meeting. She was eager, excited to please. "Nothing new from other areas either, but we're increasing patrols in the Bottoms around the Garden Center to keep an eye out in case they come back."

"And Welch's people are running traffic cams," Thomas added, more relaxed. "They've turned up in a few places while fleeing but we lost them and never picked them back up. At least so far."

Cardno frowned. "Finding this man should be top priority. It sounds as if he's the only lead we've got."

Becker gave a nod of agreement. "And we've communicated that."

"But a word from us should ensure the other divisions double their efforts," Melson added.

Word from one division to another always got the best attention it could, but at any given time there were multiple such requests to cover and with priority from headquarters, many often got treated as sidelines to whatever other business that division had given priority.

Cardno pursed his lips, body still rigid, and tilted his head. "Why haven't we brought the FBI into this?"

"We've notified them of the potential threat as always," Becker said, "but the assessment was minor risk last we spoke. We continue to pass them new information."

"We've got men with automatic weapons shooting up the streets," Cardno said through a tight jaw. "I think the threat is far more than minor."

"The assessment was for the terrorist threat, sir," Simon said. "We did not notify the ATF about the guns."

The compartmentalization of the federal government was always an issue. Whereas the FBI would act quickly on any potential terrorist activities, guns and actual explosives fell under the ATF—Alcohol, Tobacco, and Firearms—and so the FBI could only pass the word. Any need for direct involvement would be assessed by each department's local office.

"I'm sure they've seen the news," Cardno snapped, leaning forward for emphasis. "But call them again. For God's sake," he glared at Simon, "we have our own people shooting at press drones in agitation. Their help would be appreciated."

Simon shrank back in his chair. A small piece of footage from his driveway had made the news that morning, and the Deputy Chief addressing the incident directly was not a good sign regarding how the department would be reacting to any disciplinary concerns. "They endangered my daughter, almost revealed my private residence—"

Melson raised a calming hand as Cardno continued glaring at Simon. "John, this is not the time or place. We'll talk after the meeting." Melson leaned back in his chair and looked at Cardno. "I'll address disciplinary incidents with my own people, Tony."

"I hope you will," Cardno snapped and turned his eyes on Melson, who held his stare and didn't waiver.

Finally, Melson turned to Becker. "Sergeant, you found nothing at the last known residence, correct?"

Becker looked at Oglesby, who cleared his throat and nodded. "Simon and Officer George were first on scene there but called in a forensics team."

"It was basically empty, with a few old pieces of furniture, scattered food, and bedrolls," Simon said. "But we did get DNA off some cigarette butts and it's being run now."

"We expect results any time," Becker added.

Melson smiled reassuringly. "Good. But let's see if we can't track down any other addresses. And we should also use the truck as reference."

"Our people are going to all addresses connected with the

vehicle this morning," Sergeant Thomas said. "It's a priority."

"Good," Major Wilcox said, smiling. Fifties, chubby, five-five with broad shoulders, Wilcox had come up from patrol and had the bearing and swagger of a long time street cop. "There's still not a lot to go on, but I'm confident our people are doing everything they can, and we will stay in the loop ourselves now as well. Keep it priority." He seemed unconcerned and confident and meant to communicate just that to his people.

"I'll coordinate with the other divisions," Captain Snapp added. He was medium-height, thin with short brown hair and a warm smile. He'd spent a portion of his career both on the street and in community relations and was one of the better known uniforms in the division to both the public and his officers and well-liked by all. "Share it at weekly command on Thursday as well." The weekly command meeting brought together brass and officers from the various divisions in one location to discuss various priority cases and issues that affected the entire city to keep everyone aware.

"Weekly command is almost a week away," Wilcox said. "Perhaps we should call a meeting sooner." He looked at the Deputy Chiefs. Wilcox might be a street man but he was politician all the way and Simon cringed at the obvious brownnosing.

"We'll figure something out once we've reviewed all the data," Melson said, before Cardno could comment.

"We're also going to read in the FBI, Homeland Security, and ATF more fully and formally request their assistance," Cardno said.

The detectives groaned. Federal interference usually meant a takeover and frustrating extra work for everyone as support, more desk and research oriented than field work, which they all dreaded.

"This comes from Chief Weber," Cardno added, panning the room with his cold stare. He stopped when he got to Lucas. "And why is an Officer who was put on leave by Shooting Team actively involved in this? Especially when he's still in training?!"

"He has special skills we need!" Simon objected, letting his frustration show in stiffened shoulders and volume.

"I cleared it with Deputy Chief Melson," Becker added.

"We're going to review it after the meeting and set some parameters," Melson said. Cardno finally relaxed in is chair, sighing, but he kept eyeing Simon angrily.

"From what I can see," Melson continued, "you've all done outstanding work on this so far. Tough case with not a lot to go on, and you've put your lives at risk more than once and handled it swimmingly. That does not go unrecognized at HQ, I promise you."

The detectives relaxed a bit and mumbled their thanks as the Central's officers also chimed in, looking pleased.

"But this case must be resolved quickly," Cardno said. "There is great risk to the public, so we need all hands on it from now on. We'll expect your full cooperation." It was an obvious thing but someone in the brass always had to say it in such meetings. The lower echelon knew better than to react with anything but affirmative motions, grunts, nods, etc.

"Okay, Detective Simon and Officer George will meet with me in Sergeant Becker's office," Melson said. "The rest of you get back on this with everything you can. All other cases are secondary until it's resolved."

Chairs screeched and chatter broke out as everyone stood and hurried back to their various offices. Only Cardno, Simon, Lucas, Becker, Wilcox, and Snapp hung around.

"You need me in this?" Snapp asked, expecting he'd be involved in any disciplinary action of his men.

"I'll take it," Wilcox said. "You gather all the updates from any aspect of this case and get me copies, please. We'll meet in an hour."

"Yes, sir." Snapp shot a sympathetic look at Simon and Lucas, then spun and hurried out.

"Copy me and Chief Melson on everything from now on," Cardno said, hesitating beside the door to glare at Simon again.

"Yes, sir," Simon and Becker said together.

"Was there something else, sir?" Wilcox asked.

Cardno continued glaring at Simon a moment then shook it off, his shoulders relaxing as he straightened and turned to Wilcox and Melson again. "No, I'm sure Greg will handle it appropriately." With that he turned and left and a palpable tension went with him.

"When they said they'd be replacing Keller, I never thought they'd go for duplicating his attitude," Simon mumbled.

Melson laughed and the others joined in. It was a much needed release.

"Why don't we just do this here, since we're all present?" Becker suggested as the laughter died.

Wilcox stepped over and closed the door. "Sounds fine. Chief?"

"Great." Melson took a seat the table, motioning for them

all to gather around.

Once they'd all settled again and looked at him, Melson said, "Look, the drone thing. You can't do that, John. Besides discharging a weapon irresponsibly, we need the press' support as a department."

"Those pussies stalked me to my fucking house, Greg," Simon said. "You remember what happened last year? It took months and thousands to restore my house. Plus, my daughter was shot at... more than once!"

"And believe me, Detective, we are all sympathetic," Wilcox said. "But you still need to refer them to the press office."

"They were already shooting the footage," Simon objected.

"So you call it in and we read them the riot act and demand they not use it," Wilcox said. "We have ways of handling this. They don't want to risk the lives of officers either."

"You could've fooled me," Simon mumbled, looking down at the table. He was not going to win this, he knew.

"Besides, you'd already thrown it away and damaged it against the ground, which is bad enough," Melson said. "You didn't have to shoot it."

"Oh fuck those pussies," Simon said, fists clenching under the table. "They come to my house again, I'd do the same." He was struggling to control his rising fury. Cardno's attitude had just made it worse. They'd been busting their ass on this case. Did anyone see that?

Wilcox sighed. "It made the news. You need to watch yourself. Second floor took notice. More than just Greg and Tony." He meant the Chief himself. Administration, which included the Chiefs' offices, occupied all of the second floor at KCPD Headquarters off Locust in downtown Kansas City.

"Just control your temper, John," Melson said. "It's a tense situation, and with your daughter there, I get it. I do. But destroying property is not something we can overlook. It can't happen again." He locked eyes with Simon, who took a deep breath and nodded consent.

Melson nodded, satisfied. "Now, about Officer George." He looked at Becker. "I know you cleared it with me, JoAnn, and this is a special case, but Baum and Beebe and Lenz are all three pushing for suspension."

"Suspension?! Are you shitting me?" Simon couldn't believe it.

"Have you read the file, Chief?" Becker asked.

"Yes," Melson said, nodding.

"And so have I," Wilcox added.

"And we discussed it," Melson continued. "We both see a skilled officer doing his best. They're overreacting, given Officer George's special skills. But—"

Simon shot Lucas a sympathetic look. So far he'd just remained quiet, observing, but Simon had a feeling his friend was about to be called on to respond and wanted to reassure him.

"But what?" Becker asked.

Melson looked directly at Lucas. "Officer, you know you have a special burden on you."

"Sir?" Lucas replied.

"Being the first android officer," Melson clarified. "People need time to accept it and understand it. It's all new to them. Odd. Hard to fathom."

Lucas nodded. "Yes, sir." Simon and Lucas had both experienced that reality enough to know it well.

"This will blow over, but you need to keep a low profile for now," Melson said. He looked at Becker and Simon. "I'm giving special permission for him to work this case, and keep track of his hours. We'll make it right down the line."

"I don't care about the money, sir," Lucas said.

"I do," Melson said firmly but with a kind look. "No firearms. And you report to Simon and Becker. But don't wander the station."

"I'll make it known he's here under your orders," Wilcox added.

Melson grunted. "The BBs and Lenz can be intense and sometimes a bit crusading, so let's just avoid riling them any further."

"Yes, sir," the rest all agreed simultaneously.

Melson looked at Lucas again. "From what I gather, you've done outstanding work on this and added a lot. Thank you. The KCPD is lucky to have you." Melson sat back and let that sink in a minute before scooting back his chair and standing. "That's it for now."

As Becker, Melson, and Wilcox headed out, chatting amongst themselves, Lucas turned to Simon. "I get the feeling that would have gone very differently with Chief Cardno."

Simon grinned. "You'd have been fucked. Sent to the junkyard as scrap metal."

"That sounds wholly unappealing," Lucas said as they stood.

"I don't know. I was thinking your arm might make a

great door knocker," Simon teased.

"I'll be sure and leave Emma in charge of my remains then," Lucas retorted as they stepped into the corridor.

Instead of turning for the Property Office, Simon headed for the parking lot.

"Where are we going?" Lucas asked.

"Hit the pavement and drum up leads," Simon said. "They want it upped in priority—so do I. So let's raise the heat on the street."

Lucas shrugged and followed his partner.

CHAPTER 11

SIMON DROVE THEM straight to the Jackson County Detention Center at 1300 Cherry Street, near KCPD headquarters in downtown Kansas City. A tall, red stone figure-eight monstrosity with slit windows running up each side, the Detention Center had been remodeled in 2019 due to increasing incidents of escapes and riots. The average daily inmate population was 875, with 350 employees operating, protecting, and providing them services over three shifts covering twenty-four hours.

Simon parked the Explorer in the attached lot and led Lucas up to the entrance, flashing his badge. The door buzzed and they went inside where Simon checked his sidearm, cuffs, knife, and pocket flashlight. The interior was just as cold and intimidating as the outside, all the better to set an ominous attitude for all who entered. The place smelled as sterile as a hospital, except instead of antiseptic, the overall scent was of dusting, mopping, and other cleaning fluids. The surfaces of every wall and floor tile sparkled under the effusive glow of the overhead lights. Then he caught the familiar smell—the smell of stale, industrial food stuffs, industrial cleaners, and human sweat—a smell prisons and jails everywhere seemed to have. And once he noticed it, it was all his nose focused on.

He looked Lucas over as he eyed the metal detectors they were about to pass through. "This should be interesting."

Then he led the way.

Simon got through with flying colors. But you'd have thought Lucas had robbed a Federal Reserve for all the alarms.

"He's a police officer," Simon said, retrieving his belt and both their badges from the fiberglass white dish they'd deposited them in before passing through the metal detectors. The guards rushed over to wand Lucas, their faces stern and unforgiving.

"So what's he carrying to set it off?" one demanded.

"I am unarmed," Lucas said, raising his arms as they scanned him. The hand scanners added their own beeps to the alarms.

"You brought the guy with you, Detective," the guard said, frowning. "You know better."

"I'm telling you, he's got metal in his limbs," Simon said. "But no weapons."

The guards stepped back, surrounding Lucas as one grabbed him by the arm and steered him toward a private room nearby.

"Sir, we're going to need you to take your clothes off for a cavity search," the lead guard said.

"Oh Jesus Christ," Simon said and dialed the phone for Deputy Chief Melson's office.

After a few minutes of quick explaining, Melson got on the phone with the guards and cleared Lucas, then spoke with their supervisor.

Even as they released Lucas and watched him get on the

elevator with Simon to go up into the detention area, they eyed him suspiciously.

"Why are we here?" Lucas asked as the elevator door shut and Simon pushed the button for level two, where they'd check in to visiting and find the location of the prisoner they'd come to see.

"Going to work the street with a little help," Simon said.

"Someone here is an informant?" Lucas asked.

"Not willingly, but it works the same," Simon said, smiling. "Just watch and see."

As they approached the long, metal desk, surrounded by bulletproof glass windows, locked, thick armored doors to either side, Simon nodded to the guard and flashed his badge. "Master Detective John Simon and Officer Lucas George here to see Golden Boy," he said then remembered, "uh, Marcus Crebs." It was Golden Boy's real name.

"Shit. He loves when you call him Marcus," the jailer at the desk said with a grin. "Be sure and do that a lot. He's up on nine." He turned to one of the other guards behind him. "You want to take them up to a room?"

The other guard nodded and headed for the door.

Four security doors, two more ID checks, and another elevator ride later, they were waiting in a small interrogation room for Golden Boy to be brought in.

A few minutes later, leg irons and cuff chains rattling, Golden Boy was led in. His orange jumpsuit reflected the bright overhead lights, and Simon squinted. A cut in his forehead had been stitched up and he was favoring the leg that had been shot. He entered with a smug sneer, curiosity glistening in his eyes, but as soon as he recognized Simon and Lucas, he stopped and started backtracking, pulling against the guards.

"No fucking way! Not those two!"

"Sit down," Simon ordered.

"That's the son of a bitch who beat me, and the other guy shot me!" Golden Boy said, shaking his head vehemently. The guards shrugged, lifted him, and slammed him into a chair across the table from the two cops.

"Why don't we leave you three alone," one guard said with a taunting grin as they turned and left, the door clicking locked behind them. They positioned themselves outside on either side, backs to the door.

"Fuck! What you assholes want?" Golden Boy demanded.

"Your help," Simon said sotto voce and just waited, watching Golden Boy, as it sunk in.

Golden Boy was shaking his head vehemently again, stiffening in the chair. "You be crazy! What you smokin'?"

"Well, you're in for endangering the public, resisting arrest, unlawful use of an unregistered firearm in a public place, kidnapping—" Simon ticked the charges off on his finger as he recited them. "You wanna knock some time off or just take your chances?"

Unlike in their previous encounters, Golden Boy didn't suffer from his usual body odor. Clearly he'd been putting the shower time and cleaning products provided free by public tax dollars to good use. Simon was glad. Made it more pleasant to lean in and press the issue.

"Knock time off?! You two put me here." Golden Boy shot them a cocky glare and leaned back in the chair, eyes darting around. "What's the trick?"

"No trick," Simon said.

"What I gots to do?"

"Information gathering," Simon said.

"What information?"

Simon leaned forward, locking eyes with him again. He let his eyes show his sincerity though not his desperation, because that would never help. "There's guys planning an explosion somewhere in this city. Guys with AK-47s and a thirst for blood. Gathering materials. Trucks to move it. I need to know who they are and where to find them."

Golden Boy scoffed. "How I'm supposed to know that?"

"Well, Marcus—"

"Fuck you!" Golden Boy cut Simon off, kicking the table leg in response then wincing as the shifting position aggravated his injured leg.

Simon smirked and continued, "—you ask around with your boys up in here, and your pal outside when you make those phone calls you make every chance you get." Simon leaned back to stare at him.

"Shit. I don't waste no phone calls on them," Golden Boy said. "I call mama. She kill me if I don't." Mama's Boy, figured. Bad-assery was all an act. When it all came down to it, so many of these idiots feared one person above all: their mamas.

"You help me and I put in a good word for you with the judge and prosecutor, maybe get a few counts dropped," Simon said. "That'd make your mama real happy, wouldn't it?"

"Why you do that?"

"Because we need to find these people, badly," Simon said. "Get them off the street, and we both know you got the connections to get information if it's out there." Simon leaned forward across the table. "These people aren't just a threat to strangers. Their victims could be anyone...including someone you love, like your mama."

Golden Boy's scowl turned to anger now and his eyes narrowed with fear as he leaned his elbow on the table, meeting Simon's eyes then Lucas's and looking them over as he considered it. After a bit, he relaxed and leaned back in surrender. "That's it? Just ask around?"

Simon nodded. "Yep. That's all we want."

Lucas nodded, too. "Whatever you hear."

Simon shot him a smile, pleased to see him playing along just right.

Golden Boy chuckled. "Shit. I ask around, yeah. But what if I don't get nothin'?"

"You help me, I help you," Simon said.

Golden Boy frowned. "Like I said. What if I ask and get nothin'?"

"That's not going to happen," Simon said. "Someone's seen or dealt with these people. So you find out who and what they know."

"Fuck. Ain't always so easy, Simon," Golden Boy said, "especially if they're scary dudes like you describe."

"You and I both know your people don't want these types around anymore than we do," Simon said. "Bad for everyone."

"I can try," Golden Boy said. "But if someone catches on I'm talking to you, bad for business. So what's in it for me?"

"I already told you."

"I want some guarantee."

"A guarantee?" Simon scoffed. "Okay, I guarantee, you help us, you convince me you tried your best, I'll make sure the next time a BOLO's out for you, neither of us answer the call."

Golden Boy looked at him a moment, trying to decide if he was serious. "Fuck, I never see you again, that shit be worth anything, Simon."

"Can't promise that," Simon said.

"Close enough," Golden Boy said. "I'll try. But you get my mama cleared to visit up in here."

"There's visiting hours. She doesn't need my help."

"She can't walk no more and it's dangerous on them buses," Golden Boy said. "You get her a ride, regular. I'll reach out when I got something."

"I'll see what I can do," Simon said. All in all, it was fairly simple to arrange once a week transport for the old lady. But he wasn't going to let on. "You call me every two days, news or not. I need to be kept informed."

"Okay, okay," Golden Boy said. "But make sure that don't use up my phone time."

Simon chuckled. "Fair enough." He pulled a business card from his shirt pocket and tossed it across the table. "I'll see if she can come tomorrow, special arrangement, just to show my good faith."

"She like that," Golden Boy said as he pawed the card and slipped it into the top pocket of his jumpsuit. "'K then. We done?"

Simon nodded.

"Guards!" Golden Boy hollered.

Simon and Lucas waited while the guards came in and dragged Golden Boy back to his cell, then escorted them out. After that, they hit the streets.

KARL RAMON PULLED his beat-up Navy Blue 2017 Jeep Cherokee to the curb in front of the house on Canterbury Road in Fairway and shut off the engine. The entire drive over his thoughts had wandered from the set he and the boys had planned for the club gig tonight to the mysterious stranger who was blackmailing him and what "moving into" the space he'd shown him at UnderCity on Monday might really mean. What were these people's intentions? Surely not good if they were willing to threaten Karl's family. He liked his job, boss, co-workers, and fellow employees. The last thing he wanted was to lose it. He was security. He should stop them. But what could he do?

In truth, he knew he was an overtrained babysitter. The expectations of security were to keep watch, scare off burglars or thieves, stop any fights or parking or other violations and issues, and call in the big guns in KCPD for anything else. That anyone could do. But stopping real criminals with intent to kill? Way above his pay grade.

Still, Karl didn't like it. Except for a few passing thoughts of tonight's set list and a few required glances at the GPS to lead him to this location, he had little memory of the drive. His thoughts had been too preoccupied with the trouble he was facing. He'd never felt so trapped in his life.

The opening passenger door startled him almost to the

point of crying out. Then the dark stranger was next to him, staring with intense green-eyes. "We need to talk."

"What the hell are you doing here?" Karl blurted out, glancing around to make sure no one was watching them. "How did you find me?"

"I have eyes everywhere," the man said.

"How cliché," Karl said.

"Sometimes clichés speak truth," the man said.

"So you're having me followed?" Karl swallowed hard at the thought and tensed in his seat, an empty pit forming in his stomach as his muscles twitched involuntarily. God damn but these people were bad news. Intense. Scary.

"I already answered that enough," the man scolded. "We move tonight."

"Tonight? I thought you said Monday," Karl said, shaking his head.

"Plans had to change."

"Why?"

"Not your concern but we'll be there at 1:30 and I expect the cameras in your facility will be experiencing a serious twenty minute outage at that time."

Karl looked at the man. They were messing with the cameras? Then he realized what they wanted. It was an order. Karl raised his hands in protest. "I can't screw around with the security system. I'm no programmer."

The man reached into his pocket and pulled out a small red rectangular device, offering it to Karl.

"What's that?"

"A USB drive. You know how they work?"

Karl nodded.

"You insert it and a menu comes up," the man said. "At 1:29, you click the button to 'Activate' and it does the rest. Afterwards, you click "Deactivate,' pull it out, and wait for me to collect it. Which I will."

Karl swallowed again, loudly. "What if they trace it?"

"Untraceable. It will look just like any other glitch—some power surge or other thing. It resets the system and that should take several minutes to fully come back online. It will also loop footage right after for a few minutes, but to anyone who doesn't know, it will all appear seamless."

Karl licked his lips and looked away. "I really like this job. I need this job."

"Follow our instructions and you'll keep it. Guaranteed."

Karl leaned back in the seat, taking another glance around to make sure they weren't being observed then looked at the man, relaxing his shoulders, trying to seem casual. "What do you need the space for anyway? Some kind of temporary storage?"

The man's glare was so sharp Karl almost felt it slice into his flesh. "You. Do. Not. Need. To know that. You just do as you're told. Understood?"

The way the green eyes bore into him, Karl melted on the seat like a clock in a Salvador Dali piece and nodded. "Yeah, I got it."

"Okay. Tonight then." And with that, the man was gone as fast as he'd appeared. Karl didn't even catch sight of him in the rearview mirrors when he looked to see where the man went.

Then he noticed movement near the house and turned to

see Julie and a strange man, surely her friend's father, coming out of the house and heading toward him.

SIMON HAD PICKED UP Emma and her friend, Julie Ramon, from school at four and driven them home, where he and Lucas finally escaped the non-stop phones and wasted follow-ups to non-leads provided randomly by overeager tipsters and various other sources. Like his daughter, Julie was a ball of energy, always talking and laughing like life was a race. They even had similar taste in clothes. If it wasn't for Julie's long red locks being clipped up in a ponytail, he told himself he might not have been able to tell them apart until they laughed.

As they retreated to Emma's room and pumped up the volume on their favorite pop hits—none of which sounded like anything but noise to Simon—the two officers gathered in the kitchen to review their case again.

Two hours later, Simon had been watching Lucas join the girls in doing some new dance moves in the living room when he spotted a car at the curb and someone approaching from behind. He went to the window as the muscular, dark man with a military haircut climbed inside and spoke with the thin, blond-haired, pale skinned driver, who kept glancing around nervously and clearly upset.

After the song ended, Emma and Julie got curious and came to the window to look.

"Hey, that's my dad!" Julie said, just as the dark man disappeared behind the car and across the street into a copse of trees at almost a run.

Julie grabbed her backpack and gave Emma a quick hug then headed out the front door, Simon on her heels.

"See ya at school!" the two girls called to each other sing-song as they parted. Then Lucas and Emma were back to dancing as a new song hit the radio. Simon cut off the noise by closing the front door behind him as he stepped onto the porch.

Julie bounced along the sidewalk like a typical happy teen, smiling as waving as her dad looked over. He did not smile back, seeming preoccupied.

As she opened the passenger-side door to climb in, she smiled at Simon. "Thanks, Mister Simon."

Simon returned the smile and said, "You're welcome, Julie. Look forward to seeing that project."

"Tuesday!" she said, nodding. "Just a couple more touches. Dad, this is Detective Simon, Emma's dad."

"Detective?" Julie's dad said it with either surprise or distaste or both.

Simon leaned down and reached across Julie's lap to extend his hand.

Her father shook it reluctantly. "Karl Ramon. Hope she was no trouble."

"Nah! They took care of themselves. No worries. Plus it got me out of the office early on a day of routine, boring work."

"Boring work for a detective?" Karl Ramon said. "Who knew?"

"More often than you think." Simon watched the man and detected a distinct discomfort, nervousness or something. "You run into a friend?" he asked, referring to the now disappeared dark man.

Karl's eyes widened then he tried to cover it with a yawn. "Ah, no, sorry. Long hours. Just somebody from work. Wanted to talk about trading shifts."

"Ah," Simon said. "Weird to run into him like that."

Karl shrugged. "Guess he lives over here. I hadn't realized." He sighed, hands reaching for the keys. "Well, I have to be at a club to play in an hour, so better get her home and be on my way. Thanks again."

"Okay, sure, she's welcome any time," Simon said. "Nice to meet you."

With that, Karl started the car and pulled away as Julie shut her door. Simon caught the man glancing back at him nervously in the rearview mirror as he drove away and wondered why. It was almost as if the man had never met a cop before. But that seemed highly unlikely. He shrugged it off. Whomever he'd talked to had clearly upset him.

Simon went back inside to find Lucas and Emma dancing away. He rolled his eyes. "I really shouldn't leave you two alone."

"What?!" they both asked, raising their voices over the music.

"Never mind," Simon hollered back and headed into the kitchen for another beer. He knew part of what Emma adored about Lucas was his child-like energy for new things, including the latest dance crazes. For a man made of metal, he was surprisingly flexible, too. Almost freakishly so. Simon settled back at the kitchen table, going back to work on the case and ignored them.

THE STOLEN BOX TRUCKS had been painted solid black, no logos, fitted with new tires and bumpers to make them look shiny and new, then loaded with the materials to be moved to UnderCity. The final touches had been completed only that afternoon, and the man known as "the Colonel" felt great comfort in it even as his people assembled around the trucks, just outside the office, where he awaited the final phone call from the foreign leadership, giving the go ahead.

The phone rang right at midnight.

He set down his Starbucks with one hand and picked it up on the first ring with the other. "Hallo."

"We are go," the heavily accented voice said. Not the usual contact. "637Alpha," the person added. The agreed upon code. The orders were coming from the right place. Official.

"What about the diversion?" the man asked.

"We are handling that. Not your concern."

"You still need my men for the finish?"

The foreigner grunted. "Yes. They should have the truck in place by seven a.m."

"They will." And if all went well, the incident would free him of two internal problems as well as several external ones.

"Very good. May there be an awakening," the foreigner spoke, their mantra.

"An awakening indeed," the man gave the expected response and the line went dead. He sat back in his chair a moment, inhaling slowly. His body relaxing, despite his pounding heartbeat and the heat of excitement filling his body. His people had no clue the full scope of what was about to happen. All the better. Leaks could not be allowed. And the police had made far more progress than he'd ever expected. Too many mistakes. Time to eliminate some as they set about preparing for their great moment. Less than two weeks and the world would forever remember.

CHAPTER 12

A FTER EMMA WENT to her room to do homework, Lucas and Simon sat around Simon's table reviewing the case, discussing leads, trying to connect the dots in some way that would push the case ahead. Lucas even reviewed traffic footage and other evidence using his internal WiFi to connect with KCPD's mainframe. In the end, though they got a few ideas they could pursue, neither felt satisfied they'd made much progress.

On his way home along I-35, Lucas passed the West Bottoms and remembered Watters' Feed and Fertilizer warehouse at 1233 W. 11th where the trucks had been stolen. Getting off the highway at 12th, the closest exit to his house, he turned left instead of right and decided to go down and look at the warehouse area himself to see what he could find. He hadn't been to the initial call and he wanted to see if he could figure out where or how the trucks might have been snuck out of the area without being caught on camera or spotted.

Parking his chrome 2024 Outlander in the small, cracked parking lot beside the warehouse, he climbed out and walked the area, using his enhanced senses to look for evidence—tire tracks, oil or fuel drips leading away— anything that might possibly hint at a direction.

Surprisingly, his ears picked up the humming of truck motors down the block. Just as he looked up to find the source, he spotted tire tracks in dried mud and petroleum residue mix humans often oddly called "gutter goo" that led in that direction. He bent to examine it. It could have been there for several days or longer. The tires were wide enough to be truck-sized. He called up the evidence scans on his internal computer and found the impressions taken by forensics techs of tires on box trucks similar to those stolen. The dimensions matched.

Lucas stood again and scanned the tracks, using his internal GPS to find the coordinates that would take him as close to where they were headed as he could extrapolate with just a short tire impression. He began walking due west along the gutter, also the direction where the humming of engines was still coming from.

He stopped at one run-down warehouse—it sure looked abandoned—and listened at the door. No trucks. Then continued on to the next. The further he went west, the louder the humming grew. At the third warehouse, he listened at the door, and the humming sounded like it came from just on the other side.

Then, without warning, the door slid open with a loud squeal and headlights blinded him as a black box trucks, looking shiny and new, raced out and turned onto the street. He searched his mind: the other trucks had been white and these had no logos. Could they have been hidden so close and refurbished to disguise them?

Before his mind could even process that, someone yelled, "Hit him!"

Then a truck loomed down on him and Lucas tried to jump aside, but the tread from heavy, large tires grabbed his pants and pulled him down, flat on his face, and then the truck rolled over him. He cried out in fear as his circuits squealed in warning and his legs were partially crushed. Then the truck sped away with several more following. The warehouse, which looked as abandoned as many others, just stood open and empty.

Lucas winced and rolled over, trying to focus and pull up Simon's number. He had to call him. And he had to alert someone to follow these trucks.

WHEN THE PHONE rang at the Police Communications Center, across from headquarters in downtown Kansas City, traffic supervisor Angie Pedersen noticed all her people preoccupied with other calls and answered it herself. "KCPD Traffic, Technology division." The room hummed with chattering voices, machine fans and drives whirling, monitors buzzing, and other technology noises. Rows of technicians lined several counters of monitors or desks with many video screens and computer screens monitoring the traffic cameras all over the city as supervisors walked around, looking in from time to time, and jumping in where needed.

The voice on the phone was scratchy but confident. "This is Officer Lucas George. I need an immediate BOLO for black box trucks moving east from 11th and Santa Fe Street. At least six of them, headed up 12th to I-35 I believe."

"Black box trucks? Did you get a plate, Officer?" Pedersen asked.

"No," the officer grunted. "The headlights...and they ran

over my legs."

"Oh my God!" Pedersen cringed and reached for another phone on the counter nearby to call the dispatchers across the hall. "Do you need assistance? Where are you exactly, Officer. We'll send an ambulance right away and dispatch cars!"

"My partner is coming," the officer replied. "I'm fine. But we have to find those trucks. They could be related to our bombing case."

"Bombing? You think these trucks are carrying explosives?" Pedersen's heart raced and the thumping of her pulse seemed so loud she almost expected everyone in the room to stop what they were doing and stare at her.

"Potentially," the officer said. "Please find them."

"I'm issuing the BOLO now. Give me everything you can on them, okay? And then we'll get you some help." Pedersen slid into a chair at her computer as she talked and rested her fingers ready on the keyboard to type the description and whatever information he might give.

She was so busy typing that it took her a moment to hear the commotion around her.

"We've lost I-35 south and north across downtown," a dispatcher named Melissa Mattson cried out.

"The junctions with 29, 635 and 70, too!" said another with alarm.

"No street cams downtown!"

"The whole system just went down!" said another.

Pedersen typed the description for the BOLO then took down the wounded officer's address. "We'll get help out to you right away, Officer George, okay? You stay on the line while I get a dispatcher on the phone." She pushed a button on her phone to place him on hold and then started dialing dispatch when someone shouted her name.

"Angie!"

She could almost smell adrenaline in the air as she sensed their alarm. "What? I've got a wounded officer here!" she yelled back, then looked up to see her assistant supervisor Julie Frost running toward her.

"It's all down!" Julie called.

"What's down?"

"The whole traffic system!"

It took Pedersen a moment to grasp it, then her eyes went wide as she stared at Julie. "What do you mean the whole system?!"

"City wide. No cameras. No nothing," Julie said.

"Holy shit!" Pedersen motioned Julie over and pointed to her screen. "Get this officer an ambulance and some help right now, then get a BOLO out on these trucks." She stood and cleared the way, as Julie slid into her seat.

"Son of a bitch!" Pedersen continued. She motioned to her other assistant, Holly Roberds. "Holly! Call the techs and find out what the fuck is happening to my system!"

Holly waved the phone she was holding. "Trying already!"

Angie Pedersen looked around at the frozen faces and screens all waiting on her to save the day, to give them answers. In her fifteen years at the KCPD communications center, nothing like this had ever happened. And she quickly realized she had no idea what to do. But she hid it as best she could, her mind racing through training and briefings. This could be the portent of huge trouble.

LUCAS' CALL MADE Simon cranky and grumbly until the impact of his friend's words and situation sunk in. Then he was throwing on jeans and a shirt as fast as he could while stumbling for his holster and weapon and rushing for the door. He was not as used to being woken up from a dead sleep by the phone as he used to be. He texted Emma from the car to let her know he was gone and raced down for the West Bottoms Code One—full lights and siren—while calling in "Officer Down" to dispatch.

Once the dispatcher had confirmed both an ambulance and two squad cars en route plus a BOLO on the box trucks, his heartbeat slowed a bit and he relaxed into his seat. Then he realized something.

"Uh, you can cancel that ambulance," he said.

"But Detective, he sounded wounded," the dispatcher said, her frown almost audible.

"If he is, I guarantee it is nothing an ambulance can fix. I will get him to a doctor," Simon said.

The dispatcher hesitated and he understood the confusion. "Ambulance is due on scene in less than a minute."

Simon sighed. "Okay, I'll deal with it. Thank you! 186, 10-10."

The dispatcher acknowledged and he clicked off the line.

Moments later, he turned onto I-35 for a short stretch and

then headed down the ramp at 12th toward the warehouse. He pulled up, tires squealing, to see Lucas being attended by two very confused paramedics while four uniforms stood over them, watching.

Simon flashed his badge as he raced over, crinkling his nose as he noticed the stench of the nearby city sewage plant was even stronger at night than it had been during the day. Its stench lay over everything like a blanket of nastiness. "Master Detective John Simon, Central. What've we got?"

"Someone ran over him," the female paramedic, a pretty blonde with "Hicks" on her pocket nameplate said.

"His legs are smashed almost flat," said her partner, whose nameplate read "Patterson." Heavier with brown hair, he squatted beside a battered but smiling Lucas, staring at the androids legs in disbelief.

"Did you tell them?" Simon asked, locking eyes with Lucas.

"I tried," Lucas said. "They seem to be in shock."

"He should be dead," Hicks said.

"I am malfunctioning, if it makes you feel better," Lucas offered.

"He's some kind of droid?" Patterson said, shaking his head and looking up at Simon, his eyes pleading for help or at least plausibility.

"Yeah, they make them now," Simon said. "Rare but he's our first official on the force. I'll deal with him." He stepped forward, indicating for the paramedics to back off.

They stood and backed away, but seemed in no hurry to go anywhere.

"Why don't you help me get him into my car," Simon

suggested.

"I took the liberty of calling Doctor Connolly," Lucas said.

Simon grunted. "Good. I hadn't gotten there yet." He squatted, the paramedics opposite him, and together, they lifted Lucas by the thighs and back and carried him toward the Charger.

"One of you open the door, will ya?" Simon ordered the uniforms.

Two rushed over to comply, almost stumbling over each other.

"Did you see anyone?" Simon asked, nodding toward the warehouse.

"No, but we were waiting for backup to go in, then the paramedics came and we got distracted," one of the uniforms said as he opened the passenger side door and stepped clear. Simon and the paramedics slid Lucas into the seat, sitting up. Hicks reached in to fasten the seatbelt as Simon turned toward the uniforms.

"Well, this may have been a base for some potential bombers or terrorists," Simon said. "Have a look but don't touch anything."

All four uniforms drew their weapons and headed for the open door of the warehouse, using a four man assault approach.

Lucas looked at Simon. "It could be rigged."

Simon had realized it even as Lucas said it, he looked toward the uniforms. "Wait!"

But one of them was already stepping through the open door.

Even from twenty feet away, Simon heard the clicking

and dove for the ground. "Get down!" he yelled at the paramedics and the world exploded around them, debris, smoke, and flames flying everywhere.

AS WAS HIS WONT at night, Mister Information wandered the streets around the railyard and West Bottoms scavenging for anything he could use: bottles, cans, or scrap to sell or recycle, discarded clothes, food, whatever. Tonight, his regular pattern took him along Beardsley near Mulkey Square Park. He saw a couple of vagrants lying on bundles under trees there, one or two on park benches, but none looked familiar. They didn't all know each other, despite the public stereotype, and anyway, there were newbies cropping up all the time; people going in and out of shelters, coming in and out of luck or money. Besides, he was focused on his quest. He had no time for chit chat.

As he passed the park and approached West 12th, he saw the dark shadow of the familiar garden center. Ronan's was the name, if he recalled. A couple of company flatbeds were parked to one end of the parking lot, but the place was otherwise dark, all the outside display stuff having been packed up and taken inside for the night or covered over with tarps weighed down by cinder blocks. Like that would deter anyone who really wanted it. Mr. Information had meant to look under there sometime but had never gotten around to it.

He paused a moment on the sidewalk across the garden center's parking lot, staring, considering it.

Nope, not tonight. He had a mission. Another day. He made a mental note to come back over the weekend when his pattern was more random. Tonight was usual rounds.

He had just turned back to walk away when the garden center exploded in a huge orange and white fireball, the blast knocking him off his feet. He landed flat on the pavement, scraping his knees and arms as he struggled to catch himself, calling out. But nobody was around to hear.

Flaming debris flew down around him and he wondered briefly if the world was ending. Then he blacked out.

ART MABERRY LED the way out of Bobby's, a favorite off hour hangout for men in blue, just off I-670 at Truman and Grand with his partner, Jose Correia, right on his heels. Bobby's was a small bar in an old brick duplex, the other side of which was occupied by a small convenience store. The bar had booths and tables, dim lighting, a nice jukebox filled with classics, dart boards, and a small dance floor. They'd stayed out later than normal but today had been a nightmare of phones and dead end runs to explore random leads. They'd needed to unwind.

The night air filled with the sounds of nearby restaurants and bars of the Power and Light District and downtown, the smells of alcohol, spilled oil and gasoline, and the river floating under his nose as they split up in the small parking lot to head for their cars.

Correia said his name. "Art."

Maberry looked up and his partner nodded toward the

freeway passing by a few yards away above. Several black shapes moved by mixed in amongst other cars. Then one emerged from the shadows into range of the overhead lights and Maberry made out a box truck.

"Son of a bitch," he said, counting.

"I count at least six," Correia said.

"Yeah, but those were white," Maberry said.

"Could be painted," Correia pointed out.

"Should probably at least call it in," Maberry muttered. He hadn't even heard the van pull up, but as he turned for his car he saw a flash, heard the door sliding open.

Then automatic gunfire erupted and he was diving for the ground, struggling for his weapon.

He saw Correia fall, shouting for him even as his chest split open.

Maberry rolled behind a car and drew his Glock, firing back.

Then the gunfire stopped and the van took off with the squeal of tires and disappeared down the street headed south.

Who the fuck were those people?

He laid there a minute, catching his breath, making sure it was clear. He heard the voices of others coming out of the bar. Then he remembered his partner.

"Jose?" he called.

There was no answer.

He knew before he even got to his feet, as arms grabbed him under the arm to help him up.

"You okay, man?" a fellow detective from East Division asked as he and two others helped Maberry steady on his feet.

Then Maberry saw his partner's lifeless, sprawled body lying awkwardly just behind his own car nearby.

UNLIKE SIMON, SERGEANT JoAnn Becker was used to late night phone calls disturbing her sleep. When the phone rang on her beside stand, she emitted her usual groan and struggled beneath the sheets she'd twisted herself up in during the short night and reached for the phone.

"Yeah?"

She listened a bit as the desk sergeant at Central filled her in. Four dead uniforms, an exploded warehouse and garden center, a dead detective in a shooting at a cop bar, Lucas run over...

"Shit!" she said, sitting up and planting her feet hard on the floor, grateful for once she mostly slept alone in the waterbed since the divorce. She fumbled for the switch on the map as she continued, "I'm on my way. Get Oglesby and Dolby rolling to the bottoms and send anyone else who's available. Homicide and shooting teams dispatched?"

She listened again.

"All right." She hung up the phone. "Fuck!" And jumped up, hurrying to get dressed and find her car keys.

MARTIN OGLESBY PUNCHED the button to open the garage door as he raced for his Ford Taurus. He yawned and crawled behind the wheel, twisting the keys as soon as he managed to fumble them into the ignition, and reached for his seatbelt even as he started backing out.

The red sedan came out of nowhere, cutting him off at the base of the drive.

"What the fuck?" he said as he hurriedly unhooked the seatbelt and swung open the door, climbing out. "Hey! Move it!" He flashed his badge.

The automatic gunfire cut him in two before he'd even finished raising it. He flew back against the side of the car, sliding down and leaving streaks of blood as more crimson pooled at his feet.

Moments later, as his wife ran out the door and screamed, the sedan raced away. He was already gone.

"THE WORLD IS GOING crazy, Colonel," the driver, Harris, said and chuckled as the dark man rode beside him in the cab of one of the box trucks. Indeed the dispatch calls about the explosion at the warehouse, the fire and explosion at Ronan's Garden Center, and six officers down were lighting up the police scanner.

"That's why we're here," The man known as "the Colonel" said. "Our friends are doing their part brilliantly."

"Won't they come after us harder?" Harris asked. "Killing cops seems like kicking the bear."

"Well, since we're about to disappear underground until our objective is met, they won't have much luck finding us," the man said. "Anyway, most of these were pulled off by people with no obvious connection to us. You just focus on getting us there and watch your speed!" The speedometer had slipped above the speed limit and was climbing. "The last thing we need are cops pulling us over for bad driving."

"Yes, boss, sorry," Harris mumbled and applied the brakes gently, going back to his duties.

Inside, though, the boss was smiling and laughing.

Moments later, the trucks turned onto the I-435 loop and continued north toward their destination. Just ten minutes or so to go. It was a glorious night.

SIMON HAD PULLED onto I-69 south off I-35 when his phone rang. Lucas leaned against the door beside him, quiet, but alert, almost as if he had no injuries, which was unsettling, despite knowing his nature. Didn't androids feel pain or regret?

"Yeah?" Simon said into the phone.

"Where are you?" Becker demanded.

"Taking Lucas to Doctor Connolly."

"How close are you?"

"Not far. Why?"

"Is he all right?"

Simon looked over and Lucas smiled at him. "Disturbingly so for a guy with smashed legs."

He flicked on the turn signal and slid right into the exit lane as he prepared to take the exit to Johnson Drive, a few blocks from Doctor Connelly's office. The doctor was a scientist. Ph.D. And she had built Lucas and others like him. She also was his best hope of repairs. Simon had already called ahead and the doctor and her assistant, Steven, would be waiting for them.

"Good, I guess." Becker sounded tense and scared.

"What's going on?"

"You know about the uniforms."

"Yeah, I was there."

"Did you find those trucks?"

"Not yet, but BOLO's out. Maberry may have seen them. But we've got bigger problems."

Simon's mouth went dry. He knew he wouldn't like the answer but asked, "What is it?"

"Correia's gone. Oglesby too. Ronan's Garden Center. It's like a war zone. I need all hands."

"Holy shit! Jose? Martin?"

"Jose was shot at Bobby's and Martin outside his home."

"Jesus Christ! What about Art?" Simon almost forgot to slow down and had to brake hard as he reached the turn on the exit ramp.

"Somehow they missed him, probably because people

flooded out hearing the gunfire."

"Dolby?"

"Here with me. I just need you as soon as possible, okay?"

"As soon as I drop him off and can turn around," Simon agreed. He made the left onto Johnson Drive, ignoring the red traffic signal, lights and sirens still going and sped up again immediately. "Where?"

"I'm at the Garden Center but just call and find me," Becker said

"Fuck!" Simon says as he thought of Emma at home. "Emma's home, I gotta go there first!"

"I already sent Fairway PD to get her and bring her in," Becker said. "Call her if you want but get over here," she ordered and hung up.

"What's going on?" Lucas asked, looking concerned.

"World War III," Simon replied as he turned left onto Lamar, tires squealing and reached for his cell.

KARL STARED AT THE screen for what seemed like hours, his eyes locked on the digital clock at the bottom, waiting for 1:30 a.m. He'd neglected his duties but he didn't care. He was too scared to do anything but make sure he got this right.

They could find him anywhere!

He had to protect his kids.

Finally, the numbers hit 1:28 and he inserted the USB

drive into the slot, fumbling a bit, and waited, hand hovering over the mouse for the autoplay screen and the time to change over.

The guard before him, who'd left at 12:30, had left music playing on an old radio sitting by the window—some classic rock station. Karl barely noticed.

The screen popped up reading 'Activate'.

Then it was 1:30.

He clicked the button with the mouse and waited.

In moments, the cameras went to static, flicking off one by one, right after another, as the system reset. The computer beeped and the screen also went blank then he saw the cursor as it restarted, and heard the familiar Windows chimes. And then noticed the security bars at the entrance raising into the air.

He waited, frozen in his chair. Sweat tingled his skin as it slid off his forehead and made a slow arc down his face, but he ignored it.

What was that thumping?

Just as he realized it was his heart, the loud humming of truck motors drowned it out and six black box trucks, one after another, pulled in and raced past him. He didn't even have time to recognize any drivers.

Within moments after they'd passed, he pressed the 'Deactivate' button that had replaced 'Activate' and the security cameras flashed with initiation sequences and began starting up again as the security bars lowered back in place.

Karl's shoulders sunk as he let out his breath for the first time in what seemed like hours. He literally gulped up the air like he'd been without it for days.

Oh my God, what the fuck did I get myself into? Why me? he thought.

The same thoughts rotated through his mind the rest of the night as news bulletins broke in on the radio about dead cops, a bombed warehouse, blown up buildings....

Who were these people and what were they about to do at his workplace? Karl couldn't remember ever being more afraid in his life.

CHAPTER 13

AFTER CONFIRMING EMMA was safely in the hands of Fairwood Kansas PD uniforms and on her way to safety, Simon caught up with Becker, Dolby, and Maberry outside Bobby's Bar as the crime scene techs, police shooting team, assault team, and gun team members combed it and interviewed witnesses. Apparently the Chief of Police had stopped by earlier and left behind Melson to coordinate when he'd moved on to go pay his respects to Oglesby's widow. Simon had been through officer involved shootings before where an officer was killed but it had never been someone he'd so closely worked with as Jose Correia, and it was tough. Maberry kept pacing and clenching his fists, his nostrils flaring, oblivious to everyone's urging to sit down and catch his breath. Dolby had puffy eyes and splotchy skin and leaned against a car as if dependent upon it to stay on her feet.

"I'm sorry," Simon said first to Dolby, who looked away fighting tears, then Maberry. He shared their grief and anger but at the moment mostly felt numb, a sure sign of the shock and suddenness of what had just happened.

"I want these motherfuckers! I want them now!" he said over and over, almost shouting in his fervor.

"We'll get them, Art, I swear it," Simon reassured him as Dolby and Becker added their reassurances as well.

Central Property would have little direct role in the investigation, according to department policy. They were too personally involved. KCPD had a specific police shooting team made up of officers from various units with additional training, but every such incident also drew a special crime scene unit and members of the assault and gun squads as well as legal, media, and the Chief. It was unlike any other shooting because brothers and sisters in blue were family. Everyone took it personally, whether they knew the victims or not. One of their own had been struck down. End of Watch had come too soon. And none of them would rest until the culprits were found and brought to justice, however long it took, and at whatever cost.

A few moments after Simon arrived, Melson joined them from checking in with the various investigators. "No one saw the shooters except Art," he said, shaking his head. "It was too quick, but a couple did see the truck pulling away. They're checking security cameras now for the plate." The parking lot smelled of burnt rubber—probably from the shooters peeling out—and spilled gasoline and beer.

"Fuck," Maberry said, frustrated. "I was too busy dodging and diving. I didn't see them either or the plate."

"You're lucky to be alive," Becker said. "It's okay."

"Tell that to Jose's mother," Maberry said.

"Is she local?" Dolby asked, her throat scratchy.

Becker shook her head. "No. The family's from the Southwest somewhere."

"Colorado," Maberry added. "South of Denver, a smaller town."

"We'll find them," Melson said and reached over to squeeze Maberry's shoulder before hurrying off again.

Personnel records would make that fairly simple, Simon guessed. The night was beginning to brighten now for the oncoming dawn.

"Art, you should go on home and get some rest," Becker suggested. "Take all the time you need."

Maberry shook his head. "I'm fine. The paramedics cleared me."

"Fine physically and fine mentally are two different things," Becker said.

Maberry grunted. "I'd rather work. Being alone right now is not what I need."

"Dolby?" Becker asked.

"I feel the same, boss," Dolby said, baring her teeth. "Let's get these bastards."

"Why don't you go on over to Oglesby's and be with his family," Becker said. "Art, you and John get to the feed and fertilizer place and see if crime scene's turned up anything useful," Becker said. "I want everyone back at Central by nine for a powwow with the Major and probably the FBI."

"Feds?!" Simon groaned.

Becker shrugged. "We've had six officers killed tonight, another seriously injured, and a bomb went off at the Garden Center, too. Only one injured was a vagrant walking nearby and he'll be okay. When you count, that's three major incidents tonight and the bombs plus the evidence make it likely they are all connected. The FBI wants to be read in and the Chief agrees. This may be too big for us."

"I'm not taking second seat on this," Maberry said.

"Hear, hear," Simon agreed. He of all people knew just how Maberry and Dolby felt remembering his former's partner Blanca Santorios's murder at the hands of Paul Paulsen's goons the year before.

"We don't have a choice," Becker said. "Anyway, we need all the help we can get. Chief's cancelling all days off and vacations, too, at least for the next few days."

"Oh that'll go over well," Dolby muttered, shaking her head.

"We need all hands on deck," Becker said, then looked at Simon as Dolby and Maberry headed for their cars. "Take Art with you, and if he won't take a nap, at least get him some coffee."

"Will do," Simon replied.

"When's Lucas back?"

"Haven't heard yet but I'd expect no more than a day or two," Simon replied.

"Well, keep me informed," she said. "Meanwhile, you okay with babysitting Art?"

"Yeah, I've got this." He hurried after Maberry.

THE COLONEL'S NAME was Toby Derrick, and he had been an actual Colonel in the Army and served twice in the Gulf. As the city blew up around them, all according to plan, he and those of his team not otherwise occupied settled in to their new base at UnderCity, where he got constant field reports.

"One left," his field coordinator reported.

"When?" he asked, knowing the answer but always testing. He always wondered if any of his people shared his acute sense of purpose. Not that it mattered if they didn't. He would drive them toward the goal, whatever it took. Alone if needed.

"On time, nine-thirty," the coordinator replied. "Their heads are already exploding. This will send them over the edge."

"Over the edge is where we want them," Derrick replied. "Inform me as soon as it's done, and make sure Ronan doesn't come back."

"Of course," the coordinator replied then cut the line.

The space Karl had suggested was indeed turning out to be the perfect setup. They installed computers and electronics for their surveillance and communications in the front part where the drywall had already been set, and still had plenty of room for the stolen laptops and phones they'd be using as triggers. Behind that area, down one of the corridors, they found an open space like a cave, cut from stone. This space was perfect for the rest. Karl had shown them two temporary walls that had been placed where future openings had been cut. Sliding those out of the way took mere minutes, allowing them to move the box trucks fully inside and conceal them before unloading.

As he noted the progress was ahead of schedule, another man, Luis, approached with a tablet running GPS-like software via WiFi and blueprints. "We've checked the latitudes and longitudes," he said. "This location is ideal for our plans."

"As anticipated," Derrick said. "Good work on the advance scout." Then he looked at the blueprints. "What happened to the complex maps?"

"They got left behind at the feed place when the cops showed up," Luis said sheepishly.

"What?!" There was a pounding in his ears as his heartbeat accelerated and adrenaline flooded through him. Derrick knew the maps included specific notes of where they'd planned to place explosives as well as an address and the name of UnderCity. "If the cops find that...not to mention the intricate planning to chart it out!"

"It was supposed to be in the last truck, but Wheeler forgot to load it up in his rush to leave," Luis said, looking toward one of the men helping unload a truck.

Derrick hadn't wanted to leave it there after leaving the night before but the drive around with hit teams had taken more time than planned and he'd had other responsibilities, including a meeting with the European and then being first on site at UnderCity. He'd been headed back and on the phone with Luis, when Luis promised to handle it. Derrick had meant for Luis to pack the crate himself. Passing it off was utter incompetence. Yet Luis was their explosives expert, he was needed. Wheeler was not. He was one of the few men they'd hired off the street for local knowledge, and he'd turned out to be mostly an idiot.

Without further word, Derrick marched over to Wheeler, drew his pistol, a silencer attached, and shot him in the side of the head. Tension fled his body. Problem solved. As the body fell, still warm, he said, "You'd better hope it burned in the blast or he won't be the only one paying for his mistake."

"I was able to recreate things here," Luis said, laying the blueprints out on the hood of Derrick's car and motioning him over. "We had extensive notes of the calculations."

"Get out there and find all the coordinates, make sure we

have access; identify the needed preparations," Derrick ordered.

"Yes, Colonel," Luis said and hurried off with his assistant.

Derrick looked up to where the rest of the men had frozen, staring at Wheeler's fallen corpse. "Who told you to stop working?! We have a deadline! And every one of you can be replaced."

Anyone watching would have thought it was a race to see who could resume working faster. He watched a few minutes then hurried back to the communications center to check in on his field teams. Instead of coming straight to UnderCity, they were to wait until the next day, when Karl would again disable the cameras, allowing them to drive in unnoticed. But after this latest screw up, he had to be certain they followed instructions and stayed off the radar.

The Police search would be given top priority. While the diversions had bought them opportunity to move their base to UnderCity with minimum detection, they had cost them a more focused attention by law enforcement on uncovering their activities. That everything from here on out go according to plan was vital, essential. Further mistakes could risk everything and that would not be tolerated. Derrick had recruited the most qualified and skilled people for his essential posts. Nonessential personnel would soon be useless and be disposed of properly. That would leave only one weak link: Karl, but unfortunately, they'd need Karl just a little bit longer. After that, he'd be dealt with too.

DOCTOR LIVIA CONNELLY'S lab in Leawood occupied the entire bottom floor of a three-floor office complex now. A year before, it had been just two suites but the press surrounding Lucas' work on the Ashman case as well as his acceptance at the KCPD Academy had ensured her androids were now in high demand. She'd gone from a dozen orders a year to dozens overnight, and to keep up with it, she and her assistant, Steven, had quickly hired additional staff and set to work training them.

Lucas' arrival for repairs was met with a mix of excitement and concern. Many of the newer staff had only heard about Doctor Connelly's most famous creation, never met him, and so he found himself very quickly the object of a great deal of attention. At the same time, remembering his responsibilities as a police officer, he was careful to only reveal so much about what had happened to him. Spreading rumors of potential terrorists stalking Kansas City might create a panic. Fortunately, Doctor Connelly accepted his explanation without further inquiry.

Several staffers gathered around as she examined him. "I'm sorry, Lucas," Connelly said. "I'll chase them out when we begin the procedure."

Lucas smiled. "It's okay, Maker, if you want them to learn." Inside, his systems seemed flooded with fluids—a combination of hydraulic fluids and lubricants, as if pumping extra and it took discernible effort to just lie still and let them examine him. His friends had just been killed and he wanted to get back to them as soon as possible and help find those responsible.

"Well, the good news is we are upgrading you because we don't make the version of the legs you were built with,"

Connelly said. "These are upgrades."

"I will still look the same?"

"Of course," Connelly said. "Outwardly, we can fit the circuits into the same mold as your legs were made from. We just use improved materials."

Lucas nodded. "Fascinating. But what's most important is that I can get back on duty as soon as possible." To calm himself, he ran internal diagnostics and practiced complex math problems in his head.

"We'll do our best," Connelly assured him. "The procedure should take two or three hours with calibration. Ideally, we'd have you stick around for further tests to be sure everything is integrating properly—"

"I'll come back for that, I promise," Lucas said. "We just lost several officers and they need everyone on call."

"Of course," Connelly said.

Lucas wondered if humans found as much fascination with how they were made as he was. Of course, part of his programming was to perform basic fine tuning and maintenance on himself, whereas most humans didn't tend to practice complex medicine on themselves. Still, watching Doctor Connelly, his Maker, work always intrigued him greatly. To Lucas, Livia Connelly was amazing. Why the short, white female with long dark hair seemed to have only her staff and creations as family was a mystery to him. Perhaps it was the intensity of her dedication and focus. She worked the longest hours of anyone Lucas knew. She was always available to him. If he were human, Lucas certainly would imagine himself being with someone like her.

A few minutes later, Steven appeared, carrying the new pair of legs. Lucas admired their smooth sheen. "These should make you faster and stronger," he said.

"Like a *Six Million Dollar Man*?" Lucas asked. He was a big fan of classic television thanks to Emma.

"Luckily, these are a bit cheaper," Connelly said as she and Steven laughed.

"That doesn't mean we don't still want you to exercise caution and not take unnecessary risks, though," Steven added.

"Yes, exactly," Connelly said. "Just because your circumstances are special doesn't mean you are indestructible."

"A lesson I am learning today," Lucas said, smiling as Connelly turned to the gawking employees and chased them from the room.

As Lucas watched them work on his lower half, he was thankful for once he wasn't human so he could stay awake and feel no pain. Connelly and Steven worked in tandem with hardly a word passing between them—each seeming to know what was needed by the other at any given moment and providing it readily without any need to ask. He did feel a slight energy surge when the new legs had been attached to his electrical system as his internal systems increased power to his lower extremities again, but otherwise, he might have been just another outsider watching them work.

He'd heard over the radio about Correia and Oglesby and wondered how the others were handling the mix of sadness and anger these losses would evoke. He was anxious to rejoin them so he could provide whatever assistance he could in carrying out their duties, but most especially in finding and stopping the culprits before they hurt anyone else.

About an hour in, Connelly nodded to Steven, who said, "Lucas, we need to shut you down for a few minutes while we calibrate your power system and reset servos."

"For how long?" Lucas asked.

"Five or six minutes, max," Connelly replied.

"All right, I guess I will sleep after all," Lucas joked, since androids never really slept.

They chuckled and Steven assisted Connelly in turning Lucas on his side.

"You ready?" Steven asked.

"Of course," Lucas said, and sensed them fiddling with his back panel. A few moments later, he faded to black.

BY THE TIME SIMON and Maberry made it to what was left of the abandoned warehouse in the Bottoms, daylight had dawned and the crime scene crew was actively at work. Not much had survived the blast. The smoldering remains were basically a few pieces of framing with small chunks of wooden walls still attached surrounding piles of blackened ruins on the charred cement floor. If the warehouse wasn't abandoned entirely, someone might get some insurance money out of it, but there was nothing to rebuild.

As they stepped through what remained of a garage door, Simon watched as one team took photographs, measured, and made sketches as others were at work sorting and bagging in areas the first team had already finished. Another tech was examining any remaining surfaces or large pieces, probably for prints, while another grabbed what had been bagged, numbered and logged it on an iPad, then hauled it out to the team's vans. Simon and Maberry immediately found Paul Engborg, moving amongst the ruins, coordinating his team, and asked him to bring them up to date. Engborg was tall, balding, mid-forties, with a developing paunch but a warm smile.

"The place is so old, the walls pretty much disintegrated under the force of the blast," Engborg said. "The rest burned, mostly. We did get casts of some tire tracks from the gutters out front."

"Trucks? Cars?" Simon asked.

While Engborg talked, Maberry paced and turned erratically to look around the room, tense and unfocused.

"Looks like trucks," Engborg said, "but we'll know more when we've run them through the database. We also found a box of paperwork that looks like someone drove off and left it." He looked at Maberry. "Is he okay?"

"He lost his partner a couple hours ago," Simon said, looking at Maberry."Paperwork? Let's go through that."

"You can try," Engborg said. "Most of it burned to a crisp, but I suppose there's a chance a scrap or two might provide some clue."

"Any prints?" Maberry asked.

Engborg shook his head. "Not yet. Most surfaces either disintegrated or were torched as you can see. But we'll test any solid surfaces we find and see what turns up." Unless the surfaces were destroyed or severely damaged by heat from the fire—charred black—latent prints could survive, even on smaller pieces. In fact, sometimes the heat caused the print residue to darken so the fingerprints became visible after a fire—similar to the results crime scene techs obtained using latent print powders—which would just make finding them that much easier. In some cases, layers of soot could actually be removed—depending upon the nature of the soot—to reveal prints underneath, but that process could delay results for days or weeks.

Engborg led them outside to one of the vans where the box of paperwork had been taken and motioned to the tech who was approaching with another numbered evidence bag, "Can you get these detectives a tarp so they can go through the paperwork?"

"Sure," the tech said and deposited the bag in a bin inside the van then went around to the side door to get the tarp.

"Can't we just take it back to the office?" Maberry asked.

"You know the procedure," Engborg said. "We haven't sorted and photographed or printed them yet."

"I just don't want the wind destroying anything," Maberry said.

As they continued the discussion, Simon's cell rang and he answered on the third ring. "Simon."

"Detective, this is Jan Pierson over at the K.U. Med Center E.R.," a woman said. "We have a patient here named Dennis Murphy who keeps insisting he talk to you right away."

"Dennis Murphy?" Simon searched his mind.

"He was injured in the Ronan Garden Center explosion, says he knows you," Pierson continued. "Also keeps mentioning something about you owing him a bottle of Absolut?"

Mister Information! "Oh, he's a friend of mine, yeah, what

happened? How is he?" Simon asked.

"A few cuts and bruises mostly, but we're keeping him overnight for observation," Pierson said. "Any way you could come down here, though?"

"Now? We're a little busy."

"I imagine, and I'm sorry," she said. "I wouldn't normally ask but he refuses to cooperate until he sees you, so..."

"Give me half an hour," Simon said and waited until she agreed then hung up and turned to Maberry, "We taking this?"

Maberry shook his head. "Not 'til they take pictures and dust for prints, but if they find anything they'll call us right away."

"Well, we want those prints for sure, plus it's windy," Simon noted. "Wanna ride with me to the Med Center? I've got a CI who was injured and has something for me, I think."

"I think I'll stay here and see what they turn up," Maberry said. "I can get a ride in by nine for that meeting if I need to."

Simon nodded. "Okay, suit yourself. You okay?" He eyed the other detective with genuine concern.

Maberry grunted. "I'm gonna find these bastards. The quicker we process this scene, the better, so I'll suit up and help."

"Fair enough," Simon said. Maberry had actually done a stint in crime scene forensics before becoming a detective, so he knew what he was doing. "Call me if you need me."

"Just let me know the minute you get anything," Maberry said as the tech brought him booties and a protective jumpsuit.

"Don't worry. I felt the same way about Blanca," Simon

said and they exchanged a meaningful look as both thought of their deceased partners. Then they headed for the Charger, hoping whatever Mister Information had it would lead to a breakthrough. They really needed one.

CHAPTER 14

THE EMERGENCY ROOM at K.U. Med Center was on the ground floor at Cambridge and 39th, the north end of 4000 Cambridge Street in Kansas City, Kansas. Because it was the hospital closest to Ronan's Garden Center—just across State Line Road on the Kansas side—and because of the multiple victims headed to other hospitals, Mister Information had been taken there by paramedics. Simon pulled the Police placard from his glove compartment and put it on the Charger's dash then left his car in emergency parking outside and entered the Emergency Room through the automatic doors.

The smell of industrial cleaning chemicals and antiseptic struck him immediately as the chattering of staff and sounds of the injured filled his ears. He strode straight ahead toward a large admitting desk and flashed his badge. "John Simon. Is Jan Pierson here?"

A diminutive brunette in her mid-forties stepped from a room across the corridor and waved. "In here, Detective." She smiled as he nodded to the admissions staff and headed her way.

Mister Information was lying on an emergency bed under bright lights, an instrument table rolled off to one side. He had bandages around his right forearm and on his cheeks and forehead, but other than that Simon thought the nurses must have cleaned him up a bit, because he looked better—more presentable—than Simon recalled ever seeing him. Even his beard had been trimmed to give access to his wounds. Seeing another friend lying there sent his adrenaline pumping. This attack was personal, and he felt as if he'd been slapped.

The vagrant's green eyes locked on Simon's the minute he entered and he lifted his head off the pillow. "You got my Absolut?"

"You can't drink Vodka in the E.R., Denny," Simon said, forcing a smile as much in an attempt to calm himself as reassure his friend. "How are you? Are you okay?" Machines beeped and hissed softly in the background as Simon examined his CI. There was a clear IV running to his arm, but his skin looked normal and his eyes were alert.

"I'm in a lotta pain here," Mister Information said. "I need that Vodka."

"They can give you some painkillers for that," Simon replied.

"Someone blew up the garden center as I walked by," Mister Information said. "I guess I'm lucky. I'm still in one piece."

"Good. You're starting to actually look respectable," Simon teased.

"Damn it! They shaved me against my consent," Mister Information whined. "Can I sue?"

"No," Simon said, chuckling as he exchanged an amused glance with Pierson. "I think they just wanted to save your life."

"These those guys you're looking for?" His look said he meant the bombers.

"We think so," Simon said, "but this is just a diversion so they could move some trucks. We think they still have a bigger target in mind."

Mister Information nodded. "Some tourist place?"

"Maybe. Isn't that what you heard?"

"Yeah," Mister Information grunted. "Some guy named Weasel might be involved. That's the word on the street. Plus a couple illegals who get around."

"Do you have a last name?"

"He just goes by Weasel."

"Besides that? Anyone else?"

Mister Information shook his head. "Supposedly they're asking about someplace north on the east 435 loop." That was something but better if he narrowed it down.

"North or South of I-70?" Simon asked.

"I don't know where. I also heard one of them lives over on Forest Avenue."

"Yeah, we found that place," Simon said. "Gregory Ronan." It still gave them a more specific area to focus on.

"Ahhh, right," the vagrant nodded. "You said they have trucks? I didn't see any around the garden center before it blew."

"They probably wired up a car or put a device on the building," Simon said. "Don't know. Waiting on forensics. Is that all you've got for me?"

"These guys scare people," the vagrant said, shaking his head. "No one wants to talk. Out of towners, scary dudes, real dangerous."

"Well, yeah, terrorists, Denny."

Mister Information reached out a wrinkled hand and wrapped it firmly around Simon's wrist. "You promised me, Simon."

"I'll keep my word," Simon said with a nod. "We lost two cops today, too. Almost lost my partner."

"That maniac? Too bad," the vagrant said and grinned.

"You'd like him if you got to know him."

"I doubt it," Mister Information shook his head. "The only other rumor is that they had an abandoned warehouse in the West Bottoms somewhere."

"They blew that up today, too," Simon said.

"Okay, well, that's all I got."

"Keep your ears open," Simon said.

"If I ever get out of here."

Simon looked at Pierson who said, "He'll be going home tomorrow if nothing comes up overnight."

"See, Denny?" Simon said, patting his friend's back. "You're still a tough old bastard. Tonight you get to sleep indoors on nice sheets for once is all." He raised an eyebrow. "With pretty girls to tend to your every need."

The vagrant grinned as he finally released Simon's arm. "I like that."

"I knew you would," Simon said.

"Plus two bottles of Absolut!" the vagrant added. "Including the one you already owe me."

Simon laughed. "Yeah, yeah. You take care of yourself, okay? I gotta get back to work."

Mister Information grumbled something as Simon

followed Pierson back outside. "Do you know where he lives?" she asked.

"Yeah, call me if he needs a ride," Simon said. "I'll either come myself or send a car."

"Okay," she said. 'Thanks for coming over right away."

"It's a tough day for us. I was hoping he'd have a little more."

"I was sorry to hear about the other officers."

He sighed. "Yeah, I lost two good friends. You don't let him give you a hard time. Just show him who's boss."

She laughed. "He's a pussycat compared to some of them."

"He's a meth head. Wait 'til he's jonesing for a fix."

"Sadly we're used to that." She shook her head.

Simon grunted and waved as she stopped beside the admissions desk and he headed for the door, his speed increasing with every step until he was almost running.

FROM HIS CAR, as he headed back to Central along 39th Street to Southwest Boulevard, Simon called Trevor Welch at the Computer Services Unit. "Got some new information, Sarge, focus on cameras in the East 405 loop first."

"That's still a lot of area to cover," Welch replied.

"Yeah but a CI told me that's where their target is," Simon answered.

"How do we know that's where they took the trucks?" Welch asked. "They have to have a staging area."

"We don't know anything but this is something at least," Simon said. "If I were going to move my base from the Bottoms, I'd certainly be moving closer to my target, not further away."

"We've still got a ton of footage to go through, and I'm short hands 'til we get the traffic system all up and restored," Welch said, "but I'll switch our focus. Only thing is, if they went somewhere else, it will be that much longer 'til we can track them down."

"We'll just have to take that chance," Simon said. "But maybe start at I-70 and work outward from that?"

"Okay, makes sense," Welch agreed.

As he turned onto Linwood, Simon hung up and dialed Livia Connelly at her lab. "How's my partner?"

"We just finished," she said. "Just need a few minutes to run some tests. Are you coming to pick him up?"

Simon shook his head automatically then realized she couldn't see him. "I have a meeting. I'll send a unit."

"Okay, we'll be waiting," Connelly said and hung up.

Simon then dialed Becker to fill her in about Lucas.

"I'll make the call," she promised, referring to sending a car.

"And get Lucas cleared to use his WiFi for traffic cams," Simon reminded her. "We need every advantage we can get."

"DC already okayed that," Becker said. "I just hadn't had time to tell you."

"Awesome," Simon replied. "Thanks."

The phone rang again as soon as he'd hung up. Caller ID said it was from his Fairwood house. Emma!

"Where are you?" she said, sounding worried. "I saw on the news some cops from Central died."

"Yeah, I'm okay, baby. Sorry," he said, deliberately sounding calmer than he felt. "I got the call in the middle of the night. It's been nonstop since."

"You were supposed to take me to school," she reminded him.

Simon sighed. "Well, I'll call in. You can take a sick day or go in mid-day. That's the soonest I can get there."

"Who was it, Dad?" she asked.

No point dodging. It'd be on the news soon enough. "Correia and Oglesby," Simon said, wincing both from grief and anticipating her reaction. He skipped telling her about Lucas, though, knowing that would really upset her.

"Oh my God!"

"Yeah. I gotta go, babe," he said as he turned into the lot at Central. "I love you."

"I love you, too, Daddy," she said and hung up.

Simon parked in an open space for personal vehicles and hurried inside.

THE LARGEST CONFERENCE room at Central Patrol was in the southwest front corner just off the lobby where the public came to pay tickets, file reports, etc. The group that showed up at nine a.m. for the meeting was one of the largest Simon had ever attended, certainly at Central. So big, they had to bring in extra chairs.

Becker sat at the head of the table beside Major David Sanford, who commanded Central Patrol. Next to the Major were Deputy Chiefs Melson and Cardno, FBI Agents Falk and Stein, who had worked with them on the Ashman case a year before, Special Agent in Charge Hank Garner, their division chief whom Simon had never met, Tom Bailey and Jerry Tucker from homicide, Sergeant El-Ashkar, Detectives Lance Garner and Dennis Ross from the Assault squad, Sarah Miller from Legal, the two BBs, Detectives John LaDue and Jack Benson from Bomb and Arson, then Simon, Maberry, Dolby, Detectives Tom Hansen and Harry Penhall from the Gun Squad, and Sergeant Anne Ross from Media. A few aides and others from Central also joined them in chairs around the outside walls, though they wouldn't be direct participants.

"Okay, let's get started," Becker said, a few minutes after the hour. "I think we all know each other, so I won't slow us down with introductions, but please introduce yourselves as you jump in."

She waited for everyone to nod or mumble their agreement before she continued. "I believe Major Sandford wants to start us off."

Beside her, the Major nodded in thanks and said, "Thank you. What happened today is a tough hit. We lost some good people. And it's obvious what we're dealing with is going to take all our resources. We have to find these people and shut them down. Whatever it takes." He looked around the room as he said it and every eye met his.

Each KCPD patrol section was headed by a Major who often rose from within the ranks, though not always at that division. Central's was David Sandford, whom Simon considered one of the better commanders he'd ever served under. Tough but fair, David Sandford was in his mid-50s with short brown hair graying at his temples and piercing brown eyes. He was medium height with broad build but had been with the KCPD his entire career since he graduated from the academy after college in his early twenties. He'd done everything from street cop to detective and had earned his rank the hard way.

"This meeting is to coordinate our efforts with teams representing all the major squads and groups who will be involved," Sandford continued. "You'll note the Bureau folks are here. They'll be taking over lead on the terrorism aspects of the investigation while we provide support them as well as conduct our own investigation of the officer involved incidents."

The KCPD folks reacted with a mix of half-groans and half-hearty welcomes to the FBI guys, who nodded stoically. Stein was short with a paunch while his partner Falk was tall, thin, and black with a tightly trimmed mustache. Both looked they couldn't even place in a foot race against most of the KCPD cops, but they had earned Simon's grudging respect with their cooperation in busting Ashman's underlings and associates who'd kidnapped and killed his old partner, Santorios.

"Garner, Bureau," Agent Garner said. "Guys, we're not looking to step on toes, but we do have resources and expertise with terrorism we can bring to bear here that you might find useful," he speechified.

Everything about this guy struck Simon as "trying too hard," from his expensive suit and shiny, polished dress shoes, to his slicked back hair and the smooth tone and false charm. He hated him immediately. This guy was going to be in charge?! Falk and Stein were street smart and cooperative—all about helping the locals as partners. This guy smacked of D.C. suit, the very stereotype of the smug government lackey cops had years of bad experiences with. Simon cringed at his every word and stuffed down a danish to hide his distaste.

"Certainly we all want to find and apprehend those responsible before they find a bigger, more damaging target than they already have," Garner continued then raised a clenched fist like some sort of motivational speaker. "Just remember, we're on your side."

Polite nods came from around the table. Still, it was always uncomfortable when the Feds came in and took over an ongoing investigation, but when that investigation involved the death of friends and fellow cops, they resented it, domestic terrorism or not. Regardless, domestic terrorism, especially on the scale they were clearly dealing with, would draw Federal concern. This was their bailiwick and if they could help prevent tragedy and put away those responsible for murdering cops, they'd be welcome, however grudgingly.

"FBI, Stein," Stein said. "Right now, our teams are reviewing the evidence, including any and all available surveillance, with your own people to get up to speed and try and pinpoint a place to start our search. We know you lost some of your own here, and we know how that feels, so believe me, we will be including you as much as possible. I'm certain we will all need to work together to bring these people down."

"John Simon, Central. Actually, I had a CI tell me this morning that the rumors have these guys main target somewhere off the Eastern loop of 435," Simon said. "Not that that narrows it down a lot, but it's certainly a place to start."

"Who told you this?" Garner asked.

"My guy from the rail yard," Simon says. "He was injured when the garden center blew up. I visited him at the Med Center on my way here. I already called Welch."

"Good," Melson jumped in. "That at least will give us a starting point to maybe finding something quicker. Deputy Chief Greg Melson."

"I've also started going through a box of paperwork these guys left behind when they abandoned their warehouse in the Bottoms," Maberry said. "A lot of it's black from soot or burned but maybe something will turn up."

"Okay, good to hear there's some progress," Sandford said, smiling his praise at them. "Whatever you uncover, no matter how insignificant it may seem, share it with the team. You never know where it might lead." For an experienced team like this, he didn't need to say it, but Simon figured with the distraction of friends' deaths, it couldn't hurt.

"Have all the witnesses been interviewed or scheduled?" Falk asked.

"Most were interviewed on the spot at the bar," Becker said. "We're still trying to find out if there are any more witnesses for the others."

"Art Maberry, Central. We'll have a few people in here looking at books later today," Maberry said, his voice scratchy despite the forced calm he was clearly trying to project. "See if we can identify any locals working with them."

"Do we know that there are locals?" Garner asked.

"My CI says there are," Simon said.

"And we found at least one already," Dolby added, her voice faltering until she cleared her throat, "Gregory Ronan. I'm Anna Dolby, Central."

"Have we questioned him?" Cardno asked.

"We tried but he escaped and fired shots at us," Maberry said.

"We haven't located him since," Simon said, "but all of this was within the past forty-eight hours, pretty much."

"We do have a modus operandi on the break-ins we believe they conducted," Dolby added.

"They were doing break-ins?" Stein asked.

"Benson, Bomb and Arson. We believe they were gathering materials for bombs," Detective Benson said.

"That was our first encounter with them," Simon added. "They were using laser cutters."

"Residences or businesses or both?" Falk asked.

"Both," Dolby and Simon said together and there were a few laughs, which helped lighten the mood around the table, as people noticeably relaxed.

"We also know they used box trucks and we got partial plates on a few via traffic cams," Becker added.

Garner nodded. "We saw that in the files. Good stuff. You have a lot of traffic cam footage still under review, right?"

"Yes," Becker said.

"And is that from a period covering several weeks or just the past few days?" Stein asked.

"We have some of both," Simon says, "but we've asked

our people to concentrate on stuff from the past forty-eight in specific instances where we believe there was significant movement."

"Okay," Garner nodded. "Good work."

"As soon as we find some possible locations to investigate, we'll be sending out teams to check them," Falk added.

"Judging from ballistics, all our people should wear vests minimum, body armor if they have it, when knowingly going after these people," Hansen said. "They're using heavy duty weaponry." Medium height with light blonde hair that hung down past his ears, he and the chubbier, brown-haired Penhall were like the Mutt and Jeff of Gun Squad. "I'm Hansen, this is Penhall, Gun Squad," he added, motioning to his partner next to him.

"Not to mention bombs," Detective LaDue added to a few chuckles.

"We'll use what we have, for sure," Becker said.

"If needed, we may be able to loan some as needed, at least to a few key people," Stein said.

"Wow, the Feds giving stuff to us little guys, unheard of," Bailey threw in.

"Can we write rental fees off on our taxes?" His partner, Tucker joked.

Fifteen year veterans currently assigned to homicide at headquarters downtown, Tom Bailey and Jerry Tucker had been around as long as Simon. They'd also led the investigation into Santorios' murder. Tucker was early 50s and frequently mistaken for Santa Claus by local kids—a white bearded, wise, kind grandpa type. Bailey was muscular, taller, thinner, and dark haired with a warm smile and hearty laugh. It hadn't been easy being one of the first out gays in the department, but you sure wouldn't know it from his attitude.

"No charge," Stein joked back and everyone chuckled.

"What's the catch?" Simon quipped and everyone broke up.

It felt good to laugh, despite the grimness of the past few hours. No one had forgotten their losses, but they needed cheer and focus to find the energy to keep going and catch the bastards.

"Could someone run down the scenes for us?" Garner asked.

"Sure," Harry Penhall said.

For the next half hour, they did just that, describing each of the three explosion scenes in detail, various people pitching in about the aspects they were most knowledgeable of. The two Feds took extensive notes, asking questions as needed. When they'd finished, everyone leaned back in their chairs.

"Tell us what you need," Cardno said. "We'll offer whatever we can."

"We'll do coordination meetings after this general briefing," Garner said and the higher ranks all nodded. "Okay, we'll dole out more assignments as we see the opportunity," Garner continued. "We just wanted to get everyone face to face so we know each other."

He motioned to Falk and Stein. "Agents Falk and Stein are running point on the day to day, but I'll be overseeing and available as needed." He looked around the table before continuing, "That's it for now. We'll meet again once we're fully up to speed. Please continue working whatever evidence and witnesses you have and keep us informed."

As chairs scooted back and the attendees scattered, Simon joined Maberry and Dolby as they headed back for the Property office.

LUCAS HAD NEVER ridden in the back of a patrol car before, only the front. It was an interesting experience. At one point, the officers stopped at a Quick Trip for beverages and passers-by were staring at Lucas in the back, but when he opened the door and got out to greet them, they all ran away, scared. Humans could be so puzzling sometimes.

It took twenty minutes in mid-day traffic to arrive back at the station, and as they pulled into the lot at Central, Lucas spotted a familiar face that immediately set his servos spinning. He leaned forward, suddenly anxious and tense. It was the suspect from the garden place he'd visited with Simon, Maberry, and Correia. Gregory Ronan was the name he remembered. He was driving a tan cargo van onto the lot and toward the drive that passed beside the building just outside the Property detective's office.

"Stop!" he said to the uniform driving.

"What? You see something?" the other uniform asked.

"Maybe. In that van." Lucas pointed toward the drive.

"A friend?" the uniform driving asked.

"Suspect," Lucas replied.

"What's he doing here?" the driver asked.

"Yeah, that's not at all suspicious," his partner said as they accelerated again and headed toward the van. He keyed the radio mic hanging from his shoulder, "147, suspicious activity in the parking lot at Central, 1200 E. Linwood, tan van. Requesting backup."

"147, acknowledged, notifying sergeant," the dispatcher replied.

The driver stopped the patrol car beside the curb just at the end of the drive and they climbed out, the two uniforms drawing their weapons, just as Gregory Ronan climbed out of the van.

"You there, stop," the uniform driver called.

Ronan turned and saw them, then spun and climbed back in the van. They hurried toward it on the sidewalk as the engine started and tires squealed as it peeled away.

The two uniforms and Lucas had just started running when Lucas heard shouts and noticed others appearing from the building and running toward it.

Then, just as the van reached the end of the drive, it exploded in a fireball, knocking several cops who were close off their feet.

Everyone was shouting or calling out and Lucas kept running but what little was left of the van had either fallen around him as debris or collapsed onto the cracked cement drive. Soon people were shouting questions at him as he stopped and turned back to check on his companions.

CHAPTER 15

PROPERTY DETECTIVES rarely listened to the police radio in the squad room, but after recent events, they were, so Simon heard the call for assistance in Central's parking lot and headed there along with Maberry, Dolby, Becker, and several uniforms.

As soon as they left the building, Simon saw the van accelerating up the drive then heard men yelling. He had barely an instant during which the hair stood up on his nape and arms and he started sprinting. Then it blew sky high, taking out part of the curb and leaving a crater in the concrete. Several officers were knocked off their feet. Chaos ensued as tires squealed and cars crashed, horns blaring. A strong smell of ammonia mixed with burning oil, gas, and plastic filled the air.

Moments after, Becker appeared with Deputy Chiefs Cardno and Melson, along with the two FBI agents, the BBs, and several others. Simon recognized Sergeants El-Ashkar and Anthony Raymond, who had been his union rep over a shooting the year before.

"Someone call for ambulances!" Raymond shouted as Simon raced toward Lucas, who rolled over, looking a bit dazed.

"Are you okay?" Simon asked, feeling a bit dizzy himself.

"It just blew," Lucas said, then locked eyes with his partner. "Gregory Ronan was driving." Simon extended his hand and Lucas grasped it, pulling himself to his feet.

"Son of a bitch," Simon replied as Becker hurried over. Behind her he saw several uniforms hurrying toward cars that had crashed in front of the station when the van exploded.

"You two okay?" she asked shrilly.

"They just tried to bomb the fucking station," Simon said. "I am the furthest thing from okay."

"I know," Becker agreed, shocked, then wiped at her forehead absently with the back of an arm. "And what's worse, they almost succeeded." She glanced toward the wall enclosing their squad room. "If we'd all been in there—"

Simon nodded as they exchanged a meaningful look.

"What happened?" Becker asked.

"I was arriving back in unit 147 with Officers Pullman and Hill when I recognized the suspect who ran from us earlier at the garden center," Lucas explained.

"The owner's brother?" Becker asked.

"Yes," Lucas said and nodded. "As soon as we called out, he saw me and got back in the van, trying to drive away. When it got to the end of the drive, it exploded."

Simon and Becker exchanged a look.

"Remote detonator," they both said.

"And if it had been beside the station, we'd be missing half our offices," Becker said, realizing. "Sergeant El-Ashkar, we need people for an immediate search!" she called, turning and motioning to the two Sergeants standing nearby.

"Now I'm really pissed," Simon said, grinding his teeth.

"Welcome to the program," Maberry snapped.

"We've got an ATF team en route," FBI Agent Falk shouted from nearby as he and Stein inspected the hole in the concrete and what was left of the van.

"Our own crime scene people will be here in five," Deputy Chief Cardno echoed.

Sergeant El-Ashkar motioned to Raymond and several uniforms. "You get the lane blocked for two blocks each direction," she ordered. "And the parking lots, too. We don't need extra bodies until we get things well under control."

"We gotta find these motherfuckers!" Simon said.

"You and Maberry get back inside and get to work," Becker ordered as she glanced tensely around. "I'll take Lucas' statement and coordinate the other witnesses."

"Want me to give my statement first?" Simon asked.

"We'll come to you when we need you," Becker said.

Simon reached out to firmly squeeze Lucas' shoulder as their eyes met again, then turned and hurried to get Maberry and return inside.

"You ready for a full morning of questions?" Becker asked as he left.

"Of course," Lucas said, and Simon saw him nod as he and Maberry headed back inside.

IT HAD ALWAYS struck Simon as odd how police officers

could go from high stress, mile a minute drama to the most minute, boring tasks in the same day, but that's the kind of afternoon it turned into.

The minute he got inside, as Maberry started working phones for the case, Simon took a deep breath and called Emma at the Fairway police station. She'd be hearing about the explosion on the news or from cops soon enough and he hadn't had time to get back with her as promised and wanted to reassure her.

"Hey, sweetheart," he said as soon as she answered and leaned back in his chair, an attempt at forcing himself to relax a bit, or at least project that on the phone.

He could hear her exhaling. "Are you almost here?"

"There's been a change of plans."

"But you said I could go to school later if I wanted."

Shit! He'd forgotten to call the school. "I just can't get away," Simon said.

"Dad, I'm bored. When can you come get me?"

"It may be late," Simon said. "We've had a lot going on. Some really bad people."

"The school called my cell twice," she said. "You were supposed to call them."

Simon sighed. "I got busy," he said, not making excuses. "I'll call right now. Do you want me to order you a pizza or something?"

"Yeah," she said. "Be careful."

"I am, honey," he promised, hating the worry he heard in her voice.

After they hung up, he did both. Then he joined Maberry

and Dolby on phones. All of them could barely sit still, but until they got forensics back, there was little to do but try and break leads. It was always the worst position to be in on a case, but when friends' lives had been taken, it was literally painful. For the next two hours, they worked every angle—contacted every CI they had, every possible source, asking them what they knew and then urging them to ask around and keep their eyes peeled.

From time to time, they each got pulled and taken off to interview rooms to give their statements about the exploding van, but those lasted barely half an hour before they came back and went back to the phones.

Shortly after 2 p.m., Paul Engborg called from the crime lab. "We have your paperwork ready. I'll have it over there first thing in the morning. There were a couple partial addresses, but not much else."

"We might come pick it up," Simon replied, as he sat forward in his chair. "But what else you got?"

"We did find some partial prints, which we sent over to the FBI lab," Engborg said. "We got no results but they're connected to more databases."

"How soon will they know?"

"They put it on priority thanks to an Agent Stein, I'm told, so they said sometime tomorrow latest."

"Okay, thanks, Paul," Simon said.

"Let me know soon if you're coming over," Engborg added.

"Will do." Simon hung up and spun to face Dolby and Maberry who were off the phone and watching with piqued interest. He stood. "I'll run over and pick up the paperwork from the warehouse. They said they got partial addresses, not much else, but we can at least look through. Fingerprints will be back from the FBI tomorrow."

"Change of plans," Becker said from behind him and they all turned to see her striding toward them from her office. "Go home and get some rest," she continued. "We've all been up all night and there'll be plenty to do tomorrow. We're not going to get many breaks the next few days, and I need you at the top of your game."

"We're not tired," Maberry insisted, tensing again. "We need to work this."

As Maberry stood, Simon caught a whiff of him and crinkled his nose, realizing he and Dolby probably smelled just as bad.

"You're going to work it," she replied, shaking her head, "but you all look like hell, and I'm sure I'm not much better. Get some sleep and come back tomorrow morning ready for overtime."

"Boss—" Dolby protested but Becker cut her off.

"That's an order."

Maberry and Dolby sighed, shoulders sinking as they looked at the floor.

"Don't worry, we won't stop 'til we get 'em," Simon said. "Where's Lucas?"

"He had a hearing with the BBs and then he'll be going home, too," Becker said. "Go on. Get outta here."

After a few more mumbled protests, they all made their way out the door and headed for the parking lot. Simon's stomach rumbled and he hoped he'd get home to find a little pizza left.

LUCAS ONCE AGAIN found himself across the table in an interrogation room from Bahm and Beebe with Sergeant Anthony Raymond this time serving as his union rep. A career cop of twenty years now finishing out his career on desk duty, Raymond had a sterling reputation in the department. He was also one of the first "out" gays in KCPD.

"Wanna tell us why you were out fighting crime?" Beebe demanded immediately, everything about her confrontational.

"I wasn't," Lucas replied, puzzled by her animosity. "I was on a walk."

"So you just happened to be there?" she snarled. "A guy we'd just spoken with the same morning and put on a desk while we investigated a shooting?" She shot her partner, Bahm, a look of total disbelief.

"It is entirely possible and reasonable," Raymond jumped in.

"Why don't you tell us in your own words what happened?" Bahm said, much friendlier. Her eyes met Lucas' with a neutral warmth as Beebe shifted irritably beside her.

"I was on a walk," Lucas said. "My residence is just up the hill from there."

"You live in the River Market area, correct?" Bahm said.

"Yes, I have an apartment."

"Continue," Beebe snapped.

"I saw a car swerving to a stop outside the convenience store and two men running inside with guns, so I went to investigate," Lucas said.

"Were you armed?" Beebe demanded.

"You confiscated my gun," Lucas said.

"Is that a no?"

"I was unarmed," Lucas clarified.

"You went to investigate armed men without a weapon?" Bahm said.

"Yes."

"Why didn't you call it in?" Bahm asked.

"I considered it," Lucas said, "but once I arrived things moved too quickly."

"Too quickly for you to use your internal capabilities to call 911?" Beebe scoffed.

"I was focused on the customers and employees who were in danger," Lucas said.

"You should have called for help," Beebe said, shaking her head.

"Perhaps. I'm sorry." But Beebe looked totally unmoved by his apology.

"What happened next?" Bahm prompted.

"I identified myself as a police officer, hoping to diffuse the situation," Lucas said. "The two men inside threatened me and their hostages."

"And yet you still didn't call it in," Beebe said with dismay.

Lucas shook his head and focused on Bahm. "I observed a

fire alarm near me and decided to set it off as a distraction and attempt to disarm the nearest man."

"At risk of one or more hostages?" Beebe said. "In total violation of department policy—"

"I believed my enhanced reflexes would enable me to be successful," Lucas said.

"The same reflexes that weren't fast enough to call in for assistance?" Beebe snapped.

"This hostility is unproductive," Raymond jumped in. "Can we either adjourn and pick this up when Officer Beebe has better control of her emotions or—"

"I'm fine!" Beebe snapped.

Lucas raised a palm to Sergeant Raymond. "I'm okay, Sergeant. I was forewarned not to expect Officer Beebe to be friendly."

Beebe looked outraged. "What's that supposed to mean?! I have a job to do, an important one!"

Bahm put a hand on her partner's arm. "Please Lena."

Beebe leaned back in her chair and crossed her arms over her chest, taking a deep breath.

"Please finish, Officer George," Bahm said.

"I successfully activated the fire alarm, distracting the suspects, and then was able to disarm one and knock him unconscious," Lucas said.

"At which point the other suspect dropped his weapon?" Bahm asked.

"Yes," Lucas agreed.

"Other officers arrived on scene at that point as the customers and employees fled outside, is that correct?" Bahm asked.

"Yes," Lucas agreed.

"And in the process, the other robber managed to put customers between himself and you and manage an escape in their vehicle?" Bahm continued.

"Yes, I am afraid so," Lucas said.

"So the customers were again put in danger by your actions," Beebe said, pointing an accusing finger at him.

"The suspect was unarmed," Lucas reminded her.

"Yet he assaulted one of the customers," Beebe countered.

"I believe he struck the man, yes," Lucas said.

"Causing no serious injury," Raymond interjected.

"And no shots were fired?" Bahm asked.

"No, ma'am," Lucas said with a nod.

"Are you convinced, Officer George, that your decisions in handling this situation were in accordance with your training?" Bahm asked.

Lucas thought a moment. "I believe I responded to the best of my ability to create the best possible outcome."

Beebe scoffed.

"Thank you, Officer George," Bahm said. "We'll notify you if we have any further questions." She and Beebe stood and headed for the door as Lucas looked at Raymond.

"I am free to go?"

"Yes, for now," Sergeant Raymond said. "You did very well. Don't worry about Officer Beebe. But next time, you should try to place a call for assistance as soon as possible, okay?"

"I will remember," Lucas replied and nodded as he stood and headed for the door with Raymond following.

SIMON AWOKE TO a ringing phone and rolled over, glancing at the white numbers on the digital clock atop the nightstand: 12:34 a.m. He'd gotten home around 3:30 and spent the afternoon hanging with Emma, taken her to a movie, and then streamed a few episodes of shows they both liked. He'd gone to bed early by his standards at just after 9 and fallen immediately into a restless sleep. He hadn't realized how truly tired he really was, but waking up after only three-point-five hours' troubled sleep, he sure felt it now.

"Simon," he said automatically as he answered the phone, then licked his lips a bit trying to erase the sour taste in his mouth.

"Detective, this is Officer Eugene Johnson of the Independence P.D.," a man said.

"How can I help you, Officer?" he mumbled, reaching over to flip on a lamp as he scrunched back against the pillow, trying to pull himself up into a sitting position.

"Do you know a Lara Simon, Detective?"

"Yeah, she's my ex-wife," Simon said.

"Sir, we arrested her and took her to the E.R. here at Centerpoint," Johnson continued. Centerpoint Medical Center was a hospital on the east side of Independence, Missouri.

Simon sat up fully now, wide awake, his shoulders curling forward as he stiffened. "What happened?"

"We found her wandering incoherently, dodging cars on I-70, Detective," Johnson explained. "The call came in about ten. She was apparently struck by a semi's mirror on her shoulder but somehow stayed on her feet. We thought it was a suicide."

Simon nodded, flinching as he swallowed then said softly, "Shit. She's okay though?"

"They're processing her for a psychiatric hold, but there's no local next of kin listed besides a minor," Johnson said.

"Yeah, our daughter, she's with me."

"Okay. Does your ex have any history of mental illness?"

"Yeah. She's bipolar. Been on meds for about six years now supposedly."

"Well, these people sometimes get too feeling like they don't need the meds—"

Simon cut him off. "Yeah, I'll be over as quick as I can. I'm in Fairway."

"I hate to wake you up like this after the day you guys have had, but I figured you'd want to know," Johnson said.

"Absolutely. Thank you." Simon hung up and jumped out of bed, scrambling for the pants he'd thrown across a chair. He debated whether to wake Emma then decided she didn't need to see her mother like this, at least not 'til he'd assessed the situation, and let her sleep. Slipping into the pants, he gave his underarms a quick sniff and grabbed a fresh shirt off a hanger in the closet then headed for the bathroom to freshen up a bit.

Ten minutes later, he was in the Charger and on his way.

AS SIMON RUSHED inside Centerpoint's Emergency Services wing, the smell of the usual chemicals mixed with body odors filled his nose and the beeping of machines and slinking of curtains filled his ears. Doctors, nurses, orderlies and others bustled around him as he wended his way through the crowded halls looking for the intake desk. It was surprisingly busy for this late at night.

"May I help you?" a pretty but tired nurse in her late thirties said, looking up at him as he approached the desk.

He badged her. "Detective John Simon, KCPD. Someone called about my wi— ex, Lara."

She nodded and glanced down at the computer screen. "Room six, down the hall to the right."

"Thanks," he said and hurried down the wide hall.

A uniformed officer was outside chatting with a white coated doctor and a nurse as he approached. Mid-thirties, he had short brown-hair, almost military cut, with sharp blue eyes, and a crisp, pressed uniform despite the late hour. The nameplate over the pocket read: 'Johnson.'

"Detective Simon?" the cop asked as he drew nearer.

Simon nodded and extended his hand. "John." They each shook it in turn.

"Your wife is pretty wired right now," the doctor said, his name badge reading 'B. Chamber.'

Over his shoulder through the large glass window Simon saw Lara bouncing randomly around the room, her limbs and movements jerky as if she couldn't control them, which she couldn't. Immediately, his heart raced and he felt a rising sense of panic he hadn't felt in years, taking a deep breath as he struggled for control. "Yeah, manic. I've seen it before," he somehow managed. "What happened? Did her meds fail? She's supposed to be out of town on business."

"We're not sure," the nurse jumped in. Her name tag read 'C. Seder.' "She may have stopped taking them."

"Fuck," Simon said, shaking his head. "Just what we need. That still doesn't explain why this is happening here and not Memphis where she's supposed to be."

They all shook their heads.

"No idea," Johnson said. "But she's sure had a lotta nice things to say about you."

"Oh yeah, let me guess: I'm the devil who ruined her life, worst thing that ever happened to her." She'd said it so often during episodes, he could hear her voice in his head.

They all smiled sadly.

"Pretty much," Johnson replied.

"Can I see her?" Simon asked.

"If you want," the doctor said. "It might not be pleasant."

"Yeah, been here before," Simon said.

They stepped to one side and he moved forward and grasped the door knob, pulling open the heavy, secure door and slipping side. As soon as she saw him, Lara's eyes narrowed with anger. Simon braced himself as best he could.

"You! You devil!" she said, spitting the words out like projectiles. "He's trying to kill me!" she shouted and pounded on the window. "Hey! He's trying to kill me!"

"I am not, Lara," he said slow and deliberate despite how he felt. "Just calm down and talk to me."

She shook her head with jagged movements, her eyes glassy and distant—the same eyes he'd lovingly gazed into for twenty years since high school only hazy and distant, filled with rage. "Who called you?" She glared and turned to the window, shaking her fist. "I didn't say I wanted him. He's not my husband. We're divorced."

"They called me because who else would they call?" Simon said casually, resisting the urge to sound accusatory. "What are you doing here? I thought you were in Memphis."

"S'none of your business!" she snapped, pointing an accusatory finger at his chest, her speech slightly slurred. "You can go now. I don't need you."

Simon reached a hand out to touch her but she sprung back and then whirled again and started pounding her fists again this chest. "Satan! You devil!"

Simon kept his voice calm and let her pound. She wasn't that strong. It didn't hurt. But then she probably wasn't really trying. "Did you stop taking your meds? What happened—you were doing so well?"

"Fuck you. I don't need them. I don't need you either." She quit pounding and moved away again, huddling in a corner as if to protect herself.

Simon sighed. "Okay, well, they're going to keep you for a while, so when you calm down, if you want to talk, ask for me, okay?"

She chortled mockingly as he backed away and turned back toward the door, the nurse stepping forward outside to let him out.

"That was fun," he said as he rejoined them in the hall,

leaning against the wall a moment to steady himself.

"How long has she been like this?" the nurse asked.

"She was first diagnosed about ten years ago," he said. "We were still together. It destroyed our marriage, when I put her in the hospital five times in two years against her will. But she's stabilized since and stayed on her meds. I can't imagine what happened to make her stop taking them." He sighed.

"Well, we're going to send her to Research tomorrow morning," the doctor said. "They have open beds. But we'll keep her here overnight, try and get her calmer at least."

Simon nodded. "Thank you." He motioned to Johnson. "He has my numbers. Call the cell if you need me. I don't want my daughter picking up. I'll fill her in when we know more."

"Of course," the doctor replied.

Lara was pounding on the glass again, her lips moving as she raged and yelled unheard behind the sound proof glass.

"Have fun," Simon said and headed back the way he'd come in. This was just what he needed in the middle of a potential terrorist attack on the city. He'd call Lara's sister in the morning and see if anyone wanted to come out and be available to make decisions instead of him. For now, he was exhausted and felt his bed calling again.

CHAPTER 16

SIMON DROPPED EMMA off at school early the next day and was at his desk by 8:30 am. As promised, the crime lab delivered the paperwork and evidence reports by nine and the detectives went to work, Maberry, Dolby, and Simon sorting and separating papers while Lucas read them the reports. There were a couple of hits from fingerprints and facial recognition they hadn't heard before—locals named Edson Núñez and Charles Wheeler, who apparently went by the nickname "Weasel." And hits from the Feds on a Brazilian with mercenary ties names Josue Sousa. Paperwork reportedly showed partial addresses on N.E. Great Midwest Drive and Underground Road up by Worlds of Fun. At least it was new leads to track down.

The FBI lab had preliminarily identified elements they believed pointed to sophisticated electronic remote triggers and timers on the explosives as well as elements of fertilizer and C-4 amongst the fuel. But details and confirmation would have to wait a few days until the full reports once all tests had been completed.

Simon ran the names through the KCPD database IAFIS and the FBI as well, to see if any known associates and last known addresses popped up along with criminal records, and got several hits. Once they'd dug in deep enough, they all gathered in Becker's office, who'd also read the reports.

"These assholes have been busy fuckers," Simon said.

"Time to cool them down," Maberry growled, not looking any more rested than he had the day before.

"Are you okay to go in the field?" Becker asked, concerned. "You don't look like you slept a wink. I need you on your game if I send you out."

"I slept on and off, but I'm okay," Maberry insisted. "I need to do this."

She watched him a moment then relented, her eyes reluctant, and said, "You and Dolby go check out this Edson Núñez. Lucas and Simon can work Weasel, now that we have more information."

"What about those addresses up by Worlds of Fun?" Dolby asked.

"Feds want us to wait on traffic cam data," Becker said. "Since they're partial addresses, we want more information first. Can't risk scaring anyone off by poking around blindly."

"We see 'em, we shoot 'em," Maberry growled.

"Yeah, provided we see them first," Dolby replied. Everyone understood their feelings, but they were good cops, so Becker let it pass with a grunt.

"What about Sousa?" Dolby asked.

"The Feds are putting someone on him, as he'll be more difficult," Becker said. "Fewer local connections, but if anything turns up they may have us tag team as needed."

Everyone offered nods or grunts of assent except Lucas, who said, "Sounds good, boss" and smiled. The others traded amused looks.

"Just call me Sergeant, Detective," Becker said.

"He's a detective now?" Dolby asked.

Lucas grinned.

"Effectively for this case, yes," Becker said. "We have to wait for the Shooting Team and his T.O. to sign off before we can make anything official."

Simon reached over and squeezed Lucas' shoulder.

"I want you reporting in on the hour," Becker added now, meeting each of their eyes in turn. "By the book all the way. No funny business. We can't risk it."

"We're on it," Maberry said.

Becker looked at Lucas. "You're not carrying a weapon, correct?"

"I am unarmed," Lucas said.

Becker looked at Simon. "Get him a temporary department issue piece for this assignment."

"What about the shooting team—" Lucas said.

She raised a hand palm out to cut him off. "Fuck that. I'm not having any of my people going in unarmed against these terrorists. I cleared it with Melson, just try not to shoot anyone, okay? Especially not when civilians are in the line of fire." It was the first time she'd let her own anger seep through and Simon actually was glad to hear it. He knew she cared about her people, but sometimes the self-control he always admired in her became a barrier between them, too.

Lucas nodded as the others hid their amusement. "Yes, Sergeant," he said.

"But I want the paperwork on my desk by end of day,"

she added.

"Yes, sergeant," Simon and Lucas said together.

"One more thing," Becker said. "The Chief's ordered no non-official vehicles allowed within one hundred feet of the stations without an appointment until further notice, in case they try again."

"Well, that's going to piss people off," Dolby noted.

"Yes, yes it will," Becker agreed, "but we aren't taking any chances, okay? Everyone wears vests until further notice, and take whatever body armor you own."

"What about weapons?" Simon asked.

"If it's approved, you take it," Becker said. "We don't know what we might run into and I want you prepared. Just make sure you put it on reports at the end of the day."

"Yes, Sergeant," they all said and stood.

"Okay, that's it." Becker waved dismissively. "Hit the streets."

"And let's be careful out there," Lucas said in his best Sergeant Estherhaus imitation. No one laughed this time. Instead, they exchanged looks and nodded, then hurried out.

UNSURPRISINGLY, CHARLES "WEASEL" Wheeler was no stranger to law enforcement. He'd been arrested numerous times and even done time twice in prison— three years and five years—and a few month-long stints in jails. As part of their reports and interviews, arresting officers had noted several past addresses and his places of work. Simon had Lucas make a mental map of the locations so they could start with the furthest out and work their way back toward the station. That took them down to Donnolly Tire on East 83rd Street.

The manager on duty there looked just a few years older than Emma and had little to say. He hadn't known any "Weasel" but one of the employees who overheard commented "that loser was fired ages ago." So next they headed over to apartments off Pershing Road, another dead end.

"This is like a sightseeing tour of the ass end of the city," Simon muttered as they climbed back in the Explorer.

"Well, we've seen worse," Lucas commented, then added, "I actually pity those poor bastards we're going up against. By God, I do. We're not just going to shoot the bastards, we're going to cut out their living guts and use them to grease the treads of our tanks."

Simon recognized the quote from Patton, one of his all-time favorite films. "Yeah, well, first we have to find the damn tanks. What's next?"

"McGee's Muffler up on East 67th," Lucas said. "I have come here to chew bubble gum and kick ass, and I'm all out of bubble gum," he added in a gruff voice.

"What the hell is that from?" Simon asked as he pulled out of the lot and headed north on Raytown Road.

"One of Emma's horror films, They something," Lucas said.

"You're telling me with that computer inside your head, you can't remember?"

"She said it so fast, and I was distracted," Lucas said. "It was on TV and it had already started."

"Google it," Simon said.

Lucas grew eerily silent and Simon looked over to see what was the matter. He was staring off into space, then suddenly smiled, and said, "*They Live.*"

"Who lives?"

"That's the movie. I googled it," Lucas said.

Simon shuddered. "Don't do that freaky shit again, okay?"

"But you told me—"

"Not if you're gonna just go all silent like that," Simon said as he stopped at a light.

"You know, considering how much technology is a part of modern policing, your aversion to it seems counterproductive," Lucas said.

"Good? Bad? I'm the guy with the gun," Simon said, quoting Army of Darkness. "When it comes down to it, what else do I really need?"

"As you said, you have to find the damn tanks first, right?" Lucas replied.

"Do me a favor," Simon snapped. "Quote movies all you want. Just never quote me to me."

"Why? I find you very quotable," Lucas said.

"Never argue with a man with a gun," Simon snapped.

Lucas nodded and went back to looking out the window.

They turned right on East 67th and drove half a block to McGee's. As they stepped inside, a manager greeted them from behind the counter. His name tag read "Earl." "Welcome to McGee's, what can I do for you gentlemen today?"

Simon badged him. "We're looking for information on a former employee who goes by the name Weasel. Charles Wheeler." Sounds of grinding machines, hydraulics, and clanking tools drifted through the wall from the garage area next door. Through a window, Simon could see a dozen mechanics hard at work. The inside smelled surprisingly oil and fluid free at the moment, the floor shiny as if it had just been mopped, though the chairs and tables in the waiting area were aged and showed signs of heavy use.

The manager frowned. "That idiot hasn't worked here in six years at least. I'd have to go back into my books to tell you for sure."

"No need just yet," Simon said. "What can you tell us about him?"

"A lazy smartass," Earl said. "The kinda guy who does the minimum amount of work but gives the maximum lip."

"He was affectionate?" Lucas asked.

Earl scowled as Simon shook his head. "Lip means he talked back a lot."

"Oh, gave shit," Lucas said.

"Exactly," Earl agreed.

"Was he full time?" Simon asked.

"Yeah, most of my guys are, but he worked the afternoon and evening shift usually," Earl said.

"Why'd you finally fire him?"

"Incompetence and not doing the work," Earl said. "We give everyone a shot but after a certain point, if they don't keep up, they're gone. We're too busy, with too much to do, that we can't waste time on guys who just won't do the job."

"Sounds fair to me," Lucas said.

Earl nodded.

"Is anyone around who was close to him?" Simon asked.

"Oh, we had a lot of turnover in that time frame," Earl said. "Most of the people he hung with were the same type of losers he was and are long gone."

Earl gave them permission to go out in the garage and ask a few of his guys. One or two echoed his sentiments that Weasel had been a loser and lazy, but the others seemed to have never heard of him, so instead they went back inside and asked Earl if he knew Weasel's address. Earl named the same place listed on the crime reports—an apartment complex off Rolston Avenue, so they thanked him and headed out.

Rolston Meadows consisted of three brick four-story buildings side-by-side with black iron fire escapes at each end and a separate lot behind each. Weasel's address was in the third building on the second floor, apartment 203. They went inside and climbed the stairs, hands resting near their weapons, spotting the door just across from the stairs. Oddly it was open a crack.

Simon motioned for Lucas to be quiet and drew his weapon, sliding up to the right of the door, while Simon did the same on the left. The door opened inward from the left, so Simon pantomimed for Lucas to open the door on his signal and Simon would go in first. Lucas nodded that he understood.

Using the fingers on his right hand, Simon counted down 3...2...1...

Lucas sprung forward and swung the door inward as Simon rushed inside, gun extended in front of him. Lucas followed, his own gun extended.

The smell of dust and week old trash filled Simon's nose

as he entered. A pretty brunette in her late twenties sitting alone on a folding chair beside a card table gasped at the sight of them, tears streaming down her face.

Simon quickly badged her. "Detectives, KCPD. Are you alone?"

She nodded.

"We're looking for a Charles Wheeler," Simon continued.

She sniffled and shook her head. "He's not here. I don't know where he is." She said it with such an emotion-choked voice, her body trembling, hair disheveled that Simon instantly knew she was telling the truth. And she wanted to know where he was as much as they did.

Simon holstered his Glock 37 and motioned for Lucas to do the same with his substitute department issue 22.

"Are you okay?" Lucas asked.

She sniffled again and nodded. "I guess."

"I'm Lucas, this is John," he said.

"Hi, I'm Lucy," she said. "Is he in trouble again?"

"Maybe," Simon said. "We're looking for him to find out."

"That asshole," she said, more firmly this time. "He told me he had a special job and had to go away for a while. Real sudden. Out of state, he said. Then my friend's brother saw him over here. He lives in the next building. So naturally, I came to find out what was going on, but he's not here."

Simon looked around. The card table and four folding chairs were the only furniture in the room. He glanced over her shoulder and saw the kitchen just had a microwave and the stock fridge and through a door to her right was a bedroom with two bedrolls on the floor. "Not real settled in, are they?" he said.

"Yeah, I know," she said. "His stuff's at our place mostly. It's really odd."

"Has he ever done this before?" Lucas asked.

"Not really," Lucy said. "My dad hates him. Says he's a loser. And he has struggled with jobs. But he's been trying harder since we found out I'm pregnant. Was really trying to turn it around. He promised me. He said this was a huge score that would take care of us for a long time. But he lied to me about it, so now I'm wondering."

"Of course," Simon said. "Not cool."

"Exactly," she agreed.

"How long has it been since you've seen him?" Lucas asked.

Lucas was cool and calm. Simon was impressed with how well he was doing at picking just the right tone and questions to put her at ease. Of course, her state of mind helped, too. Still, Lucas had soaked up his training well.

"A couple of weeks," Lucy answered. "I miss him so much."

Lucas nodded. "Sure you do."

"Do you mind if I look around?" Simon asked.

She waved an arm. "Go ahead. Not much here."

Simon motioned for Lucas to keep her talking and went into the kitchen past the smelly trash can to open drawers and cupboards. The fridge had half a case of Budweiser, some cheese slices, a third of a loaf of bread, and a few apples. The cupboard next to it had jars of jam and peanut butter, some canned refried beans and peas, and pasta. The rest were empty. One drawer below the microwave had plastic utensils and paper plates. Whoever lived here was temporary in every respect. Just like Ronan's apartment at Guinotte Manor.

He heard Lucas ask, "Do you know who lives here with him?"

He came back out and glanced in the trash to see used paper plates with mold growing on them and discarded utensils and beer cans. Not much else.

Lucy shook her head and said, "No. I didn't even know where he was, but obviously there were two of them."

Lucas nodded as Simon slipped behind her and headed for the bedroom. "They were sleeping on opposite sides, though," Lucas said.

"Right, so not another woman," Lucy said and smiled as she drew a wrist across her forehead. "Whew."

A quick search of the bedroom turned up a checkbook in Wheeler's name, a few Mexican pesos, and some sort of storage or lock key, a half-used box of tissues, and two piles of dirty laundry.

Lucas looked at Lucy. "When was the last time you heard from him?"

"A week ago, on Sunday afternoon," Lucy said. "For like ten minutes. Just to check on me and tell me he was okay. He was all rushed and stuff."

As Simon came back out to join them, she looked pleadingly at Lucas. "If you find him, can you please tell him I miss him and to come home?"

"Of course," Lucas said and pulled out a small notebook and pen from his pocket. "Let me get your name and number."

As Lucas took down the information, Simon checked the main room one more time, looking for anything he might have missed. It almost looked like the people were squatters, and he wondered what the apartment staff might know or think of their sparse belongings. The place was stuffy, an air unit in the window near the kitchen currently switched off. The place clearly needed to breathe.

Lucas stood. "We'll certainly let you know if we hear anything."

"Really? That would be great," Lucy brightened, her eyes hopeful.

Simon shook his head at Lucas. Androids could lie? Had they taught him that at the Academy? Detectives weren't in the habit of reporting to families unless there was a compelling reason—death notification or something similar.

Lucas realized his mistake and reached over to gently touch her arm. "We'll do what we can, of course. You take care. Good luck with the baby."

"Thank you," she said, reaching up to pat his hand.

Simon turned and led the way back out as Lucas followed.

"Don't make promises you can't keep," Simon whispered.

Lucas shrugged. "I got carried away. She was so sad."

"That happens. You gotta be prepared for it."

"Where to now?" Lucas asked.

"We should check the office and see if they know anything," Simon said, checking his watch. "Then we'll head back to Central and check in with Becker."

Simon led the way to the office and found it locked with a plastic clock sign on the door declaring they were out to lunch until 1 p.m. He wrote down the office phone number off a sign on the door and turned back toward the parking lot, Lucas following.

SIMON AND LUCAS STOPPED at Subway on East 63rd then took Troost north to Central.

"The FBI cleared us to check out Underground Drive and N.E. Midwest Drive," she said. "Why don't you two take a look at the cam footage we have from up there and then go knock on some doors."

So Simon and Lucas sat down and watched surveillance footage as Simon consumed his foot-long meatball sub. The first clips showed several box trucks exiting 435 at 210 Highway then turning south on Randolph and right on Underground Drive to head East. Others an hour later showed box trucks turning north off 210 Highway onto N.E. Midwest Drive. There were several business in the area that used large trucks, including HuntMidwest, Hallmark, Bayer, and Vanguard, among others.

"Well, this should occupy the rest of the day," Simon said.

"Where do we start?" Lucas asked.

Simon leaned forward and typed on a computer terminal, pulling up images of the specific trucks and license plates they were searching for. "Let's print some images and go start showing them around, see if anyone's noticed them."

"This could take a while," Lucas said.

"Yeah, days," Simon said.

"So we just start at one end and work our way?" Lucas asked.

"Well, there's two possibilities," Simon said. "They're hiding the trucks in plain sight or they actually concealed them inside a building."

"How will we know for sure?" Lucas asked.

"We start with the most likely targets and hope we get a break," Simon said. "If we're not that lucky...we'll still be at it next week."

"Is this why they say cops like donuts, they need sugar to keep going?" Lucas asked, totally sincere.

Simon burst out laughing. "You're not wrong," he managed after a breath. "Coffee works, too." He stood and tossed the Subway wrappers in the garbage, then tapped Lucas' shoulder. "Let's hit the road, partner."

The drive up to Underground took about twenty minutes in early afternoon traffic. On a hunch, Simon decided to start on Underground Drive. The bigger shipping and trucking companies on Midwest Drive seemed more likely to use bigger rigs than box trucks, and something just told him in his gut that was the place to start. After fifteen years on the job, a cop learned to trust his gut on such things. It didn't always pan out, but it often seemed to increase the odds.

Simon decided to start at the gas station on the corner of 210 and Randolph before hitting the big three. When he showed the images of the trucks to the clerk behind the window and asked if he'd seen them, the clerk shrugged.

"We get trucks like that past here all the time. Who knows?"

"Want me to try French Connection on him?" Lucas asked, referring to the time he'd broken Mister Information by dangling him inches from a passing train and reciting dialogue from one of the movie's interrogation scenes.

Simon grunted. "No, we're good."

Lucas narrowed his eyes at the clerk in warning. "You got lucky, punk."

The clerk scoffed as Simon grabbed Lucas by the arm and led him outside again.

"That's what got you in trouble with your T.O., remember?" Simon said.

"I thought maybe if I made him laugh, we'd win him over," Lucas said.

"First, I don't think he knows that movie," Simon said. "Second, he doesn't know anything useful, trust me."

"How can you be sure?" Lucas asked.

"Gut feeling," Simon said.

They climbed in the Explorer and continued on down the street past a small strip of offices and then took a three minute drive over to Northeast Underground which led to the cave-like entrances to Kansas City's famous underground complexes—a mix of storage and office space that made use of the rich limestone deposits under the city.

"What's in there?" Lucas asked.

Simon explained. "Former mines turned business complexes." Simon had heard about them but never been inside.

Lucas shrugged and stared at one of the entrances, narrowing his eyes a moment. Simon got the feeling he was computing something. "The opening would seem to be large enough for the trucks we are seeking."

Simon shook his head. "I don't think most of the tunnels are big enough."

As they passed another underground site's entrance, a large construction truck pulled out and turned right, headed back toward the interstate. Lucas shot Simon a curious look. "My gut says we should ask," Lucas said.

Simon chuckled. "Well, I guess it can't hurt to ask. Hang on." He slowed the Explorer and turned back around toward a small lot beside the entrance to the underground site the truck had just left. As he parked, he noted a sign that read "Parking for UnderCity only."

Simon turned off the car and reached for his door. "Let's go ask someone."

Together they walked back toward the entrance.

KARL HAD SEEN the news about the explosions and dead cops, and he knew who'd done it without being told. The minute he'd activated the USB to shut down the security systems and then watched box trucks arrive, it had occurred to him that those very men might be the ones who'd bombed and shot cops. Then he thought of his children and shuddered, his throat gone dry. He'd seen the leader's face. How long would they leave him alive knowing that? He fought a sudden urge to scream. That was nothing he could afford to think about, so he went back to work.

Then that cop and his partner appeared, walking in from off Underground Drive. The one whose daughter was friends with Julie. What the fuck was he doing here? Karl fought the impulse to jump under the desk.

The detective approached and showed his badge, then smiled when he recognized Karl. "Hey, John Simon. Your daughter was at my house a couple days ago studying with my daughter, Emma."

Karl forced a friendly smile and nodded. "Yeah, right."

Simon looked around. "So you work here, huh?"

Karl nodded his shoulders stiff, elbows pressed to his side.

Simon motioned to his partner. "This is Lucas George. What can you tell us about this place?"

Karl tried to relax. He couldn't let them see his fear. Cleared his throat. "Uh, it's storage, office space, that kind of thing."

"People actually like coming to work down here, huh?" Simon seemed puzzled by the idea.

Karl nodded again. "Yeah, it's quite popular. There are several companies that do this."

Lucas said, "We saw that."

Simon held up pictures of some box trucks and license plates. They looked just like the ones the man and his friends had brought in and Karl's heart jumped into his throat as Simon asked, "You ever seen any trucks like this come in?"

How the fuck did they know? Karl coughed, sputtering as he tried to answer, then swallowed, and finally said, "We get them occasionally."

"Any recently?" Simon asked.

"Maybe some that didn't come back out?" Lucas added.

Karl's legs wobbled and he put a hand on the desk to steady himself as he shook his head. "People don't store vehicles here. We have parking outside and across the street." His voice sounded shrill and shaky. Fuck. They'd know he was lying.

Simon didn't react. "People drive them in though and drop off stuff, take deliveries and such?"

Karl licked his lips and grunted. "Yeah. Sometimes."

"Maybe some came in during another shift?" Lucas asked.

Karl shrugged. "Always possible."

Lucas motioned to nearby cameras. "You keep the video? Maybe we could take a look?"

"I'm sorry. You'd need a subpoena," Karl said. "The owners are strict about the privacy of our customers. I could lose my job."

Simon nodded. "Sure. Wouldn't want you to lose your job."

"Had to ask," Lucas added.

Karl braced himself for more questions, but they looked around a little more, seeming just as relaxed as when they came in and Simon said, "Well, if you see anything suspicious, give me a call, okay?" He pushed a business card through the slot into the guard booth. "You probably have my number from the other day, but just in case."

"Do you mind if we look around a bit?" Lucas asked.

Karl heard the muffled ring of a cell phone and saw Simon pulling one from his pocket.

"Yeah?" Simon said, then listened. He reacted, looking at his partner. "Shit. We've gotta go. They found a body."

Lucas nodded and started for the door as Simon waved at Karl. "Thanks, pal. Have a good one."

And then they were gone and Karl fell back into the chair like the wind had been knocked out of him and tried to catch his breath. Jesus Christ. What had he been dragged into? And what was he going to do?

CHAPTER 17

THE CALL HAD COME from Tom Bailey of Homicide, who'd responded with his partner, Jerry Tucker, to a private landfill owned by Watson Waste Management off Gardner Avenue near Nicholson Park at the north end of Kansas City to investigate a corpse. Due to Waste Management laws and regulations, everything that could be recycled or incinerated had to be dealt with, the rest being buried in the actual landfill. So what had once been the province of one city-owned company, over the decades, had now grown to the responsibility of numerous companies, and private contractors greatly outnumbered the public ones.

The call to Bailey and Tucker had been inspired by the return of a Watson garbage truck which dumped its load only to reveal a corpse inside. The corpse in question was that of a white male in his mid- to late thirties with neck-length sandy blonde hair and a mustache. He'd been shot in the head at close range, his body wrapped in a tarp and tied with ropes, and then placed in a dumpster somewhere along the truck's route. The Watson people had seen the tarp come out, gotten suspicious—it wasn't the first body tied by ropes in a tarp they'd seen—and investigated.

By the time Simon and Lucas arrived, Bailey and Tucker were well into interviewing the Watson employees involved in the discovery, while a crime scene team led by Paul Engborg tagged, bagged, and loaded evidence. Incredibly but necessarily, this would include the many bags and piles of garbage that had arrived with the body, which would be taken to a warehouse, spread out and searched, looking for any identification of the businesses or locations the body might have come from. Given the latest technology, trace elements on the tarp could potentially be used to identify which bag or bags the tarp had come into close contact with as a way to narrow down the likely locations. It was all very scientific and a very big pain in the ass Simon was glad he didn't have to be involved in the processing of.

"Whatcha got?" he asked Bailey as he and Lucas navigated the lumpy, smelly landfill to join the two homicide detectives and their witnesses. Half-buried bags of garbage poked up out of the ground all around them along with pieces of furniture, glass bottles, and waste of every shape and size imaginable as they made their way along a winding path.

"You saw the body," Bailey said. "ID says he's one Charles Wheeler."

"You're fuckin' kiddin' me," Simon said.

"Feds sent us to Becker, so we called you. He involved with the bombers?" Tucker asked.

"We think so," Simon said. "We were just visiting his old employers and apartments."

"His girlfriend was quite upset," Lucas said.

"Yeah, well, this is going to make her real fuckin' happy," Bailey added, shaking his head.

Working landfills was one of the worst parts of the job— overwhelmingly unpleasant sights and smells everywhere.

Simon envied his partner the lack of olfactory senses, the first time he could recall actually being jealous of the android.

"So they shot him, rolled him up, dumped him, and left his ID?" Simon said, puzzled.

"They wanted the guy found," Tucker said. "And they wanted him IDed."

"Either that or they don't give a fuck," Bailey added. Simon figured that was the more likely scenario.

"Perhaps they were rushed or forgot?" Lucas said.

Tucker and Bailey laughed. "We should be so lucky," Tucker added. "But we never are."

"How long did Engborg think it would take to go through all this?" Simon asked.

"Go through what?" Lucas asked, puzzled.

"The garbage," Bailey and Simon said together.

"They take everything he came in with and look for clues as to where he mighta been dumped," Tucker said. "The crime scene team expects several days, maybe a week."

"Fuck," Simon said.

"Hey, I'm sure you'd be welcome to jump in and help," Bailey said and grinned.

"Don't hold your breath," Simon snapped.

"Hell, if we're stuck here much longer, I won't have a choice," Bailey said, crinkling his nose and making a face.

"Right, well, I hardly noticed it over your usual smell," Simon said and Tucker laughed.

"Hey, I'm the cleanest, best-groomed guy in Homicide," Bailey protested.

"Well, that sure is a high standard," Simon replied.

"He's on his game today," Tucker said, chuckling.

"Okay, we'll leave you to it," Simon said, relieved he didn't have to stick around. "Let us know as soon as you have reports we can skim."

"Hey, my reports are quality reading, no skimming," Bailey said.

"Yeah, yeah," Simon said and led Lucas back toward the Explorer.

"Where to next?" Lucas asked.

"Back to Underground Drive," Simon said. "Do me a favor—call Becker and have her get subpoenas for the camera footage at UnderCity, okay?"

"Okay," Lucas nodded and made the call as they climbed into the car.

They'd resume their list for now, but Karl Ramon's behavior had piqued Simon's interest. He was looking forward to an excuse to pay another visit. The man had been afraid, despite his attempts to conceal it. Whether he knew anything or just didn't like cops was the question. He'd acted odd outside Simon's house when he picked up his daughter that day, too. And then there was the weird visitor Simon had seen him chatting with. Either way, Simon was determined to talk with the man again.

SIMON AND LUCAS SPENT the rest of the afternoon visiting area businesses along Northeast Great Midwest

Drive and showing pictures of the trucks and license plates with no success then headed back to Central to check in with their fellow detectives. They huddled in Becker's office.

Maberry and Dolby had found similar results on Edson Núñez—old apartments, workplaces. But in Núñez's case, his former employers provided no insight because they barely remembered him. He'd been the kind to keep to himself. He showed up, did his work, hassled no one, talked only when spoken to, and that was it. Not exactly the kind of personality that is helpful for making one memorable and easy to track. But both teams had come away with lists of a few names to talk to, so that was something at least.

"How soon do we get reports back from the landfill?" Maberry asked.

"Feds put a rush on it and divided it between their lab and ours," Becker said, "but everyone's overloaded with all these crime scenes, so it won't start trickling in 'til tomorrow earliest."

"How long is it going to be until one of these bombs takes out a large group of people?" Dolby wondered.

"We have no way of knowing," Becker agreed.

"We've got to get the public working for us," Simon said.

"I agree," Becker said, "but there's concern about a mass panic."

Simon shrugged. "It's the best option for generating as much data as we can as quickly as possible. Do we have a choice?"

Becker shook her head. "Yeah, no one thinks so, which is why the Feds are working on a statement right now coordinating with our media office. We have to handle it sensitively, so keep it close to the vest for now. And get us pictures of Núñez and Wheeler. We want to get whatever help we can to pin down a location as soon as possible."

"We picked up several today," Maberry said.

"We can call Wheeler's girlfriend," Lucas suggested.

Simon hated the idea of bothering a woman who was just finding out she'd lost the possible love of her life, especially when they knew where Wheeler was, but grunted. "We'll ask. We can at least find out who he might have been seen around with."

"Good," Becker said. "The FBI press conference is going on right now and that should mean our phones will be lighting up."

Groans and mumbling came from around the room. They all knew what that meant.

"Here come the crazies," Dolby said.

"Thank God for overtime pay," Maberry added.

Becker chuckled. "Yeah, so rest while you can."

Simon debated whether to let them all in on his personal situation or just tell Becker. They'd all been around when he'd gone through the divorce and for at least part of Lara's earlier treatment. And regardless, they'd all heard about it. Finally, he decided they all should know, because as much as Dolby and Maberry were already dealing with in the loss of their partners, it was only fair he make them away of his own complications, too.

He cleared his throat.

"You've got something?" Becker asked.

Simon nodded. "Got a call last night. Lara's back in the

hospital."

They all reacted with surprise and worry.

"Where?" Dolby asked.

"Research," Simon replied.

"I'm sorry, John," Becker said.

"Yeah," Maberry agreed.

Lucas looked confused. He was the only one who hadn't been there and knew very little. Simon would tell him later. "I thought she was out of town?"

"So did I," Simon said. "And so does Emma."

"You haven't told her yet?" Dolby asked.

"Wanted to wait until Lara was back on meds and evened out a bit," Simon said. "She's worried enough with all the shootings and the bombs."

They all nodded with understanding.

"Whatever we can do," Becker said.

"Well, she's not my responsibility anymore," Simon said, "so I won't be taking any days, but I do have Emma to think of, so I'll at least be consulting with doctors and staying abreast."

"Good luck," Maberry said.

Simon exhaled. It was a relief just to have others knowing and supportive. "Thanks."

"Okay, well, unless you guys have other leads that need immediate attention, go home and get some rest," Becker said. "We don't know how many chances we're going to get until this is over." She stood and the rest followed.

"I'm going to be taking Emma over to Lara's to stay 'til

her mom comes home," Simon said. "Just to be closer to her school and such, so my commute may get a bit trickier for a bit."

"Fine," Becker said. "Just let us know."

"You bet," Simon said.

And they all dispersed back out toward the cubicles, Lucas following Simon. "I don't understand. What's going on with Lara?" he asked.

"Long story," Simon said. "How about you come over later and I'll tell you all about it?"

"What about Emma?"

"I'm going to tell her as soon as I check in on Lara," Simon said. "She's been at Research since this morning and should be under treatment by now."

"Okay," Lucas said.

"Just don't let the cat out of the bag until I tell you," Simon said.

Lucas' brow furrowed. "Cats do not like bags."

Simon chuckled. "Colloquialism. Guess you haven't heard that one, huh?"

Lucas shook his head. "What does it mean?"

"I'll explain that later, too," Simon said as he turned and gathered his wallet and keys from his cube.

ON HIS WAY TO pick up Emma at school, Simon called

Research and identified himself, asking to speak with person in charge of Lara's treatment. After a few moments, a woman with a heavy accent came on the line.

"This is Doctor Lidia Agbeblewu," she said.

"Doctor, Detective John Simon, Lara Simon's ex-husband," Simon said. "I'm calling to check on her condition and treatment so that I can fill in her daughter."

"Ah, yes, Detective," Agbeblewu said, "your ex is fine. We have her back on medications and she seems to be calming down. She even slept for several hours today."

"That's good," he said. "I'm sure she was exhausted."

Agbeblewu grunted. "I'm sure she is. Of course, it takes several days sometimes for them to really start getting back into a normal rhythm after an incident like this. Maybe even a week."

"Or longer," Simon said, recalling past experience.

"Well, whatever it takes, we are ready," Agbeblewu said, though Simon had his doubts. He had seen Lara kicked early with doctors insisting she was fine only to immediately lapse into manic behavior and violence once Simon got her home. Bipolar patients were exceptionally good at faking normal behavior, and mental health personnel, who tended not to know them very well, seemed to be exceptionally easy to fool. But in this case, Simon hoped Lara's regular doctor, Robert Nickell, would step in and take charge, because he had been treating her for six years and would know what's what.

"Has Doctor Nickell been notified?" Simon asked.

"Yes, and he came to see her this afternoon," Agbeblewu said.

"Is she up for visitors?"

"Maybe tomorrow," Agbeblewu said. "She is still angry with you for 'imprisoning her' again, as she puts it. And with us."

"Yes, well, what else is new," Simon said. He'd been through this before. "I'll check with him and call again tomorrow. Let me know if there's anything you need."

He gave her his information and hung up, immediately dialing Doctor Nickell as Linwood Boulevard changed to Highway 40 and he stopped at a red light.

Nickell's office transferred Simon to his cell. "Hi, John," he said when he answered. "It's been a while. How are you?"

"Okay, considering I'm reliving a nightmare," Simon said.

Nickell chuckled. "Well, this time it's not your responsibility, so if you want me to take charge, I will."

"Well, given the case we're dealing with, I'll probably be doing that, but I have Emma, and she's going to be asking a lot of questions, so I want to be in the loop."

"Of course."

"So what's your prognosis here?"

Nickell thought a moment. "I think she's been playing with her meds, perhaps because of weight gain, or maybe some other reason," he said. "I won't be able to know for sure until she's somewhat under control again and capable of truly rational discussion, of course."

Simon grunted knowingly.

"I expect her to be in the hospital for two or three weeks," Nickell continued, "but she's got good insurance through work, and I've spoken with her employer. They were aware of her condition because of health forms and annual physicals."

"She won't lose her job, will she?" Simon asked.

"No, she actually was on vacation and has enough sick leave and vacation to cover her time away, plus they said she's been an excellent employee and they'd like to see her back," Nickell said and Simon sighed in relief.

"That's good to hear," he said as he turned off 40 onto Blue Ridge Cut Off. "Thanks, Doc. I appreciate the update."

"Anytime," Nickell said. "Call me anytime. I'd wait a few days to bring Emma, though."

"I don't know," Simon said. "I'll see her again alone myself first, but it might be good for her to see what her mom's like, to better understand. She's old enough."

"Whatever you think is best," Nickell said. Simon agreed to call him again the following afternoon and hung up.

Five minutes later, Simon pulled up in front of Nowlin Middle School to find Emma and her friend, Julie Ramon, dancing on the sidewalk.

"Hey," the girls said as he rolled the window down.

"Aren't you two supposed to be studying?" Simon teased.

Emma made a face as she opened the door and folded the seat forward for Julie. "'Hi, honey, how was your day? How was school?' That's what a loving parent would say."

Simon chortled. "Yeah, right, not caring about homework equals love. I suck."

"Exactly," Emma teased as Julie got in the back and she folded her seat back up 'til it snapped in place.

"Do you need anything from my house before we go to your Mom's?" Simon asked, even though he'd told Emma his plan the night before.

Emma rolled her eyes as she closed the door and buckled her seatbelt. "Can we eat out at least?"

"We'll order a pizza," Simon said as he pulled away. "I need to see what your mom has in the fridge anyway."

"Fine. There's no beer."

"Figured," Simon said and then Emma flipped the radio to her favorite station and she and Julie started singing along and bopping to the beat.

AFTER PIZZA AND a beer run, Simon settled down to review the evidence file via KCPD's online database while Julie and Emma switched between studying and dancing around with a good approximation of hyperactive distraction.

Lucas called Simon's cell about seven and asked when would be a good time to come over. Simon told him eight, knowing Lucas would arrive on the dot as usual, so he went to Emma's room to tell Julie she'd need to leave about that time.

The girls were currently dancing and singing along to the latest Carnie Hayes smash, "Dream Lover." Emma's generation's Taylor Swift, Hayes was a third generation country pop star whose hits like "Born To Be Lonely" and "Walk Away From Me, No Run" provided the perfect narration to Emma's teenage life.

"What time's your dad coming?" Simon asked, looking at

Julie.

"I'm supposed to call," Julie said.

"Can you make it eightish?" Simon said.

"'Kay," Julie replied, never missing a beat.

Simon remembered their last encounter and figured it would be the perfect chance to catch Karl Ramon off guard and maybe figure out why he'd seemed so nervous at work when Simon and Lucas had stopped in.

He went to the living room to watch TV and wait. NCIS: Miami was on tonight and that was always good for a laugh—TV cops making miracles.

Karl Ramon arrived first at ten minutes to eight. Simon met him on the drive. "Seen any box trucks since we talked?" he asked.

Karl didn't look any more comfortable with the question now than he had before. He avoided eye contact, shifting back and forth on his feet, his voice barely a whisper. "No."

"Just curious," Simon said. The trick was to figure out how to get him to open up without him running off. "We just had some bad people associated with similar trucks and we're trying to find them. So please keep your eye out and call me if you see anything that might help, okay?"

Karl nodded. "Sure."

"Thanks."

Karl stood there an awkward moment, still avoiding silent eyes but saying nothing, his right hand rubbing the back of his neck. "You expect to find these people up near UnderCity?" Karl asked finally.

"Some trucks like that were spotted up that way," Simon replied.

Karl grunted. "There are several shipping companies and factories up there. We probably have hundreds go by on a daily basis. Seems like you'd better have more to go on."

"That's why we're talking to people like you," Simon said.

Karl shrugged. "Well, sorry. I can't be much help."

Simon smiled. "Well, we had to ask. Part of the job."

"Sure. I get it." Karl drew quiet again, restless, but silent. Obviously still uncomfortable. After a minute, he asked, "Is Julie ready?"

"They're in Emma's room," Simon said. "Let's go get them."

He turned and opened the door, motioning for Karl to go in ahead of him. Once they were inside, Simon motioned to the hallway to the left off the entryway that led to Emma's room and the men headed that way. The door was open and the two girls were lying on Emma's bed sharing headphones and giggling loudly.

"They were dancing and singing loudly with the music up full blast earlier," Simon commented as the dads entered the room. "Not sure why the headphones now."

Karl shrugged. "Teenagers."

Simon chuckled. "Tell me about it." He stepped forward where Emma could see him, and when she looked up, pointed at Karl.

Emma flipped over and turned down the volume. "Well, thanks for hanging out."

"Always a blast," Julie said as they stood and hugged. Julie turned to Simon. "Thanks for the pizza."

Then she joined her dad who led her out quickly,

avoiding further words with Simon, and headed for the car.

"What?" Emma asked as she came up behind Simon, who was watching them from the doorway.

Simon shook his head. "Nothing."

Just as Karl pulled away from the curb, Lucas' chrome Outlander appeared and pulled into the drive. Emma squealed and ran to meet him. By the time they got inside, Emma and Lucas were so engaged in conversation that Simon didn't have the heart to interrupt with bad news about Lara. Instead, he waited for them to finish, watching TV, and when Emma went to bed, Lucas joined him.

For the next hour, Simon told the story of his disastrous final three years of marriage and his ex's illness. After he'd finished as they walked to the door, Lucas looked at him sadly and said, "I feel like you need a hug."

Simon laughed. "Nah. It's ancient history really. Just Lara having a relapse so I have to keep an eye on things and help Emma." Truthfully, it still hurt sometimes, especially when he'd stood in that hospital reliving it. But he was doing his best to move on, and he'd long ago accepted he and Lara would never rebuild what they once had. They could only push forward separately.

Simon opened the door and exhaled. It felt good to let someone in, especially the partner who was becoming such an important part of his and Emma's lives. Even if he wasn't quite human. "Thanks for driving over."

Lucas nodded. "My pleasure. I will see you tomorrow."

"Bright and early," Simon agreed and watched until Lucas' feet touched the driveway before closing and locking the door.

LUIS WAITED UNTIL the black cop drove away to pull out of his parking spot in the shadows and head back to UnderCity. He'd seen it with his own eyes—Karl Ramon met with the detective leading the case against the Colonel's team. It was inexcusable. Ramon would have to be dealt with, and probably the cop, too. It appeared the distractions they'd tried to create had not deterred anyone or steered them clear. Instead, they'd drawn even closer to locating the team's activities, and they weren't ready. Not for a few more days. So he'd report to Derrick and let the Colonel decide what he wanted to do.

Luis had a pretty good idea what that decision would be, of course. The Colonel was not one to waste either words or time, which was one of the things that Luis liked most about him, most respected. This was a man of vision and singular dedication, and following a leader like that was not only uncomplicated but inspiring. Some of the men had their doubts, sure. But fuck 'em. They were just in it for money and the sense of power. Their mission had so much more to it, and when it was over, they'd see that. It would historic, unforgettable, its impact felt for years to come. Most criminals only got to work small time with little impact except on themselves and direct visions. But this mission was a higher calling. And Luis couldn't wait to see it play out.

The car he was driving had been rented from Enterprise by the airport the day before. Rented for a week. Only it would never be returned. It was a tan Toyota sedan, as nondescript and common as they come, which allowed him to blend in easily in traffic and around town. Even the staff at UnderCity could hardly take note. And that made it perfect.

Luis had been riding in the back of a truck as they arrived there, too, so not even Karl Ramon knew of his association with the Colonel. That's why he was the perfect front man and would remain that way.

He pulled onto I-70 and brought the car up to the speed limit slowly and evenly, so as not to draw any attention. The windows were down and the cool night air refreshing as it caressed his skin. Twenty minutes to UnderCity. He flipped on the radio to a Spanish station and started singing along. Anyone who saw him would think he was just another Hispanic driver casually moving about. But soon the world would realize his significance. Fear his existence. And he looked forward to watching it unfold.

CHAPTER 18

THE PROPERTY DETECTIVES arrived at Central the next day to find themselves inundated with new leads thanks to the FBI press conference the afternoon before. The phones in the squad room rang constantly, and the department had called in several temps to take messages so the officers could continue investigating.

Simon and Lucas spent some time scanning the spreadsheet of messages, a work in progress constantly growing, and then joined the others in Becker's office to prioritize leads. Most, they all knew, would lead nowhere—either simply crazies desperate for attention or frightened citizens grasping at anything their paranoia deemed a possibility—but others could well take them closer to finding the bombers, and unfortunately, that meant they had to check them all out, or at least as many as they could manage. Of course, the FBI and detectives from other squads and sections would also be roped in. Even Becker herself planned to return calls.

First priority for Simon and Lucas was to go back to UnderCity, Hallmark, and other businesses around Underground Drive and Great Midwest and deliver subpoenas for their security camera footage. It was going to pull in a lot of footage, even though they'd limited it to the past week, but Agent Falk felt it essential that they get whatever they could in an attempt to nail down the needles in a haystack for which they were searching.

Simon had to admit he also liked the idea of staying on Karl Roman, especially after seeing him the previous night. That man had tried to put on a casual face but his body language and face had given him away. He knew something he was worried about the police finding out, whether it had to do with the present case remained to be seen, but either way, Simon wanted to know what it was, and he was tired of waiting.

On the way over, Simon took Lucas through the process of serving papers, which was fairly simple, telling him what to say and to whom. They would technically serve the manager or one of the higher ups, not Karl Ramon himself. But Simon wanted Lucas to handle it so he could take the opportunity to pressure Karl again.

Simon parked the Explorer in the lot outside UnderCity and strolled confidently inside with Lucas following.

As they approached the security booth, Lucas badged Karl, who was on duty there, and asked, "Where's the manager's office?"

Karl pointed to a yellow metal door on the wall to the right beside a sign that read, "Office." Lucas nodded and headed that way as Simon stopped beside the booth and nodded at Karl. "Long time no see. What's going on?"

"What's he doing?" Karl asked, eyes darting toward the door Lucas had just disappeared through.

"Serving a subpoena to your bosses," Simon said. "Video footage."

Karl's eyebrows darted together as his hands rubbed his legs.

So the mention of video footage makes you nervous, eh? Simon thought, then said, "Routine. We're gonna need all the footage for the past week."

"I don't think we save it that long," Karl said, nonchalantly.

"We'll find out," Simon said.

Karl shrugged. "Okay." His darting eyes said it was anything but.

Simon heard footsteps behind him and turned to see a tall and bulky man with a military haircut and toned muscles on his chest, arms, and legs, approaching and motioning to Karl. The man's intense green eyes seemed to stab at anyone he looked at. When he spoke, he had a slight accent, it sounded Southern but Simon couldn't quite place it.

"Karl, that stupid problem with the locks is happening again. Can you come take a look?" the man asked, and Karl turned ashen at the sight of him.

"Sure," Karl said, his voice a bit shrilly. He cleared his throat. "Be right down. Let me get someone to cover the booth." He looked at Simon as he picked up a red phone. "Excuse me, Detective. Work calls."

Simon nodded and stepped away toward the door to the office, but kept watching. Moments later, a woman appeared from the office and stepped into the booth, using an access card to let herself through the secure doors. She and Karl exchange a few words he couldn't hear and then Karl stepped out of the booth and walked away with the muscular man, both ignoring him in a way that was a little too obvious.

Simon considered following them but they got in a golf cart labeled 'Security' and raced off through one of the tunnels. Behind him, the woman, a short, chunky brunette in her late 30s, keyed a microphone and asked, "Can I help you with something? We really don't allow people to loiter there." Her voice was tinny through the speaker as she spoke loudly to be sure he could hear her.

Simon started back toward the booth to answer her when Lucas appeared.

"How'd it go?" Simon asked.

"Simple and easy," Lucas said. "We will have footage to pick up tomorrow by mid-day."

"Perfect," Simon said. "You gave them our number?"

"Yes, and the FBI," Lucas replied.

"Okay."

"Sir?" the woman asked again, impatiently.

"We're good," Simon said and badged her. "Just on our way out."

"Have a nice day," she said in a way that came across as very insincere.

AS SOON AS THEY got down the tunnel a ways, Derrick turned to face Karl and snarled, "Why are you spending so much time with the police lately, Karl?"

Karl's skin turned pallid, his lips trembling as he stuttered, "I-I-I-they-they-they came here with a subpoena for security camera footage. I didn't tell them anything. They dealt with the office."

Derrick smirked and shook his head. "That explains their showing up here today, but not your being at the white detective's house twice now."

"M-m-my daughter's friends with his daughter," Karl managed to say, his hands turning white from clasping the steering wheel as he shifted back and forth on his seat.

"You better not be helping them, Karl," Derrick said. "That would be very unfortunate for you and your family."

Karl shook his head several times adamantly. "I swear, I am not. They were asking about box trucks. I told them twice I never saw any."

Derrick stared into Karl's eyes a moment, Karl's eyes dodging direct contact. The man was a weasel but he was probably telling the truth. He finally said, "I think I believe you, Karl. For now. But consider this a warning. Stay away from the police. And perhaps your daughter would be best to find new friends."

Karl nodded repeatedly so fast Derrick wondered if his head might fall off. "Okay, okay."

Derrick reached up and grabbed Karl's shoulder firmly, causing him to wince. "Now walk with me down to one of the doors and act like you're doing your thing. Don't want anyone to know we didn't have a real issue, right?"

"Okay, okay," Karl said, nodding again as he and Derrick started walking again and the other man let go of his shoulder. He mumbled, stuttering for words, "Wh-wh-what about the tapes?"

"Did you do as we ask with the USB drive?" Derrick asked.

Karl grunted. "Of course."

"Then there's nothing for them to find," Derrick said.

"Won't they ask about the places the tape loops?" Karl wondered.

"It doesn't loop exactly, there is static and a frozen image," Derrick said. "They may ask the office to investigate, but it could just as easily be a malfunction. By the time they have enough information to decide, this will all be over. So don't worry about it. Just keep doing as you're told."

"All right," Karl said, exhaling. They stopped beside the doors to a newer office and climbed out, walking together toward the secure entry door. Karl made like he was examining the keycard security panel and making adjustments. This took several minutes and Derrick thought he put on a good show. Karl even mimicked asking him questions a few times, to which Derrick mumbled responses, just to look good for any cameras that might pick up the interaction.

When he was finished, Karl opened the door for Derrick and Derrick stepped into the doorway, holding the door open. It wasn't his office, but the management wouldn't know and he could always leave through the side exit and use one of the pedestrian tunnels to head out like he was on another errand before making his way to the undeveloped area to rejoin his team off camera.

"Now, go find a place to kill time. At least half an hour," Derrick said. "And remember, we're watching."

Karl nodded as Derrick shook his hand and acted like he was thanking him. As Karl turned to head off, Derrick walked into the office. A couple secretaries looked up, surprised.

"May we help you?" one asked, puzzled.

"Hi," Derrick said, putting on his warmest smile. "I was just preparing to rent space and they said this layout was the closest to the one we'll be getting. I just wanted to take a peek."

The other secretary crossed her hands over her chest, frowning. "Shouldn't someone from the office be with you?"

Derrick chuckled. "Yeah, they had some kinda crisis over the radio and she had to rush back to check something. Said she'd be right back. 'Go ahead, these people are really nice.'"

The secretaries looked as if they were still suspicious but noticeably relaxed.

The second one said, "Well, we'd prefer they escort you, but I suppose given the circumstances, we can show you around quickly. It's a slow day."

"Thank you so much," Derrick said, still smiling. He made sure to ask lots of inane questions as they did, just to sell it, and they never seemed to suspect a thing before he finally made a quick exit through the pedestrian walkway, explaining they told him to use it to get back to the office because it was safer with the vehicle traffic.

The truth was, Derrick always used the pedestrian walkways, when he could, because he blended in with everyone else on security footage. He entered through an unrented office unit down near the one he and his team had been guided to by Karl, an area where security cameras were not fully installed yet. It took extra effort but best ensured his activity would go unchallenged by other staff unaware of his presence. Some security cameras had been placed but not connected in the newer areas, and Derrick and his team had fed those into their own security feed so they could keep an eye on any activity around them and the caverns where they were working. They'd also installed a series of others of similar make in the caverns still under construction just to help them keep an eye on comings and goings. Others were hidden to blend in with walls—tiny in size—or in shadows or holes in the rock where no one would be likely to look.

He walked a bit of the way back down the walkway toward the office until they closed the door behind him, then turned and hurried back the other way, slipping the earpiece to his personal comm out of his pocket and back into his ear as he went.

POP'S BAR SAT at the corner of Prospect Avenue and 36th in a building built in the 1940s that showed every bit of its age. The paint was faded and peeling at the borders, the plastic sign atop a pole out front reading "Pop'" because the S had faded over the years. One of the few functional pay phones still in the city hung on a wall ten feet from the door, but it was often in need of repair since the neighborhood and clientele were prone to disliking the requirement that they actually pay for its use. Simon parked the Explorer in the red zone out front and smirked at the disparaging looks thrown at the two cops as they strode ambivalently toward the front entrance.

They were there following up on a tip Becker had passed on from one of the temps. Someone named "Lucky" claiming to have heard something about the bomb suspects.

As he pulled on the faded faux brass door handle to open the door, Simon whispered to Lucas, "Let me take the lead, okay? These people can get quite rough. This is a favorite place for certain types."

"Criminals?" Lucas asked a little too loudly as they stepped inside and Simon silenced him a little too late with a glare. Every eye in the place was now focused on them.

Up tempo hip hop blared from a classic jukebox in the corner that looked like a relic from war torn Beirut, while three skimpily clad dark skinned women and a Hispanic male worked behind a long oak bar with black faux leather stools spaced out along its front. The same faux leather colored the booths lining the outside wall and the chairs at the tables in the center of the floor, except for the small portion near the jukebox clearly designated as what passed for a dance floor. If it weren't for his higher class dress, Lucas, whose presence was met with some puzzlement, might have fit right in except Pop's catered to a clientele whose concern for the latest fashion was almost nonexistent. They only dressed up when required by church or the latest criminal enterprise. Simon, on the other hand, was met with angry stares from every corner. His wasn't the only white face in the room, but they were definitely a minority.

He went immediately to the bar and stood between two stools as the occupants reacted like he stank of skunk and stood, slinking away to distant corners. The place smelt of spilt beer, cigarette smoke, sweat, and cheap perfume—a potent combination. The floor was sticky from spilled alcohol and crushed peanuts, chips, and pretzels from the bowls set out on the bar and several tables.

"Whatcha want, cop?" one of the barmaids asked, none too friendly.

Simon badged her and smiled. "Looking for information."

The barmaid scoffed as a drunk wobbling on a nearby stool laughed and said, "You fuckin' crazy comin' here."

Simon shrugged. "Maybe. Maybe not."

"What makes ya think anyone here'll talk to ya?" the barmaid asked, her mouth twisting smugly like someone who already knew the answer.

"Depends how worried they are about terrorists bombing the city, I guess," Simon said. "Anyway, we got a tip from a 'Lucky' who said to find him here."

"Shit," the barmaid said, shaking her head, then turned and raised her voice as she looked at a man in his 30s on a stool at the end of the bar. "Lucky, you sonuvabitch, yo' callin' cops in here?"

The man grinned, his all gold teeth reflecting the light of a nearby bar lamp as he did. "Fuck yeah. So get me anudder beer whilst we talk, 'k?" He stood and motioned for Simon and Lucas to follow him to an open booth in a nearby corner.

To Simon, Lucky looked like just another loser ten years older than he probably was, maybe even twenty. His vocabulary was all street as were his clothes and look— mostly unkempt, wrinkled, and cheap with signs of dirt and wear on everything. He scooted into one side of the booth with Simon and Lucas sitting across from him. Simon stopped and urged Lucas in ahead of him so he could keep his eye on the rest of the room and be ready, if necessary. Fortunately, Lucky also took the side facing away from the door, so Simon was positioned ideally in case of trouble.

"How ya doin'?" Lucky asked cheerfully as they sized up each other across the table.

"You had information?" Simon said, not wanting to waste much time given the resentment toward cops filling the room.

Lucky grunted. "Maybe. Figured ya'll'd be lookin' for dem bombers, and I'z heard a few things around."

"Like what?" Lucas asked. "Time to let the cat out of the bag."

Lucky looked at Lucas with confusion as Simon stifled a laugh. A different barmaid than the one they'd talked with before strolled over and looked at Lucky then Lucas, ignoring Simon. "Can I get y'all sumthin'?"

Lucas shook his head. "No thank you, ma'am."

Simon waved dismissively. "We're on duty, but get Lucky whatever he wants."

"'Nother Miller, sugar," Lucky said and winked at her.

She rolled her eyes and sashayed back toward the bar. In the background, the jukebox switched to the latest Tupac Jr. hit. Rap. Simon cringed and did his best to tune it out. Torture for his ears. "What you got for us?" he asked, staring at Lucky.

"White dude was in here coupla months back," Lucky started in.

"What did he look like?" Lucas asked.

"Big dude, muscular, haircut like dem military dudes, ya know?" Lucky said and Simon and Lucas nodded. "Anyway, he's talkin' 'bout some big job he needs people for."

"Out loud? In front of everyone?" Simon asked, skeptical.

"Nah, just to a select few brothers," Lucky said. "But I hears 'bout it after."

"So this is second or third hand then?" Simon asked.

"You wants this or not?" Lucky said, eyes narrowing as he leaned back on the bench until the barmaid returned with a bottle of Miller and slid it along the table top to him. He leaned forward, picked it up, and savored a long sip.

Simon motioned for him to continue.

"He wuz talkin' all about some higher mission er sumthin'," Lucky said. "Buncha bullshit, yo' ask me, but anyways, pay was really good and it was short term, so lotsa talk and interest, only he didn't want just anyone. Wasn't interested in referrals. Jus' those he handpicked, ya know?"

"And who were they?" Simon asked.

"Have you seen any of them around lately?" Lucas added.

"Nah, theys all disappeared," Lucky said. "The ones he took. But a coupla fellas who went to some orientate thing he threw said there was all this talk of some weird philosophy."

"Weird philosophy? Like what?" Simon asked.

"All that 'Make America Great' shit but without the racism," Lucky said. "A coupla o' brothers actually got excited about it."

"They did?" Simon said.

"Yeah, totally bought into the shit," Lucky said.

"Can you help us find them?" Lucas asked.

"Not sure," Lucky said. "Like I said, they disappeared."

"When was the last time you saw them?" Simon asked.

"Not for at least two or three weeks I'd say."

"Anything you can tell us would sure help," Lucas said. "We're trying to stop these people before they kill a whole lot more people."

Lucky nodded. "Right. Which is why I called you."

Lucky gave them a few names—not just people who may have joined up, but a couple of others who'd attended the orientation and showed interest and some known associates of all of them as well. He also provided possible work and home addresses, or at least last known.

"Are you not afraid of trouble from talking with us?" Lucas asked when he'd finished.

Lucky waved it off. "This here's important for all o' us. Let them talk if they wants. People dyin'."

"Good man," Simon said and smiled as Lucas nodded beside him. "Are any of these people in here tonight?"

Lucky's eyes searched the room for a few minutes, squinting against the shadows as he took a long draw finishing his beer, then he finally turned back to the two cops and shook his head. "Nah."

"Okay. We'll check it out," Simon said as he slid out of the booth and pulled a business card from his pocket, sliding it across the table for Lucky.

"Thank you," Lucas added.

Simon threw a few bills on the table for the beer and the barmaid and they headed for the exit, ignoring the unfavorable looks that followed their every step.

SIMON DROPPED LUCAS back at Central around noon and headed over to Research to check on Lara. On the way, he'd called Doctor Agbeblewu to let her know he was coming. She agreed to meet him in the lobby and escort him up, so she could fill him in on the way.

The lobby was typical rows of chairs with tables and magazines, a couple of TVs blaring, various people around, many with kids, many elderly, a few staff—mostly nurses or orderlies—checking on people or bustling back and forth, receptionists behind a curved counter handling check in and calls. Agbeblewu was a short, dark-skinned woman in green scrubs, her hair up above her head in circles to create a sort of Marge Simpson-esque tower, her lips were larger than his but framed a warm, welcoming smile as she shook his hand, her grip firm.

"Welcome, Detective," she said. "Sorry to meet under these circumstances."

"It happens," he said. "Your name sounds African."

She nodded. "Yes, I'm from Kumasi, Ghana."

"How'd you wind up here?"

"In my country, opportunities can be limited," she said. "I wanted to train with the best, so I came to the U.S. and here I am."

"I imagine they need doctors there, too," he said as she used a keycard to let them into a stairwell and they headed up together.

"Yes, of course," she agreed. "But I can gain more experience and learn better techniques and technology faster working here for a few years, then going back."

"Is that your plan?"

She chuckled. "Who can know the future. But yes, I do hope to return one day."

Her voice, despite the British accent, was lilting, almost lyrical and filled with joy. That amazed him given the kind of patients she was surrounded with daily. Mentally ill people were taxing even at their best, yet here she was in good spirits. She must have the patience of a saint.

"How's she doing?" Simon asked, finally getting around to Lara.

"Better today, though still mad at you for putting her in here," Agbeblewu said.

Simon shrugged. "She's been pissed at me for years for one reason or another. Just another day."

The doctor's eyes gleamed with a mixture of amused recognition and sadness. "Patients often blame loved ones. It comes from fear and uncertainty and the frustration they feel over a condition they can't control."

"And don't deserve," Simon added. "Doesn't make it much easier sometimes. Though I'm sadly used to it."

She stopped at the fourth landing beside a door, holding her key card and met his eyes. "I hope not. I hope most times she is living a more normal life."

He grunted. "She has been. This is the first episode in years. Just been through it before."

"Ahhh," Agbeblewu keyed the door and held it open for him as they entered. "She's down the hall in room eighteen. By herself at the moment. Do you want me to come with you?"

The halls echoed with shouts, cries, screams and mumbling of the distressed—some of it babble or nonsensical, much of it angry or pained. The usual antiseptic smell of a hospital filled his nose mixed with that of sweat and bodily fluids.

He shook his head. "No, I'm okay. Where can I find you after?"

"I'll be making rounds," she said. "Meds time for most of them. The nurses can always use a hand."

"I hear you," he said as she stopped beside the nurse's station and he continued on toward room 18.

The walls were pastels, calming tones, mostly off white with highlights in yellow or aqua blue. The patient rooms he passed were aqua green with yellow highlight walls at the heads of the beds.

Lara was lying in bed reading a worn harlequin paperback. Her hair was stringy and wet from a recent shower, her skin pale. Simon stepped inside and stood in the doorway.

"Hi," he said as she continued reading.

"What the fuck do you want—to laugh at me?" she demanded without looking up.

"No, actually, I was here to see how you're doing," Simon said. "Maybe see when you'd be ready to see your daughter."

The book dropped into her lap, her hands still on it as her angry eyes met his. "Aren't you going to come closer? What are you—afraid of me?"

He strode into the room a few feet, facing her. "No, just giving you space. I know you're mad at me."

"Put me in prison again! Bet you loved that," she spat.

"Not really," he said. "I wish you were home or at work, frankly."

She scoffed. "Right."

"I thought you were on a business trip," he said.

"Well, I was out of town," she said, eyes darting away. "None of your business why." She wasn't telling him something and he wondered what.

He raised his palms in surrender. "I was just caught off guard when they called me. I had no part in the decisions to bring you here. That was already done, believe it or not."

"Right," she said and laughed.

"Lara, I'd be more than happy to see you out of here as soon as possible. So take your meds and listen to the doctors. I'll drive you home myself."

"No thanks. Uber or cab preferred."

"Okay."

She went back to her book and he continued watching her, until she lowered it again, shooting him an annoyed look. "Why are you still here?"

He exhaled. "I don't have to be. You call me if you need anything. Emma is at your house with me."

"Oh great. Don't leave me a damn mess."

"I'm treating it like I would my mom's, okay? I promise. Besides, Emma keeps me in line."

She guffawed. "Someone has to."

He turned and strode out then, not bothering to waste words on "goodbyes." He found Agbeblewu down the hall outside another room a few minutes later.

"How'd it go?" she asked.

"About like you'd expect."

"The meds take a while."

"When can I bring Emma?" he asked.

"She's never seen her mom like this, right?"

"Yeah, but it might be good for her. She's a teenager. She needs to know."

The doctor shrugged. "Visiting hours are 6 to 9 every evening. But if you call me, I can make special arrangements."

Simon nodded his thanks. "I may do that with the craziness at work. Thank you."

She smiled. "Have a better day, Detective. You can find your way out?"

"Yes," he replied and waved as he headed back down the hall toward the stairs.

CHAPTER 19

FROM THE HOSPITAL, Simon went back to Central to pick up Lucas. As they got in the Explorer again, Simon behind the wheel, Lucas looked over. "I didn't get the chance to ask. How's Lara?"

Simon sighed. "Angry as hell, especially at me. Says I put her in jail again. Meds are calming her somewhat—no manic shakes or frantic movement—but she's not happy to be there and resents that I am involved."

Lucas frowned. "Don't you have to be?"

"Not really," Simon said. "We're divorced. I have more standing as a detective and Emma's father than I do as an ex-spouse. But I am technically family, and someone has to communicate with the doctors. It's not a burden anyone wants to put on a fourteen-year-old, so it falls to me."

"When will you tell her?"

"Tonight," Simon said. He'd already decided. "For one thing, if I put it off any longer, Emma will be mad as hell when she finds out. Second, she's old enough she needs to start seeing how this works with her mom. Maybe she'll be lucky and never have to deal with this again, but that's unlikely. Most people with bipolar have episodes throughout their lives, so she'll need to be ready for when it falls on her."

"Poor Emma," Lucas said, and he meant it.

Simon grunted. "Yeah." He slowed at a light and turned the car onto 71 Highway headed north, accelerating to speed as he wove into the heavy afternoon traffic

"The case is a good distraction," Lucas said.

"Fuck. What case? We're chasing ghosts, and it's scary as shit," Simon said.

"You are afraid?"

"Hell yeah, so is everyone," Simon said. "Besides losing our friends, partners, these people clearly want to kill people, innocent people, and a lot of people are about to get hurt. We want to—need to stop it."

"How?" Lucas asked.

"That's what scares me," Simon said. "We don't know where they are, and we don't know who they are to figure that out. If they're ex-military, these are heavy duty dudes probably with access to heavy duty weaponry and explosives and capable of stealth and intense tactics. It's like we're about to go to war against an unknown enemy."

"They've got all the time in the world, while we're ice skating uphill," Lucas said, combining movie quotes from Man on Fire and Blade, Simon thought. It was a damn good analogy.

"You got that right," Simon agreed.

"Well, I guess instead of doing things the nice way, we gotta do things the hard way," Lucas said.

Simon recognized it from A Bronx Tale. "You got a quote for everything?"

Lucas shrugged. "It's a hobby."

"Well, keep talking, if you want, it helps me think."

"Where are we going?" Lucas asked as Simon took an exit ramp and turned left onto 11th Street.

"Just driving," Simon said. "That helps me think, too." He thought a moment, then continued, "What we need's a real break. But I'm starting to lose hope." And he was. It had been a while since a case had him so discouraged.

Most criminals were so stupid, their mistakes gave them away. All you had to do was put enough time in and the leads would reveal themselves, but it was taking much longer on this case than normal with so little to show for it that he was beginning to wonder. And the ex-military angle meant they were dealing with a different class of criminals than usual on top of it, which meant smarter, craftier, with different techniques and approaches and more worrisome, different goals and attitudes about killing.

That last part was what really scared him. Most criminals dreaded jail time and trials and prison. They had families, drug habits or other addictions—reasons to stay outside—and thought long and hard about how far they were willing to risk that in their criminal behavior. But these people might just be the type with nothing to lose or at least no concern about it. If that was the case, the city would be headed for disaster if the KCPD didn't track these criminals down and stop them.

"What do you usually do to break cases?" Lucas finally asked, interrupting his thoughts as Simon took the exit.

"We've been doing it," Simon said. "That's the problem. Though usually there's better human intel to work with. Nobody seems to know anything. It's like hitting a brick wall day after day."

"People don't want to let the cat out of the bag," Lucas

said nodding that he got it.

"No," Simon said. "That's not really how you use that phrase."

"To tell people things you know that they don't is not what it means?" Lucas asked, his brow furrowing.

"Well, yeah, but more in a good kind of secret way," Simon said.

"A good secret?" Lucas asked.

"Yeah," Simon said. "Like one you keep to surprise someone with something that will make them happy."

"Like when I did the robot and you were surprised and it made you happy?" Lucas said, beaming like he understood at last. But he was referring to a time he'd done karaoke to distract some clients while Simon questioned a potential witness. Not really what the phrase meant, but Simon decided to let it go.

"What do we do now?" Lucas asked, his voice sounding sad.

"Try to shake things up somehow," Simon said.

"How?" Lucas asked again.

"I'll tell you when it comes to me," Simon said as they turned right on Locust and cruised south beside KCPD Headquarters and the Jackson County Court building. Then he turned left on 12th and took Holmes south, turning on 13th and then Cherry Street, and into the parking lot at the Jackson County Detention Center. Deep in thought the whole time. He was looking for something—he'd know it when he saw it—anyone or anything out of place. But first, it was time to shake the tree a bit.

SIMON AND LUCAS LEFT the car in the lot and walked over to the Jackson County Detention Center to chat with Golden Boy again. They wound up waiting for him in the same fifth floor interview room where they'd met with him before. It took almost twenty minutes for the guards to locate him and escort him into the room. This time, his limp was less pronounced and he was not wearing leg irons, though they had put him in cuffs. His orange jumpsuit had sweat rings under both arms and around the neck. Simon guessed he'd been pulled from work duty to talk with them.

The minute he saw them, Golden Boy scowled. "What the fuck dey want?"

"You'll see," one of the guards said, dragging him into the room by an arm and pushing him into a chair across the table from them.

Simon smirked. "Hey, Marcus, how you doin' today?" Simon snapped in his best imitation of the tough street tone Golden Boy and his cohorts loved to use.

Golden Boy chuckled. "White boy be a poser."

"White boy got a license to kick your ass, now shut up and listen," Simon said.

Golden Boy rolled his eyes. "I din't ask for you. So why you here?"

"We can't wait forever," Simon continued. "I thought we had an understanding."

Golden Boy scoffed. "Hey. I'm in here. Not on da street. You wants the real scoop, you get me outta here."

Simon snorted. "Yeah, you wish, asshole. How about I just let my partner here have at you again?" He motioned to Lucas and Golden Boy shrunk back in the chair as best he could.

"No way, man. I'm tryin' but no one wants to talk about these dudes. Scary shit. All ex-mil fuckers."

"Ex-military?" Simon asked.

Lucas leaned forward in the chair and smiled, playing along. "What did you hear?"

Golden Boy eyed him warily. "These dudes were in Afghanistan or somewhere. They all into dat bullshit about making America great and making some big statement, but not racist. They got brothers on their team and shit."

"Who told you this?" Simon asked. "Someone in here met them directly?"

"A bro of a dude in here did," Golden Boy continued. "Some kinda presentation. Said they had a sacred mission but wouldn't give details except to those who signed on and swore to secrecy."

"So this guy didn't work with them?" Lucas asked.

"Nah, he took one look in their scary eyes and walked his bro said," Golden Boy added, looking only at Simon, ignoring Lucas. "I don't know much more, but whatever these dudes are doin' scared some brothers big time. And he said it will fuck up the city major and kill lots of people."

"If they didn't tell him details, how does he know?" Simon asked.

"You can just tell assholes like dis ain't into no street crime," Golden Boy said. "They wants to do real damage, you know? Make a statement. Talkin' 'bout changin' the world."

"None of this helps us find them, though," Simon said.

Golden Boy grunted. "I jus' passin' on what I hear, man. All I can do."

Simon leaned forward this time, locking eyes with him. "Cut the bullshit. We need to stop these guys or it may be your family who dies next and mine, too. You want me to help you—you get me something I can use. I don't hear from you in twenty-four hours, deal's off, okay? Seriously. I could put in a real good word with the prosecutor, maybe even get some charges dropped if you helped. This is that important. But you gotta make an effort."

Golden Boy shifted in his chair, his brow narrowing, eyes intense. "I'm tryin', Simon! I swear!"

"We got a dead guy named Charles Wheeler, street name Weasel, another named Gregory Ronan, an Edson Núñez and very little else. Get me names, get me descriptions, locations—something that'll help me find them," Simon said. "I don't have time to wait around, and so far you've done nothing to incline me to do shit for you."

"Fuck. You never were gonna keep your word," Golden Boy said.

"Bullshit. You ask around about me," Simon said. "My rep is solid with people who deal with me. But I need actual useful info. This ain't squat."

"Not my fault—"

Lucas' hand shot across the table and grabbed Golden Boy by the collar, pulling him chest down on top of the table so their faces were inches apart. "Now, you let the cat out of the bag right now or you'll be sorry, pal," Lucas said in a very John Wayne-esque way.

Golden Boy's eyes looked ready to pop out of his head as he struggled to pull away and escape. Behind him, the waiting guards were peering in with concerned looks.

Simon held up a palm to signal all was okay as he relaxed again. "Just a little motivation, Marcus. You have my number."

As Simon stood, Lucas suddenly let go of Marcus and scooted back the chair beside him, motioning dismissively to the guards. "We're done with him."

Then he walked around Golden Boy as a guard opened the door and strode on down the hall. Simon following.

As they reached the elevator, Simon grinned and pressed the down button. "That oughta get results. Because we're coming up empty, and we're running out of time."

"There is no one more full of shit than a cop except a cop on TV," Lucas said, quoting some unknown movie.

Simon grunted. "Or a low life in jail." The elevator dinged as the doors opened and they stepped inside, pressing the button for the first floor.

WHAT WAS LEFT OF Ronan's Garden Center was a cratered parking lot and the wreckage of maybe a third of the former building. A double-wide trailer had been set up in the parking lot and a crew was at work clearing rubble from the crater. Chainsaws and a generator buzzed as men with hoses suctioned up debris and others swept or shoveled. Simon wondered how far away Mister Information had been. From the looks of it, he had to have been almost across the street to survive the blast and its shockwaves and walk away, he figured.

As he parked the Explorer near the trailer and got out, he smelled hints of ammonia and even stronger tar. He'd read these were typical of C-4 craters, the tar coming from the C-4 while the ammonia came from the bomb fertilizer. He and Lucas glanced around, taking in the destruction. Poor Mark Ronan must be devastated. He wondered if they'd rebuild or just call it a loss and start over somewhere else.

The answer came when the trailer door opened and Mark Ronan appeared on the steps, his face gaunt and shadowed, his hair uncombed. He recognized them and came down the stairs to meet them. "Those motherfuckers ruined my life!"

"We're very sorry," Lucas said.

"Was anybody hurt?" Simon asked.

Ronan shook his head. "No. Thank God. Except a vagrant who was walking on the sidewalk over there." He pointed across the street. Simon was sure he meant Mister Information. "But what a mess. It will take us months to rebuild."

"I hope you can," Lucas replied.

Ronan grunted. "Good insurance, thank God. But some of my employees will take other jobs and not come back, so I'll have to retrain quite a few. That will slow us down, too."

"Well, hopefully you'll start over better than ever," Lucas said and smiled.

"Or at least become that eventually," Simon added, knowing it was always easy to say but hard to do. Many businesses like this would never survive such a setback.

"Eventually," Ronan agreed. "What brings you here?

Surveying the damage?"

"We came to ask about your brother," Simon said.

"He's dead," Ronan replied, "and I wish I was sorrier."

"Whoever did this, we think he was working with them," Simon said.

"Yeah, it sounds like it, so no loss," Ronan said. "How a loser like him could come from our angelic mother is beyond me." He sank down on the trailer's steps, hands on his chin. "He just never got himself together. From the time he was four, it was one trouble after another. Of course, they just got more serious as he got older." He looked across Beardsley to Mulkey Square Park where kids were laughing and playing on a playground as parents watched. The complex housing the FBI's local office rose in the background.

"Do you know why?" Lucas asked.

Ronan laughed. "I could venture a guess or two, sure. Lazy, selfish, greedy. But—"

"Usually it's more complicated," Simon added.

Ronan exhaled. "Yeah, that's what the shrinks would say. But to be honest, he was spoiled. Dad's favorite. Mama's boy."

"Really?" Lucas said.

"Yeah, I broke the parents in and he got the breaks," Ronan said. "But you know, I got dad's work ethic and mom's sense of dedication, and he just didn't. No matter what any of us tried."

"What can you tell us about the people he was hanging around with the last few weeks?" Simon asked.

Ronan's brow creased and he made a sour face as he thought a moment. "Buncha losers as always."

"Same people he'd known for a while?" Simon asked.

"No, they were new," Ronan said. "But the same types really." He grunted then added, "Except..."

"Except what?" Simon asked.

"These latest were tougher," Ronan said. "Maybe even ex-military, I think."

Simon and Lucas exchanged a look.

"Did you hear any names?" Lucas asked.

Ronan thought again. "Not really much. But they did talk about this guy a lot. They called him 'the Colonel.' I got the feeling he was some kind of leader. And then there was a guy named Luis and something about foreigners."

"Foreigners from where?" Lucas asked.

Ronan raised his hands in puzzlement. "Got me. That's really about all I know. They'd swing by to pick him up or drop him off on occasion when he was bothering me about something—usually money or freebies from damaged shipments, and then he'd disappear with them again. Hardly showed up for work the past month. I'd have fired him if he wasn't family."

"What kind of freebies?" Simon asked.

"We had some dented fuel oil drums that sat in the back he wanted," Ronan said. "Those we usually return for credit. Most people just don't like to buy dented stuff. He wanted torn bags of fertilizer, too, but we tape those up and they sell as long as most of the contents are still there."

"So you said 'no'?" Simon asked.

"Well, yeah. I wasn't much inclined to help the bum for lots of reasons," Ronan said. "Least of which being his job performance. But then some of it just disappeared one day."

"It disappeared?" Lucas said.

"Yeah. Greg denied knowing anything about it, of course, but I was pretty sure, and he was warned," Ronan said. "On thin ice."

"When did you notice it was gone?" Simon asked.

"A week or so later," Ronan said. "After he asked. He hardly showed up after that. The day you came in I was shocked to see him."

"But he was working, right?" Simon said.

"If you call it that," Ronan said. "I got the feeling he was just there to see what else we had around. Kept finding him in the back room and warehouse poking through stacks."

"Can you make a list of the stuff that went missing?" Simon asked.

"Probably. Why?"

"It actually might have used to make bombs," Simon said. "It would really help us."

"Jesus. You think they blew up my life with my own product? Bastards," Ronan said.

"It's a possibility," Simon said. "How soon could we get a list?"

"Tomorrow?" Ronan said.

Simon nodded. "That would be really helpful."

"And if you think of anything else that might help us," Lucas added.

"Finding these people is difficult at best with what we have," Simon continued. "But we think they are planning some sort of major attack on tourists somewhere in the city."

Ronan frowned. "Fuck. Okay, I'll get to work on it. Want me to email it over?"

Simon pulled a card from his pocket and handed it to Ronan. "Yeah, that would be even better. Thanks." He looked around as Ronan stood again and looked at the card. "Good luck with all this. Really."

"Yeah, thanks," Ronan said. "I hear they bombed your station, too. Everyone okay?"

Did he not know his brother was there? Simon wondered. "We got lucky," he replied. "Thank goodness."

"God is merciful," Ronan said and headed back up the stairs to the trailer as they headed for the car.

Simon glanced back as he opened the driver's door and Ronan waved then disappeared inside.

"That was interesting," Lucas said.

"Yeah," Simon agreed.

"We shook the tree well," Lucas added as they both climbed into the car.

Simon chuckled. "Yeah, stuff is falling out. Now we just have to put the puzzle together piece by piece."

SIMON AND LUCAS WERE called back to Central for a 3 p.m. meeting to go over evidence with the FBI and leaders from all the teams, including homicide's Tucker and Bailey, Bomb Squad's LaDue and Benson, Assault's Garner and Ross, and Gun Squad's Hanson and Penhall, along with Becker, Melson, Maberry, Dolby, and El-Ashkar.

Agent Stein led the meeting. "We have several reports in and I wanted to go over them with everyone," he said as Falk handed out folders around the table. The meeting was once again held in the front conference room off the lobby at Central. Coffee, tea, and sodas were available on a side table with danishes, fruit, donuts, and crackers on trays scattered around the table.

"Let's start with the lab's analysis of the explosive components found at the bomb sites," Falk said as he slid into a chair between Stein and Becker. Everyone opened their folders and looked at the top sheet as Falk read from the report. "We found traces of C-4, bomb fertilizer, and fuel oil as well as steel plating."

"Traces of C-4, fertilizer, and fuel oil were also found on the vagrant injured at the garden center as well as Wheeler," Becker added.

"With both the Garden Center and the warehouse, it appears they got access and wired the buildings," Stein added.

"Well, they were using the warehouse, so that makes sense," Ross said.

"What about the Garden Center?" Dolby asked.

"They got access somehow," Falk said. "Probably from someone who worked inside."

"Gregory Ronan, the owner's brother," Simon jumped in as he swallowed a bite from a cherry danish. "We were there today and his brother ran when we tried to talk to him several days back."

"And shot at us," Maberry added, mouth full of donut.

"Or at least someone did," Lucas said.

"So this brother lets our guys in and they wire the place," Falk said. "Do we have a location on him?"

Maberry motioned to the window. "What's left of him are particles out there on the lawn and drive."

"He was seen driving the van that exploded here," Becker added.

"Ah," Stein said with understanding.

"Our lab thinks the items reported in your burglaries and the components found are obviously the sign of people with serious bomb making skills and knowledge," Falk said.

"We could be looking at multiple and sizable devices," LaDue added.

"Enough to do potential damage to an area the size of a football field," Stein said.

"Provided they have sufficient quantities and know what they're doing," Benson added.

"I don't think there's any doubt about that last part at this point," Deputy Chief Melson said.

"No," Becker agreed.

"How sophisticated and skilled is still a mystery," Stein said, "But yeah, we'd agree with that assessment. Next is the Watson West landfill." He looked at Bailey and Tucker.

"Crime scene and our team finished going through the garbage we believe was from the load in the dumpster where Wheeler's body was found," Tucker said. "We found mostly the usual, but there were several pieces of correspondence and letterhead with address off Underground Road at UnderCity, a storage and business complex cut from limestone."

"We've been there several times," Lucas commented.

"We subpoena'd their camera footage," Simon added.

"You saw something?" Bailey asked from behind them as he poured a cup of coffee.

"Not really," Lucas said.

"We went in doing the routine check of the area for anyone who'd seen box trucks," Simon added. "The guard on duty has a daughter who's friends with mine, and he acted like he's hiding something. Beyond that, nothing of substance."

"Did you talk with him again?" Stein asked as Bailey rejoined them at the table.

Simon nodded. "Twice. No luck."

"Seems suspicious it would be a coincidence," Dolby said and sipped from a can of Pepsi.

"At least as far as the finding of the body," Becker said. "But worth taking a look."

"Can't be a coincidence," Melson interjected. "When do we know about the security footage?"

"Agents picked it up an hour ago, so a day or two," Falk said. "But we've brought in extra people from St. Louis and Chicago to help process it, and more from Denver are en route."

"So what we've got so far are enough explosive components to do major damage, a potential site, and a few possible suspects, at least two of which are dead?" Penhall said.

"Well, whether we have a site remains to be seen, but UnderCity seems worth checking out for sure," Stein said.

"Can we stake it out?" Hanson asked.

Stein looked at Becker and Melson. "We were hoping

your people could handle that."

Becker nodded. "We'll set it up."

"Just for a day or two until we see if anything suspicious turns up," Falk added.

"Well, we have to investigate Wheeler regardless," Tucker said.

"So that gives us an excuse to get people inside," Melson said.

"Right, but there are several hundred tenants and miles of corridors and tunnels in there," Simon said. "We'd have to know a lot more even to narrow down search warrants."

"All we can do is see if anyone saw Wheeler or anything suspicious," Bailey said.

"We could send in dogs," Benson suggested.

"All of those things are possibilities," Stein said, holding up a hand to stop them, "but we'd like to observe for a few days first for probable cause before we risk scaring these guys. We can't risk them blowing the place early before we get it cleared."

"Or moving again," Falk said.

"I don't get why these guys would be there, anyway," Dolby said. "Weren't they supposedly after some kind of touristy target?"

"Yeah, not much of value around there, other than the casino," Ross added.

"Vatterott College, a couple of hotels, Oceans and Worlds of Fun," Garner said.

"Those amusement parks are pretty big tourist-filled targets," Maberry said.

"We'll at least send someone over to ask their security if they've seen anything suspicious, show the pictures we have," Stein said.

"And keep in regular contact, until we can pin it down for sure," Garner said.

Becker looked at Simon and Lucas. "Did you find any other likely locations for them to hide out around there? There's a chance UnderCity could be another temporary base to hide out and prepare before hitting the target, like the warehouse."

"Several underground storage places, warehouses, factories," Simon said. "None of them seem like places anyone could go unnoticed for long."

"We did get a new name today," Lucas said.

"Right," Simon added. "Mark Ronan said his brother was hanging out with military types. Several other witnesses said the same thing."

"He mentioned someone his people call 'Colonel,'" Lucas said.

"So a potential ex-officer," Falk said. "Did we get descriptions?"

"None but those we already have," Simon said. "No one so far has seen this Colonel, just heard him mentioned."

"Gregory Ronan did steal fertilizer and fuel oil from the center," Lucas said.

"The brother's supposed to email a full list of items he thinks Gregory stole by tomorrow," Simon said. Across the table, Maberry swallowed the last of his donut and popped open a Diet Coke.

"Maybe there'll be something new we don't already

know," El-Ashkar added hopefully.

"We definitely need something," Melson said. "Jesus Christ. How are we supposed to stop these people with so little information?"

"They're good," Stein said. "Possible professionals. So we have to keep looking—"

"Shaking the trees," Lucas interjected.

"Exactly," Falk said.

"Let's stake out UnderCity for a couple days at least, see if anything turns up," Stein said. "And we'll go take a look around at the casino and the amusement parks, too."

"Our people can do whatever you need," Melson said.

"Can homicide hold off on questioning UnderCity staff about Wheeler for a few days?" Falk asked.

"Sure," Bailey said with a shrug. "We have a girlfriend to talk to and some others."

"Great. See what turns up," Stein said. "By then, we should know about UnderCity."

"What can you tell us about this guard?" Falk asked, looking at Simon.

So Simon filled them in about Karl Ramon.

As Stein finished the meeting by meting out assignments and offering a few more updates, it occurred to Simon there was one place he'd failed to go back to where someone knew something. But if he were going to go there again, he'd need major backup. So, as the meeting adjourned and he walked out with his fellow cops, he gathered several of them in the parking lot, including Maberry, Bailey, Tucker, Ross, Garner, Penhall, Hanson, and Lucas.

"What's going on?" Ross asked.

"There's a bar Lucas and I went to where there are people who refused to say anything, but they knew one of the suspects," Simon said.

"What place?" Hanson asked.

Simon told them about Jimmy's bar and Mr. Clean.

"Fuck," Garner said.

"If we go, we have to go off books, late at night, kinda unofficial," Bailey suggested.

"Exactly," Simon agreed. "Who's in?"

"I'm in," a female voice said and they turned to see Dolby standing nearby beside her blue Prius.

"This place is pretty rough," Maberry said.

"Those bastards killed my partner, too," Dolby said. "I'm in."

Maberry grinned. "Me too."

"Count on us," Tucker said.

"Us too," echoed Penhall.

"When and where?" Ross asked.

Simon gave them the address and arranged to meet them all there around ten-thirty. "Bring your rumbling clothes," he said.

"Let's kick some ass," Lucas echoed and the other chuckled.

Then they all headed off.

CHAPTER 20

THAT NIGHT, SIMON took Emma down to Taste of Brazil, her favorite restaurant at the City Market off 3rd and Walnut in the River Market area. Just north of downtown off the Missouri River, the area dated back to the 1850s and included the original land on which Kansas City itself had been founded. It had endured several name changes through the years including River Quay. As the River Market, it had been revitalized with a thriving farmer's market, restaurants, shops, a steamboat museum, and more. It was now an active place for music, people watching, and shopping, especially on weekends and holidays, and from 2016 on, it had been serviced by Kansas City's revived street cars, allowing residents easy and cheap access to the entire downtown through the Union Station and Crown Center areas.

Lucas walked over from his nearby apartment to join them at the restaurant. With an open kitchen area that looked out on scattered tables filling the inside and a patio out front, Taste of Brazil was a fun little spot with excellent samplings of authentic cuisine. Emma had taken to it immediately after going there with a friend's family and asked Simon or Lara at least once a month to go back.

The tables were wood grain of various shades with matching chairs, there were plants of various Amazonian

types with large leaves—some bigger than a person's head—
and Brazilian art and flags decorating the walls. The luscious
offerings included classics like picanha, frango doido (orange
chicken), Brazilian pork sausage, tilapia, Brazilian cheese
bread—pão de queijo, coxinha, yucca fries, empanadas, and
delicious flan and other desserts. Simon had yet to find a
menu item he didn't savor thoroughly, and he tried to order
something different each time, hoping to eventually work his
way through the entire menu. Emma was more conservative
in her choices. She particularly favored picanha—a juicy cut
of steak—and the various chicken dishes along with
Brazilian pot pies called empadinhas. They both loved the
flan—Pudim de leite.

Lucas and Emma chatted like the old pals they were,
comparing notes on the latest music or movies they'd
discovered, discussing her schooling, and even her friends.
Simon was lost some of the time, but he didn't mind, because
by the time dinner was over Emma was in a great mood, and
that served his purposes well. The time had come to tell her
about her mother, and he wasn't sure how it would go.

After Simon paid for the meal and they started walking
across the market, Lucas made the excuse to go look at an
exhibit nearby, leaving them alone.

"Lucas is the best, dad," Emma said.

"Yeah? He's becoming a pretty good partner, too," Simon
agreed.

"Cool," Emma said with a smile. "He makes me laugh."

"I'm glad," Simon said. "There's something I need to tell
you."

Emma also loved the River Market for its people
watching. There was always a crowd and lots to see around
them. The clothes, the couples, the outdoor vendors, games,

artists, and more created an energetic atmosphere. There were also the cornucopia of smells from restaurants, people, the city air, and the river. "Oh yeah?"

Simon stopped her with a hand on the shoulder and stepped in front of her so they were facing each other.

"What's going on?" she asked, frowning.

"Your mom's in the hospital," he plunged in.

"What?!" Her eyes widened, her posture stiffening.

"She had an episode, bipolar," he went on.

"On her trip?"

He shook his head. "I don't know what happened exactly but she's here."

"But she's not supposed to be back for a few more days."

"I know, but maybe she never went," he explained. "We won't know for sure until she's back to her old self, but she's at Research, under treatment."

"Can I see her?" Emma said immediately, her eyes meeting his.

He nodded. "Yeah. I want you to."

Her face fell. "But not until she's better?"

He shook his head. "No. You're old enough you need to know how she gets. In case anything ever happens when I'm not around."

She brightened. "So when?"

"Actually, we can go tomorrow night, if you want," Simon said, checking his watch. "Visiting time is up in an hour, so we wouldn't have time tonight."

Emma nodded. "Okay. You promise?"

He put a hand gently on her cheek. "Yes."

She reached up and took his hand in hers, surprising him. It was something she rarely did now that she was a teenager. As they started walking together, Lucas rejoined them.

"Perfect timing," Simon muttered.

"Are you okay?" Lucas asked, shooting Emma a concerned look.

"He knew?" Emma looked slightly annoyed at Simon.

"I had to tell them at work because of what's going on, in case I had an emergency," Simon said.

"How long have you known?" Emma's eyes narrowed as she let go of his hand.

"Two days," Simon said.

Emma shot him a look, then turned and smiled at Lucas. "I'm okay. But you need to tell him to stop treating me like such a child."

"He treats me the same sometimes," Lucas said.

Emma rolled her eyes. "He's such an old man." Then her eyes wandered to a circle of people gathered around some dancers and a drum circle ahead.

"Hey!" Simon said.

Emma grabbed Lucas' hand and started pulling him as she ran. "Come on!"

Simon stood there alone a minute, watching them, then muttered, "Well, that went well." Actually, it had and he was relieved. Still, he wouldn't have done it any differently, no matter how Emma reacted. She was a child and always would be to him. Then he rushed to catch up with them.

THE GROUP MET at a Phillips 66 station a mile from Jimmy's Bar. They were all wearing street clothes—jeans or shorts and t-shirts or button downs. They briefly discussed whether to put on vests, but Simon suggested that would be overkill.

"After what happened last time?" Bailey said. "This place had a rep for rough patrons."

"Who could be armed," Penhall added.

"Vests and sidearms are fine but we don't want to go in looking like vigilante rogue cops," Simon said, "so everyone except Lucas put on vests if you must but sidearms only." Lucas didn't need one. Everyone grabbed extra ammo for good measure.

"Let's go," Tucker said and they headed for the bar, Simon and Lucas in the lead. They'd decided to approach it casually but ready to act, hoping the show of force would be enough to curtail any violence. No one put a lot of stock in the idea that would work, but it sounded good.

They parked a block away in the red zone, cars spread out over both sides of the street, then walked in together. Simon could hear outlaw country blasting from the stereo as they crossed the street at the nearest corner—something new from Krystal Keith, Toby's daughter, the latest break-out star. From inside, voices sang along, others laughed and chatted.

Through a window they saw a busy dance floor and packed tables and bar stools as they approached the front door.

"You ready for this?" Simon asked.

The others nodded and grunted.

Hanson got the door and Simon led them inside. As they went through the door, the smell of beer, sweat, and peanuts dominated the atmosphere. They spread out and quickly all eyes turned toward them, faces turning hostile. Then someone killed the music as the dancers stopped to stare at the detectives.

"What the fuck are you doing back here?" a gruff voice demanded and Simon turned to see spotlights gleaming off Mr. Clean's bald head as he ambled over in the same spiked leather jacket, his friends following behind.

Maberry stepped forward, eyes narrowing at Mr. Clean. "Not this time, asshole."

"We had some questions we still need answered," Simon said.

Mr. Clean and his buddies guffawed.

"We told you before, we're not talking," the bartender called from behind the bar.

"We have two dead cops and several civilians, including your buddy Weasel," Simon said. "And hundreds more including your families and kids could be next if you don't tell us what you know."

"We can do this the easy way or the hard way," Lucas said in his best Eastwood impersonation.

Chortling came from around the room.

"I've always been partial to the hard way." Mr. Clean sneered and swung a fist straight at Maberry's jaw.

"Art!" Bailey called out as Maberry ducked and swung his own right hook straight into Mr. Clean's stomach. Maberry might be overweight but his muscles were toned.

Like most police officers, he made healthy use of the gym at his station. Mr. Clean had leaned in with his punch and couldn't pull clear in time. Simon could hear his teeth clack together as Maberry's fist made contact, bending him over with a loud groan.

Hanson and Garner quickly grabbed Mr. Clean's arms and held them behind his back as Bailey cuffed him.

Mr. Clean's buddies and several patrons swung into action then jumping on the three cops restraining their friend. Mr. Clean fell to his knees as the detectives spun to defend themselves. Simon, Dolby, Ross, Tucker, Penhall, and Maberry also moved in to cut off other would-be attackers.

One man picked up a stool and swung it at Simon's head, who ducked. Another punched Hanson in the back, causing him to let go of Mr. Clean. Meanwhile, Maberry, Tucker, and Penhall exchanged blows with two others.

Simon yanked the bar stool from the man's hand and threw him over the bar where he flew into stacked glasses and bottles of liquor with a loud crashing. Then he saw two patrons drawing weapons from their waistlines.

Before anyone else could react, Lucas rushed in and grabbed the armed bar patrons, banging their heads together and tossing them aside as if they were children instead of grown men. He kicked their weapons away, then ducked as one of Mr. Clean's cohorts swung at him and flipped the man head over heels to land atop a table, which collapsed beneath him. Next, he intercepted a pool cue another Mr. Clean friend was swinging at his head and snapped it in two, throwing both pieces back to hit the guy in the face and chest.

All of these disabled attackers were quickly pinned or subdued by his fellow cops, who looked at him with amazed faces.

"Jesus Christ," Tucker said, shaking his head.

Simon shrugged as he and Dolby quickly snapped up the two patrons' fallen weapons. "Partner's got a gift." Then he looked around the bar, meeting the eyes of whoever shot defiant looks his way. "Anyone else want a piece?"

A few grumbled, others shook their heads, several just stood staring and pondering.

"Look!" Simon finally said. "We didn't come here to bust anyone. We just need information. Good people are dead and more could die if we don't find the people who did it. So tell us what you know, and we leave. Otherwise, we'll call in every car available and make this a very bad night for you,"

"I already told you I don't know shit," the bartender growled.

Dolby, who'd wound up beside the bar, grabbed him by the collar and dragged him up over the bar to land at her feet in a heap. "I don't believe you," she sneered.

"I didn't spent sixteen years on this job not to know when someone is lying to me," Simon said, his gaze drilling into the bartender. "Talk to me or talk to someone else here or downtown. Your call. But you will tell us what you're holding back."

Lucas stepped toward another group of angry-looking patrons. They raised their hands in surrender and backed off. Dolby reached for the bartender again.

He scooted away, raising his hands. "Okay, okay. We don't know much."

"Start talking," Dolby said.

For the next hour, the cops spread among the bar's

patrons and questioned them about Weasel and any known associates or anything and anyone else they knew who might either be associated with the bombers or know something about them. After ninety minutes, they came away with a few leads and more information and descriptions than they'd had before. One even claimed he'd seen "the Colonel." He'd heard the last name "Derrick" once or twice, he swore.

It wasn't much, but every little piece gave them more to work with.

At the end, as they gathered to leave, Simon tossed the bartender two fifty dollar bills. "For the table and the pool cue," he said.

And then they all headed for their cars, the patrons now watching them with far more relief than resentment or anger.

"I hope you get the bastards!" the bartender called after them.

STAKEOUTS WERE THE bane of any cop's existence, but nonetheless a necessary evil. Often they were the only way to pin down enough evidence to nail elusive suspects and shut down their criminal enterprises. Simon took the Charger, picking Lucas up at his apartment around five-thirty, and bracing for a long day. Simon didn't have to worry about getting Emma to school while they were staying at Lara's, because she rode the bus regularly from there. She was old enough to get breakfast and get herself going, so he'd checked on her before he left and trusted she'd make it on her own.

He parked down the Underground Drive half a mile from the main entrance to UnderCity in the lot opposite HuntMidwest's larger complex Subtropolis—a location with a good view of the comings and goings. Both had binoculars. Simon had also packed a cooler full of Cokes and two Subway foot-longs he'd picked up the night before. Over the hill at UnderCity's other entrances, Maberry and Dolby and Hanson and Penhall were taking day shift. Others would rotate on at night.

A light breeze blew through the Charger's open windows as puffy cumulus clouds floated overhead in an ever brightening blue morning sky. Daylight was coming on fast as it did in the Spring, and there was steady traffic along Underground as workers arrived for shift changes or to open the various offices around them.

Lucas was far too cheerful and energetic for a time of day Simon wished he was still in bed, singing along with the radio as they drove and attempting small talk the whole way. As they settled in for the stakeout, Simon would teach him the ropes, hoping that distraction might focus him for a while. Those hopes were dashed after about fifteen minutes.

"Do you want to play the license plate game?" Lucas asked.

"What? No, we're watching UnderCity," Simon said. "We can't distract ourselves, we need to focus."

"Oh," Lucas sounded disappointed.

"How do you even know about that?" Eventually, Simon would talk to him about how detectives traded off during stakeouts but for now, he wanted him to focus on how stakeouts were run.

Lucas brightened. "Emma told me. I was asking about

ways to pass the time in a car."

"When did you speak to Emma?" Simon asked, hiding his annoyance as he watched several cars parking in the lot in front of UnderCity and the drivers heading inside.

"I called her last night, as I was preparing for the stakeout," Lucas explained.

"The license plate game requires us to watch the cars passing by," Simon said.

"We have binoculars," Lucas said helpfully.

"Which we need to use to see who comes and goes and what happens at UnderCity. How can we do both? What if we miss something?" Simon crinkled his nose as a large truck with a carburetor issue spit out a cloud of smelly exhaust smoke right in his face as it passed, and he waved an arm to clear it away. "Be glad you have no olfactory capabilities, pal."

Lucas shrugged and quieted as Simon cracked open a Coke and settled in with his binoculars.

"Would you like to count VW bugs instead?" Lucas asked after another minute.

"No! Jesus. Can you just watch the building?! That's what we're here for!" Simon snapped.

"Perhaps I should get you coffee," Lucas said. "You seem quite cranky."

"It's too damn early and we need to work," Simon said.

"A Xanax?"

"No!"

Lucas frowned. "This is what Emma calls a 'chill pill,' correct?"

"Just shut the fuck up and watch the building, okay?" Simon said.

Lucas flipped on the radio and started singing along to the latest Wolfie Van Halen hit as he aimed his own binoculars and adjusted the focus.

Simon flipped off the radio and shot him a glare. "No distractions."

"Sorry."

"We don't want to call attention to ourselves," Simon added. He keyed the police band on a private channel and said, "Team One in position."

"Team Two, copy," Dolby said moments later.

"Team Three, copy," Hanson said after.

Lucas stayed silent and watched the building.

THOUGH THEY WERE still using the office cavern Karl had directed them to for computer and tech work, the box trucks and most of the supplies had been relocated to the cavern Derrick had scouted out six weeks before. Karl was a loose end. It was safer if he didn't know their main base of operations. Meanwhile, he and Luis had gotten the team to work on digging out other pre-selected spots and preparing them for explosives, either in steel reinforced box trucks filled with fertilizer, C-4 and fuel oil, or with directed charges designed to bring down the ceiling and everything above it.

His men were demolitions and ordinance experts, Special

Forces trained, as was Derrick himself. They'd had years to perfect the craft of designing controlled explosions and this plan was their masterpiece; the culmination of two years of planning and rising anger. This would make history not just in Kansas City but beyond, and no one was going to fuck it up any more than they'd already tried.

The teams worked in pairs and all of them wore masks like Derrick had on to protect themselves from the dust and debris their work generated. He couldn't have his people falling ill just when he needed them. All demo teams were ahead of schedule, but they still needed forty-eight hours to be ready. Right on time. Oceans Of Fun was open weekends only in the Spring season, so Saturday would be the perfect day. He finished his rounds in two hours then slipped off the mask and hopped into the golf cart he used for transportation in the unmonitored areas and headed to check with Luis in the electronics room.

He arrived to find Luis nowhere in sight.

"Are the units ready, Private?" he asked the nearest electronics team member.

"Twenty-four hours, Colonel," the man, Jonah, replied.

Derrick gave a pleased grunt. Perfect. "All right. Very good," he said. "Where's Luis?"

"He got called next door," Jonah said as they heard a commotion from the room next door where communications and security were being coordinated.

Rather than calling Luis on the comm channel, Derrick hurried down the short corridor to investigate. As he arrived, the room was erupting with chatter and motion as people hurried around, pointing at monitors, checking the various feeds.

"What's going on?" he demanded.

"Colonel, we're being watched," Luis said and motioned Derrick to a monitor with security camera feeds. Simon and Lucas, the two cops who had been hassling Karl, were sitting in a car down the street with binoculars. "There are two more teams at the other entrances," Luis added.

"How long have they been there?" Derrick asked.

"Since early this morning," Luis said.

"Forty-eight hours, that's all we need," Derrick muttered.

"Sir?"

"Execute Plan D," Derrick ordered.

"Plan D, Colonel?" Luis asked.

Derrick glared at him. "Are you questioning me?"

Luis shook his head. "It will take a few hours to get all elements in place."

Derrick checked his watch. "You have until three p.m."

Luis nodded. "Yes, sir."

Plan D was a distraction he'd hoped to never use. It was just one more complication they didn't need. But this team prepared for all contingencies, and when called upon, they were ready. And this could no longer be ignored. The cops were a problem. Karl was a problem. Plan D would neutralize both. At least long enough for the plan to put into effect, and in the end, that's all that mattered.

He heard Luis sending out the Plan D code over the frequencies as various units called in acknowledgment. Two hours from now, these intruders' determination would be fully tested. They clearly underestimated who they were dealing with. That was fine. Their mistake.

Derrick didn't get where he was by making mistakes.

ABOUT NOON, AS SIMON tore into one of the subs and Lucas kept watch on UnderCity's main entrance, Simon called Doctor Agbeblewu on his cell to check on Lara in anticipation of Emma's visit with her that night.

"She's better today," Agbeblewu said immediately after they exchanged greetings. "The meds seem to be stabilizing her, though it'll be a while 'til her chemistry evens out to normal again."

"Understood," Simon said. "Planning to bring our daughter to visit her tonight, just wanted to be sure I can prepare her."

"Well, redose with dinner," Agbeblewu said, "so she should be well into the dose if you come around seven or eight."

"Okay," Simon said.

"She's been asking for you," Agbeblewu said.

"She has?"

"Would you like to talk with her?" she asked.

"Well, I don't have long. I'm working. But I guess—"

"Hang on." The phone went silent as she transferred the call, then he hear Lara's voice saying, "Hello? Johnny?"

"Hi, Lara," he said.

"You son of a bitch! Get me out of here right now!"

Simon held the phone away from his ear as she left off a string of curses that made him reconsider taking Emma to see her.

Then he heard Agbeblewu in the background, "Lara, that's enough of the abusive language. If you want to talk to people, you need to calm down."

"Calm down?! Is that what you say to all your prisoners here?!"

"No one is a prisoner," Agbeblewu replied.

"Good, so I'm going home now," Lara said.

"Not quite yet," Agbeblewu said, ever patient. Simon was impressed. "We still need a few more days for your meds to stabilize."

"Bullshit! Fucking bitch!"

"Hang on," Agbeblewu said into the phone then the line went dead until she picked it up again, obviously outside at a nurse's station or somewhere else away from Lara. "Sorry about that."

"You call that stable?" Simon said.

"Well, she's very angry with you, and that seems to supersede her normal control, at least at the moment," Agbeblewu said.

"Really makes me want to bring our daughter in there," Simon said.

"I hope you will," Agbeblewu said. "I think she will be pleased to see her. She asks about her a lot, and I think she'll be softer and calmer with Emma than she is with you."

Simon agreed with her but couldn't help still feeling gunshy. "Emma won't forgive me if I don't, so we'll be there."

"Okay," Agbeblewu said. "Don't worry. We'll talk with her about that. See if it makes any difference."

"Good luck," Simon said and hung up, taking another bite of his sub. His past experience was Lara's anger rose at the sound of his voice or mention of his name. With other people, she was calmer. For him, bipolar Lara was a nightmare. She seemed to save most of her rage and resentment to direct at him. He certainly hoped Emma would be spared. Having her mom yell at her like that could devastate her.

"How is she?" Lucas asked beside him, interrupting his thoughts as Simon swallowed the latest mouthful.

"You couldn't hear that?" Simon grunted. "Angry."

"Why?" Lucas shot him a puzzled look before turning back to his binoculars.

"She blames me for being held against her will in the psych ward," Simon says. "Old baggage."

"She needs new suitcases? Shall we buy her some to make her happy?"

Simon chuckled. "Not that kind of baggage. It's a term that means 'old issues between us,'" he explained.

"Oh," Lucas said but sounded just as confused.

Simon's cell rang and he saw Federal Bureau on the Caller ID and answered. "Simon."

"Agent Stein, Detective," Stein said on the other end. "We've identified a Colonel Tobias Derrick who may be involved with your bombers."

"Tobias Derrick?" Simon repeated. "What is he—Special Forces?"

"Rangers," Stein confirmed. "Explosives and ordinance specialist along with his entire squad. Several of them, including Derrick were dishonorably discharged after an incident in Afghanistan that's classified."

"Does that mean not even you can get details?"

"So far, yes," Stein said. "We're working on it."

"Okay."

"He's dangerous, and if he's recruited his old team, they could be capable of anything," Stein added.

"Well, we know they want to kill a whole buncha people, so I'm thinking 'no fuckin' surprise there,'" Simon snapped.

"Fair enough," Stein said. "We'll email a file on him, partially redacted, and some photos. Let us know if you see him there, okay? As soon as possible."

"Will do," Simon said then hung up and finished his sandwich.

A few minutes later, his phone beeped and he found a new email message with attachments from Agent Falk. Simon clicked on it and opened the jpegs. The face staring back at him was the client who'd interrupted his talk with Karl when they'd dropped the subpoena at UnderCity.

"Son of a bitch," he said.

"What's going on?" Lucas asked, still watching through the binoculars.

"I just confirmed we're in deep shit," Simon said.

CHAPTER 21

AFTER SIMON CALLED Stein and Falk to let them know he'd seen Tobias Derrick at UnderCity, the next three hours passed like molasses. Simon finished the other sub about two and then resumed watching the building while Lucas took a break. One of the nice things about Lucas being his partner was he didn't stink and he didn't bring food or other items to add odor to the car. All Simon had to tolerate was what he brought himself, and that was a pleasant change for a stakeout. It gave them less to bitch about with each other, but certainly kept the time from dragging any more than it already was.

The next time he checked his watch, it was getting close to three, which meant Emma would be calling him a little after the hour as she headed home, his request on days when he had to work late and couldn't pick her up. Then he noticed people flowing out of UnderCity looking a bit frightened.

"What's going on?" Lucas asked.

"We have movement," Maberry said over the radio.

"Here, too," Penhall reported seconds later.

Simon rolled down his window and heard the distant blare of a fire alarm. "Fire alarm," he said into the radio. "Anyone smell smoke?"

"What the fuck?" Hanson said back.

"We should help them," Lucas said, reaching for the door.

Simon shot a hand out and pressed him back against the seat. "No. We're undercover."

"But we are police—"

"Others will come," Simon said, and then they heard the first sirens. "We keep our cover and see what happens."

Lucas shifted in his seat, clearly uncomfortable with the idea. "Are you sure?"

"Trust me," Simon said.

"Hmmm," Lucas said, making a face.

"What?" Simon asked.

"Emma said you are always lying when you say that," Lucas said, looking back toward UnderCity.

"Why would I lie about this?" Simon snapped.

Lucas shrugged. "Perhaps you are playing a joke."

"You've really gotta stop talking to my daughter behind my back," Simon said and went back to his binoculars, watching the people milling around UnderCity's parking lot, looking for familiar faces.

IT WAS THAT time of year when it got harder and harder to concentrate the later in the day it was. It was late April and school had less than a month left 'til summer break. Like everyone else, Emma couldn't wait.

She met Julie Ramon at her locker ten minutes after the end of day bell rang at 3:05 p.m. and they planned to walk home together.

"You ready?" Julie asked.

"Almost," Emma said as she finished stuffing the books she needed for homework in her backpack and stacked the rest back in her locker. "Just gotta call my dad real quick."

"Checking in?" Julie teased. "My dad used to make me do that more. Now he just does it with Matt." Her younger brother was two years behind her. She'd told Emma she looked forward to being in separate schools again the following year when the girls were freshmen.

Emma waited until they were through the crowd and outside to dig out her cell phone. She followed Julie off to the side along the curb as they chatted with a couple of friends.

Emma was dialing the phone when a dark van darted out of the line of cars waiting to pick up students and barreled toward them as students, parents, and teachers jumped clear or yelled at the driver. Tires squealed as the van skidded to a stop right in front of them and four men jumped out, grabbed her and Julie, yanking their backpacks off their shoulders and letting them drop to the sidewalk as they shoved them toward the van.

"Get in the fucking van!" one of them said. All four were wearing black ski masks that concealed their heads and faces.

"Who are you? What do you want?!" Julie screamed. "Emma!"

"Get your fucking hands off me!" Emma yelled and fought against the men who'd grabbed both her arms. She managed to press dial on her cell phone then watched as it clattered to the sidewalk ignored.

"Hey! Stop that right now!" a school security guard yelled as he and two male teachers ran toward them.

One of the men drew a gun and fired at the guard and teachers and students and parents screamed and dove for cover.

Julie was already in the van and yelled, "Emma!" again with desperation in her voice.

Emma struggled harder to free herself as the same man said, "Get in the fucking van!" then punched her hard in the stomach and threw her threw the back door, clambering in after her.

"Help!" Emma and Julie both screamed as the van's metal door slid loudly shut, leaving them in shadows. The smell of body odor and sweat from the men abducting them mixed with exhaust leaking into the van and made her cough.

Another man yelled, "Go! Go! Go!"

And the driver took off, tires squealing again and raced around the curved drive and out onto the street. In the distance, Emma heard sirens as the men pressed her and Julie down on their stomachs against the floor of the van with their feet, not very gently.

"Stay the fuck down!" someone commanded and then she felt a sharp pain as a particular blow landing against her lower back and she cried out and stopped struggling.

Her last hopeful thought was maybe her dad had answered the call and heard something. He'd find her. Whatever it took.

Julie was sobbing beside her, her eyes wide and filled

with fear as Emma whispered, "It'll be okay. My dad will come for us."

The men chattered and laughed, drowning her out and she settled in for the ride, trying to figure out what to do.

SIMON AND LUCAS KEPT their eyes peeled on the activity at UnderCity. The firemen would go through the entire building before they cleared it, and given its six miles of tunnels, that could take a while, so Simon expected the employers involved would soon send everyone home. But right now, people were still sitting on or in cars or milling about the parking lot, looking frustrated or worried. Meanwhile, Lucas watched with rapt fascination while Simon monitored the police emergency band.

"They stand outside in case of a fire instead of running?" Lucas observed. "This seems odd."

"Fire alarms can be set off by wiring problems, someone pulling a handle, or even a triggered or faulty smoke detector without there being a real fire," Simon explained. "And kids in school do fire drills to prepare for emergencies, so people are fairly accustomed to alarms being fake. They don't want to leave and find out it was a false alarm and then get in trouble with their employers."

Lucas hrmmphed. "Humans have puzzling rituals."

"Why is this puzzling?" Simon asked. "It seems common sense if you've experienced enough fire alarms."

"Are people not afraid of fire?" Lucas asked.

With the windows down, Simon could smell no smoke. "Yes, but only when they feel the imminent threat," Simon said. "There's no smoke and no flames, so they're feeling safe where they are and anxious for it to be over. Not fear."

Lucas said, "Hmmmm" and kept watching.

Simon's cell vibrated on the dash and he reached for it as the ringer clicked on. The Caller ID read: "Nowlin Middle School," so he clicked to answer. "Simon."

"Detective Simon, this is Cindy Koepp, Assistant Principal at Nowlin," a woman said.

"Yes, I remember you," Simon said. "What can I do for you?" He had expected it to be Emma calling because her phone was broken or its battery dead. He figured this was about academics or volunteer recruitment.

"I'm afraid there's been an incident," Koepp said next.

Simon stiffened on his seat. "What happened?"

"I'm afraid some men have taken Emma and a classmate in the circle drive," Koepp said slowly with hesitation probably resulting from dread.

"What? Taken her?" Simon asked as he reached for the keys and started the Charger. "When?"

Beside him, Lucas dropped the binoculars and looked over, concerned.

"A few minutes ago as school let out," Koepp said. "They shot at one of our security guards when he tried to interfere."

"Son of a bitch!" Simon said and flipped the car into gear, pulling out onto Underground Drive and racing away. He motioned to Lucas, "Notify the others." Then asked into the phone, "Who was the other classmate?"

"Julie Ramon," Koepp said after a short pause, probably

as she debated student privacy then relented because he was a cop.

"Fuck me!" Simon said, then added, "Any description of the vehicle? Make or model?"

"We're reviewing security footage for a clearer view of the van. We think it was a Chevy cargo van, black or dark blue, but the plate seems to be blocked," Koepp said.

"On my way!" Simon hung up and flipped on the siren then hit the switch to turn on the flashing red light on his dash as he wove through traffic backed up by the emergency vehicles partially blocking the road near UnderCity.

"What's going on?" Lucas asked, holding the radio mic in one hand with a puzzled look.

Simon grabbed the mic and keyed it. "Team One 10-7 en route to Nowlin Middle School. My daughter's been kidnapped. Send someone to cover our position. Over."

"Holy shit," Dolby replied. "One of us is on the way. Good luck!"

"Simon out," Simon replied, then dropped the mic and went back to driving as he raced up the on-ramp and into busy afternoon traffic on I-435, headed South.

"Get on the traffic cams and see if you can find a dark blue or black Chevy cargo van in Independence near Nowlin," Simon said to his partner.

"Independence PD has a different traffic system," Lucas protested, but Simon cut him off.

"Hack it!" Simon snapped.

"What about my T.O.—"

"DC Melson cleared you per Becker a couple days ago to use whatever resources you can on this case," Simon said.

"Oh, no one told me."

"This is the first time it's come up," Simon said and Lucas went to work.

It took nine minutes, with Simon pushing seventy-five as often as he could to reach the Middle School from north Kansas City. Lucas reported no luck with traffic cams, but Simon knew it was like searching for a needle on a silver-colored floor so he kept driving.

Reaching Nowlin, Simon pulled up into the circle drive behind several emergency vehicles, jumped out, and ran up to where Koepp and a school security guard were talking with several officers and a detective from Independence P.D. He recognized Emma's backpack lying on the sidewalk near a similar red one he thought was Julie's nearby.

He badged them as he hurried over and said, "What've we got?"

"Detective Simon's daughter was one of the victims," Koepp quickly explained as Lucas joined them. She motioned to the IPD Detective. "This is Detective McCain and Officers Craig and Jones." McCain was late thirties, with short red hair and a cheap three-piece suit, his shoes shined to perfection. Craig and Jones wore uniforms. Craig was short and chunky with a trim goatee and mustache, Jones black with no facial hair but taller, his muscles toned. Both looked to be early forties.

"Not a whole helluva lot yet," McCain jumped right in. "A dark brown Chevy cargo van jumped out the line and swerved over to here where your daughter and her friend were standing." He motioned to where the backpacks had fallen, acting it out as he continued, "Four men jumped out, forced the girls inside, one of them saw the security guard running up and fired six shots, then jumped in the van and they raced south down Hardy there." He pointed.

"Anyone hit?" Simon asked.

McCain shook his head. "Two slugs in the wall behind those bushes over there, two more in that bench in front of them, and the others ricocheted off the cement stoop."

"Two teachers, the guard, and several students were in the line of fire," Craig added.

"Fortunately, they all missed," Koepp said.

"Descriptions?" Simon asked, continuing to systematically run down the list of obvious questions.

"They wore ski masks, but two were white and two black," McCain said. "We got security camera footage there"—he pointed to one camera and then another high up on the school's outer walls—"and there."

"And one of the students shot film on her cell phone," Jones added.

"Can I see it?" Simon asked.

The three cops exchanged a look, then McCain nodded. "Sure."

"Did you get a plate?" Simon asked.

"On the cell," Jones said.

"You issued a BOLO?" Lucas interjected and they all glanced at him.

"My partner," Simon explained.

Craig nodded. "Yes, and dispatch is calling it out to other local agencies."

"Get it to the Feds, too," Simon said. "These may be suspects related to our bombing investigation and two murdered cops."

Craig nodded again and stepped back to key the shoulder mic on his radio and call it in.

McCain held up an evidence bag with a phone that looked like Emma's. "We found this on the ground just inside the curb. The last call was to you."

Simon cursed to himself as he fumbled in his pocket for his cell. He and Lucas had been jarred so suddenly from total focus on the case to alarm at Emma's kidnapping he'd forgotten to check it. He pulled it out and hit a button to turn on the display. It showed a missed call from Emma. "Fuck." He dialed voicemail and put it on speaker.

They heard a man yell, "Hey! Stop that right now!" Then six shots being fired and screams. A girl yelled, "Emma!" Simon recognized Julie Ramon's voice and heard her desperation. Next a man said, "Get in the fucking van!" followed by sounds of a struggle and both girls crying "Help!" A van door thundered shut and a man yelled, "Go! Go! Go!" then tires squealed and they heard Koepp and other students and adults talking over each other, discussing what had just happened.

"That's pretty similar to the cell phone video," Koepp said.

"I wanna talk to that security guard," Simon said.

"That's me," the school guard standing beside Koepp said, hand raised, speaking for the first time.

"Show me those videos please," Simon said.

They all headed together into the school toward the security office.

THE CELL PHONE video was more illuminating than the school security videos for sure, but in the end, they all basically showed the visuals to Simon's recording with a few additions—people dodging the racing van and then bullets, men grabbing the girls, more yelling, and most, importantly, a good shot of the license plate on the van. Simon raged when he saw one abductor punch his daughter in the stomach. He'd never so badly wanted to kill anyone. Lucas put a gentle hand on his arm, sensing it.

When the videos had run a couple times, Simon asked IPD to send copies over to KCPD to help the bombing investigation and they headed back to Central. IPD promised to run the plate and pass along the info as soon as they had. Afterward, they'd run him through the usual questions, of course: Who might want to harm him or Lara or his daughter? Did they have any enemies? Notice any strangers lurking around? Any odd occurrences? Simon answered these and a dozen more with great impatience. It was so hard to focus when his world was falling apart. He felt like a garment ripped and torn on a clothesline after being left outside in a storm.

Finally, when they'd exhausted their list, he gave them his phone numbers and hurried back to the Charger with Lucas on his heels. Lucas insisted on driving because of Simon's state.

"These motherfuckers are going to pay!" Simon said over and over as Lucas drove. Simon was perched on the edge of the passenger seat, his hand tight on the door as if ready to spring out at a moment's notice as his eyes darted about looking for any sign of Emma.

"We will find them," Lucas offered again and again.

When they got back to Central, fifteen minutes later, Lucas followed as Simon stormed into the squad room to find Agents Falk and Stein meeting with Becker, LaDue and Benson from Bomb Squad, Maberry, and Dolby.

"What happened?" Dolby asked immediately as Simon and Lucas pushed into the crowded room.

"Those motherfuckers took my daughter and Julie Ramon!" Simon shouted.

"The daughter of the UnderCity security man?" Falk asked.

"Yes," Lucas confirmed.

"I'm sorry, John," Becker said and others offered similar sentiment.

"Tell us what happened," Stein said. "What leads do they have?"

Simon ran it down for them in detail then said the BOLO and videos should be forwarded shortly, along with details on the van's plate.

"Jesus," LaDue said when he'd finished. LaDue had a daughter of his own in middle school.

"It's every cop parent's worst nightmare," Benson added.

"I want these fuckers," Simon said. "I want them now."

"We were just discussing how to proceed," Stein said.

"Our people will grab up Karl Ramon as soon as he's located," Falk said.

"He wasn't at the school," Simon said. "Where did he go?"

"We're not sure," Becker said. "He slipped out sometime after you did amidst the chaos."

"It might have been while I was moving around to cover your position," Maberry said.

"Fuck," Simon said. "Get a BOLO out on his ass right now!"

"Already done," Becker said.

"We'll grab him as soon as he's located and bring him here," Falk said.

"Good. I need to talk to that bastard," Simon snapped. "No more holding out. He's going to talk."

"We'll handle it," Stein said.

"Oh, I'm in the room!" Simon said through gritted teeth.

"John, you're too close to this one," Becker said gently.

Simon glared at her. "I'm in that fucking room, JoAnn!"

Becker and the FBI Agents exchanged a look that said they'd discuss it again later, then moved on.

"We've got a call in to management at UnderCity," Stein continued. "We're asking them to close down for three days over the weekend claiming water damage from sprinklers triggered by the alarm."

"Won't renters want to get in and assess damage?" Dolby asked.

"We're giving them a story that most of it was in the UnderCity offices and storage and that they want the chance for maintenance and cleanup crews to work without extra traffic," Falk said.

"It won't stop the questions, but it should buy us time," Stein added.

"The biggest problem is locating Derrick and his team in such a large complex," Becker said.

"Right," Falk agreed. "We have people reviewing further security video footage pulled from UnderCity today and we've got blueprints and rental agreements."

"We're going to send in dogs to see if we can locate C-4, fertilizer, or fuel oil," Benson said.

"With drones to confirm any finds with GPS and video," LaDue added.

"We're also sealing off all exits," Becker said. "No one goes in or out without our okay and subject to searches."

"Which means they can't take the girls to UnderCity," Lucas said.

"Not unless they slipped in before we put units in place," Becker said.

"And slipped past our surveillance teams," Maberry added.

"There was only a small window for that to happen," Becker said. "They'd have had to come straight back from Nowlin."

"I thought the firemen were keeping people out?" Lucas said.

"In theory, yes," Becker said. "But it got a bit chaotic once they decided to send everyone home."

"Get the description of that brown van out to the teams and see if anyone saw one like it," Simon said.

"Absolutely," Becker said and turned to LaDue and Benson. "When do you send in the dogs?"

"Tomorrow morning," Benson said.

"First thing," LaDue added.

"We'll be there," Simon said.

"Actually," Becker said, "Lucas needs to meet the Shooting Team at the range first thing tomorrow."

"Why?" Lucas asked.

"They want to do some tests to verify your statement from the Golden Boy incident," Becker said and looked at Simon. "I want you with him. You know him best and someone needs to look out for him. The union rep is coming, too."

"I need to be at UnderCity," Simon said, shaking his head. No way was he sitting on the sidelines for this.

"You can come there as soon as it's finished," Becker said. "If anything comes up before, we'll call you."

"Don't do this to me, JoAnn," Simon snapped. "No way I'm sitting this out."

"What you need to do right now is go home and see if they call you," Becker said.

"You really think these are the types to ask for ransom?" Simon scoffed.

"No, but they obviously want something," Stein said. "Or why bother with your daughter and her friend?"

"Leverage," Simon said. "We're getting too close."

"Still, they may call," Falk said.

"I have my cell," Simon said, leaning forward in the chair, his jaw set, one hand on a knee. "I'll be waiting."

Becker sighed. "John, go home. Lucas can stay with you. There's nothing you can do right now but wait. Let us do some follow up."

"God damn it—"

"That's an order, Detective!" Becker snapped. "Don't push me. I promise I'll get you in on it as much as we can."

"Meaning I'm sidelined!" Simon stood stiffly, fists clenched. "Fuck that. Call me if you need me." He darted out the door and headed for the parking lot.

"Lucas, stay with him!" he heard Becker call and then Lucas was hurrying to catch up. Simon just kept walking.

"Where are you going?" Lucas asked as he caught up at the Charger and Simon unlocked it and opened the driver's door.

"Go home, Lucas," Simon said, slamming his door. "I don't want you getting into more trouble because of me."

"Where will you go?" Lucas asked.

"To shake some trees, do whatever it takes to find Emma," Simon said and climbed into the Charger. The passenger door clicked open and Lucas slid in beside him. "What are you doing?!"

"We're partners," Lucas said matter-of-factly. "You go, I go."

"Get out," Simon said, motioning sharply.

"No," Lucas insisted.

Simon glared at him.

"Emma means a lot to me, too," Lucas said and met his gaze, unwavering.

"Fine!" Simon turned the key and started the engine, then shifted into reverse and backed hurriedly from the space.

"Where are we going?" Lucas asked again.

"I don't know," Simon said. "Just shut the fuck up. I need to think."

"Okay," Lucas said and didn't say another word as Simon threw the Charger into drive and headed out onto Linwood headed west.

THE FIRST THING she noticed was the air was filled with the overwhelming odor of chemicals or was it poison? Whatever it was she could breathe and the smell was fading, even in the mere two hours since they'd arrived here, but it was far from gone. Her captors had blindfolded them in the van, shortly after leaving the school, and when they'd been dragged from the van fifteen minutes or so later, the blindfolds had been left on. Since then, Emma had heard several male voices with various accents and tonal differences, but seen nothing.

She felt the hard stone floor beneath her and she felt Julie pressed against her right side. They were sitting in chairs inches from some sort of wall, she could sense that, but with their hands and feet bound, exploring the area around them was impossible for the moment.

They sat that way, waiting, occasionally whispering back and forth to reassure each other—Emma doing most of the reassuring because Julie was fraught with fear—until the voice drew closer again and someone kicked lightly at their feet. Then the blindfolds were yanked free and bright lights flooded their eyes, blinding them.

Emma squinted and blinked, her eyes adjusting as she tried to see around her, see faces. The closest, staring down at her was a Hispanic man in his thirties, around her father's height, bulky with muscle, his hair crew cut military-style. His piercing green eyes bore into her as he smiled. On someone else she supposed it would be warm, but on him it was menacing.

"Well, ladies, how nice of you to join us," the man said.

"Who are you?" Emma demanded.

"Where are we?" Julie muttered from beside her.

"Neither question is of any matter to you," the man replied. "But you are our guests for the next day or two. Don't worry, we have no desire to harm you. We just need you with us for safekeeping for a time."

"You kidnapped us, beat us, tied us up, blindfolded and scared us half to death!" Emma spat. "Is that the no fucking harm you're talking about?!"

The man chuckled, his men guffawing behind him. Now that she could see them they were muscular, too, with military cuts, and like him—the leader perhaps—were all dressed in plain black with military-style boots. But there were only two now. Some of those who'd abducted them had apparently left or were outside.

"You're a feisty one, aren't you, Emma?" the man grinned. "Good. That means you keep your old man on his toes. No one deserves it more." He leaned down and cupped her face in one hand, then suddenly squeezed hard, not quite to the point of hurting her but enough to silence her protests and get her attention. "Well, you save that for daddy, girl, you hear me? You just behave yourself for us and you'll have no problems. Make yourself a pain in the ass and you won't find us tolerant, okay? Understand?"

He held her a moment, locking her gaze on his, then let

go, shoving her head away as he stepped back and stared down at her again with the same smile he'd shown when she first saw his face.

"Got it," she snapped.

"Okay, okay," Julie hurried to add.

The man gave a satisfied nod and turned to his men. "Get them rations and keep an eye on them."

"What about our assignments?" a Hispanic man asked.

"Trade off," the man ordered. "They are never alone. One of you at all times until you get the signal. I have to get back."

"Yes, sirs" echoed from around the chamber—she saw it now, they were in some sort of office. There were file cabinets along one wall and a couple of cubicles with computers on desks and a printer beside one.

Then the Hispanic man left, leaving the two men to watch over them. One, an Asian, sat in a chair across the room and sneered at them as if daring them to make trouble and give him an excuse to do his worst. The other nodded to him and slipped outside a door, shutting it behind him.

Emma looked down at her body, checking herself. Her clothes were wrinkled and a little dirty, but she otherwise looked fine. So did Julie. Her dad would come. He'd never stop until he found them. This she knew for certain. So she'd bide her time and try and keep Julie calm. Look for a chance to send a message if she could get a phone or find a computer, but wait, pretending to be the obedient, scared little girl.

At least until the time came she had to do what her father had been teaching her in case of trouble. That she would save until she needed it, and she'd make them sorry.

CHAPTER 22

THEY DROVE AROUND for a while before Simon finally wandered back to Nowlin to look over the scene again. It was after six p.m. but there was still daylight, so he parked and walked around with Lucas following. Thanks to Lucas' inbuilt memory recorders, he was able to reenact the abduction while Simon watched from different angles, using the Charger as a stand-in for the Chevy van. Lucas played back the recordings in his head and matched every player move for move, pausing as he took each position, while Simon examined the lines of sight. When he came to the shooter, Simon then traced the potential trajectories looking for missing bullets IPD's crime scene team had not recovered.

Over and over, again and again, they reenacted it, until Simon was so exhausted he sat down on the school's stoop to think, and that's when Lucas found the bullet, one of the two that had ricocheted off the stoop—this one ending up embedded in a short tree newly planted around a corner a few feet away. From its position, it had to have traveled an odd trajectory. It was a miracle it hadn't hit a person instead. Lucas pointed it out and went to the Charger for an evidence bag from the trunk as Simon stood and came over to kneel and dig it out with his car key.

"9 mm," he said as Lucas came and held the bag open.

Simon popped it out and watched it fall into the bag then took it from Lucas and examined it. "Common Special Forces use." Of course, it was also one of the most commonly shot rounds in the world period, so that made it significant only with what they already knew.

"I'll call the Independence Police," Lucas offered.

"No," Simon said, "we'll drive it over there and see if they found anything else."

This time, Simon took the wheel and drove them north on Hardy then east several blocks on 78, then north again on Noland Road to IPD headquarters. He parked in visitor parking and then badged his way past the front desk into an elevator for the detective's squad. McCain was still at his desk.

The squad room smelled like most did at night—the odor of stale coffee and dusty files mixed with stale boxes and overloaded trash bins. Simon held up the evidence bag as they approached. "Found one of your missing bullets."

"Where was it?" McCain asked as he held up the evidence bag and examined its contents. "Nine mil."

"A tree around the corner," Simon said, nodding.

McCain's brow furrowed. "Odd that our people missed it."

"It was an odd place, very small tree," Lucas explained.

"And the trajectory was odd, almost as if it zigzagged," Simon said.

"But we know it didn't so some freak thing," McCain said.

"Exactly," Simon agreed.

"It's a miracle no one was hit," Lucas added.

McCain grunted. "Was going back tomorrow to look for it with a couple of crime scene techs, so thanks. Any sign of the other one?"

Lucas shook his head. "No."

"Well, thanks," McCain said and slid the bag inside his top drawer. He'd deliver it to the crime scene person tomorrow when the lab opened again, Simon figured. That's what he would do. McCain leaned back in his chair. "Nothing new on our end, though we did talk with a couple witnesses who saw the van speeding by before it hopped onto the highway."

"Where?" Simon asked.

"Blue Ridge Cutoff," McCain said.

So I-70, Simon noted. That could take them anywhere.

"Go home," McCain said. "You look exhausted."

"He is," Lucas agreed.

Simon leaned against the side of McCain's cube, shaking his head. "I'd just be going crazy."

"I understand, but not much you can do 'til we get more leads," McCain said. "Your people searching UnderCity?"

"Bomb squad's sending in dogs tomorrow morning," Simon said.

McCain nodded. "Good. I heard they found the other girl's father at a bar somewhere, he was playing a gig." He shook his head, nose wrinkling with disgust as his lip curled. "Guess he wasn't too worried about his daughter."

"What time?" Simon asked, glancing at a clock on the wall.

"About half an hour ago," McCain said. "They filled me

in on your possible suspects in case anything helps."

"Shit," Simon said and hurried for the door.

"He shouldn't go down there," McCain said with a concerned look at Lucas, then raised his voice to call, "They'll handle it, Simon. Feds are all over it!"

But Simon was out the door, cutting him off and hurrying back toward the lobby. Lucas caught up with him as they got to the car.

"They won't want you to talk to him," Lucas said.

"Let them try to stop me," Simon said as he slipped behind the wheel.

"John—"

"Shut the fuck up or get out, Lucas," Simon snapped. "They've got Emma, okay? No way I'm not going in."

Tires squealed as he spun the car in reverse out of the space and raced onto the road, headed west.

AS THEY RACED UP the sidewalk toward Central from the rear parking lot, Simon and Lucas met Dolby, who was headed for her car.

"Which room?" Simon demanded.

Dolby looked surprised to see him. "They're not here."

"Where?!"

She exhaled. "Headquarters."

Simon turned and hurried back for his car, Lucas

following as Dolby called after them, "John, they won't let you near him. Becker and the Feds are there. We were barred, too!"

The slamming driver's door of the Charger cut her off and moments later, Simon was racing out of the lot headed downtown along 71 Highway. The entire way flashbacks to moments with Emma played in his brain like home movies— Emma as a toddler taking her first steps; Emma holding his hand as he walked her to the school bus one of her first days of kindergarten; Emma in a tutu at a dance recital as Simon looked on with pride; Emma and Lucas doing a silly dance in her bedroom—all moments that captured his most precious thing, his little girl. A little girl who was now in danger all because of him.

And with each memory his rage grew that much more.

Five minutes later, they were racing into KCPD Headquarters on Locust through a side entrance, headed for elevators up to the seventh floor, where the homicide unit was based.

The seventh floor walls were white, the lighting low, Simon immediately headed for the interrogation rooms just outside the key coded entrance to the homicide squad room and burst through the door.

A very distressed, disheveled and tired Karl Ramon was at a white table with LaDue, Bailey, and Stein surrounding him.

"We don't believe you, Karl," Bailey was saying. "You were seen with this man, Derrick—"

They turned, reacting to Simon as he raced up, leaned across the table and yanked Karl onto its surface by his lapels, holding his face inches from his own. "Enough bullshit, Karl! Your daughter and mine are about to be killed because you're helping these assholes! You talk or I'm going to do terrible things until you do!"

Hands grabbed at him, voices speaking urgently: "Simon, stop." "This isn't the way, man." "Let him go, John."

Simon ignored them as Karl sputtered for words.

"Tell us what you fucking know!" Simon demanded again.

Then hands were pulling him off as Bailey grabbed Karl from beside him and slid him back down into the chair.

"Enough, Detective! You get out of here," Stein was scolding. "We're handling this!"

"John, this isn't the way," Bailey urged.

The whole time Karl's eyes didn't leave Simon's, and he saw the grief, the fear, the desperation, and the complete sense of loss there but felt zero sympathy.

He heard others bursting into the room behind him through the open door. Then more hands on him.

"John, come with me," Becker said sternly.

"John, it'll be okay," Lucas added. "Come with us please."

"He came to a club," Karl finally said.

And everyone stopped.

"Who did?" Simon said.

"Derrick, I guess," Karl said. "I didn't know his name."

"Which club?" Simon asked. Becker, Lucas, and the others released him, stepping back.

"The Waterfront," Karl replied.

"I know it," Bailey said. "Inside the Crossroads Plaza,

right?"

Karl nodded. Simon hadn't recognized the club but he knew the hotel.

"What did he say?" Simon slid into a chair across from Karl and took a deep breath. Behind him, he heard people leaving and the door closing. Probably Lucas and Becker. Bailey was still beside Karl, and he felt Stein and LaDue standing over his shoulders on either side.

"He threatened my kids," Karl said. "He knew their names, their schools, where we lived. He said if I didn't do what he said, he'd hurt them."

"What did he want you to do?" Bailey asked.

"They wanted an open space in UnderCity, someplace they could set up and use without anyone taking notice. For some kind of job, but they never told me that," Karl continued. "It had to be big enough for box trucks though, and they gave me this thumb drive to disable security cameras when they came in and out."

"How many were there?" Stein asked.

"I only saw one or two at first," Karl said, "but I'm pretty sure a few others came and went after they'd settled in."

"When was this?" LaDue asked.

"About a week ago, maybe a little longer," Karl said.

"Can you show us which unit they're set up in?" Simon asked. "On a map."

"Sure," Karl said.

"And we want you to look at some footage, see if you recognize any of their faces," LaDue said.

"Okay," Karl said and nodded.

"What else?" Bailey asked.

"That's it," Karl said. "Just they saw me with Simon, our daughters are friends from school, and they warned me about it. I think that's why they took her." His hands shot across the table and grabbed Simon's as his eyes glistened, taking on a pleading, sad look. "Are they going to hurt them? Please tell me they won't hurt my baby girl!" And he started crying, sobs bursting out as tears shone on his cheeks.

"I don't know," Simon said and pulled his hand free as he leaned back in the chair. "That's why you need to tell us everything so we can try and stop them, try and save our girls, Karl."

"I don't know anything else," Karl said through sobs, shaking his head again and again. Then his eyes widened and chair legs squealed against the floor as he jumped to his feet. "My son! I have to get home!"

"We sent people to pick him up, Karl, don't worry," Stein said then motioned to LaDue. "Let's get him some water."

As LaDue turned and headed for the door, Stein slid into a chair next to Simon. "Karl, we need to ask you some questions—about details, anything you remember. Even the littlest thing might help, okay? We're gonna get you some water, and then we need you to calm down if you can and talk to us."

Karl nodded again, his voice cracking, "I'll try."

LaDue returned a few minutes later with a white plastic cup of water. Karl drank it down and LaDue went for another one as Bailey handed Karl some paper towels and he wiped at his face.

For the next hour, they sucked Karl dry like a parched

mosquito on a tourist—every piece of information, no matter how small, that he knew from descriptions of suspects to vehicles and anything else. When they were finished, he collapsed on his chair, spent, and Simon and the others went down the hall to converse with Becker, Tucker, Benson, Lucas, and Hanson and Penhall who were sitting on chairs in a waiting room.

"He pointed out where he set them up," Stein said. "But that doesn't guarantee they haven't moved."

"We have descriptions of vehicles and people—he thinks a dozen at least," Bailey said.

"So what next?" Becker asked, looking at the FBI Agents.

"I think we still send the robots," Stein said.

"It seems the best plan," Falk agreed. "We need to know for sure where they are to plan any assault or action. And it would help if we had some idea how much explosives we're dealing with. The robots can't tell us exactly but they can give a damn good estimate, and we can get a good idea of how many locations they've wired."

"So far," Penhall added.

"What about the girls?" Simon asked.

"If they're there, the drone can probably tell us," Hanson said. "It will pinpoint locations with GPS, but it also has cameras and sound. Hopefully, we'll hear something that clues us in."

"Which means it's a long shot," Simon said and turned toward the large bay window that looked out on the city at night. "God damn it! I want these fuckers!"

"We all do," Becker said.

"We'll do everything we can, Detective," Falk said. "Use

every resource."

"Go home and get some rest, John," Becker said, then off his look, added, "If you can. You go with Lucas to the range in the morning then check in with me and we'll hopefully know by then what the robots found."

"I'm not going to just stand by and do nothing, Sergeant," Simon said, facing her again. "No way."

Her eyes showed clear understanding.

"We'll be checking with our surveillance team again shortly and take it from there," Falk said.

"Someone will be working all night," Stein said. "We're taking Karl right now to look at videos."

Simon waved a hand dismissively and headed for the elevators, Lucas following. It was like the adrenaline fueled energy that had been driving him had suddenly been sucked out. He wobbled a moment as he reached for the elevator button and Lucas reached out to steady him.

"You okay?" Lucas asked.

"You drive," Simon said and tossed him the keys.

The elevator opened and they stepped on. And Simon remembered very little after that until he woke up the next morning in his bed.

THE KCPD GUN RANGE was located near the Police Academy and Shoal Creek Station off N.E. Pleasant Valley Road and I-435 in north Kansas City. It was also not far from the unsightly LDS Temple, a big glaring white monstrosity dominating the horizon straight north of Shoal Creek. At 8 a.m., the sky was crystal clear and bright blue with scattered cumulus cloud banks and warm sunshine highlighting the abundant trees and foliage that prospered in the area surrounding Shoal Creek itself.

The gun range was in a large, square one-story building of white stone with an angled brown metal roof down the hill behind the Academy itself. It was large and the air around it was filled with the humming of its large power generators and air conditioning system. There was a small parking lot in front of it. If you continued on past, you'd drive past the hill holding the running track behind the Academy and enter the driving training course with its orange cones and white lines where officers and trainees alike practiced defensive and offensive driving skills.

Simon parked the Charger in a space across from the range's dark brown front entrance and they walked over together. A brown handicap sign was next to a keypad entry but during regular business hours, the range was unlocked so they walked right in.

Lucas was scheduled to meet the two BBs and his Union rep, Officer Doaa, inside the KCPD gun range which had rows of numbered lanes with targets featuring various criminal personas that could be adjusted to different distances depending upon the particular test or skill the shooter wanted to focus on.

Firearms Instructor Larry Hightshoe met them beside lane number 6 with a nod. After shaking everyone's hands, he handed everyone sound-muting headphones and Lucas the Glock 19C that had been confiscated after he'd shot Golden Boy. "What we need you to do, Officer George, is to stand here—" he positioned himself in shooting stance in lane 6 motioning to Lucas "—and shoot like you did that day. I'll position the targets. The ladies are going to take some pictures and do some measurements as they observe. Then, when we're satisfied we have what we need, we'll try the shooting gallery for a bit, okay?"

Lucas nodded. "I understand." Hightshoe stepped clear and Lucas assumed the position he'd demonstrated in lane 6.

"What's this supposed to prove?" Simon asked.

"It's part of our investigation," Beebe said sternly, holding a tape measure in one hand and an iPad in the other.

Her partner, Bahm, held a camera and another iPad. Her face was gentler. "We want to test Officer George's accuracy and ability under some conditions so we can satisfy ourselves about the claims his reaction times and abilities differ from those of other officers."

Lucas nodded again. Simon only grunted.

"I am ready," Lucas added.

"Let me position the first target," Hightshoe said. He pushed some buttons on a column behind and across from the lanes and slid the target in lane 6 toward them about ten feet. Then he adjusted the targets to either side different distances. "What we want you to do is shoot all three in any order as fast as you can as if you were reacting to a threat."

"How many times?" Lucas inquired.

"Once should be enough," Beebe said sternly.

"We'll run it two or three times, yeah, so once each is fine," Hightshoe agreed. "Okay?"

Lucas checked the Glock quickly, following his training in how to prep a weapon, then readied himself. "Ready."

"Fire at will," Hightshoe said.

Within seconds, each target fluttered as a bullet hole appeared center mass of the figure shown on the target. Hightshoe shot Simon an awed look. Simon smiled.

"Weapon down," Hightshoe said and Lucas held the gun in safe position, pointed down.

Beebe handed Bahm an end of the tape, which she held next to Lucas, then walked forward. They measured all the way to each target, one at a time, with Beebe recording figures onto a chart on her iPad.

When they'd finished and Beebe had returned to her position behind them, Hightshoe looked at the two BBs. "Did you get that?"

"Yes," Bahm and Beebe said together.

"Okay," Hightshoe said. "Let's try it again. Same targets, same positions."

They did it three times with the same setup but at the end, the targets showed one hole each. Slightly enlarged, of course, but Lucas had nailed it exactly the same each time. Hightshoe looked stunned. Bahm nodded. Beebe remained stern.

After that, they tried a few more setups and distances, some just focused on the same lane, some spread out. Same measuring and recording with occasional redirection from Bahm or Beebe to Hightshoe as he set up targets.

After about forty minutes, the two BBs relaxed a little, studying their iPads.

"Okay, I think we're ready for the gallery now," Hightshoe said.

"Yes," Bahm agreed.

As Hightshoe led them from the lanes out through a

corridor into the nearby room where he'd set up a temporary shooting gallery, Simon's cell buzzed in his pocket and he pulled the headphones off his right ear as he answered it. "Simon."

A man grunted. "How are you today, Detective?" The voice had a slight accent that seemed familiar but Simon couldn't place it.

"Who is this?" he asked.

"If you want to see your daughter again, listen very carefully," the man said and Tobias Derrick standing near the security booth in UnderCity flashed through Simon's head. He stiffened, his hand clenching around the phone.

"Derrick?" he asked. "Where's my fucking daughter, you son of a bitch?!"

Derrick chuckled. "Very good, Detective. You've done some work, I see."

"Where's Emma?" Simon demanded. "If you hurt one hair on her head—"

"Yeah, yeah," Derrick said and tsked. "You follow instructions and she won't be harmed."

"What instructions—some bullshit about backing off? Looking the other way? No way I do that," Simon said defiantly.

"You'll hear from us when the time is right," Derrick said, ignoring him. "If anyone tries to interfere or comes inside our location uninvited, one call is all it would take..." He let his voice trail off but the meaning was clear.

"I'm coming for you, motherfucker!" Simon shouted into the phone, his voice rising even as his throat felt dry and parched and his vision clouded over, his heartbeat pounding in his ears. "You and everyone with you! You understand?! You fucked with the wrong city and the wrong cop!"

By the time he'd finished, his arms and legs were shaking and he had to plant his feet to steady himself as the line went dead and he looked up. Hightshoe, Beebe, and Bahm were staring at him.

"Can we get this over with?!" Simon snapped, popping his headphones back in place. "We have real work to do!"

He turned and marched over to stand by Hightshoe, motioning harshly toward the shooting gallery path which was marked with large white letters on the floor reading "START".

Hightshoe spoke into a headset microphone, pushing a button on the cord that dangled down around his neck. "Okay, Officer, let's run it," he said.

Inside the shooting gallery, Lucas wore a similar headset and held his Glock ready as he moved through a maze. Targets in various guises would pop up suddenly from positions all around him. His job was to assess them as friend or foe, danger or not, and react accordingly. Once again, Lucas only shot the targets representing criminal threats and he shot them in seconds of popping up, straight in center mass. The boom of each shot echoed off the walls despite expensive soundproofing and headphones. Again, Hightshoe looked amazed. Simon was pretty impressed himself. Not a single mistake, not a single miss.

When he was done, Bahm and Beebe walked through the gallery and took various measurements, referring often to playback video on their iPads of Lucas' run through the gallery, while Lucas stood with Simon and Hightshoe, waiting. They ran it three more times with different variations to the same results, before dismissing Lucas and

Simon to return to work. Both took off their headphones and handed them to Hightshoe, then Lucas handed him the Glock and followed Simon to the car.

"How did I do?" Lucas asked as they climbed into the Charger.

"You kicked ass and took names," Simon said.

Lucas' brow furrowed. "I did not kick anyone, but I remember their names."

Simon laughed. "Ask Emma to explain it sometime, okay?" He shifted the Charger into gear and backed out of the parking space, then shifted again and accelerated onto the main drive, headed out toward Pleasant Valley Road and 435 again.

"I hope Emma will be okay," Lucas said with an innocence and sincerity only he could pull off.

"She'll be," Simon said. "When I get those men who took her, they're the ones who'll be hurting." He said it with such intensity that Lucas looked over, assessing him, but remained silent, despite a sudden look of concern.

Simon took the on-ramp to 435 and headed for UnderCity.

DERRICK HEARD THE robots before his men reported seeing them on their cameras. The noise of their whining servos echoed through the tunnels and walls around him. The first thing that came into view was the long tank-like tread over wheels, followed by a reinforced chassis and body, with 4-axis arms with giant vice-like claws at one end and smaller stabilizer arms at the rear. Derrick had seen similar models in Afghanistan.

"The cops," Luis said.

"Not unexpected," Derrick said calmly. "They never listen."

"Can we have some fun?" one of his men asked with an eager grin.

Derrick nodded. "Don't waste too much ammo."

Three of his men grunted, grabbing weapons, and heading for the door.

Derrick and Luis watched on the security cameras as the police dogs, followed by two black drones, made their way into camera range in the undeveloped areas of UnderCity moving in the direction of where his team were hard at work.

Luis got on the comm channel, "All teams, stand by. We have search robots and two drones. Hold position."

Derrick keyed his mic. "Do not reveal yourselves under any circumstances. If the robots spot you, take them out, but only if absolutely necessary. We have a team already on task."

"Copy," the responses came back, one after the other for the next couple of minutes.

On the screen, the robots were halted and their sensors beeping as they clustered around one of the walls near where one of Derrick's teams had been working, indicating they'd caught the scent of fuel oil or fertilizer, Derrick figured. He watched as the pack moved along the tunnel, spread out, then slowly converged, honing in on the blocked entrance to the cavern he was in right now, where they clustered and activated their sensors again.

Then he heard gunshots and one of the robots was stalled mid-roll as automatic fire raked across its body, denting metal and sending up sparks as it beeped in protest.

"Get the drone!" Luis said beside him, even though none of the shooters could hear. "Get the drone!"

More shots rang out, and more robots were hit, one even falling over. Then Derrick heard a ricochet and thought it looked like something had struck the drone and deflected. The men around him cheered.

"Do it again!" Luis shouted.

THE COMMAND POST had been set up on 42nd Street, one of the back entrances to UnderCity, much closer to the undeveloped areas. A uniform admitted Simon through the barrier and he parked beside two unmarked cars and hurried with Lucas to join Becker, Hanson, Penhall, Stein, and Falk as they monitored the drone's feed on a video screen with the dog handlers.

The screen jumped and one of the screens spun as its robot source tipped over.

"They're shooting the fucking 'bots!" Hanson said.

"I think they're shooting for the drone, too," Penhall said from his seat at a control panel Simon figured was operating the drone.

The screen jumped again as the drone shook from a

stream of bullets. Then a round black object flew across the screen and landed at the base of one of the robots.

"Is that a fucking grenade?!" Penhall shouted, rocking on his feet.

"Oh fuck no. Pull them outta there," Hanson said as he and Penhall worked the controls. On camera, the robots hesitated as one more shook from incoming automatic fire, dents appearing across its body, then fell as its companions turned and began rolling back the way they'd come.

"Fucking bastards!" Penhall said, and the image on the screens began retreating backwards.

"I thought these things could withstand sizeable explosives," Becker said.

"Depending where they are when it goes off, but not two hundred rounds at once," Hanson snapped.

"Or a grenade right under them," Penhall added.

Becker raised her hands in apology as Simon asked, "Did they find anything?"

"We got some readings," Hanson said. "Didn't get far enough in to find much."

"They're either there or were there," Falk said. "Did you get the coordinates?"

Penhall nodded and pointed to a figure on the screen. "Captured."

"That doesn't help us if we can't get in without getting shot," Becker said.

"It's a start," Stein said. "We know where we are. Now we have to figure out how to take them down."

"Looks simple," Simon joked and they all stared at him as

he chuckled. They were truly fucked.

CHAPTER 23

EMMA AWOKE WITH a start, unable to remember when she'd managed to nod off. As she lifted her head, a pain shot through her neck and she cried out. "Ow!"

"What happened?!" Julie said, startling awake beside her.

"Nothing," Emma whispered, suddenly worried they'd draw attention from their abductors. "Slept funny."

"Oh," Julie whispered back. "Don't scare me like that."

"Sorry."

Footsteps approached and the Hispanic man sneered down at them. "Since you're awake, we got you sub sandwiches. Man's on his way back right now. Hope you like ham and cheese and Diet Cokes." Then he chuckled. "If not, tough shit."

"No tomato!" Emma snapped.

"Eat what we give you and be glad you have anything," the man replied.

"I'm allergic," Emma replied even though she wasn't. "I'll break out in hives and maybe even have a seizure."

The man scoffed. "Yeah right."

"It's true," Julie said, realizing and playing along. "I can't have olives. Same reason."

"Whatever," the man said and walked away shaking his head like he didn't believe them.

"He'll know when we eat them anyway," Julie whispered.

"Hang on," Emma said, watching the man across the room.

A few minutes later, he picked up his cell and dialed, then after a few seconds, said, "Bitches say they have allergies to tomatoes and olives... So what if you already got them? Go back and make sure they take them off and rinse the tomato juice to be sure!... Just fucking do it, man!"

He slammed the cell back into his pocket and glared back at the girls as Emma turned her head to hide her grin. Fucking with these bastards was fun.

"See?" she whispered. "Why make it easy for them."

"I just hope they don't kill us for all the trouble," Julie whispered back.

"They won't," Emma said and meant it. "They still need us 'til they do whatever job they came for."

"Yeah, but after that..." Julie shivered beside her.

"My dad will find us. I know he will." Emma truly believed it, too. They just had to wait. Meanwhile, she'd think up a few more ways to frustrate the assholes holding them.

THE LEADERS, INCLUDING Stein, Falk, Hanson,

Penhall, Simon, Lucas, Becker, Bailey, and Special Agent in Charge Garner, who'd just arrived back on scene, met in the large mobile command unit to go over strategy.

The larger, black-painted equivalent of a mobile home, the mobile command unit bore the KCPD logo on the side in white beside the words "Command Center" and contained several rooms, including a conference room, a communications and computer room—the largest—and two small interrogation rooms in addition to the cockpit, where a driver and one other person could ride.

"Okay, what do we know so far?" Garner said, eager to get up to speed as they sat around the conference room table.

"We're majorly fucked," Simon said.

"The biggest problem is we know their intention was to blow through the limestone and effect a tourist target," Stein said. "So what does that give us?"

"The only touristy targets anywhere near here besides hotels are the casino and Worlds of Fun-Oceans of Fun," Hanson said. "But both seem a stretch."

"Wait," Simon said. "This place is six miles, right? Just like SubTropolis next door?"

"Something like that," Falk said, nodding. "But that's road length. There are many twists and turns."

"Right. The roads kind of wind through there," Simon agreed. "Has anyone looked at a map?"

Becker and the Feds exchanged puzzled looks, then Falk got up and ran over to a nearby file cabinet, pulling open the top drawer and digging through.

"Of UnderCity, yes," Garner said. "But not the city."

As Falk returned with a large map and unrolled it across

the table before them, Lucas sat forward. "Doing calculations in my systems, I conclude the back side of UnderCity should sit under Hunt Midwest and Oceans of Fun, at least in part."

Falk traced the route on the map as they all leaned into look. "Son of a bitch."

"By my calculations, the complex could stretch to at least Parvin Road," Lucas said.

"It's Oceans of Fun!" Penhall said. "It has to be."

"Fuck!" Becker said.

"You can make those calculations in your head?" Garner asked, shooting Lucas a skeptical look.

".75 miles worth to be exact," Lucas added, confident.

"He's like a fucking walking computer," Simon said, frowning at Garner.

"He's never been wrong with math yet," Becker added.

Lucas beamed. "Thank you, Sergeant."

"And they open it weekends in April," Penhall said.

"We need to get people over there and clear out the entire complex," Becker said. "Right now."

"What about the hotels across the highway?" Hanson asked.

"Those, too," Stein said, "and we should close the highway just to be safe."

"Oh, the mayor's gonna love that!" Bailey said, his face saying the exact opposite.

"He'd love dead civilians even less," Garner said.

"What about the casino?" Penhall asked.

"It should be far enough out to be safe, but SubTropolis and surrounding houses and businesses—" Falk said.

"And the quarry," Simon added, cutting him off.

"Yes," Falk continued. "Those we have to clear."

Becker got on the radio and issued the orders. When someone on the other end balked, she added, "Tell them it's on my authority and the FBI. Send the Mayor and the Chief and anyone else to us if you must. There is a strong danger to the public." She disconnected and the discussion continued.

"We're sure they have enough explosives to do this?" Garner asked.

"These people are former military explosives experts," Lucas said.

"They know what they're doing," Bailey added.

"Doesn't mean they don't just want to scare people to make a statement," Garner pointed out.

"They've already murdered two cops and several civilians!" Simon snapped.

"And we lost two robots," Hanson added. They were disabled and could probably be recovered if they stopped Derrick and his men in time, but Simon decided not to argue details.

"We can't afford to take that chance," Becker added.

"What's our strategy here, besides evacuations?" Bailey asked. "Do we just sit and wait, try to negotiate?"

"We'll try to get them on the phone for sure," Garner said.

"Yeah, that seems like it'll work," Simon said, then rolled his eyes.

"We have to try it at least," Garner said, irritated.

"Diffusing is always the first goal, but the other problem is: if we send people in, we risk them being caught in an explosion."

"Or the assholes blowing it early," Falk added.

"We can probably risk sending people in part way, just to see if we can figure out how to get to them," Stein said.

"Risking my people again is not something I'd take lightly," Becker said.

"Fuck it! Send me in," Simon said. "My daughter's in there!"

"Me, too," Lucas chimed in.

"Maybe," Becker said. "We don't know for sure."

"That's the other thing," Garner said, looking uncomfortably at Simon, then turning to the FBI and Becker. "We have to make stopping whatever explosion our priority. Everything else is secondary."

"Meaning, fuck my daughter and her friend!" Simon snapped.

"Not what I'm saying at all," Garner snapped back, brow creasing. "The explosion is the bigger danger."

Becker put a hand on Simon's arm. "We'll do whatever we can to resolve both, don't worry."

"The real issue is there's no way to reach them quickly without being seen by their cameras," Bailey said. "We just can't surprise them."

"So what stops them from blowing it at the first sign of trouble," Penhall agreed.

Simon grunted. "Once again, we're majorly fucked."

"Let's have someone get them on the phone while we consider other possibilities," Stein said.

"I'll make the call," Garner said, dialing the number Simon had provided after Derrick's earlier call.

"Or do we want to keep it local? We don't want to feed their sense of importance," Bailey said.

"They'll already figure we're here," Falk said. "They may already know after we gave the order to shut down UnderCity, if someone talked."

"Like Karl Ramon," Lucas added.

"Right," Hanson agreed.

"Either way, they know enough to know how these situations are handled," Falk said.

"Okay, so phone call it is," Garner said as he stood and headed for the door, Simon glaring after him icily.

"Meanwhile, let's do some thinking," Becker said.

"I don't trust that guy," Simon said.

"Hank's good people," Stein said. "Just not very tactful."

"He has daughters of his own," Falk added.

"Only his are safe and far away," Simon snapped, looking away.

Becker put a hand on his arm. "Do you want to get some fresh air?"

Simon shook his head. "No, I'm all in."

"We need to focus here, keep our cool," Becker said.

"I'm not going, JoAnn," Simon insisted. They locked eyes for a moment in a silent impasse, until—

"Okay, so what's everyone thinking?" Stein asked.

Then they began brainstorming possibilities.

"THERE'S ANOTHER DRONE!" Jonah called from his station monitoring the security feeds.

Derrick and Luis joined him in time to watch the black drone swoop down outside the cavern and drop a bundle, then zip away again, back the way it had come.

Seconds later, they heard a phone ringing.

Everyone checked their phones but none of them were ringing.

"Where's that coming from?" Luis asked.

"I think it's outside," another man near the door said.

Derrick marched over and yanked open the door. The ringing was coming from the bundle the drone had dropped. Derrick motioned and the man who'd alerted him stepped out and scooped up the bundle, bringing it back inside as Derrick closed the door.

"Gotta be the cops," the man said. He untied straps to reveal a small cloth sack and then dug inside, pulling out a burner phone. It was still ringing. "Do we answer?"

Derrick took the phone and looked it over. The Caller ID read "FBI Command" before it ran out of space. "Feds," Derrick said and clicked the call button to answer. "Hello?"

"Colonel Derrick, please," a man said.

"Who's calling?"

"This is Special Agent in Charge Hank Garner of the FBI," the voice said.

"Ooooo, are you as mighty as your title?" Derrick taunted then snapped, "What do you want?"

"The question is what do you want, Colonel?" Garner said. "How can we bring this situation to a peaceful resolution as quickly as possible?"

Derrick laughed. "There is no peaceful solution except success. Once America is reminded of what it should be and can be, only then can change occur."

"And what is that?" Garner asked, annoyingly calm and placating.

"Consider this a demonstration," Derrick said.

"No one else has to die, Colonel," Garner said. "Surely we can come to an arrangement."

"The time for negotiations was over long ago, Agent," Derrick snapped. "Don't call me again." And he hung up the phone and tossed it onto a nearby desk. "Idiot."

Luis and several others chortled.

Seconds later, the phone rang again but they ignored it.

Then Derrick's comm beeped. He answered, "Go."

"They're making us evacuate, Colonel," Edson Núñez said, sounding a bit distant through the hand radio the local hires had been issued in lieu of the more expensive personal comms Derrick and his own men wore.

"Say again?" Derrick replied, confused. "Evacuate?"

"They're clearing the area—Worlds of Fun, Oceans of Fun, businesses, all hotels," Edson reported. "We have to get out."

"Shit."

"They even shut down the fucking highway, sir."

"Use the alternate location," Derrick ordered.

"Yes, sir."

Then he heard commotion on the other end—shouting, shuffling, arguing.

"Fuck!" someone said. "Shut it!"

A car door slammed.

"Núñez?" Derrick demanded. No response. "Núñez, report!" he said again.

"Fuck, Colonel, we think someone saw the girls," Edson finally said as tires squealed in the background.

"What?! Who?"

"Some tourist or hotel staff, not sure," Edson replied.

"Handle it!" Derrick ordered.

"Too late," Edson said. "We're gone. En route to alternate location, sir."

"Son of a bitch!" Derrick pounded his fist against a stone pillar. A major fuck up. "Just get there fast and don't let the cops or anyone else see you!" Derrick shouted, then disconnected.

"What happened?" Luis asked.

"Someone saw them," Derrick said.

"They didn't handle it?" Luis asked.

Derrick shook his head.

"Fuck!" Luis responded.

Derrick motioned. "Go check our escape route, right now! Make sure it's still secure!"

Luis motioned to Jonah and two others and they grabbed

rifles and slipped out into the corridor at a run.

They'd scouted early on and found the tunnel up to the quarry, just large enough for workers, not for vehicles. The plan was to extract themselves then call the helicopter and hit the air before calling in the code to the cell phone chain to trigger the explosive cycle. But it counted on the quarry being secure. A copter could land there and pull out quickly with minimum observation and no one from the police and Feds surrounding them on Underground Drive and the other exits. It was still a risk, but minimal. The copter would lift them out to vehicles Edson and another team would have waiting north, from where they'd head straight for the airport and a private plane waiting on the tarmac. All with such speed amidst the chaos of the explosions, they'd be gone before the police could track them and follow.

But people knowing Edson's team's location was a major problem. They had to get to the alternate location—an abandoned office building awaiting new renters just north of Worlds of Fun—unseen.

The Fed's cell phone continued ringing, an annoyance, but one he'd ignore for now. They might need to talk to them again, to cause confusion or create a diversion. It could still be of use. But he had to be sure other aspects weren't compromised.

He got on the comm to check in with all his teams.

"WELL, THAT WENT WELL," Garner said, frustrated as he hung up the phone yet again.

He was standing outside the N.E. 42nd Street exit from UnderCity with Becker, Simon, Lucas, Bailey, Tucker, Stein, Falk, Penhall, and Hanson. They were behind several unmarked cars beside an FBI van, semi-protected from random fire should the bombers decide to try sniping. With the quarry and area buildings cleared out, the air was eerily quiet compared to earlier. They could actually hear themselves breathing, and in the distance, they heard the sound of helicopters doing passes over the area.

"About like I expected," Simon snapped.

Garner spun, nostrils flaring. "What exactly is your problem with me, Detective?"

"Where do I start," Simon replied, glaring back at him.

"Enough!" Becker said. "This is not going to help."

"The UnderCity staff told us cell phone signals are spotty at best in the complex. Everything has to be hard wired or run off of WiFi," Stein said.

"Well, they're doing something," Becker said.

Hanson and Penhall whispered a moment, an idea brewing. "You know, if we could block the WiFi, maybe that would interfere with their triggers and communications," Hanson said.

The others reacted, considering it.

"We could just cut off power altogether," Garner said. "The only reason we haven't is we wanted lights and it would disable the carded security doors."

"These guys are prepared," Tucker said. "They probably have a generator."

"Or two," Hanson said. "Blocking the WiFi would be an extra step."

"And sealing security doors to block their movement sounds smart," Bailey added.

"Maybe," Falk agreed. "We can get there entirely by tunnels and blast through a door."

"There's probably a manual override," Becker said. "Most of these systems have them."

"So we could still communicate with them," Garner said. "Our sat phone wouldn't be affected."

"Yeah, that's going well!" Simon snapped.

"We don't know for sure what kind of triggers they're using," Tucker said.

"No, but cell phones or computers are the most likely, given their MO and background," Garner said.

"And certainly it will affect their communications regardless, which will slow them down," Hanson said.

"If only we had that kind of technology," Becker said.

"Doesn't the government have the technology?" Penhall asked.

"We do," Garner and Falk said simultaneously.

"They could still trigger explosives manually," Penhall pointed out.

"But that would require them to sacrifice themselves," Bailey said. "These people have been planning this for a long time. They're planners. They won't just go off half-cocked."

"Unless we back them in a corner," Simon said.

"You think they have a way out of there that we don't have covered?" Stein asked.

"They've got something figured out," Tucker said. "These are smart people."

"And they don't seem suicidal," Bailey added.

"Their plans may have changed since we surrounded them," Becker said.

"I'll make a call," Falk said and turned away, pulling out his cell phone.

"So, we block the WiFi," Garner said. "It won't take long for them to figure that out."

"But it may buy us time while they reconsider what to do," Hanson said.

Simon could hear Falk discussing the blocking technology with someone at the Bureau as Penhall said, "Right, and if we can confirm their triggers are disabled, we might be able to take them out before they can manually trigger."

Becker shook her head. "Still plenty risky. They may have teams all over the place, in position. The biggest problem here is how little we know."

"Can the equipment for blocking even reach through all that rock?" Lucas asked.

Falk hung up the phone and rejoined them. "On its way."

"The WiFi and cell blocking system can be set up just outside their security camera range inside," Stein explained. "It should work fine as long as it's close to the source."

"Plus, we're trying to find out who's supplying the WiFi to the complex. Have that shut off, too," Falk said.

"Okay, it's a plan," Becker said. "I guess we see how they react."

"What if how they react is to kill hostages?" Simon asked.

Everyone exchanged looks but no one would meet Simon's eyes. He grunted. "Fuck that," he added.

Becker's cell rang and she answered. "Becker." She listened a moment. "Where?... How many?... Did he see where they went?... Okay, thank you." She hung up.

"What's going on?" Lucas asked.

"Well, the girls are not in there with them," Becker said.

"What?" Simon asked.

"That was Maberry," Becker said. "Someone at one of the hotels thinks he saw them being shoved in a van over at the Holiday Inn and driven away by two men."

"Where?!" Simon demanded.

She shook her head. "He's not sure."

"But it's something," Lucas said.

"He only saw them for a few seconds, from the side, as the hotel was evacuated," Becker added.

"Let's go!" Simon turned and hurried off toward where he'd parked. Lucas followed.

Becker turned to Bailey and Tucker. "Go with them. Make sure he doesn't screw up."

"We're on it," Tucker said as he and Bailey hurried off after Simon.

"How sure are they it was the girls?" Falk asked.

"Apparently Maberry and Dolby showed the guy pictures and he thought it was them," Becker said. "Got a decent look at them from the side."

"If he's right, that would take some pressure off," Stein said.

"Right," Falk agreed. "What do we care if the bad guys blow themselves up?"

"Do you realize how much damage that could do to the area?" Becker said.

Falk shrugged. "It's not ideal, but better than having those girls die with them."

"Or anyone else," Garner said.

"I still say the priority is to talk them out of there," Becker said. "Let's not give up just yet."

"Absolutely," Garner and the other FBI Agents agreed together.

AS SIMON PULLED off N.E. 42nd Street onto North Doniphan and headed for Northeast Parvin Road, well over the speed limit, his cell rang. He hit the green button to answer and placed it between his shoulder and ear. "Simon."

"Detective Simon, this is Doctor Agbeblewu at Research," a familiar accented voice said.

Oh shit. Simon had forgotten all about checking on Lara since Emma's abduction.

"The nurses said you and your daughter didn't come by to visit last night," she said.

"My daughter has been kidnapped," Simon said.

"Oh my God!" Agbeblewu exclaimed.

"Do not tell her mother."

"Of course not," the doctor agreed. "What happened?"

Simon slowed at the corner and turned sharply onto N.E. Parvin Road headed west as he replied, "Long story. Related to a case. I'm a little preoccupied."

"I imagine. Do you know where they took her?" Agbeblewu asked.

"I don't," Simon said. "That's what I'm preoccupied with."

"Oh yes."

Oceans of Fun was passing by on the right, its round twisting red and orange tube-encased slides rising into the air behind a black metal fence as they passed by. "Is Lara okay?" Simon asked.

"Oh, yes, she's fine," Agbeblewu said. "Slowly progressing."

"Good," Simon said. "It may be a few days before I can get back in there, but thanks for calling to check."

"Of course," Agbeblewu said. "If there's anything you need..."

"Thanks, Doc," Simon said. "Just take care of, Lara."

"I will."

Simon hung up and flipped on the lights and siren as he reached the intersection of Randolph Road, sliding onto the shoulder and moving past waiting traffic and on through, under 435 to where Randolph Road continued on the west side with hotel after hotel. It paralleled 435 but for some reason the city engineers had it running east of 435 south of Parvin and west north of that intersection.

"It's there," Lucas said, pointing to the "Holiday Inn" sign up ahead on the left.

Simon grunted and slowed slightly as he made a sharp left turn into the parking lot and raced up to where Maberry and Dolby were standing beside an open hotel room door with a blonde woman in her late twenties who was gesturing animatedly as they talked.

Simon flipped off the lights and siren and jumped out, hurrying to join them. "Where did they go?!"

"Ms. Brewer, this is Detective John Simon," Dolby said. "His daughter is one of the missing girls."

"Oh," Brewer said, her mouth turning down, her eyes sad. She was wearing a uniform shirt with the Holiday Inn logo above her heart. A badge on the opposite side read: 'Lindsay B.' "I'm so sorry."

"Where did they go?" Simon asked again, insistent.

"She doesn't know," Maberry said. "She just got a glimpse of them."

"She was just going over what she saw with us," Dolby added.

"Start over," Simon said. "I'd like to know everything."

"I guess," Brewer said and then repeated her story with Simon and the others interjecting questions from time to time. She'd been going room to room to ask people to evacuate on police orders. Room 107 where they were standing was the room where two men with a brown van had been staying. She was several doors down, explaining the situation to other guests, when one of the men appeared and asked what was happening. She explained again and then hurried off to alert other guests.

It had been when she came back a second time to double check on everyone that she saw the two men shoving two girls, hands tied behind them, hurriedly into the van. One of them, a Hispanic, had been speaking urgently on a cell phone and he stiffened, his face taking on a worried look, when he saw her.

Brewer had called out, "Is everything okay?"

"We're fine!" The Hispanic man insisted as his companion shoved the girls into the van then hurried around to the driver's side.

Then he'd glared at her and she'd noticed a gun in his waistband before he slammed the door and they raced off, headed away from her.

"It was the wrong way to go, since the street is one way," she said. "It was like they didn't want me to see in the van."

"So they had to go south once they turned onto Randolph?" Lucas asked.

She nodded. "Yes, it's one way here."

"And you didn't see which way they turned?" Simon asked.

She shook her head.

"Fuck!" Simon said before she could speak.

She quickly added, "I was too busy worrying about the other employees and staff. I'm the assistant manager."

"Thank you, Ms. Brewer, we appreciate you giving us a call," Dolby said.

As Simon turned back toward the Charger, Tucker and Bailey arrived in an unmarked Explorer.

"What've we got?" Bailey asked as they hurried to join them.

"Nothing," Simon said and climbed into the Charger, Lucas hurrying to join him.

"Where are we going?" Lucas asked as Simon started the engine and began backing out of the parking spot.

"To see if anyone saw the van down at the hotel on the corner," Simon said.

"You think someone was watching?" Lucas asked.

"Fuck! I have no idea," Simon snapped as he maneuvered the car toward the nearest lot exit. "It's all we've got!"

And he whipped the car right onto Randolph and raced south.

CHAPTER 24

SIMON DROVE DOWN N.E. Parvin Road headed west, searching every vehicle, every lot for a brown van, Lucas doing the same, even as he searched area traffic cams on his internal computer at the same time. He scanned the area as Simon keyed the radio beside him.

"186."

"Go ahead, 186," the dispatcher came back.

"186 headed west on northeast Parvin Road," Simon said. "What's the plate on that BOLO for the brown van?"

"Echo-Whiskey-Echo-Seven-Three-Six, 186," the dispatcher replied, pronouncing each letter and number of the plate one at a time.

Simon slowed to a stop beside a large lot, his eyes and Lucas' searching the vehicles. "Subject has been seen in the area of the Holiday Inn off Randolph at Parvin," he said. "Any units available for assistance in searching?"

"182 joining," Dolby's voice came over the radio.

"Copy, 182," dispatch replied.

The lot was clear. No sign of the van. Simon accelerated again, moving on as Lucas scanned the opposite side of the street. "182, you take east on Parvin, we're searching west,"

Simon said into the radio.

"Copy, 186," Dolby replied.

Simon spotted something across the way and swerved sharply left, cutting off the other lane west then through a turn lane and across two eastbound lanes as horns honked, tires squealed, and cars swerved. He bounced up onto a lot and slowed, cruising around as they searched the vehicles.

"Do you want me to drive?" Lucas asked. His friend was very agitated and aggressive, clearly worried about his daughter, as any parent would be. Lucas thought it would be easier to let him look while he drove.

"I got this!" Simon snapped.

"She will be okay," Lucas said because he really believed it. They would find Derrick and stop him. Too much depended on it and they had the resources and training.

"Is that what your many years of experience tells you then?" Simon replied.

"It is what I believe," Lucas replied.

"I wish I had as much faith as you," Simon said as he circled back around toward where he'd entered this lot. No van here either. "God damn it!"

"We will find them," Lucas said.

"Just keep looking," Simon snapped, clearly not in the mood for Lucas' cheerful optimism. Somewhere out there his baby girl was in danger, and he had to find her.

Simon sped out across two eastbound lanes again and swerved onto the west lane just in front of a pickup that braked and honked, the driver yelling obscenities. Lucas wrapped his hand tightly around the door handle, trying to steady himself as Simon flicked on his emergency light and flipped the driver the bird, speeding onward, his eyes always searching for any sign of the van.

After eighteen years on the force, Simon had seen a lot of depravity—humans hurting and endangering other humans like it was nothing, like they were nothing. For seventeen years though, his family had been safe. Protected, at least in theory, from the harsher realities Simon saw every day. But then Paul Paulson and Miles O'Dell came along, shooting at his house when Emma was home. And now Tobias Derrick abducting her. Lucas knew the man would never give up, but no one would have blamed him if he'd stayed back at the command post. Simon was driven by pure fury, that much was obvious, aggravated by the frustration from days of little progress on a case that involved dead friends, and now the desperation and helplessness he was feeling as a parent with a missing, and possibly in danger, child. These people were crossing a line. And he'd do whatever it took to get his daughter back safe and punish those who dared threaten her and put her in danger. Lucas would help him. He wondered if his friend could ever recover the sense that his daughter would be safe again.

BECKER CLIMBED THE stairs into the FBI's mobile command post and hurried to where Agents Falk and Stein were huddled with SAIC Garner on a bench behind several FBI techs monitoring computers and communications equipment. The cramped room was stuffy with heat from all the electronics and the closer quarters filled with body odors mixed with hints of cologne and other scents she refused to ponder long enough to identify.

"Simon seems to have found that van," she said as she hunched down beside them. UnderCity's manager had given them the password and ISP info on UnderCity's WiFi network and service and they'd called the company and arranged to have service cut off at a phone call. They were just waiting until the FBI's jamming and scrambling equipment was in place and ready to activate.

"The kidnappers?" Garner asked.

"Yeah." Outside, people were getting anxious, but during a siege, restlessness always set in pretty quickly, and so far, this one had lasted twenty-nine hours.

"He chasing them?" Stein asked.

"Disappeared. But they're on the trail, more cars coming," she replied.

"Good," Falk said. "I hope he gets the bastards."

"We'll get the rest," Stein added sipping coffee from a generic white styrofoam cup with a plastic lid.

"How long?" she asked.

"They're sending it in with a robot now," Garner said. "Twenty minutes maybe."

"Half an hour max," Stein said.

"Hope we have that long," Becker said.

"Yeah," Falk said as they exchanged looks. It could happen any time. That was the risk. But they all hoped they had enough time.

"They still won't take my call," Miller griped.

"They aren't the types to want to talk, I think," Falk said.

"Exactly," Becker agreed as she stood again and stretched.

"So we'll communicate in other ways," Stein said. "We're about to get their attention."

Falk grabbed his own cup from a mug rack on the wall and stood, motioning toward the conference room down the hall toward the back of the command post. "You want some?"

Becker shook her head as Falk slid past her and headed back to refill his cup. "Let us know before you turn it on," she said to Garner and Stein.

"Absolutely," Garner said and she headed back outside to update her people.

AT SEARCY CREEK PARK, Simon turned the Charger back and headed east again. There were only residential areas and they were getting further and further from any likely target. Given the siege and time factors, it made no sense to take their hostages that direction. He and Lucas continued searching as they returned the other way, their eyes poring over again and again places they'd already checked, hoping for any sign of the brown van.

Simon strained himself to concentrate—he was looking but not seeing, his stomach clenched so tight he wondered if it would be permanent. His heart threatened to explode from his chest at any moment and it took every ounce of strength to keep his hands from shaking on the wheel and remember to breathe.

"Anything on the cams?" he asked Lucas, who was intensely focused beside him, multitasking on the window and his internal searching.

"No, but I am searching as rapidly as I can," Lucas replied, and Simon knew that meant a search rate much faster than even several humans working at once could accomplish.

As he drove on, he keyed the mic and radioed the KCPD helicopter searching overhead on a designated channel for the search. "186 to 692."

"Go ahead, 186," the pilot came back.

KCPD currently had four MD500E helicopters, each manned by a pilot and an observer, who also was FAA certified to fly. Their call signs were 690 to 698. The observer of the pair assisting with the search was the on duty Sergeant for this shift, Jason Brock, who Simon knew well. He had three teenage daughters of his own.

"Any brown vans out there?" Simon asked, exhaustion and desperation leaking into his voice.

"Negative, 186," Brock replied. "Plenty of vans, no brown ones yet."

"Fuck," Simon said to himself, then keyed the mic. "Copy."

"We'll find them, John," Brock replied. "We won't stop 'til we do."

When an officer's family was at stake, the entire force took it personally, so Simon knew he meant it. Coming so soon on the heels of two Detectives gunned down off duty, it had even more urgency. Every cop out there wanted a win on this one and to punish those responsible. It wasn't just about protecting the public anymore. Now it was personal, an attack on them all.

"182, what's your location?" Simon asked, keying the radio again.

"Parvin at Doniphan," Maberry replied.

"We're coming back your way," Simon said.

"Copy," Maberry replied.

Simon blinked and took a deep breath, pushing back the worst case scenarios that kept wanting to play out like moves in his head. Come on, baby, where are you? Give me a sign! Simon silently pleaded, sending all his mental energy toward Emma, hoping for just a moment telepathy would cross the distance, riding on the love of a father for his baby girl.

THE COPS WERE getting restless. Derrick could tell that much just from his security feeds. And that made Derrick's people increasingly nervous, so the time had come to finish things. It wasn't the way he'd wanted. There'd been too many screw ups. The chance of making a statement with large casualties had diminished, but there was still a chance they could take out some cops, and that would be satisfying. It would serve the cause just as well.

Derrick motioned to Luis as they watched the security feeds. "Final sequence, give the orders. I'll radio air support. It's time."

Luis nodded. "Yes, Colonel." And he got on the radio sending out orders to each of the teams as Derrick dialed his cell.

Edson answered after three rings. "Yeah."

"Are you ready?" Derrick asked.

"Yeah, been ready. Can we place the assets and blow this joint?" Edson asked eagerly.

"Go. Rendezvous at the pick-up point in point-four-five mikes, departure in sixty mikes." Forty-five minutes to make the rendezvous. The plane would leave in sixty no matter what.

"Copy, Colonel," Edson said. "We're on our way."

Derrick hung up and switched his comm to another frequency as Luis continued issuing orders to the teams.

"Eagle," a voice answered one of the pilots.

"Is the Eagle awake?" Derrick asked, using a predetermined code phrase.

"The Eagle is awakened," the pilot replied, indicating the plane was standing by, probably refueling and doing preflight checks at Kansas City's Downtown Airport. It was twenty minutes away, less by copter, but he'd wait for his teams. No man left behind. Not if he could help it.

"Point-sixty mikes, rendezvous in forty-five," Derrick replied.

"Copy," the pilot said.

Finally, Derrick switched to yet another channel. "Baby Birds mark, Corporal," Derrick said as the copter pilot answered.

"Baby Birds en route," the copter pilot, Counts, replied.

Derrick hung up again. The wheels were set in motion. Two copters on their way. Now, they could watch everything they'd worked for play out. Even without the victim count, the massive explosion would send a signal. He hoped it would still be enough to inspire others to join their cause. He turned and motioned to the team around him.

"Set autosequence eleven," he ordered. "And prepare to depart."

The men sprung into action around him and he watched them work. Their disciplined precision still made him proud, screw ups aside. Most of those had been hired hands. He'd learn from that and avoid involving locals in execution in the future. If it came down to it, he'd abandon them to fate without hesitation, but the men who'd been with him for over a decade were top notch. They were his men. Men he could rely on.

"Orders given, Colonel," Luis said as he finished on the comm.

Derrick smiled. "Very good, Lieutenant. The time is now."

Luis smiled back, looking pleased, then sprung into action with the others, finishing final preparations.

THE MEN HAD HELD them in an old garage somewhere not far from the hotel. They'd raced there after shoving the girls roughly in the van and threatening some witness at the hotel. Emma had heard their concerned chatter over the handheld radio. Someone had seen.

Please God, let them call the cops so my dad will come! she'd prayed as they'd been forced to lie face down on a dirty floor in silence, then men pacing around them and yelling at them any time they made a sound. Emma found it ironic, given their own yells would surely carry farther to potential witnesses than the two girl's whispering.

Less than an hour later, they were shoved back in the van and headed off again, the men mumbling about "final sequence" and something about a "rendezvous," though where and what any of that meant remained unclear.

Julie whimpered beside her as they lay on their stomachs in the back of the van, cheeks resting against the torn and stained carpet in the cargo area.

"It'll be okay," Emma whispered.

"He's taking too long! They're going to kill us," Julie hissed.

A gun barrel pressed hard against the back of her head and Emma looked up to see the Hispanic man sneering down at them. "Shut the fuck up, bitches. No one said you could talk."

"She's just scared," Emma snapped, glaring up at him.

"Good!" He chortled, eyes sparkling as he glanced behind him at the driver. "The back way, by the office," he directed, motioning with an arm. "We can make our way across."

The driver mumbled a reply as the Hispanic man turned back to the girls. "It's almost over anyway, just relax." And then both men grunted and laughed in a way that made the hair stick up on Emma's head and arms.

Hurry up, daddy, she plead silently, focusing all her energy on reaching him somehow, wherever he was. He'd find her. He had to. That was who he was.

Julie whimpered again and Emma leaned her head to one side, pressed against her friend's cheek to offer what little comfort she could. Neither of her parents were particularly religious, but they believed in God, and her grandparents were church regulars. She closed her eyes and prayed like they'd taught her, asking for mercy, asking for rescue. If you're out there, I need you, God, she prayed. It was the most sincere prayer she'd ever uttered in her life, even if it was said silently. God could read our minds, the Bible said. He'd hear her.

Now she needed Him to answer, too.

She glanced up at the side window and saw the large towering metal frames of roller coasters and thrill rides passing by as the van sped along. Worlds of Fun! We're at Worlds of Fun! She hadn't been to Kansas City's equivalent of Disney in a couple of years. She'd have to get on her dad about that. But how could they be driving in the park? What about all the people?

Opened in May 1973 to the city's north off the 435 loop that circled Kansas City, Worlds of Fun consisted of 235-acres packed with rides, restaurants, kiosks, shops, and other amusements, including an amphitheater. A water park, Oceans of Fun, had been added directly adjacent in 1982 and expanded in 2013 to add rides and more large attractions, including a 65 foot tall slide complex with 6 new slides.

The van wound its way through the park taking various twists and turns at a steady pace for several minutes, until the driver slammed on the brakes and pulled to a stop.

"There! Just across that fence," the Hispanic man pointed out the window.

"What—we just leave them?" The driver asked, sounding confused.

"Just help me, Kareem," the Hispanic man replied.

"Don't say my name, you fuck!"

"Doesn't matter now," the Hispanic man replied. "They'll never tell." His voice took on an ominous tone and Emma was worried.

The girls were yanked out of the van and onto their feet then led, each by one captor, through a connecting gate and along walkways past Monsoon, Castaway Cove, volleyball courts, and then past Splash Mountain to the boat dock near Buccaneer Bay. The air smelled strongly of chlorine. The men helped the girls into two lime green fiberglass kayaks and laid them down on their backs, then pushed the kayaks out into the lake amidst other drifting kayaks and a couple white swan-shaped boats that somehow hadn't been secured in the rush to clear the park.

"We just leave them here?" Emma heard the driver ask as she floated out toward the middle.

"Yeah, we don't have much time, we gotta go!" The Hispanic man urged and they both turned and disappeared again.

"Oh my God! We're going to drown!" Julie said, panicking, as her kayak angled away from Emma's. They were about ten feet apart right now.

"No, we're not," Emma said, thinking. Then she lifted a leg and bent it over the side, gently kicking at the water. It pushed the boat where she wanted. "Use your leg! Carefully! Don't flip yourself. But see if you can get to the shore so we can roll off."

Emma kept pushing the water with her foot and the kayak turned, heading toward the shore again.

She heard Julie struggling beside her and then a yell and stopped, her head snapping over to look. Julie was still on the kayak but frozen with a look of fright.

"What happened?" Emma asked.

"Oh my God! I almost tipped over!" Julie replied.

Julie was her best friend but Emma was starting to get

annoyed. Julie was way too panicky. That was the last thing they needed right now. She took a deep breath and tried to reply calmly, "I told you to be careful. Just move slowly. It's working. Look at me?"

Julie glanced over, saw Emma's progress, then took a breath and tried again. This time more slowly. "It's working!" she shouted as her kayak turned.

"Just stay calm and take your time," Emma urged her. If either of them fell in they were fucked.

SIMON AND LUCAS WERE headed north on Worlds of Fun Ave parallel to the amusement park when a brown Chevy cargo van shot out of the drive leading to the amusement park's administration offices and turned in front of them.

"There!" Lucas said.

"I see it," Simon replied as he flipped on the lights and siren and gave chase. "Call for backup."

Lucas keyed the radio mic hanging from his shoulder. "186 in pursuit of a brown van. North on Worlds of Fun at—" He looked outside for a street sign.

"Northeast Forty-Eighth," Simon said.

"Northeast Forty-Eighth," Lucas repeated.

"Copy, 186," a dispatcher replied.

"Requesting backup and air support," Lucas added.

"182, on our way," Maberry replied.

"Copy, 182," dispatch said.

"692 en route," Jason Brock said.

"Copy, 692," dispatch said. "Sending available cars."

The van turned left as they reached the intersection and Simon followed as Lucas keyed the radio again. "186, West on Northeast 48th."

"Copy 186," dispatch replied.

They were speeding along a residential street pushing sixty past housing clusters with I-35 approaching fast ahead. A few scattered cars pulled over the side to let them past—far more common in this part of town than more urban areas. Chases were more and more dangerous these days because more and more drivers just didn't bother pulling over at the sign of emergency vehicles moving Code 1 despite laws and driver training to the contrary. Everyone had somewhere to be and couldn't be bothered.

They passed a church on the right, a high school on the left. Then a Mercedes 600SL suddenly turned left off a side street, moving across the lanes.

The van driver braked then swerved in a wide arc out into the opposite lanes and around the Mercedes, whose startled driver came to a fast stop. Fortunately, the cars in the opposite lane were still fifty feet ahead and slowed but not enough to leave it clear for Simon, who slammed on his brakes to avoid hitting the Mercedes and honked, waving his arm at the stunned driver. "Get clear! Get the fuck outta there!"

After a few seconds, the woman nodded and continued her turn, heading slowly back the way they'd come in opposite lanes as Simon accelerated again, trying to catch up with the van once more. "Jesus! Idiot!" he cursed.

"We should cut him off before he hits the highway," Lucas suggested, stating the obvious.

"Good idea, if anyone was in position to do it," Simon said as he made up some lost ground, but the van still kept a good lead.

"If someone else comes out of a side street, we will be in trouble," Lucas said, and glanced at the speedometer. "Department policy for chases on city streets—"

"I know the fucking policy! Emma's in there!" Simon snapped.

Lucas snapped his lips shut and looked out the window again, watching the van, then sat up and keyed his shoulder mic again for the radio, "182, 692, what's your positions?"

"692, North Choteau Trafficway and I-35," Brock replied, the chopping of the copter blades noisy in the background.

"We're coming up Brighton from Parvin now," Dolby replied.

Simon reached up and keyed his radio, one hand still on the wheel. "182, go up Prather Road and get ready to cut them off on I-35 at Antioch."

"Which way are they going?" Dolby replied.

"Not sure yet," Simon said. "Just be ready to hop on when we know."

"Copy, 186," Dolby replied.

"What if they don't take the highway?" Lucas asked as Simon returned both hands to the wheel.

"Then we compensate," Simon said as he glanced in the rearview mirror to see a black and white several blocks back speeding toward them Code 1–full lights and sirens.

As the van reached Brighton, it turned right and sped over the top of the freeway.

"They're gonna get their education today," Lucas said, quoting a movie, though Simon couldn't remember which.

"Do you really think this is the best time for quoting movies?" Simon asked.

"I am trying to help you relax by amusing you," Lucas said.

"Not helping," Simon said. "You gotta pick your moments."

"It was just one mistake," Lucas lamented. Another quote.

"Just stop it!" Simon snapped but he suppressed a smile.

"Sorry," Lucas said, looking apologetic. Then he added, "Let's go get 'em, partner!"

"Shut the fuck up!" Simon said but then laughed. "Just be ready on the radio, okay?"

Lucas grinned. "Roger, Dodger."

Simon shook his head. "Now you're just quoting anything to annoy me."

The van turned sharply left just past the highway, tires skidding and leaving black trails on the street, then raced along Northeast Winn Road toward the onramp to I-35 south. Simon followed, slowing to turn left on Winn and dodging a minivan that had turned on from the opposite direction on Brighton, then accelerating again as Lucas keyed the radio.

"186, continuing pursuit south on I-35 from Brighton," Lucas said.

"182, we'll be ready," Maberry replied.

"692, I'm almost overhead now," Brock said.

"623, right behind you 186," a uniform replied.

"Copy, we see you, 623," Lucas confirmed.

As they came up the offramp onto I-35, Simon began weaving quickly through traffic following the van. "No fucking way you get away from me. No fucking way!" he said aloud but more to himself, then glanced back to see the black and white following up the onramp and into traffic behind them. 623 he assumed.

"Wish we had a way to clear some of this traffic," Simon muttered.

"623," Lucas said in to the mic, "hang back and slow this traffic if you can please."

"Copy, 186," the uniform said.

"Gonna need more than one car," Simon said.

Lucas shrugged. "He can try."

Simon grunted, wishing the uniform luck as he sped around a semi and closed on the van as traffic thinned a little as they crossed the intersection with Chouteau, where another black and white appeared to join the pursuit.

"620, joining pursuit," the uniformed driver called over the radio.

"182 is in position," Maberry called.

Simon keyed the radio. "Copy 182, 620. Get ready on that onramp at Antioch, 182, and cut him off. I'll PIT him."

The PIT maneuver (Pursuit Intervention Technique), or TVI (Tactical Vehicle Intervention) developed by the Fairfax County Police in Virginia was basically a pursuit tactic by which a pursuing car forced a fleeing car to turn sideways abruptly, causing the driver to lose control and stop, often involving them spinning out, and sometimes flipping or crashing. The idea was to end a high speed pursuit without further possibility of injury to anyone else on the road. And usually the criminals survived it as well.

"Copy, 186," came several replies.

A few cars were pulling to each side as they sped past on I-35, but others ahead just kept going as the van and Simon dodged around them. Just past Antioch, I-35 split to join I-29 going south while ramps led to state highway 71 North, so Simon wanted to stop the van before it got there.

Groves of trees lined the right side of the freeway as they sped along and Simon saw the sign for exit 8C. "That's where they'll be," he pointed out to Lucas.

"I hope we can stop them," Lucas said as Simon maneuvered around a semi that had been trying to get over when the van cut it off by speeding around to its right.

"Didn't you learn tactical driving at the Academy?" Simon said, frowning. "The PIT is textbook now."

"Yes, developed in Virginia, I believe," Lucas said.

"Yeah, okay, just relax and watch," Simon said.

As they approached the exit, he sped up past a few more scattered cars, closing in on the van.

"I have to get my front end up beside him as soon as the other cars cut him off," Simon narrated.

"186, we're almost there," Lucas called into the radio.

They passed exit 8C now, moving over Antioch and past the Islamic Center of North Kansas City, and then the unmarked explorer and black and white appeared Code 1, lights and sirens, and sped out on I-35 in front of the van, applying their brakes and forcing the driver to slow. He tried to go around them but they continued angling across the lanes in front of them.

As they did, Simon managed to pull up on the van so the Charger's front wheels were even with the van's back wheels, then he turned sharply right into them and the van began spinning out. It bumped into the back of a box truck, pushing it sideways, and then the driver tried to recover, pressing the accelerator and turning the wheel sharply back and forth. Just as he seemed to be getting control again, he pulled out to go around the box truck on the right and ran right into slowed traffic. He braked, swerved and plowed right into the large pole holding up one half of the large freeway navigation sign, his van twisting like a pretzel as it spun around again.

Simon pulled the Charger to a stop on the shoulder with Maberry and Dolby and the two black and whites close behind. "Go! Go!" he yelled as he and Lucas jumped out weapons drawn, and ran toward the van. The right front and left rear wheel were now raised off the pavement, the van was so twisted, and Simon feared for the worst for anyone inside.

His heart pounding, Simon raced up and yanked hard on the side door, cursing as he tried to pull it open and finally managed a crack, peering inside. Then he gave up and yanked open the passenger door. "Where are they?!"

The driver was crumpled across the twin front streets, his face and hair bloodied, clearly dead. Simon glanced past him as Lucas finally managed to yank open the sliding side door and saw another man, Hispanic, pinned between the twisted back seat and the backs of the front seats, also dead.

"Fuck!" Simon yelled.

"They're not here," Lucas said.

"Damn it!"

"The must be back near where you picked up the van," Dolby suggested.

"Worlds of Fun," Lucas said.

"The park is cleared out," Dolby said.

"In case of explosion," Maberry added.

Simon and Lucas realized the possibility at the same time.

"Holy shit!" Simon said as both spun and started back toward the Charger.

"Where you going?" Dolby asked.

"Let the uniforms handle this," Simon called back. "I gotta find Emma!"

And then they were climbing into the car and pulling back out into traffic, Simon looking for the nearest off ramp.

CHAPTER 25

EMMA AND JULIE HAD managed to kick their kayaks almost to the edge of Buccaneer Bay after a few false twists and turns and collisions with other boats, when Julie got to the edge and tried to grab hold but as she pulled to lift herself over onto the land, the kayak slid in the opposite direction and her legs fell in the water as she screamed and scrambled with her tied hands and upper torso to stay on it.

"Oh my God! I don't wanna die! I don't wanna die!" she kept saying.

"Calm down," Emma tried to soothe her with a soft tone. "Easy goes it. Pull yourself back up."

Finally, in desperation as she started to slip, Julie kicked out with both feet against the shoreline and pushed enough of her back on the kayak to steady herself. Slowly, she shifted to recenter herself and pull herself back on as Emma reached the shore.

Emma lifted a foot onto the cement dock and used it to pull her kayak parallel with the shore, then pushed quickly with her other foot and rolled at the same time, managing to roll right off the kayak onto land. She cried out in victory, then looked back at Julie. "Okay, that worked. You try it."

Julie shook her head. "No way. I'm fine here."

"You gotta try, Julie!" Emma urged.

"No! You go get help. I'm fine," Julie insisted.

Emma cursed to herself and debated whether to risk leaving her friend or staying. With no cell phone and her hands tied, she ultimately decided to stay put for the moment. "Come on, Julie, I know you can do it," she encouraged.

Julie shook her head even more adamantly and stayed where she was.

IF SIMON HADN'T violated KCPD policies before when chasing the van, he certainly had in getting to Worlds Of Fun at speeds pushing ninety miles per hour. To his credit, Lucas kept his mouth shut, sitting beside him. When they reached the amusement park, he headed back up Worlds of Fun Avenue and turned right where they'd seen the van emerge from the park's administrative entrance, crossing a large employee parking lot toward the admin buildings at the far end.

"The park is very big," Lucas said. "Very strange architecture."

"Yeah, it's an amusement park, with rides and games for people to have fun on all day," Simon explained with amusement.

"That's what those tubes and tracks are?" Lucas asked.

"Yes, they have rollercoasters—like little trains—that travel on them at high speed," Simon said.

"People don't fall out?" Lucas looked worried.

"They have safety harnesses and seat belts and bars," Simon said as he pulled to a stop in front of the admin building and they looked around for any sign of the girls.

"Where do you think they will be?" Lucas asked.

"I have no idea," Simon said.

"That gate is open," Lucas said, pointing to a maintenance gate behind a smaller building nearby. A drive lead through it and into the park.

Simon immediately drove the Charger toward it. A gate being left open when the park had been cleared for an emergency was certainly suspicious. "Good call. At least that'll get us in."

"And we can move faster in a car," Lucas said.

"Until we run out places we can drive at least," Simon added as he steered through the gate and followed the maintenance road.

"How will we find them?" Lucas asked as they drove inside, passing under the towering Steelhawk thrill ride with its ferris-wheel-like suspended seats that spun people 301 feet up in the air at incredible speeds, the yellow towering Timber Wolf coaster on the left and Patriot coaster on the right.

Simon had no answer to Lucas' question as they both looked around. The air was still filled with the smell of popcorn and hotdogs and funnel cakes and all the usual thrill park foods with carts abandoned where they stood and restaurants and stores barely closed behind steel gates that dropped from the ceiling. Clearly the staff hoped to come back when it was clear and properly secure things—if the park was still here. They'd had to balance the need to obey the evacuation order with some sense of minimum security. A few strollers and toys were also abandoned as parents had no doubt grabbed young children and rushed toward the nearest exit.

Finally, Simon keyed the radio. "186 to 182 and 692. Can either of you join us at Worlds of Fun?"

"182, we're almost there," Maberry replied.

"Come through the maintenance gate off the admin area," Simon instructed. "We'll go right, you go left."

"182, copy," Maberry said.

"692, overhead," Brock replied then as Simon heard the whirring of blades above them. "Going left."

"Okay," Simon said and released the radio button, then stuck his head out of the car and yelled, "Emma! Julie!"

Taking the hint, Lucas joined him, calling their names. Simon wasn't even sure they could be heard now over the chopper, but the effort made him feel better as he took the right fork in the maintenance road and drove past Ripcord, another towering ride, this one that swung riders on bungee-like cables at fast speed high overhead, toward the CocaCola freestyle sign.

"Emma! Julie!" Lucas called beside him.

Simon feared they'd never find them if they didn't get out and search, but where would they start? It could take hours. Fuck.

"WE'RE READY," SAIC GARNER said as he clicked off

the radio beside her and nodded to Becker. They were standing outside the mobile command unit now under a canopy with Penhall, Hanson, Bailey, Tucker, Deputy Chief Melson, and FBI Agents Stein and Falk.

Robots had placed the WiFi jammers at strategic points near enough to where Derrick's team was holed up that the cops hoped they'd be effective. The FBI had employed robots with signal detectors to locate the source of the WiFi and detect the frequencies. The jammers would render the WiFi useless by transmitting synchronized radio waves at the same frequency to increase signal-to-noise ratio and blur the signal. Fortunately, this time, none of them had been shot at.

"Notifying teams," Stein said behind him as he and Falk got on their radios and Becker did the same.

"Holding for confirmation," Garner replied. They at least wanted all law enforcement personnel aware of what was happening so they could anticipate a possible reaction from Derrick or his people. What form that might take was anyone's guess, but at least they'd be ready.

"LET'S GO!" DERRICK ordered over the comm as the last of his teams called to confirm their readiness. Seven minutes earlier, Edson had called to confirm the two hostages had been secured and that he and Jackson were headed for point Omega, their final rendesvous. They'd be first at the Downtown airport and aboard the plane.

"All personnel converge on route Zebra," Luis repeated over the comm channel as confirmation. The personnel around him confirmed final settings on their computers and equipment then headed for the door as Luis and Derrick followed.

The tunnel to the surface was three yards from their mine cave and wide enough for two men to walk out at a time, provided they weren't wearing big packs or carrying anything large between them. The climb was steep but took about a minute for men in good condition, which all of his men were.

Derrick waited at the bottom as his command team and the first remote team converged and started toward the surface. Then the lights flickered and went out.

"They cut the power!" one of the men said.

Derrick smirked. "Generators are on," he said, not even remotely concerned, and the man grunted and hurried on into the tunnel.

Two more teams appeared, moving at a fast pace along the main tunnel, among them was Harris.

"V-Day!" Harris said and raised a clenched fist.

"Hooah!" shouted several others as they too filed into the tunnel.

It was a day they'd all looked forward to, despite the setbacks. They'd anticipated the Feds' and cops' every move, even if things hadn't gone as planned. Soon they'd be in the air and laughing as the idiots floundered as usual. They were no match for Derrick or his team.

He waited for two more teams, then headed into the tunnel himself. The rest were further out and would follow shortly. He wanted to be up top when the copter arrived.

BECKER HUNG UP the phone. A Kansas City Power and Light rep had confirmed they'd killed power to the grid feeding Subtropolis, UnderCity, and the surrounding neighborhood. "Power's out," she reported to the others.

"Now we see if they call us," Garner said.

"Get teams ready to infiltrate on our command," Stein said into a radio beside him.

Becker signaled to Penhall to call to KCPD's own assault teams who were standing by. Then they heard gunshots from overhead and everyone scrambled for the nearest cover—ducking down behind vehicles, a few racing for safety under the mobile command center's canopy with Becker and the others.

"Where's it coming from?!" Falk yelled.

"Is anyone being shot at?!" Deputy Chief Melson called out.

Radio chatter clouded the airwaves as people reported in. Then a voice broke through. "We think it's coming from the mine above us."

Everyone looked in the direction of the mine atop UnderCity and Subtropolis.

"Who's up there?" Becker asked.

"A couple of ours," Stein said as Falk keyed his radio and hailed that team.

EMMA HAD MANAGED to stand and was trying to loosen the ropes securing her hands behind her by rubbing them against the edge of a stake-like sign pole near Buccaneer Bay, all the while keeping her eyes on Julie who was still frozen atop her kayak and starting to drift out again.

"You've gotta at least kick and stay close to shore, Julie!" Emma called.

"I might fall!" Julie shouted.

"Just do it slow like we did before," Emma urged.

"Emma!"

Emma stopped, looking around. Was someone calling her name? Then she heard chopping overhead. Was that a helicopter?

"I think the police are here!" she shouted excitedly to Julie as she moved away from the sign post to the open, looking up, craning to see any hopeful sign.

"Do you see something?" Julie called back in desperation.

"Hang on!" Emma said. The chopping was nearby but she couldn't see the copter or any cops. "Dad! Over here!" she yelled at the top of her lungs three times, wishing her arms were free so she could wave overhead the minute a person or vehicle appeared.

After a minute, with no sign of the helicopter and no more shouts of her name, she rushed back over to the post again and began working the ropes even harder, slipping a little because her hands and arms were starting to sweat now.

"What are you doing?!" Julie demanded.

"Trying to get my hands free so I can signal them!"

"Go find them! Get help!" Julie yelled back.

But Emma hesitated. She wasn't sure it was safe to leave her friend. Their captors had been away several minutes, so they were probably gone, right? Still, without knowing where the copter or help might come from, should she risk it?

She threw every ounce of her strength into rubbing the rope against the sharp stake-like pole faster and faster, up and down.

"EMMA! JULIE!" SIMON and Lucas kept calling alternately as they made their way through the park, stopping to check the rides and buildings as they went. They'd made it past International Plaza to the park's Scandinavia section and Lucas was checking the Viking Voyager with its log shaped boats while Simon checked the Nordic Chaser, which had pirate-style boat shaped seats for two that flew around a central axis at increasing speeds, when a call came over the radio.

"I think I've got something," Brock said.

"692, what is it?" Simon answered immediately.

"Someone on a kayak in Buccaneer Bay," Brock said, then paused. "I think it's a girl...Wait! There's another on the shore. She's jumping up and down, yelling at me, I think."

"Emma!" Simon said and rushed back for the Charger.

"Where's Buccaneer Bay?" Lucas asked as they climbed in.

"Fuck if I know," Simon said and keyed the radio again. "Where's Buccaneer Bay?"

"Oceans of Fun," Brock replied as Simon turned the ignition and the Charger's engine roared to life. "We pulled up a map on google."

Simon pushed the accelerator as he asked, "How do we get there?"

"Where are you? I'll guide you in," Brock said.

"Over in Scandinavia by the—" Simon looked around as he slowed the car, waiting for directions.

"Viking Voyager," Lucas said.

"Viking Voyager," Simon repeated into the radio. "The log ride."

"Gotcha," Brock answered. "Give me a few seconds. Turning back."

"182, where are you?" Simon said into the radio as he listened for the chopper blades to come overhead again.

"186, we're over by Planet Snoopy," Dolby replied. "Heading that way."

"No," Simon said. "Keep looking in case it's a false alarm. We're running out of time."

"Copy, 186," Dolby replied.

The chuffing of the blades drew nearer and Lucas pointed. "He's there!"

Seconds later, Simon saw the copter circling overhead. "We see you, 692," he called.

"I've got you, too, 186," Brock replied. "Okay, go straight ahead around past Scrambler and under the railroad bridge."

"Copy," Simon said as he accelerated again and followed the winding path, narrowly missing a few trashcans and benches at one of the turns. There was a bridge to the right over a water channel that seemed to be pedestrian only, too narrow for the car. To the left was the Boomerang thrill ride with its winding track that formed multiple loops in the air, but that looked like a dead end. "692, are we at a dead end?"

"Copy, 186," Brock replied. "I thought I saw a maintenance road but it was partially covered. Doesn't go through."

"182, do you copy?" Simon said as he shut off the engine and opened his door, standing, as Lucas followed.

"Copy, 186," Dolby replied.

"We're proceeding on foot," Simon replied. "Proceed to assist."

"On our way," Dolby said.

Simon rushed across the pedestrian bridge into an area marked Africa with a Dinosaur store and a Moroccan-named souvenir stand. "Where to, 692?" Simon called into the radio as he looked up to see the chopper overhead.

"Straight ahead then left, under the next railroad bridge," Brock said.

Simon ran, Lucas on his heels, and found himself between another row of stores with the railroad track visible up ahead, elevated above the ground on pillars past an African game store, ATM, and restrooms. Simon had never run so hard in his life. His lungs strained for air and his feet ached, but he wasn't stopping for anything until he got to Emma.

He glanced over at Lucas who was keeping up with ease. Motherfucker. If the guy wasn't so damn nice, he'd be easy to hate.

They passed together under the railroad tracks again as the chopped stayed with them overhead. Simon keyed the radio again, "Where now?"

"Keep going straight," Brock said. "Up ahead around the next curve. Past Fury of the Nile, there's a gate linking the two parks, and it's open."

As they ran, Simon heard a car behind them. Lucas turned back as he kept running, and said, "182."

Simon didn't care. He just kept running. Let Maberry and Dolby follow. And they did.

They ran past the back edge of the amphitheater which hosted in-park concerts and then saw the waters of the Fury of The Nile circular raft ride to their left on the opposite side as they started to round a bend. The mamba rollercoaster's huge arcing tracks climbed steeply into the air high above them up ahead its red tracks supported by large white metal poles and beams. High up at the top, Simon saw the tail end of one train that had been left parked there when the park was cleared.

Then they rounded the bend and went back the other way between Fury and the Mamba, seeing signs labeled "Oceans of Fun Access Ahead."

"Straight ahead!" Brock called encouragingly.

"Emma! Julie!" Simon and Lucas shouted again, ignoring the fact the chuffing helicopter was probably drowning them out.

They pushed through the gate as they heard car door slamming behind them and footsteps and Maberry and

Dolby ran in pursuit.

"Right! Go right, under the blue flumes of Monsoon!" Brock instructed.

"Dad!" Simon thought he heard several times. Was that Emma's voice? Despite exhaustion, he found a sudden reserve and sped up, racing around a curving walkway right under the aqua blue curved flume tubes passing overhead and around a corner past a fence labeled Buccaneer Bay through which Simon saw a giant pond and then spotted Emma jumping up and down on the dock, yelling for him, her hands tied behind her back.

"I'm coming, baby!" he yelled, starting toward the fence, then realizing it was too high to jump.

Lucas simply leapt over it without even slowing and headed right for Emma as Simon took the long way, mumbling, "Show off!"

His breathing eased, just from the knowledge his daughter was alive and relatively unharmed as he jogged past a sign for "Crocodile Isle" and headed right again toward volleyball courts and the large "Buccaneer Bay" sign rising in the air behind them.

THE FIRST SHOTS rang out as Derrick reached the top of the tunnel, just before he stepped out into the afternoon air. Men yelled and scrambled, ducking for cover behind piles of rock and abandoned mining equipment as they drew or raised their own weapons and prepared to fire back.

"Sit rep?" Derrick demanded of Luis who'd been one of the first up the tunnel.

"When we came out, two men—Feds, I think—asked who we were and told us to stay where we were," Luis said. "When they started over, Anderson and Dawson tried to take them out."

"They missed?" Derrick asked, frowning.

"Got one in the leg, missed the other," Luis said. "I'd signaled them to wait but—"

"Goddamnit! We can't afford these kinds of fuck ups right now!" Derrick said as he drew his own sidearm. "Get air on the sat phone and get me an ETA."

As Luis dialed beside him, Derrick popped his head out from behind the large yellow excavator where he'd sought cover and spotted the two Feds, then carefully took aim just as one of the men raised his arm from behind a black sedan and flashed a badge. "FBI!:"

Derrick and his men opened fire and the hand flew back down as bullets tore into the side of the sedan, one after the other, windows shattering, tires flattening.

"Three minutes out," Luis called over the comm as everyone looked at Derrick for instructions.

"Kill them," Derrick said and nodded his head toward the Feds.

Everyone opened fire again. One of the Feds tried to fire back but as soon as he lifted his head, bullets tore across the trunk of the sedan straight at him and he ducked down again.

"We're drawing too much attention," Luis said, wrinkling his eyebrows, his body tense.

"By the time they get here, we'll be gone and blowing it," Derrick said. Overhead, they could hear the chuffing of the blades as the helicopters approached.

"I hear they cut the power," Luis said.

"Not our generators," Derrick said and heard a cry as one of the Feds fell back, dead, shot in the chest dead center multiple times.

"What if they use signal blockers?" Luis asked.

Derrick smiled. "Backup plan." All the timers had been built with a failsafe that would trigger the bombs within twenty minutes of being set. The plan had been to trigger them in a preplanned cycle before that. Nothing could stop it now. The damage wouldn't be as great this way, but it would keep the cops busy and help cover their escape.

Derrick watched as his men took down the last Fed across the quarry, then rocks jangled and blew across the dusty ground as the choppers lowered down into position.

"Everyone load up!" Derrick ordered and watched as his people scrambled aboard the copters, their spinning blades cutting through the air around them as they ran.

BECKER FELT HERSELF relax a bit as the gunfire from above in the quarry went silent.

"Shit! They're not responding," Falk said as he released the talk button on his radio.

"Assault team is reporting two choppers taking off," Penhall yelled from nearby as they all heard the helicopters whirring overhead.

"Son of bitch!" Stein said.

"Let's get after them!" Becker ordered, motioning to her people, who scrambled into action, some heading for vehicles, others getting on radios.

Then they heard a rumbling as the ground shook beneath their feet and UnderCity exploded in front of them.

SIMON RACED PAST Splash Island with its playground slides surrounded by jets that shot water straight up out of the ground and from all directions and turned right toward the dock of Buccaneer Bay as Lucas finished untying Emma's hands and she raced into his embrace. The air was filled with the musky smell of stale water and chlorine, the clouds puffy and white amongst a clear blue sea overhead that belied the danger unfolding below.

"Daddy!"

"Thank God you're okay," he mumbled, pulling her tight. No embrace from her had ever felt so good and they held it a minute before she turned back as Maberry and Dolby arrived.

"Kick, Julie! Come on!" Emma screamed as Julie yelled from the kayak out almost in the center of Bucanneer Bay again.

"We'll get her," Simon said, motioning to Dolby and Maberry as Lucas moved toward the edge of the dock. "Get her outta here, back to your car."

Dolby put a gentle hand at the small of Emma's back, guiding her back away from the water. "Come on, honey."

Simon didn't wait to see if they were gone before hurrying to join Lucas.

"Come on, Julie, we're right here waiting. Let's go home," Simon called.

Then there was a vibration as the ground shook beneath them and rocked them on their feet, sending small waves across the water. Julie kicked frantically and then suddenly screamed and fell off.

"Her hands!" Lucas yelled and dove into the water, swimming toward her and ducking under a swan boat then weaving between two kayaks.

Simon looked back to see that Maberry, Dolby, and Emma were gone, then prepared to jump in after his partner but Lucas had Julie around the neck with an arm and was gently swimming and pulling her back to shore with him.

Simon got down on his knees and pulled her onto the dock where she sputtered and coughed, spitting out water as Simon clasped Lucas by the hand and pulled him up onto the dock beside him.

Then the ground shook again twice in a row.

"Fuck!" Simon said as he stood and pulled Julie to her feet. "We gotta run!"

Without a moment's hesitation, Lucas scooped Julie up into his arms and took off running, Simon on his heels, out past Splash Island and the volleyball courts and then around past Crocodile Isle and under the flumes of Monsoon once again, the ground shaking and rumbling as they ran. Lucas just kept running, Simon gradually falling behind.

Jesus Christ, they're blowing it up! he thought as he stumbled and fell to one knee.

Lucas stopped and turned back, clearly debating whether he should help his friend.

Simon waved him forward frantically. "Go! Go! Go!" Then got back up and raced after him.

He glanced back as he ran and saw the ground giving way behind them as Buccaneer Bay disappeared into an expanding hole and the ground shook again and again from rumbling explosions.

The last thing he saw before he fell again was Emma partway into Maberry and Dolby's Explorer, looking back at him and screaming, "Daddy!"

Then he was falling and the world went black.

CHAPTER 26

IT HAD JUST BEEN one explosion at first, ironically the calm before the storm. That turned out to just be the beginning, because shortly thereafter came a whole set of explosions, one after another—at least twenty by the time she lost count. Someone else had said thirty-two. Becker didn't doubt it. Altogether it had lasted around three minutes, and afterwards, she had been too busy to worry about it—checking on her people in person and by radio or phone, issuing orders, and generally trying to pull the pieces back together and respond to the ongoing danger posed by the escaping helicopters and the bombers presumably aboard them.

They'd probably lost an assault team and most certainly two FBI agents. None of which could be confirmed until they'd stabilized the scene and were sure it was safe. No one else had more than minor injuries so far but there were homes and businesses destroyed, and God only knew how far the damage stretched—reports were still coming in piece by piece.

Once everyone around here was back at it, her thoughts turned to her team: Simon, Lucas, Dolby, Maberry. Where they? Last she'd heard over the radio they'd been pursuing the brown van up near Worlds Of Fun. She needed to find them or at least make contact and confirm they were okay.

She keyed the radio. "180, Does anyone have a location on 186 and 182?"

"Last reported location for 186 and 182 was Worlds Of Fun, a dispatcher responded.

"180, 692."

"Go ahead, 692," Becker said.

"692 is over Worlds of Fun now," the helicopter observer—she thought it was Jason Brock—reported. "Last known location of 182, 186. We are trying to confirm status now."

Becker took a deep breath. God, let them be okay. "Copy, 692, please confirm ASAP."

"Copy, 180, will do," Brock replied.

Becker turned to the FBI agents. "How soon until we're secure to check on our assault team?"

"It could be a while," Falk said. "We're sending robots with explosive detectors now. We have to make sure nothing live is left."

"Jesus," Becker said. "We need to get someone after those helicopters, too." She keyed the radio again. "180, TAC Air now." She was requesting the TACTICAL Air channel that went out system wide to all units, regardless of channel or location.

"Copy, 180, TAC Air," dispatch said, indicating what Becker said now would go out system wide.

Becker continued, "All units, be on the lookout for two large helicopters headed from our location at Northeast Underground Road to unknown location. Suspects believed to be aboard. 16:01 hours. 180, clear."

"Copy, 180," dispatch replied, indicating she was off TAC Air.

Around the city, every available unit was now keeping watch for the two helicopters and would report in. Becker wished she had more details, a better description, but any unit that spotted them would report those as well, keeping everyone updated through dispatch until someone called for TAC Air again.

Now she busied herself with her duties and waited for word on her people.

THE WORLD WAS BLACK and silent. Then he opened his eyes and realized someone was touching him. It took a moment to grasp that they were checking him for injuries.

Screaming. Multiple voices. It was like a switch flipped and his ears came back on.

He groaned and tried to roll over.

"Take it easy, John," someone said. Art Maberry, his fellow detective.

"Let me help you," said another—Lucas, his partner and friend. They pulled at his arms and side, gently helping him as he rolled over and looked up into Lucas' blue eyes. The android was kneeling beside him, and Emma was standing nearby, hugging Dolby and crying.

"Emma?" Simon said, his voice cracking.

"Daddy!" Emma rushed over and knelt, throwing her arms around him.

"I'm okay, baby," Simon said, patting her head. "It's okay." Then he looked at Lucas. "What happened?"

"Explosions," Lucas said. "Oceans of Fun is gone."

"We were lucky to get out when we did," Maberry said.

"How long was I out?" Simon asked.

"Two minutes, tops," Dolby said.

"I thought you were dead!" Emma said and embraced him again.

"Takes more than that to take out your old man, babe," he said, rubbing her back as he held her. "I'm fine."

"692 to 182 and 185, what is your status, over," Brock's voice came over Simon's shoulder radio, crackling and barely audible.

"Get on the radio and tell him we're all okay," Maberry said, looking at Lucas as Simon noticed Maberry's shoulder mic was cracked.

"On it," Lucas said and keyed his own radio, calling it in.

Simon looked toward Dolby and Maberry's Explorer, which was nearby and thought he heard crying. He saw a girl sitting there, blinked to clear his vision. "Julie?" he asked.

"Yeah, she's fine," Emma said.

"In the car," Dolby added.

"You seem to be all in one piece," Lucas said next as he finished on the radio and went back to examining Simon.

"Good, then help me off this fucking ground," Simon said and reached up as Emma let go and stood.

Simon bent and grasped Simon's hand then heaved, pulling him to his feet. Simon wobbled a bit and Lucas steadied him with a strong hand on the shoulder.

"I'm okay," Simon said, realizing the air smelled of sulfur, dirt, chlorine, and smoke. He turned around and looked back toward Oceans of Fun. It was in shambles, most of it sunken into a giant crater now. "Jesus Christ! Those motherfuckers!" He looked around. Some rollercoaster tracks and rides had partially collapsed, a couple of nearby roofs showed damage, but it appeared to be relatively unscathed by comparison and the ground was cracked but still holding solid.

"Luckily we cleared the civilians and staff," Maberry said.

"How many did we lose?" Simon asked as he checked his radio and sidearm. No visible damage but he readjusted the volume to his earpiece.

"Not sure yet," Maberry said. "Our shoulder units got damaged when we fell."

"We gotta get these bastards," Simon said and headed for the Explorer, grabbing Emma's hand and dragging her along. "Get me to the Charger."

Maberry climbed in the driver's seat as Dolby led Julie around to the passenger side and helped her in followed by Lucas. Emma got in next to her with Simon behind the driver.

"Well, this is a tight fit," Emma said as Maberry pulled the car into a turn and headed back away from Oceans of Fun.

"Just for a few minutes," Simon said.

"They lost some Feds and maybe an assault team," Lucas reported.

"What about Derrick?" Simon said, realizing he hadn't heard it, then remembering his radio was on a side channel during the pursuit.

"Escaped in two helicopters with his men," Lucas said as they passed between the amphitheater and Worlds of Fun railroad and Detonator, another towering ride rising high into the sky, appeared ahead on the right. Radio chatter filled the background. Maberry was pushing forty miles per hour around narrow turns, but Simon couldn't care less. Derrick and the other assholes were getting away.

"Fucking assholes!" Simon said as he put his radio back on the main channel and it crackled to life again. "Can you two get Julie and Emma back to Central?"

"No fucking way we're missing this!" Maberry snapped. "I want a piece of these motherfuckers!"

"Units are already in pursuit," Dolby said.

"Get back on and have 692 meet us in the parking lot out by the admin building. We have to go after them," Simon said.

"You sending the girls with them? They can only hold four," Maberry said as he took a sharp right through the Wild West area and narrowly missed hitting a Coca Cola refresh kiosk, arcing on right and out toward the fountain at the center of Americana.

"Actually, five, but the weight limit is an issue, especially for speed," Lucas said like something out of a textbook he'd read out of the Academy.

Meanwhile, Dolby was on the radio calling the chopper.

"They don't know where they're going," Dolby said as she finished.

"No one's located the helicopters yet," Lucas added.

Maberry shot past the fountain and curved right again, Ripcord and Patriot looming on the left as they followed signs toward Orient and International Plaza. "You left it up here somewhere, right?" Maberry asked.

"In Africa, past Scandinavia, just beyond the railroad bridge," Lucas confirmed. Simon was glad because his memory was still a bit hazy and he was too busy making a plan in his head.

They passed the International Plaza as the Viking Voyager loomed on the right, and in two minutes were at the Charger. Simon and Lucas raced over and led Maberry and Dolby back out via the maintenance gate, the way they'd come in, both cars running Code 1—lights and sirens.

MD500E's were smaller copters than the more common military ones like the Hueys. With room for two up front and three in back, depending upon weight, they had four large round windows in the cockpit and two on each side designed to allow maximum line of sight and five-bladed main rotors designed for fast lift and greater speed. An MD500E could reach maximum speeds around 152 knots, or 171.6 miles per hour, compared to the Huey's 140 knots (161 mph). The helicopter was waiting in the open area of the parking lot, blades spinning, Brock standing twenty feet out, waiting for them.

They pulled up alongside and Simon jumped out, handing Brock his car keys then shouted to be heard over the chopper, "You take my car and get these girls back to Central, okay? Have them checked out at the ER."

"What? I have to get back aboard," Brock shouted back, looking confused.

"We're going to find Derrick and his men," Simon snapped. "Please, that's my daughter." He didn't wait for an answer but rushed toward the chopper, bending to clear the blades as he headed for the front seat, Lucas on his heels.

For a moment, he thought he heard Emma calling after him, then he was climbing through the open sides of the chopper and into the observer's seat. "Get us in the air and headed to the downtown airport," Simon said to the confused pilot.

Maberry rushed over and handed him a hand radio. "We got this off one of the men in the van. Maybe you can eavesdrop."

Simon nodded. "Thanks."

Maberry grunted and hurried back toward the others and the Explorer.

"What about Brock?" the pilot, Schaefer, asked.

"We're after the men who tried to murder my daughter and just killed an assault team and two Feds," Simon snapped as he slipped on Brock's abandoned headset with microphone and headphones. "He'll take my car in." He glanced over to see Brock looking angry and arguing with Maberry and Dolby.

Technically, Brock outranked him and Simon had no real authority over the chopper but Schaefer didn't argue. The bird lifted into the air and headed off. Simon would smooth it out later if he could.

"Why the downtown airport?" Lucas asked from the back. He wore an identical headset and was using the internal comm system of the chopper.

"That's where I think the van was headed," Simon said. "It wasn't toward KCI."

"So we're guessing?" Schaefer asked.

"Until someone spots them," Simon said. "The downtown airport is closer and it's almost a straight shot north from there to KCI. If we don't spot the Hueys downtown, we'll go there next." It had to be one or the other. "Choppers and ground transportation won't get them out fast enough with everyone looking for them."

"Makes sense to me," Schaefer said and turned the chopper southwest as Simon tried to listen over Derrick's men's radio.

THE CHOPPERS IN THIS case were actually Bell 412's, the civilian equivalent of Hueys, designed to hold two crew and up to thirteen passengers and heavy equipment. The Bell's were fifty-six feet, 1 inch long compared to the MD500E's thirty feet ten inches. They were also 7 feet taller and had four-blade rotors, and were a lot noisier and rougher ride.

The rotors whop-whopped overhead as the signature smell of exhaust filled his nose and made Derrick feel right at home. He contacted his pilots aboard the rented Lear jet again, speaking loudly to be sure he could be heard over the constant whine of the transmission. "We're four minutes out. Be ready to lift off as soon as we're aboard."

"Roger, Colonel," the pilot replied.

A direct route to the downtown airport was five minutes but to avoid quick detection, they'd taken a wider arc north over less populated areas and turned south, lengthening their journey by several minutes. As they neared the airport, though, for safety, the pilot was swinging back around to one of the authorized approach channels for copters which took them back east before they came in.

Next Derrick hailed the other chopper. "ETA four minutes. Set us down as close to the Lear as you can then leave the birds. They're ready and waiting."

"Okay, Colonel," the other pilot, Rogers, answered.

"They'll be looking for us with everything they've got," Luis said.

"They have no idea where to look," Derrick said. "We got out too fast and they got started too late." By the time the cops figure out where they were, he and his men would be half way to Mexico.

"They could send fighters after us," Luis said.

"Why we're switching planes in the panhandle," Derrick said. "By the time they figure out who we are, we'll be out of U.S. airspace."

Luis still looked worried but Derrick wasn't. The plan was too well organized, the pilots too skilled. Fake papers and flight plans had been filed, the plane's IDs changed—they'd thought of everything. There was even a playbook for dealing with nosey air traffic controllers if it came to that. His team had too much experience at infiltration and extraction. This part was what they did best. His only regret was not being able to survey the damage. He'd have to wait for the news reports for that. Maybe he'd check the internet once they swapped planes in Texas.

He smiled at the images of destruction flashing through his imagination. America may have lost her way, but brave souls like his men wouldn't give up without a fight. To be strong, she had to be ready. She had to be alert and ready for trouble around every turn, from every unexpected quarter. Like they had after 9/11 briefly when America came together with united focus and purpose for the first time in decades. This America was weak, afraid, too easily offended, too quick to attack each other and speak out about rights for their enemies. America the great knew its position and its place, as well as its superiority and power. Forget those who couldn't keep up. We had to take care of ourselves and our own. We were not the world's babysitters or gatekeepers. We were the best of the best, the sole superpower, destined to show them all how it's done, not be at their mercy.

Today was just the beginning. America was about to get a series of wake up calls that would remind her of what mattered. Maybe then she could remember who she was supposed to be and truly be great again. He'd die for that cause like his father and grandfather before him. It was the least he could do to protect their legacy, to give their sacrifice meaning.

SIMON HAD HEARD Derrick on the radio and Lucas was running quick calculations.

"The downtown airport is the most likely destination given the factors of time and distance," Lucas said, sounding more like an android than he had in a while. He was talking loudly despite the radio to be heard over the noise of the chopper.

The wind flying by outside whistled as the chopper wound its way. The choppers usually didn't travel at such high speed when the sides were wide open. From above them came the steady popping of the blades as the tips flexed and hit friction time and again and the steady whine of the transmission filled his ears. Altogether though, Simon thought the ride was a lot smoother than the military copters he'd been on a few times. Those jerked you around like marionettes in a tornado, whereas the MD500E seemed to compare more to a sports car.

"So, they're headed downtown," Simon said. "See if you can get ahead of them, Schaefer. We need to delay them if we can while people get in place."

"I'll do my best," Schaefer said, pressing the yoke and a few buttons as the helicopter picked up speed.

Simon keyed the police radio. "Dispatch, 692, I need TAC Air, stat!"

"Copy, 692, go for TAC Air," dispatch replied.

"692, we have confirmation the helicopters are headed to the Downtown Airport," Simon reported, his voice going out to everyone on KCPD's radio bands, broken up a bit by the wind. "Look for a Lear Jet with engines running. We need to hold all planes. We have three minutes!"

"Can we make it?" Lucas asked as Schaefer said, "I'll notify air traffic control," and spoke into his radio to the airport tower.

"We have to try," Simon said. The MD500E was faster and lighter, with far less passengers giving it an advantage. And

Schaefer was pushing the speed to top safety limits in the skies over a city at the moment.

"692, 137, we have visual on your targets going over 29 at Bedford," a female cop reported.

"Where are we?" Simon said aloud as he looked down below them for landmarks.

"210 and 29," Lucas said just as Simon got visual confirmation of the same.

"Damn it," Simon said. "We'll never catch them."

"Actually, I think I've got visual ahead," Schaefer said and Simon's head snapped back forward as he squinted out the cockpit windows. He could see a couple of dots in the distance ahead.

"Got any more speed?" Simon asked, looking at Schaefer.

"There are safety limits and regulations, bro," Schaefer said.

"Test them," Simon snapped and Schaefer adjusted controls once more, speeding up again. The popping of the blades became more frequent, but Simon knew from experience it was normal to fast flying copters. He glanced out the front again and could make out what looked like the civilian equivalent of Hueys, the type seen in so many war films, though he couldn't remember what the civilian type were called.

He turned in his seat to look back at Lucas and motioned to a rifle in a rack between the seats. "Okay, buddy, it's up to you. See if you can slow them down."

Lucas frowned as he pulled the rifle from its slot and examined it. "Where do I aim?"

"You don't want to bring it down over the city," Schaefer said. "It might crash into people or traffic."

"Right, so try and hit the people or at least force them down," Simon said. "But if we get them over the river or a large undeveloped area, go for the tail rotor, the rotor up top, or the fuel tanks in the lower rear. Any of them would have a chance of bringing her down fast."

"We're too far away," Schaefer called.

"Maybe he can distract them at least," Simon said.

Schaefer shook his head. "He'll never hit them."

Simon ignored him and locked eyes with Lucas. "You'll have to account for wind resistance. But you're the only one of us who might stand a chance."

"I will try," Lucas said and loaded the rifle, before moving into position so he could hang out the side of the copter without falling.

Simon leaned back forward toward Schaefer. "Get us as close as you can then a bit of an angle," he said.

"This isn't going to work," Schaefer said, shaking his head.

"We just need to buy a little time," Simon said. "Headquarters is downtown. The airport will be swamped with KCPD."

"I'll do what I can," Schaefer mumbled with a small nod, resignation on his face.

As Schaefer maneuvered the helicopter, Lucas did his best to line up a shot. Simon jumped in the back and wrapped one arm around an overhead bar, while grabbing onto Lucas' belt with the other. Lucas shot him a puzzled look.

"If you need to lean out further, I've got you," Simon said.

"I think I've got this," Lucas said.

THE HELICOPTER DESCENDED and the pilot, Counts, nodded at Derrick. "We're coming up on the airport now, sir."

"You know where the plane is?" Derrick asked.

"Yes, Colonel."

Derrick turned to his team and shouted to be heard over the wind whistling in through the Huey's open sides. "Okay, prepare to disembark and get on that plane. In a few hours, we'll be sipping on margaritas and dancing with señoritas!"

The men whooped, grunted, or cheered, then there was a metallic thunk and a whoosh and something hit the edge of the Huey's passenger bay door. Derrick turned, puzzled, to examine it.

"Someone's shooting at us!" Counts yelled.

"What the fuck?!" said Harris, who was seated near the bay door in the back.

"They won't risk taking us out over the city," Derrick said. "Too many civilians. They're just trying to force us down."

There was another whoosh followed by a thunk as another bullet hit the fuselage just outside the bay doors.

"That was too close!" Harris yelled.

"Find them and shoot back!" Derrick yelled back, pantomiming to be sure they understood him over the noise, but as the men grabbed rifles and moved to position themselves, the copter suddenly arced right and began climbing again, throwing them back against the benches and bulkhead and forcing them to grab on to handles or dangling handholds to steady themselves again.

Derrick whirled around toward Counts. "What the hell, Sergeant?!"

"There's fuckin' cops all over the runways," Counts replied.

"What?!" Derrick said and strained to look out the window at the airport as it faded behind them. Vehicles with flashing lights were surrounding the plane. Then his earphone beeped.

"Colonel, we've got trouble here!" the plane's pilot reported.

"Where are we going?" Derrick demanded as he turned to Counts again.

"Anywhere but here," the pilot said.

Derrick cursed then saw his men watching him, rifle stocks resting on the copter's floorboards. He waved curtly. "Shoot the fuckers! Luis, get me a map."

Luis scrambled for a map as the first man leaned out and aimed his rifle, but before he could fire off a shot, there was another whoosh and thunk as a red dot appeared in the center of his forehead and the rifle dropped as he fell sideways out the side of the bird without another sound.

"They shot Jacobs!" Harris yelled.

"Get in position and fire!" Derrick screamed, pantomiming again as his men scrambled.

"THEY'RE TAKING OFF AGAIN!" Schaefer called over the copter's internal channel as Lucas leaned out for another shot. Lucas had never been on a helicopter before and it was an odd feeling—like hanging from the air. As the copter banked and yanked, it flung them around a bit like the ends of a pendulum, the movement having a few seconds' delay to transfer from the rotors overhead implementing each move to the cabin below.

"Why?" Lucas asked, responding to Schaefer via his mic. He had to concentrate to hear over the popping of the rotors overhead and the droning whine of the transmission. With the air passing through and blowing everything that wasn't nailed down, especially clothing and hair, his sense of balance seemed off. The whole experience was quite disorienting, at least for a first timer.

Simon motioned below them as they followed in the Huey's wakes, looking down to see KCPD cars with lights flashing surrounding a Lear jet, men with guns pointed and ready. "They didn't like the welcoming committee."

"They're kinda fucked," Lucas said and Simon burst out laughing.

"What?" Lucas asked, frowning.

"It's just funny hearing you curse," Simon said.

"Why?"

"Because you're like a kid doing it and you don't do it often," Simon said.

Lucas shrugged. "Let's get these fuckers."

Simon laughed again then tightened his grip on Lucas' belt as Lucas leaned out for another shot.

"You hitting anything?" Schaefer asked.

"Took out a sniper," Lucas said, feeling lucky he'd accomplished even that. His precision might be far superior to humans but with the wind and the constant sharp, abrupt movements of the copter, plus the wind and noise, it was far from the training environment in which he'd gotten used to shooting rifles.

"Shut the fuck up and let the man work," Simon snapped then grinned.

"Hooah," Schaefer said, smiling as he focused on flying.

Lucas leaned out again and heard a whoosh and thunk as his arm jerked. Something had struck it. A bullet? Lucas popped back in. "I am hit."

"You are?" Simon began examining him. "Where'd they get you? Are you okay?"

Lucas pointed to a hole in his shirt sleeve. "I am fine."

"Get back out there and let them know how much that pisses you off," Simon said.

"Perhaps I could dance and sing a song to distract them," Lucas teased.

Simon chortled then gently shoved his friend toward the window. "Would you shoot those assholes already?"

Lucas steadied himself into position again then took

careful aim and fired a series of shots just as the Bells turned and exposed their open passenger bays from the side.

"I GOT THAT FUCKER!" Harris yelled and high fived several others.

"They're still after us. Hit 'em again!" said one of the others when Derrick heard another whoosh and thunk before the man fell bleeding and writhing to the deck.

"Get us down low by the city where they can't risk collateral damage!" Derrick ordered Counts as the Bell took another round of rifle fire and Harris fell wounded onto the passenger deck.

"I can hug the river or go downtown," Counts said.

"Downtown," Derrick snapped back right away as the Bell arced right into a long turn and headed for the skyscraper and hotelscape that made up downtown Kansas City.

The radio lit up with an alarmed call from the other copter, "Taking heavy fire!"

"Get down low!" Derrick replied. "Near to the river or the ground. Collateral damage." He knew he didn't have to explain further. He glanced back as he released the mic button and saw the other Bell 412 diving sharply toward the water, the flashes of gunfire from aboard firing back at its attacker, and he knew it was one copter so his own was safe for now.

"Get us as far from them as you can as fast as you can," Derrick said to Counts. "So they can't find us again."

"They have others," Counts said. "And everyone in the city will be looking for us."

"Just do it!" Derrick snapped.

"692, DO NOT BRING the bird down over the city!" Becker said over the radio. "Do you copy? That's an order from the top! It's too dangerous!"

Simon turned down the radio and motioned to Lucas. "Keep hitting them!"

The second Huey dove down low above the Missouri River, its fuselage showing holes now, a few of its passengers having fallen spinning toward the ground. They were close enough now that Simon heard a few whooshes and thunks as bullets hit the MD500E's fuselage.

"What about the other one?" Lucas asked.

"694 and 695 are honing in on them now," Schaefer replied as Lucas fired a barrage again, the automatic rifle pumping out shot after shot, the copter weaving side to side and rising and falling in attempts to dodge the fire.

"Take them down, Lucas!" Simon said and then Lucas landed a direct hit on the rear rotor and the Huey faltered, its tail wavering as the pilot struggled to maintain control. The Huey banked left and went nose down for a bit, then seemed to be leveling out again, but it was too late.

Seconds later, it crashed in a fiery explosion against an abandoned railroad bridge that crossed the river and Schaefer took them up again and off toward downtown after the other Huey.

"695, we have the suspects over Sprint Center," Maberry said over the radio. Simon had heard them on the radio earlier but not realized they'd gotten a ride on another chopper.

"Get us over there!" Simon called.

"On my way," Schaefer replied as he steered the copter left and accelerated.

Simon looked down to the see the River Market and the trolley tracks passing below them, then the chopper rose above several taller hotels and office buildings headed for the Kansas City Power and Light District.

"ANOTHER BIRD COMING IN," Counts reported.

Derrick cursed and keyed his mic. "Find us somewhere to set down." They'd do better blending in to the city, maybe hijacking a few cars and running for it. "Get as far east as you can, maybe north of the river. Somewhere we can run to cover and disappear."

"Copy," Counts replied and put the Bell into a leftward arc.

It was all going bad. He'd lost half his men. Their big objective had been compromised. Now they couldn't get out without heavy risk of further losses and capture. They'd just have to take their chances. His men wouldn't talk. They were too loyal, too well trained. But he'd had other plans for them. He didn't relish the idea of having to start over or recruit fresh. Still, they'd been in worse spots. They'd do what they must. They had a rendezvous plan out of state for such a contingency Derrick had never planned to use. He was always prepared for anything. But this was nearing worst case, and they hadn't scouted for it properly.

God damn it! Fucking Karl Ramon! Just because his daughter was chummy with a cops daughter. When they got out of this, someone would come back and pay him a visit. Karl Ramon had cost them the extra day they'd needed. Brought the cops down on them too soon. If they could at least get to where the KCPD were far enough away that they'd need time to get there.,, Maybe a suburb with a smaller force that wasn't ready for them. Give them a chance.

"Hit that other bird before she can fire at us!" he ordered his men over the radio.

"THIS IS OUR BEST CHANCE," Simon said as he saw the last Huey turning north across the Missouri River. "Just beyond the levee is an area with nothing but the dump. If we're going to bring them down, it has to be there."

He got on the radio. "695, let's bring them down by the dump. It's our best shot."

"Copy, 692," Maberry replied. Then the sound of automatic fire came over the radio. "We're taking fire!"

"Back off until we catch up," Simon said. "We're almost there. Get above them if you can!" At least up high, they'd be harder to hit.

Simon grabbed another rifle and slid back up to the front passenger seat. "Two minutes," he said over the radio so everyone could hear.

"Ready," Lucas said.

No response from 695.

"Shit. Did they go down?" Simon wondered as Schaefer shot him a worried look.

"We're ready," Maberry replied at last, the automatic fire having died out for the moment.

"There they are!" Schaefer called, pointing, and Simon saw 695 and the Huey ahead, the KCPD MC500E flying to the left and above the Huey with a good two hundred feet separating them.

"Get us to their right just behind and we'll drop down and coordinate fire," Simon ordered.

"On it," Schaefer said.

Simon keyed the radio again. "We're going right, you stay left and drop back, 695. We'll get them between us." They'd have to angle it so they wouldn't hit each other but if they stayed just behind and weren't firing directly across each other, it should be safe enough and make it that much harder for Derrick's people to hit them back.

"Copy, 692," Maberry replied.

The two KCPD copters moved quickly into position and then opened fire. The Huey pilot managed to weave and dodge but then another Huey bearing the logo and letters of the FBI rose into view right in its path and the pilot hesitated, choosing his course.

The detectives fired again, seizing the opportunity. Bullets raked the tale of the Huey and Simon got off a few shots into the passenger bay as well, causing Derrick's men to duck back inside.

Then Lucas scored a direct hit on one of the top rotor tip caps, causing chunks of it to break away which made the Huey jerk and vibrate. Simon and Maberry fired shots at the engine and smoke started pouring out of the fuselage.

With his next shot, Lucas hit a fuel tank and liquid started trickling out and falling behind as the bird descended, its pilot seeking both cover and regained control.

"It'll take a while for our people to get here," Schaefer said as Simon put out a call on the radio beside him.

Lucas fired one more shot that hit one of the tail rotor pitch links and caused the Huey to shimmy and spin just as it was crossing over power lines.

"Lucky shot," Lucas said.

"Fucking androids," Simon teased. "God damn technology."

Lucas grinned. They watched together as Derrick's pilot fought the stick, trying to keep it steady, but the tail suddenly jerked down and made contact with wires, setting off a series of sparks like mini-fireworks. The pilot fought to free and steady the copter, turning it as more sparks flew, then they made contact with the draining fuel. In seconds, flames ignited.

"Oh shit," Simon and Schaefer said together as the KCPD pilot averted quickly, steering clear.

A string of fire shot up the stream of fuel and moments later, the Huey exploded in a fireball. The copter's burning remains fell apart and descended down toward the ground below.

Lucas hung out the side one more time and hollered, "Yippppeeeeekayayyyyyy, motherfucker!"

Simon laughed as Schaefer shot them a look. "Nicely played," Schaefer said. "I'm guessing we won't be seeing those guys again."

"Good riddance," Simon said and motioned. "Take us down." Then he radioed directions to dispatch and asked for a heavy response including a crime scene unit as Schaefer started a slow descent.

CHAPTER 27

IT WAS ALMOST SEVEN before Simon made it to Research Hospital on Prospect at Meyer Boulevard to check on Emma. First, he'd had to talk with a shooting team and others called in to process the crash scene, then he'd made sure Lucas got to Livia Connelly's lab for repairs on his arm. He found Emma on the fourth floor in a patient room where she and Julie had been taken after the doctor examined them so they could rest under observation after their ordeal.

Emma was sitting up in the bed on the right reading a Wonder Woman comic book. The walls were the typical stale white, two brown lounge chairs against a window facing each other, a dining tray on wheels pushed against a wall beside Emma's bed, the wall behind its headboard filled with tubes and electronics. Thankfully Emma didn't need any of it. She wasn't wired up at all and though the noise of electronics and people leaked in from the hallway, the room itself was fairly quiet.

"You get some sleep?" he asked.

"Daddy!" She tossed the comic book aside on the bed and jumped down, running over to hug him as he met her halfway. He held her a moment and kissed her on the forehead then looked at the room's empty second bed.

"Where's Julie?" he asked.

"She went home already, when her dad came," Emma said. "He was in jail all night and her brother had been home alone, so they were anxious to get back. Did you get them?"

"They went up in flames," he said, knowing she'd be quizzing him later for the details.

"Good," she said. "I hope it was painful."

"Hey! That's not the way I want you thinking," Simon said.

"They tried to kill me. Fuck 'em," she said.

Simon grunted. She was so much like him. Maybe he'd apologize to Lara later.

"Now, let's go see Mom," Emma said, grabbing the comic book and taking his hand. "Where is she?"

"The psych hospital off 63rd," he said. "Just a short ride."

RESEARCH PSYCHIATRIC CENTER was around the corner off Prospect and 63rd. They were there and parked again in two minutes and headed up the elevators. Simon had called ahead and Doctor Agbeblewu had happened to be there on evening rounds. She met them as they got off the elevator on Lara's floor.

"Emma meet Doctor Agbeblewu," Simon said. "She's your mom's doctor."

"Hello," Agbeblewu said warmly as she and Emma shook hands.

"Nice to meet you," Emma said.

They walked down the hall together.

"How is she?" Simon asked.

"A lot better, but she's been asking for you and Emma," Agbeblewu said. "She's a little upset no one's come to see her."

"Well, with what was happening—"

Agbeblewu gently patted his arm. "I know, and it was only twenty-four hours since she was even aware enough to ask, but we didn't want to tell her that, so just be prepared."

"Where is she?" Emma asked.

"Well, we put her in a private visiting room since she's upset and this is her first time seeing you with her meds relatively stable," Agbeblewu said and led them to a door marked "Visitor's B." She tapped the door. "In here. You ready?"

Emma nodded eagerly.

"I'll be out here if you need me," Agbeblewu said to Simon and smiled.

He thanked her and followed Emma inside.

Lara was waiting at a round cafeteria-style table dressed in a pink sundress with light blue flowers on it and white tennis shoes. She looked up as they came in and smiled as Emma ran to hug her.

"Momma!" Emma said and wrapped her arms tightly around her mother. Lara hugged her back then glared over her shoulder at Simon.

"It's about time," Lara said. "I've been asking for you for days."

"Sorry," Emma said. "I'm here now." She let go of her mother and stepped back as Lara examined her.

"Are you okay?" Lara asked, ever maternal. "He's feeding you okay?"

Simon fought the urge to roll his eyes.

"I'm fine, really," Emma said then shot her dad an amused look

They stayed with Lara for over an hour as she and Emma chatted like hens with Simon jumping in occasionally, mostly when they asked him a question. Neither Emma nor Simon brought up events of the past few days. There'd be time for that later, when it wouldn't add to Lara's stress and she could process it better.

That night, Simon slept like he hadn't been home in a week. The next day, by special arrangement, he took Emma to spend a few hours with her mother at Research again while he and Lucas reported to Central per Becker's orders for a special meeting.

"We're in big trouble, right?" Lucas asked as they walked in from the parking lot. His arm was fully functional and he'd simply dismissed it as "fine" and "like new" when Simon asked about it.

"Deep shit," Simon agreed as they went inside and headed for the squad room.

Becker was already in her office. As Simon and Lucas arrived, Maberry and Dolby joined them and they headed in to face the music together.

"What the fuck were you thinking—trying to shoot down helicopters in the middle of the city!" Becker yelled as she sat stiffly behind her desk, shooting them dead with a look. Her eyes had rings under them and she looked tired, despite presenting her usual well-oiled appearance with hair and clothes fresh and professional.

"We were trying to slow them down and get them to land," Simon said. "The first one was an accident. The second we waited until they were over a clear area."

"You had no business being on those helicopters in the first place, and sidelining Jason Brock!" Becker scolded, undeterred. Simon couldn't remember when he'd last seen her so angry. They deserved it. As their commanding officer, she could face discipline, too. Simon hadn't really thought about the consequences too much when he was in the moment. He just wanted Derrick and his people stopped whatever it took, but he'd had plenty of time since then and the shit was going to drown the fan, for sure. "They don't work for you. The Chief is furious. Expect to be written up and you'd better pray you don't get demoted or sent down to traffic or worse."

"They took my daughter, JoAnn," Simon protested.

"And that's the only thing mitigating here," Becker replied. "Maybe we can make a case for temporary insanity, put you in counseling." She turned to Maberry and Dolby. "You lost partners. But we are not in the revenge business."

"It wasn't revenge," Dolby said. "Look what they did to UnderCity and Oceans of Fun!"

"The assault team! FBI!" Maberry added.

"Yes, we lost a lot of good people," Becker said. "A lot of businesses are destroyed and people without homes. It'll take the city a long time to recover. But I can't have my squad going out of control like this. I'd expect they'll probably be breaking us up now."

"What?!" Simon said as Maberry and Dolby offered their own protestations.

"You guys know policy! You went off the reservation here!" Becker said. The others just went quiet, looking away. There was nothing to say. They all knew she was right. "I wanted those fuckers dead, too. Just as much as you. Oglesby and Correia were good people, like family. But there are rules we have to live by. Most of all we have to have the public trust."

"The public is better off without Toby Derrick and his kind running loose," Maberry said.

"No doubt," Becker said. "But you took a huge risk. People are pissed. Did I mention the Chief?"

"Yeah," they said in unison and nodded.

"Twice," Simon added.

Becker glared at him, then turned to Lucas. "And you. On report and under investigation by a shooting team. You were supposed be a consultant, keeping a low profile."

"The city is safer for what he did," Simon snapped.

"That's beside the point," Becker said. "It was against policy."

Lucas refused to meet her eyes. "I'm sorry, sergeant."

"He did what I told him to do. Catching bad guys is what we do, damnit!" Simon said.

Becker silenced him with an icy look. "Don't tell me our job, Detective." She turned to Lucas again. "We all respect your amazing skills. Hell, I admire them and I thank God I'm the lucky one who gets you on my squad, but there have to be boundaries. You can't go rogue. No matter what nonsense your idiot partner feeds you."

"Yes, sir," Lucas said.

Becker sighed and put her face in her hands, taking a deep breath. It was a moment before she looked up at them again. "Whatever happens, I'll put a good word in. You've been top notch for too long, even if you did screw up. But this is going to hurt for a while. Restricted duty or sheets in your jackets. You'll have to watch yourselves for a long time."

"Understood," Dolby said.

"Yes, sergeant," Maberry and Simon said.

Becker leaned back in her chair and nodded, pulling a file from beneath a stack on her desk and looking at Lucas again. "Believe it or not, in the midst of this there's good news. The shooting team cleared you." She pulled out a draw and took out Lucas' gun, sliding it across the desk. "You get your gun back and you're off restriction. At least until the shit hits the fan over this."

"Thank you, sir," Lucas said as he reached for his Glock 19.

Becker's eyes met his as she slid another folder across the table beside the gun. "Read this."

"What is it?" Simon asked.

"New policies and procedures pertaining to your partner's special gifts and how the department expects them to be employed in accordance with department policies and practices," Becker said.

"He's got his own regs?" Dolby said.

"Yes," Becker snapped. "And after yesterday, don't be surprised if you each get one too." Her stare was serious but after a moment she relaxed and they saw she was joking.

"Damn, you scared me a minute there," Maberry said.

"She's good," Simon said, nodding.

"You should do theatre," Dolby agreed.

"Funny people," Becker said. "The shit will be deep but your service records will make a difference. Just keep your fucking noses clean in the meantime, okay? You're giving me migraines. I don't need a heart attack on top of it."

They chuckled and nodded as she waved dismissively and they headed back out into the squad room.

"What now?" Lucas asked.

"Well, now we gotta get you back on patrol," Simon said. "Probably tomorrow. But first, we're going to lunch to celebrate while we still can."

"I do so enjoy watching you eat," Lucas snapped.

"We'll find a nice place with a power outlet so you can recharge, okay?"

"Sounds like a party," Lucas said, repeating a phrase Simon assumed he must have picked up from Emma.

Together, they headed for the parking lot.

LUCAS COULDN'T BELIEVE he'd been cleared. He didn't know why, but he'd started to doubt himself, despite Simon's and several others' unwavering faith in him. He felt like he was walking on air, assuming this must be the equivalent of what humans called joy, because he imagined he was at the top of the world and hoped nothing could ever knock him down again.

Simon took him to lunch at a favorite burger place downtown in the Power and Light District off 14th and Main, BRGR Kitchen and Bar. With black leather booths and dark brown faux wood tables and a huge bar at the center of a moderately lit dining room, it was fancier than most burger joints Lucas had been in so far, and the burgers looked thick and juicy. Simon sure enjoyed his and so did the many other patrons who kept the dining room mostly full while they were there.

As Simon ate, they talked about Lucas finishing his training. Simon promised to talk with Gil again and show him the shooting team's final report, urging the Training Officer to give Lucas another chance. Either way, Simon assured him he'd finish. Lucas was too close with too much going for him now. Worst case, he might have to do a few weeks longer with a new T.O. to sign off on him but Simon didn't think it would come to that.

Afterwards, as they navigated their way through downtown construction and crosswalks to the lot where Simon had left his car, they saw a commotion outside a convenience store. People were milling about, looking worried, but still peering inside. Several were talking frantically on cell phones. It sounded like they were calling 911.

"What's going on?" Simon asked as they passed through the crowd.

"Some cops are getting their ass kicked by a guy in there," a man said.

"We called 911, officer needs assistance," a woman offered.

Simon and Lucas exchanged a look and turned quickly, heading for the convenience store's front entrance.

"Is he armed?" Simon asked.

"Not that I saw," the woman said. "But the cops ushered us out as soon as they arrived."

"Where is he?" Lucas asked.

"In the cashier's booth," the man said.

"You all stay clear in case he has a gun," Simon warned and then he and Lucas drew their weapons and rushed inside.

There were bottles of water and soda scattered in one of the aisles along with some bags of pretzels and chips all of which looked to have been knocked off either by fleeing customers or the perp.

The minute they entered they heard yelling and other sounds of a struggle.

"I'm not going back! No fuckin' way!" a man was yelling over and over.

"Get the fuck off me!" another man yelled. Lucas was sure it was Gil Lenz, his T.O. "Shit! He's got my eye!"

"I'm trying! What's this guy on?" a third voice said.

As Simon and Lucas rounded the third aisle, they saw the booth with steps leading into it and a black man's head popping up from behind the glass and back down again, like he was struggling with someone.

They got to the steps and could see Gil Lenz on his back

with the black man pinning him, one finger poking into his right eye as another cop—Lucas recognized him as a classmate named Metz—was on top of the man, trying to pull him off.

"Jesus Christ! My eye!" Gil called out.

"Get off the officers and put your hands up!" Simon yelled as he and Lucas moved in.

"Fuck you!" the black man said, eyeing them warily. "I ain't going back!"

"You're going to jail, no matter what, brother," Simon said. "Don't make this any harder than you already have by hurting a cop."

Lucas assessed the situation and realized Metz's efforts weren't working because he'd forgotten his training. He was trying to pull the man off with sheer strength instead of using tactics to try and incapacitate like a choke hold or a baton around his neck. Without hesitation, Lucas rushed in, pushed Metz aside, and grabbed the perp in a choke hold, pulling him up so his legs were in the air—forcing him to release Gil Lenz's eye—and swinging him around and against the wall hard.

The perp cried out and twisted and fought, but Lucas managed to hold him there as Simon helped Gil Lenz to his feet. "You okay?"

"I thought the motherfucker was going to blind me," Gil said.

Simon motioned to a stunned Metz, who was standing limply by catching his breath. "Call an ambulance and we'll have paramedics look at that. Also, get a wagon here."

Metz just stood there as if he hadn't heard.

"Now!" Simon yelled the last in a way that shook Metz out of his haze and sent him into action.

Metz got on the radio and called in as Simon hurried over to help Lucas with the perp just as they heard sirens outside.

Moments later, other cops rushed in and hurried to check on Gil Lenz and then help Simon and Lucas get the perp into restraints, including a straight jacket at Simon's instructions.

Ten minutes later, as other cops took charge of the perp, Lucas hurried to the ambulance to check on Gil Lenz, Simon right behind him.

"Are you okay, sir?" Lucas asked.

Gil looked at him a moment, frowning, and then finally nodded. "Yes."

"Thanks to you, pal," Simon said, patting Lucas on the back. Then he looked at Lenz. "The shooting team cleared him. Becker will send you the report."

"I saw it this morning," Gil said.

"Good," Simon said and they waited for more but Gil just sat silently as the paramedics wrapped his eye carefully under a gauze pad.

Lucas shot Simon a worried look. What should he do?

"Hey, pal, this officer just saved your eye and maybe your life," Simon said. "Don't you think he deserves another chance to pass training?"

Gil looked at them a moment and then sighed. "I gotta deal with that joker first." He motioned to where a dejected and confused-looking Metz waited leaning against a cruiser. Then Gil turned and extended a hand to Lucas. "Thank you, George."

"You're welcome," Lucas said as he shook the hand firmly and smiled.

"Report to me tomorrow morning in roll call at eight, okay?" Gil said.

Lucas stood straight, trying not to look too happy or eager and nodded. "Yes, sir. See you then. I hope your eye is okay."

"It'll be fine," a paramedic said. "They'll flush it and treat it with antibiotics to prevent infection. He'll be up and around in a day or two."

"Okay, maybe not tomorrow," Gil said as the paramedics helped him up into the back of the ambulance. "I'll notify you."

"Yes, sir," Lucas said. Graduation was two weeks away. He could still make it, and he felt encouraged for the first time since the incident at Crown Center.

As one paramedic climbed in the back of the ambulance with Gil and the other closed the double doors behind them, Simon led Lucas back toward the sidewalk.

Lucas glanced at Metz. "He's a good man. I feel bad for him."

"Some people just aren't cut out for this job," Simon said.

"They'll fire him?" Lucas asked, feeling bad for his classmate.

"I don't know," Simon said. "He may just need more training. If it was his first time in the fire, it might make a difference." He patted Lucas on the back again. "You have it, my friend."

"Have what?"

"The stuff," Simon said as they continued along the sidewalk toward the parking lot again.

"The right stuff? I can be an astronaut?" Lucas asked.

"You can be anything you want," Simon said, looking amused.

"I want to be a cop," Lucas said, sure he'd never wanted anything more.

"Awesome. We're lucky to have you," Simon said as they reached the Charger and he used the clicker to open the doors.

CADET CLASS GRADUATIONS took place in Chief James Corwin auditorium in the main building at the Regional Police Academy in north Kansas City. The auditorium had rows of seats that could accommodate an audience of several hundred and a large stage with a podium in the center bearing the image of a KCPD badge. A U.S. flag and the flag of Missouri were on stands at either end of the stage against a wall on the floor in front with a large blow-up of the KCPD logo next to one and an enlargement of a badge next to the other. The audience sat in shadows and darkness while the stage was lit up like Broadway.

Lucas' class of twenty-five and several instructors occupied chairs on the stage along with dignitaries such as Chief Weber, the various deputy chiefs, and a few Majors and Captains, typically whoever was available at the time given what might be going on in the city. Tonight was a quiet night so the stage was well filled.

Simon and Emma sat with Becker, Maberry, Dolby, and several others amidst the various cadets family and friends and a few fellow officers—friends of the cadets, training officers, or others who liked to check out the new blood. There were also a few members of the media, KCPD media staff, Academy staff, and various others in attendance. Over half the seats in the audience were full.

They sat through the various pomp and circumstance as the Academy director spoke, then introduced the Chief of Police, who talked about the mission of the KCPD, the privilege of public service, the public servants' oath, and so on, with several statements intended to inspire bravery and dedication and so on. After that, the director introduced a few instructors who praised the class and its abilities, and then the Chief, two Deputy Chiefs, including Melson, and several instructors lined up beside the podium where the director would hand out diplomas and the graduates were called up by name to accept their accolades as the audience applauded.

Simon watched as KCPD and media photographers took photos of the assembled VIPs and every graduate as they went up, politely clapping for each himself along with the rest of the audience. When Lucas went up, Simon, Emma, and the Central crew jumped to their feet and cheered, applauding like crazy. Lucas beamed, ignoring them, as he shook hands one by one and accepted his diploma.

When the last graduate had finished, they lined standing in a group for a few more photos and then for the Chief to take them through the public service and KCPD oaths and finally give them their charge as duly appointed officers of the KCPD.

Afterwards, as the lights came up over the audience and the cadets filed down to greet their friends and family, Simon and Emma waited as Becker, Maberry, Dolby, and various others shook hands, hugged and praised Lucas. Then the Chief and head instructors took Lucas aside with the press for a few interviews. Altogether it was about twenty minutes before he finally made his way to his waiting friends. Emma gave him an especially long hug and big smile. They even did a little jig together. Simon chuckled.

As they walked out together, Simon said, "You're a real cop now. Congratulations."

"Thank you," Lucas beamed.

"So I guess you guys are equals now," Emma said.

Simon grunted. "I'm an eighteen-year veteran and he's a rookie. Hardly equals. He has to listen to everything I say as I break him in."

"But I'll do the driving," Lucas said.

"I don't think so, pal," Simon scoffed.

"I have a tactical advantage with my better defined reflexes and response times," Lucas countered.

"Your driving scares the shit out of me!" Simon snapped.

"I can always quit school and drive," Emma teased.

Simon and Lucas exchanged a worried look.

"It's fine. You drive," Simon said as he opened the door and allowed Lucas and Emma to exit before him.

"Well, you are the eighteen-year veteran," Lucas said on the sidewalk as they continued toward the parking lot.

"I'll only drive when it's my car," Simon said.

"Deal," Lucas replied and Emma laughed, shaking her head.

"What?" Simon tousled her hair. "Look at us. We're already agreeing on something." They waited at the curb as a few cars departed then walked across and down a row to where Simon had parked.

"Shut the fuck up, dad," Emma said and rolled her eyes.

"Hey, you know I don't like you using that language."

"Can I at least drive to dinner? Using the autodrive?" Emma begged.

"You know how much I hate that fucking thing," Simon said, shaking his head.

"I'm almost fifteen," Emma said. "I'll have my learner's permit next year."

"And you can practice then," Simon said as he pushed the clicker and the car beeped as its doors unlocked.

They continued arguing even as Lucas opened the door and pulled forward the passenger side seat so Emma could climb in the back.

Lucas smiled as he lowered the seat again and climbed in after her. "Ah, it's good to have a family," he teased.

"Shut the fuck up," both Simon and Emma said together and then they all cracked up.

Simon had to agree with him. Lucas was family and he couldn't have been happier.

THE END

ACKNOWLEDGEMENTS

A S USUAL, THERE are many people to thank. First, Guy Anthony DeMarco, Caprice Hokstad, and Wendy Delmater Thies for editorial notes and Anthony R. Cardno for proofreading. Guy again for his formatting expertise and template creation, Audra Crebs for her excellent design, and Gil Carter and Doaa El-Ashkar (thank you for your service) of the KCPD for their research assistance. Additional research assistance came this round from Lt. Col. Keith Haskin (thank you for your service), commander of the 1st Battalion 58th Aviation Regiment (Airfield Operations Battalion), a military helicopter pilot, who helped me greatly with the helicopter chase and equipment details, and Agent Jeff Heinze of the Federal Bureau of Investigations Public Information Office (thank you for your service) for help with FBI procedures and equipment details.

Thanks also go to my core street team of Martin L. Shoemaker, Wendy Delmater Thies, Caprice Hokstad, Benn Liska, Anthony R. Cardno, Dayton Ward, Eugene Johnson, Lindsay Brewer-Munoz, and Marisa Dutton Means for helping me launch this series well and providing early reviews and ready feedback on various ideas as requested. Thanks to the many friends I tuckerized. I used so many, I don't remember all the names so just know I included you because I like and value you—even if I made your character a bad guy or a boob—and inclusion is meant as a compliment and tribute, not an insult. With the possible exception of Hank Garner, who might not know what to do with himself if I didn't insult him daily as that back and forth is the foundation of our friendship.

Louie, Amelie, and Lacy—much more than pets, but my rock and my calming influence to keep me reminded I am loved, and keep me getting out of bed for trips outside not to mention food and treats on a regular basis. Anita for new love and hope for the future.

As always, the books are meant to entertain but that doesn't mean I don't try hard for accuracy, particularly in how I represent the Police and law enforcement officers and their policies and practices as well as the city of Kansas City and the various businesses and locations included herein. Any errors as always are mine and unintentional, with my apologies.

AUTHOR BIO

Bryan Thomas Schmidt is a national bestselling author editor and Hugo-nominee who's edited over a dozen anthologies and hundreds of novels, including the international phenomenon *The Martian* by Andy Weir and books by Alan Dean Foster, Frank Herbert, Mike Resnick, Angie Fox, and Tracy Hickman as well as official entries in *The X-Files*, *Predator*, *Joe Ledger*, *Monster Hunter International*, and *Decipher's Wars*. His debut novel, *The Worker Prince*, earned honorable mention on Barnes and Noble's Year's Best science fiction. His adult and children's fiction and nonfiction books have been published by publishers such as St. Martins Press, Baen Books, Titan Books, IDW, and more. You can find him online through his website www.bryanthomasschmidt.net or Twitter and Facebook as BryanThomasS. He lives in Ottawa, KS with his canine bosom companions, Louie and Amelie and a cat named Lacy.

Lightning Source UK Ltd.
Milton Keynes UK
UKHW010615130220
358664UK00002B/347

9 78162

Coming in May 2020

COMMON SOURCE

JOHN SIMON BOOK 3

For a sneak peek at the first two chapters, visit

http://www.bryanthomasschmidt.net/CommonSourcePreview

AUTHOR BIO

Bryan Thomas Schmidt is a national bestselling author editor and Hugo-nominee who's edited over a dozen anthologies and hundreds of novels, including the international phenomenon *The Martian* by Andy Weir and books by Alan Dean Foster, Frank Herbert, Mike Resnick, Angie Fox, and Tracy Hickman as well as official entries in *The X-Files, Predator, Joe Ledger, Monster Hunter International,* and *Decipher's Wars*. His debut novel, *The Worker Prince,* earned honorable mention on Barnes and Noble's Year's Best science fiction. His adult and children's fiction and nonfiction books have been published by publishers such as St. Martins Press, Baen Books, Titan Books, IDW, and more. You can find him online through his website www.bryanthomasschmidt.net or Twitter and Facebook as BryanThomasS. He lives in Ottawa, KS with his canine bosom companions, Louie and Amelie and a cat named Lacy.

Coming in May 2020

COMMON SOURCE

JOHN SIMON BOOK 3

For a sneak peek at the first two chapters, visit

http://www.bryanthomasschmidt.net/CommonSourcePreview

Lightning Source UK Ltd.
Milton Keynes UK
UKHW010615130220
358664UK00002B/347